Dominoes, Danzón, and Death

Also available by Raquel V. Reyes

The Caribbean Kitchen Mysteries
Barbacoa, Bomba, and Betrayal
Calypso, Corpses, and Cooking
Mango, Mambo, and Murder

Dominoes, Danzón, and Death

A CARIBBEAN KITCHEN MYSTERY

Raquel V. Reyes

CROOKED
LANE

NEW YORK

Published in the United States by Crooked Lane Books, an imprint of The Quick Brown Fox & Company LLC.

Crooked Lane Books and its logo are trademarks of The Quick Brown Fox & Company LLC.

Library of Congress Catalog-in-Publication data available upon request.

ISBN (hardcover): 978-1-63910-904-3
ISBN (ebook): 978-1-63910-905-0

Cover design by Joe Burleson

Printed in the United States.

www.crookedlanebooks.com

Crooked Lane Books
34 West 27th St., 10th Floor
New York, NY 10001

First Edition: November 2024

10 9 8 7 6 5 4 3 2 1

To Miami and Biscayne Bay

May we honor and learn from
its history.

May we take care of its natural
resources and residents so that there
is a beautiful and sustainable future.

Chapter One

I t had been one thousand one hundred twenty-nine days since my last brush with death and crime. It wasn't like I was counting. Truthfully, I rarely thought about it. I'd been too busy with life.

And life in the Quiñones-Smith household had become beautifully chaotic. Case in point and why I'd thought of those warehouse safety signs that counted the days since the last accident. Camo, our calico cat, had jumped onto the patio dining table with a rather large lizard. *Is that a baby iguana?* She'd dropped the still-twitching lizard onto Manny's plate of guayaba y queso panqueques. It was a gift to the human she loved the most. He'd yelped in surprise. Sirena, almost three, startled and knocked over her jugo de mamey causing the blood-orange-colored juice to drip over the edge. *That's when I thought about the deaths.* Tom, our neighbor's dog that we were watching for a few days, began lapping it out of midair. It wasn't the errant bacon the Vizsla had been waiting for, but all table crumbs were manna from heaven to a canine.

"Mami," Manny said, on the verge of tears over his ruined breakfast. The guava and cream cheese pancakes, a favorite of his, had been per his request.

"What's wrong?" Robert asked, turning from his bacon-frying station at our outdoor stove.

"Zero days since our last spill," I replied.

It was then that the lizard awoke, ran through the juice stream like it was hot lava, and launched itself over Tom's head and onto the grass. High-volume laughter bubbled from Sirena. Camo ran the length of the table in pursuit. *No animals on food surfaces. House rule.* The dog, not to be left out of the fun, galloped after her.

"¿Qué paso aquí?" my mother asked. She was at the French doors, carrying a tray of coffee, hot milk, and cups.

"Camo, the lizard hunter. Don't worry about the mess, Abuela. I'll clean it up." Robert called my mom, Abuela. It was just easier to call her what the kids did. She and Papi, aka Abuelo, my dad, lived with us. Like I'd said, beautifully chaotic.

Manny, in Spanish, told Abuela about the cat, the lizard, and his ruined pancakes. Mami —*I mean Abuela*—gave the tray to Robert, waved away his protests, and began cleaning up the mess.

"You Americanos do not know how to clean," Abuela said.

"But they do know how to make crispy bacon," I said. I gave Robert a nudge to check that his deserted bacon didn't burn. He took the strips out of the pan just as smoke curled from the grease. I made Manny a fresh stack of pancakes, and we sat down to eat.

"¿Mami, puedo ir a trabajar contigo?" Manny asked. During the pandemic, our patio kitchen had become a TV studio set. Delvis, the director of my show *Abuela Approved*, had come up with the idea to keep us all healthy and in production. Having just had Sirena, I'd appreciated it. Manny and my mom, a certified abuela, got to be on the show a slew of times as tasters or helpers. Manny had loved it and the viewers had loved it more. Now, whenever I said I had work, he wanted to "trabajar contigo."

"No, no, mi príncipe, you have a soccer game today, and I might not be back in time," I said. Today, I was shooting a special for a network. Restaurants, the ones that had survived, were struggling to bounce back. People had gotten used to curb-side pickup and delivery. Ileana, the host of *La Tacita*, UnMundo's popular morning show, had asked us to do a series of food tours. Today's was one of two planned for the Little Havana neighborhood.

"Do I have to go to soccer?" Manny asked. Sophia, his best friend, was on the team and loved it—our son, not so much. We'd ask him to stick with it until the end of the season. We'd put him in the activity when indoor activities were masked so he could get some kid time and play.

"You can come to work with me," Robert said.

"Are you really working, or are you breaking in your new clubs?" I teased him.

"Work. The excavator uncovered something they need me to check," Robert replied.

"Tell me, why it is taking so long to build a little hotel?" Abuelo asked.

"First, it was the permits. Coral Shores is very, *very* particular. Every change had to go before the committee, and if there wasn't a quorum, then it got postponed until the next month's meeting," Robert said.

"What is a quorum?" my dad asked. I explained it in Spanish and added that every person on the committee had gotten the virus at some point. One person had died. It had taken six months to find a replacement.

Robert continued with the saga. "Then we never had a full crew for more than a few days at a time. We had to wait for an engine part that was on that ship that got stuck in the Suez Canal." He groaned. "And then the finances dried up, and the bank wouldn't fund us. It's been one problem after the next. But finally, we are all systems go." Robert gave a thumbs up.

"Ah, very good, hijo." He patted Robert's forearm affectionately. "It will be the very best little hotel in all of Miami."

My dad's English still had a Cuban accent after thirty-plus years. I loved that his v's were b's because, in Spanish, they make the same sound when they are the first letter of a word. And whenever Papi called Robert son, I knew the first few months of feeling crowded with three generations under one roof had been worth it. We had a warm, loving, intergenerational home. Robert and I had adjusted to losing a little privacy. It hadn't ended our love life. We'd learned to take advantage of an empty house when the abuelos took the kids to the park. And to lock the bedroom door.

Sirena exploded with giggles. I looked over to her corner seat and saw Abuela was responsible. She had pieces of banana on forks and was beating the air to the rhythm of the nursery rhyme. "De Tin Marín de Do Pingüe, cúcara mácara títere fue. ¿Cuántas patas tiene el gato? Uno, dos, tres, cuatro." It was a sorting song, the equivalent of *eeny, meeny, miny, moe*. On the last word, Abuela offered the down piece of fruit to Sirena, who opened her mouth to take it.

A lot of nursery rhymes had morbid origins. "Ring Around the Rosie" was probably about the bubonic plague. In preschool, I'd learned all the Mother Goose nursery rhymes. *I bet I drove Mami loca singing them constantly.* I'd recited the rhymes without understanding their coded meaning. As an undergrad, I'd taken an American Studies elective about folklore that had blown my mind. "Eeny, Meeny, Miny, Moe" had awful racist origins in its original form. "Mary, Mary, Quite Contrary" was about Bloody Mary, the Catholic queen of England who tortured Protestants. There was a version of Tin Marin that had an alternative line that was not as sweet as *How many feet does a cat have? One, two, three, four.* Instead, it said, "Yo no fui, fue Teté. Pégale, pégale que ella fue." It translated to English as "It wasn't me. It was her. Hit her. Hit her."

Dominoes, Danzón, and Death

My friend Jorge had sent me a video supposedly explaining the violent lines. The PhD after my name dismissed the macabre retelling as the birth of an urban legend. But the narrator was convincing. The anthropologist in me wanted to see research, citations, and documentation. Was there proof that Martin Marin and Maria Esther-Marin had adopted a child named Reinaldo Pingüe? Were Martin and Reinaldo killed? Was the culprit Reinaldo's pet monkey or the possessed marionette?

"Mami!" Manny said.

"Miriam," Robert said. "the dog!"

I snapped to attention too late to stop Tom from stealing the bacon from my hand. It had been midway to my mouth when I'd gone down the rabbit hole of my tangent thoughts.

"*Tom!*" I stretched out the dog's name. He'd won his treat through vigilance and patience. It was my fault, not his.

Robert leaned close to me. "You okay? You were in deep space. What's on your mind?"

"Murder."

Oops. I didn't mean to say that out loud. I hope I haven't jinxed myself.

Chapter Two

Delvis and our UnMundo film crew were on Fifteenth Street and SW Eighth Street, better known as Calle Ocho. The open space beside the 1926 Deco theater had two-foot-long domino pavers that snaked through the area like a hopscotch game.

"Makeup, mi'ja," Delvis barked.

"Hello to you, too," I replied.

"Sorry, it's the weather." She pointed to the moody gray clouds threatening to blow over to us from Key Biscayne. "We need to shoot the outside stuff quick."

"Okay." I spun around, looking for the makeup tent.

"That one. Corre, corre." Delvis clapped her hands.

I broke into a mock run, which didn't get a smile from my usually chill and cheery boss. Opening the tent's flap, Jorge greeted me with a raised finger. He was getting off a video chat.

"Besos, mi amor," Jorge said to the screen. He pressed end and slipped the phone into his apron. "Okay, chica. Sit down. Let me fix you before the blue meanie yells at us."

I knew he meant Delvis with her bright blue hair. Wardrobe had a yellow V-neck wrap dress for me to wear. It was hanging from the tent's armature. I slipped into it quickly and sat down.

"What is up with her today? I've never seen her like this," I said. "She says it's the rain, pero I think something else is going on."

Although not formally trained in cosmetology, Jorge was great with hair and makeup, thanks to his love of drag. He'd stepped in for the studio's regular person when they'd gotten the flu. Later, we'd found out it was probably early days coronavirus. Since then, he's been my makeup artist for the backyard kitchen series and all location shoots. He still taught his Mambo-cise classes. But he'd done a pandemic pivot to virtual and subscription classes.

Jorge tamed my frizzy waves—*thank you, 80% humidity*—with some magic product that smelled like almonds and sandalwood.

"Do you want the chisme?" Jorge asked.

"Of course," I replied. I always wanted to know the gossip, as long as it wasn't mean-spirited. And usually, Jorge's chisme was of the celebrities' follies kind. His boyfriend Lucas Palo was a telenovela star, so they lived a more glamorous life than my pancakes and wild iguana morning.

A loud motor rumbled outside, followed by the squeak and hiss of air brakes. Chattering erupted, but not the local parrot cacophony we were used to. This was human, and it sounded like it was at our tent flap.

"Halt!" Delvis yelled. "This area is off limits!"

I heard German and Canadian accents replying in befuddlement.

"This is a film set. I need you to exit immediately."

I poked my head out of the tent and saw Delvis pointing to the broken orange tape that the UnMundo crew had strung around to cordon off our area. The tourists had ignored it completely. A sporty looking woman with dark blonde hair and an amplifier slung crossbody split through the crowd and squared up to Delvis.

The pair were toe to toe, and neither was going to budge. Terse words were exchanged.

"My tour comes through here every day. It's a public space." The tour guide spoke with a flippant New York accent.

Delvis patiently explained that it was a film set, but exasperation got the better of her. "That's why it is roped off! *And* it says, 'Crew only!'"

"What's going on?" Jorge asked. He pulled the flap from my hand to see for himself. "Oh my God, are they going to fight?"

"It looks like it. Should we intercede?" I asked.

Deus ex machina did the interceding for us. A lightning bolt split the sky, and simultaneously, a clap of thunder reverberated between the buildings. The clouds let loose, and rain pelted the concrete like a water balloon offensive. The tourists moved in circles like frightened pollitos looking for cover. Jorge and I stepped into our tent and zipped it shut.

"Everyone back on the bus." The tour guide's voice was boosted by the book-sized loudspeaker. "Don't push. Single file."

We heard steps and splashes. Once the people were back on the bus, I expected it to pull away, but it didn't. The hum of the motor added to the storm's volume. Water seeped under our temporary walls. The zipper tab flew upward, and a yellow-cloaked Delvis entered the tent.

"Here." She thrust two folded raincoats at us. "Put these on. Jorge, grab your tools and bring them with you. I'm taking you to the restaurant."

"Can't we just wait until it stops?" I asked.

"I don't think it is going to stop," she replied.

I nodded that there was credence to her assertion as I inched away from an encroaching puddle. We hastily grabbed our belongings, donned our plastic ponchos, and dashed through the lot to the awning-covered businesses on Calle Ocho proper.

Delvis led us to a Cuban restaurant. Through the glass folding doors, I could see the film crew unwrapping their equipment and drying it off. Delvis tapped on the glass, and the restaurant's manager let us in. Cubatón played at low volume in the background. I recognized the song by El Chulo. Jorge had used the rap mixed with lyrical romantic verses as a cool-down song in one of his virtual classes. Presently, it was competing with the roaring squall outside.

"We'll start in the kitchen. You'll watch the chef prep the meat and cook the frita. The second shot will be you eating the burger. It will be a tight shot since we don't have a full house of patrons," Delvis explained.

"I'm sure you could get that busload of tourists to fill the seats," I said innocently.

"Hell, no," she said. "I can't believe Ileana sent us out here to film *struggling* businesses. De verdad, I am this close to calling off the shoot, pero like, this place is new and woman-owned, so I know they need the exposure. At least, they are Latinas and from Miami, not some New York venture capitalist group con fotos de Che y Fidel porque they didn't do their homework. Idiotas." Delvis huffed.

"Is something going on? You seem really sensitive today," I asked. "Jorge and I thought you were going to punch that woman."

"I'm sorry. Not very professional of me. It's just a lot of little things setting me off today. Did you read the *Herald*? About the theater? The city has it up for sale. It's ridiculous. Where is the film festival going to go?" Delvis adjusted the headphones resting around her neck.

"What festival?" I asked.

"The Latinx Film Festival. I have a documentary in it. And one of my students' films made the honorable mention list," Delvis replied.

"You teach?" I'd never heard her mention anything about teaching.

"I mentor some students and teach an intensive during the summer session."

"At Dade?"

Delvis nodded.

"They have a lot of good programs and some amazing facilities." I'd toured the culinary institute at Dade College a few weeks ago, contemplating teaching a class as an adjunct. I'd worked hard for my PhD in food anthropology. I didn't want to leave academia completely. While on the tour, I'd seen the fashion design workshops, the computer animation department, and some of the film production studios.

There was a commotion at the front of the restaurant. A tour bus idled in the street, blocking one of the three traffic lanes. *Honk. Honk. Honk-honk-honk!* Miami drivers used their horns more than their turn signals.

Delvis and I stopped talking to watch the action on the sidewalk. The bus door opened, and the tour guide from before stepped out. She had her loudspeaker on and was leading her group in an off-key rendition of the "piña colada song." The restaurant's manager quickly checked that the door was locked before they pulled down a privacy shade using a pole with a hook.

Waves of aggravation pulsated from Delvis. I wasn't psychic, but I could read my director's moods. She was not happy.

"You don't like tourists?" I asked.

"I don't hate them. I don't love them. They are just part of life in Miami. Little Havana residents put up with it because tourism brings in money and jobs. My abuela rolls cigars at the Bohío Cigar Factory." Delvis waved her hand in the direction of the street.

I think I knew the place she was talking about. They had what looked like a rustic writing desk in the window. But instead of sheets of stationery and a fountain pen, there were dried tobacco leaves and a chaveta knife. People passing by could look in and see the tobacco being manipulated into the world-famous (almost) Cuban Cigars. Genuine Cuban cigars were illegal to import and sell in the United States and had been for over sixty years. The Cuban cigars made in Miami were usually from Cuban seed grown in the Dominican Republic and elsewhere. There was a black market for smuggled ones, half of which were probably fakes. South Florida had a new scam every day.

Delvis continued venting. "Little Havana is a tourist trap pero at least it is still a neighborhood con comunidad, you know, like Domino Park. Pero now that's in jeopardy, también. Ay papá, el alcalde es un criminal." Delvis blew air out the side of her mouth.

I wanted to ask her what the mayor had done that had her so irate, but a PA, production assistant, informed us the kitchen was ready. Jorge touched up my hair and shiny forehead before I went into film.

"Action," Delvis directed.

"Estoy aquí con Yuvisleidys una de las Reinas de Las Fritas." I made the introduction to the camera and then turned my gaze to the chef-owner, after a few questions about the new restaurant and why hamburgers, we got into the making and cooking. Yuvisleidys mixed half ground pork and half ground beef with cumin, paprika, grated onions, minced garlic, and a pinch of homemade sazón. She pinched off a mound of meat, rolled it between her palms, and then patted it into a fat disc.

At the griddle, she squirted a runny sauce onto the hot surface and dropped the meat on the pool of it. *Sizzle. Pop. Smoke.* The smell whetted my appetite.

"¿Qué hay en esa salsa?" I asked the chef about the sauce. Her answer about its ingredients was vague. But she did expound upon the baked-in-house buns. They were crackery outside and pillowy

11

inside, like Cuban bread. She lathered one side of the bun with a Thousand Island-colored spread. Chef Yuvisleidys called the spread her special recipe. Figuring she wasn't going to give up her secret, I took a taste with a spoon. "Mmm. Pimentón dulce, ajo, vinagre y tomate." The chef's smile was as good as a yes that I'd gotten it right.

She topped the glistening patty with a handful of shoestring potato sticks and leaned the bun top half on, half off the burger. "La frita de Las Reinas." She presented the plate to me, and I held it to the camera for a zoom-in.

The next scene was at a table set with a Materva soda. I sat with my back to a mural of a 1957 Chevy underneath a Royal Poinciana tree. I took a bite of the juicy burger and had to dab my chin with a napkin before I could look into the lens. "¡Deliciosa!"

"Cut," Delvis barked.

The crew swiftly began dismantling their gear. I cut the burger in half and gave the other piece to Jorge. His yums and noms would have been good advertising for the restaurant if we were still filming. The manager raised the privacy screen and told the line outside that it would be another few minutes before they opened.

"It looks like the rain has stopped," I said.

"Good. I'll send you out with Alex to get some B-roll," Delvis said. "I need to talk to the owner and chef about something." Delvis walked away from me on a mission.

"Okay, jefa." Usually, when I called her boss, she'd reply with a funny and snarky *that's right* or *jefa know jefa,* or she'd twerk and say *jefa moves.* But today, she was disinterested in our regular banter.

Alex, the cameraman, signaled he was ready to hit the streets. We went out a back door to avoid the hungry tourists waiting for tables. He shot B-roll of me with several of Calle Ocho's five-foot-tall fiberglass rooster sculptures. Over fifty gallos dotted the fifteen-block area. After I kissed the one with a heart painted on its wattles, Alex and I spent a few minutes filming at a ventanita, where I drank an espresso for the camera and ordered a colada (espressos to share) for the crew. The sky looked like it was going to rain again. So, Alex called it done. He took the colada and its stack of plastic shot glasses from me when we got to our tents. Jorge had texted me he'd packed up and gone home to Lucas. I changed into my regular clothing and dashed to my car in the sprinkling rain.

I got turned around trying to get to I-95. *Thank you, one-way streets and neighborhood traffic circles.* The drains couldn't handle the heavy rain, and ponds had formed. Visibility was low. The risk of hydroplaning was high. I began to worry about lightning at Manny's soccer game. I accelerated through an intersection so as not to get hit by a police car barreling through the red light sans sirens. In my rearview mirror, I saw it followed by a Fire Rescue truck with horns wailing.

Caridad, please get me home where my worst problem is spilled juice. Also, help whoever it is they are on the way to.

Chapter Three

The Coral Shores weather was partly cloudy. Manny's soccer game was in its last half. Walking to the sidelines, I spotted my parents sitting with Pepper. Sirena and Pepper's daughter Elliot were in a canopied wagon between them. The two girls had due dates within a week of each other, but Sirena came early (something my MIL hasn't forgiven me for) in March, and Elliot came late in May. It was only February first, but I was looking ahead to spring. Our two families had four kid birthdays between us. Manny already had the menu planned for his party. He wanted croquetas, mariquitas with a lime-garlic mojo dip, and a cake with meringue frosting.

I looked onto the field for Manny's number ten jersey but didn't see him. Sophie scored a goal, and Pepper stood to cheer. That's when I heard my son's voice. "You go, girl!" He was on the bench, his preferred spot. He was reading *El Club de Cómics de Supergatito*, the Spanish version of Cat Kid Comic Club that he'd borrowed from his classroom's library. I loved that his Montessori school supported its multilingual students. Manny noticed me, tucked his book under his arm, and trotted around the playing field to meet me.

"Mami, I saw bones!"

"¿Qué?" His statement and the soccer game noise made me lean in.

"Yo ví huesos."

I hadn't needed him to repeat it to me in Spanish. He was speaking to me in Spanglish more and more anyway. As long as he kept his language skills up with his abuelos, I was okay with bending my Spanish to Mami—English to Papi rule. What I'd needed was clarification on bones.

"Bones? Like chicken bones?" I asked. *Probably chicken bones.* Groundskeepers were always finding chicken bones either from the wild chickens or from offerings by ill-informed, desperate people who didn't formally study La Regla de Ocha or Vodou.

"No, like human bones! It was so cool." My son hugged my neck and then cheerfully skipped back to the team bench.

"¿Que qué?" My befuddlement was a shout into the void. Sophia had scored another goal, and the applause surpassed the noise ordinance. I looked around for Robert. When I didn't see him, I texted him two words with an interrobang. *HUMAN BONES?!* I stared at the screen, waiting for my husband to respond. I got nothing.

"Miriam! Come over." Pepper waved, and I went to join her. "Did you see Sophia make that goal? She's a little Megan Rapinoe."

I smiled like I knew who that was. "Have you seen Robert?" I asked.

"He dropped Manny off and told your parents he had to get back to the site. There was something important he had to oversee or something," Pepper replied.

"He didn't say what, did he?"

Pepper shook her head. "Maybe Bernice is mad at the earth movers." She laughed.

Hmm. Gators are people-sized. Could the bones be reptilian?

The boutique hotel was being built at the edge of the country club's golf course that had a resident alligator the club golfers had named Bernice. The creature collected the balls that landed near the water's edge and placed them in its nest in the middle of the pond.

"I promised Elliot ice cream after her sister's game. Can Sirena join her?" As Pepper spoke, she was packing up her area, storing her chair, cooler, and camp stool in the family's push wagon, which was the size of a stagecoach.

"Sure. We'll all go," I replied.

Manny and Sophia came running up. I congratulated Sophia on her goals.

"It's a team effort. Manny tired the other team out in the first half. That's probably why I made the goals so easily," Sophia said, patting Manny's back.

She was being gracious. Even though I hadn't seen Manny play that day, I'd seen him enough to know that he had great footwork. You couldn't get the ball away from him, but he'd often run in the wrong direction because he didn't care about the game. He'd realize it at the goal line and would have to run the ball in the other direction. Only when Sophia was on the field with him telling him which way to go, did he pay attention to the sport.

Pepper was having a hard time getting the wagon to roll. With two toddlers and all the camp stuff it was at max load.

"Let me help you, señora," my father said.

"Mr. Quiñones, you don't have to," Pepper protested in vain.

My dad took over and got the wagon moving with minimal effort. He was very fit from his years as a Jack-of-all-trades handyman, landscaper, and property manager. Manny and Sophia skipped ahead, and Pepper, Mami, and I became the middle of the procession. Papi entertained Elliot and Sirena in the wagon with a Cuban folk song.

Dominoes, Danzón, and Death

"¿Mami, qué dijo Roberto cuando dejó a Manny?" I asked my mother as we walked to the field house.

"He said the—" My mother made a clawing motion. "Found bones, and he had to wait for the authority." When there was an English-only speaker like Pepper in Mami's company, she liked to speak in English for their sake. But I wished she'd make an exception at the moment for the sake of the finer details she was leaving out.

"The authorities? You mean the police," I said.

"No, someone from the Groovy college," Mami said.

I couldn't help but smile at my mother's malapropism. She meant Grove College, Coral Shores' private institute of higher learning.

Pepper, who'd been listening to our exchange, piped in. "I bet it's Dr. Bell." She made a face.

"Who is that?" I asked.

"Dr. Gregory Vander Bell. He heads the museum at Grove," Pepper replied, using a highfalutin accent.

"The college has a museum? I didn't know that," I said.

"It's small, mostly Florida history stuff. They have a nice-sized collection of Tequesta Indian artifacts. I think the kids' class is taking a field trip there soon. Oh, and your in-laws donated an exhibit hall. There's a plaque with Marjory and Senior's name on it." Pepper fluttered her eyelids and grinned at me.

"Of course. I should have known."

"Speaking of The Smiths. I think I see Sally and Drew over there." Pepper pointed toward a group of parents and kids walking in from the opposite side from which we'd come. The field house, which held the registration office and a few activity rooms, divided the soccer fields from the softball and basketball courts. It also had a snack bar that sold frozen treats. It appeared that Savannah, Sally and Drew's eldest, who'd recently taken up softball, had just

17

gotten out of practice. "Join us," Pepper shouted and waved. Sally, Drew, Savanah, and her younger sister, Reagan, joined us in line for ice cream.

"Hello, strangers," Sally said.

We gave each other hugs. With six adults, six kids, and an oversized wagon, we took up more space than was polite. Pepper, Sally, and I took the kids' orders and sent the rest of our group off to the bleachers. Manny fell in stride with his cousin Rae, who was dressed in Sleeping Beauty pink, from hair bows to shoelaces. Vana showed Sophia her glove. Despite the two-and-a-half-year age difference, the two sporty girls chatted like besties. Papi steered, and Mami retrieved the toys the toddlers were tossing onto the ground. As soon as she threw a toy back into the wagon, Elliot threw it out, causing Sirena to laugh hysterically.

"Esa niña." I chuckled to myself. "My daughter thinks *everything* is funny."

"That's better than a tantrum," Sally said.

"Oh, don't worry, we have plenty of those too. Sirena is a meltdown drama queen. I expect there will be one right around nap time," I said.

My friends nodded knowingly. We moved up a few paces in the line.

"Off topic, but maybe not since we're talking about tantrums. Have you spoken to Marjory lately?" Sally asked.

I gave my sister-in-law a why-would-I-do-that look. I was not blonde nor from the right family for my mother-in-law Marjory's liking. I'd tried my best to be nice to her when Robert and I first moved to Coral Shores when Manny was four. After all, she lived only three blocks away. My fantasies of a grandmother baking cookies with us and crocheting stuffed animals were quickly squashed. Marjory had taken every opportunity to be passive-aggressive about my heritage, my career, and our choice to raise Manny bilingual. Robert hadn't believed his mom could be so xenophobic until he saw it for himself. He gave his mom a literal "time-out" and asked her to do some introspection. She checked out a few antiracism books from the library. We had been considering lifting her ban when Sirena made her early appearance. I was in the Dominican Republic helping my parents tie up loose ends after losing their dream property management position. The owner had sold the vacation rentals but had given them a respectable severance. Sirena hadn't been due for two months. Marjory accused me of planning the early birth.

"You know, she says I had a premature delivery just to spite her," I said.

"*What?*" Pepper's eyes got big.

"Yeah, I had a medical emergency so that her granddaughter would be born a foreigner." I smiled sardonically.

"Sorry about that. That was *way* out of line even for her," Sally said. She'd had her own run-ins with Marjory. She wasn't a member of her fan club, but Sally had more ticks in the acceptable-to-marry-a-Smith-son tally than I did.

"You've got to be kidding me," Pepper said. "Why didn't you tell me?"

"You were in babymoon with Elliot. I wasn't going to taint that with my MIL's poison." I squeezed my friend in a side hug. "So, no, I haven't spoken to Marjory," I told Sally. "Why do you ask?"

We'd reached the counter. Pepper placed our group's order.

"Well, she canceled family dinner this week. And she skipped the Women's Club Tea where she was scheduled to give a talk about the Smiths in early Florida," Sally said.

"Maybe she caught the virus again and is too embarrassed to admit it," I said.

19

"No. Drew was at the house to see Senior the next day. He said she looked fine. But that she had all the windows covered." Sally offered Pepper some money to cover her children's ice cream.

Pepper didn't accept Sally's twenty-dollar bill. She paid for everything and passed each of us a flimsy paper box with ice cream sandwiches and treats.

"Covered? Like with tinfoil?" I asked.

"Is she into conspiracy theories and alien stuff?" Pepper asked, bewildered, as we headed toward the bleachers.

"Ay Caridad, I hope she hasn't fallen off the edge of reality, for Senior's sake." I looked at Sally for assurance.

"No, not tinfoil. She had the curtains drawn and the blinds tightly shut. A little weird. But what has me worried is that she asked Drew if he could get her a *gun*." Sally whispered the last word.

Chapter Four

The lightning detection alarm sounded before the kids had finished their ice cream sandwiches. Families dashed to safety, ours included. My mother, the kids, and I made it to the car before the rain started. But, my father, pobrecito, was getting drenched while helping Pepper collapse her wagon. I'd upgraded from the Prius to a Chrysler Pacifica hybrid. *Ay Caridad, I'm a soccer mom with a minivan. I never thought that would happen.* My phone rang, and I touched the car's screen to answer the call.

"Are you close to home? Can you pick up your parents from the game?" Robert asked. "It's raining cats and dogs, and I can't leave the site yet."

"I've got them. And I've got you on speaker," I replied.

"Hi, Papi," Manny said from the third row. Sirena, next to him, was pointing and laughing at her abuelo, who was running hunched over toward the van. He got in, slid the door closed, and shook like a wet dog, causing Sirena to giggle more.

"Sorry I missed your game, Manny," Robert said.

"It's okay, Papi. Did you find more bones? Is it a caveman? Did you find a saber-toothed tiger, too?" Our son asked.

Robert laughed. *Is that a sarcastic laugh? He sounds weary.* "I'll tell you all about it when I get home."

"Cuidate con esta tormenta, hijo," my father said.

"Yes, please be careful in the storm. The lightning horns keep blasting," I echoed my father's sentiment. Florida's golf courses were notorious for lightning strikes.

"I hear them. I'll be safe. See you at home, ASAP," Robert ended the call.

Turning onto Manatee Lane, a combination of lightning and thunderclap hit like a bomb exploding. I parked in our driveway but kept the motor on. There was no point getting out at the apex of the storm. I was certain the worst of it would pass in five or ten minutes. Plus, Sirena had fallen asleep from the steady beat of the rain. Manny regaled his abuelos in Spanglish about the woolly mammoth he'd seen on Friday at the Frost Science Museum. It was ten feet tall— "and only a teenager." Manny used his pointer fingers as fangs. "And I saw a saber-tooth tigre skull."

Bones. I didn't want to think about what kind of bones the construction crew had found. *I really hope they're animal and not human.* I clung to the thought that they could be alligator bones. *I hope it's not what an alligator ate.* The local news had recently reported finding a man's leg in the belly of a Fort Myers alligator. *At a golf course.* I shuddered at the gruesome reality and stared out the window at the river our front path had become. Red twinkles in the sideview mirror caught my eye. It was a police car rolling to a stop in front of our house.

I checked my messages for a text from Gordon, Robert's police officer cousin. I'd introduced him to his fiancée, Omarosa. He often dropped by for coffee when he was on patrol. On closer inspection, it didn't look like a Coral Shores police car. The decals were placed differently. The officer stayed in his car as well. I shifted in my seat to get a better look at the situation but couldn't see much through the car's foggy windows and the outside haze. I put the defrost to max. A bolt of lightning lit the front yard up like a stadium. It was then that I saw the driver. He was looking at me—directly at me. My heart began to pound. *Ay, Caridad. Is it bad news? Is someone hurt? I just spoke to Roberto, and my parents and the kids are with me. Oh no, no, no. Is it Alma? Has something happened to my best friend?*

I shot off an '*¿En qué estas?*' text to Alma. She replied, 'nada.' She was drinking coffee and watching her backyard become a lake.

So, if it's not Alma, then who? I tried to read the city name on the car's door. *Coño.* It was impossible to decipher. *I hope it isn't my tíos or Yoli y Bette.* "¿Mami, haz hablado con Tía Elba hoy? ¿Como van los planes para la fiesta?"

"*Hable con ella hace un rato*," my mother replied. She'd spoken to her sister-in-law a little while ago. The plans for Yoli and Bette's marriage celebration had hit another roadblock. *Bad luck. Unless the cop is coming to tell me about the banquet hall not refunding Yoli her deposit, that isn't why the fuzz is lurking in front of my house waiting for me.*

Fifteen agonizing minutes passed before the storm let up. When I turned off the car and opened my door, the police car did the same. But when Manny hopped out, the officer pulled his leg back into the car. *Wrong house?* Mami used her keys, and Papi went in first, carrying a still-napping Sirena. Manny splashed up the path in a zig-zag.

"*Te vas a enfermar*," Abuela said to him. She'd given me the same warning all my life. *Playing in the rain doesn't give you a cold.* I didn't tell Manny to stop his fun, but I did encourage him to get inside and take off his wet socks before Abuela got out the vic-vapo-rú.

"That stuff is stinky," Manny said.

"I know. But Abuela swears Vicks can cure anything and everything. So, if you want to avoid the stinky then dry your hair and change quickly." I shooed him over the threshold.

"Ms. Miriam Quiñones?" said the voice coming up my driveway.

"*Yes.*" I responded, facing the officer.

"Do you have a moment to answer a few questions?"

I motioned to a dry area under the garage's overhang, away from the house's large front window. "Sure. What's this about?" Ever since my run-in with a dirty cop in Puerto Rico, I'd lost some of my trusting nature. Not all police were good. Not all police were bad. But the favor of power was theirs, and I'd learned to be cautious. I covertly pressed video record on my phone with the lens poking out of my pants pocket.

The officer's shield had a palm tree with the words "Incorporated 1896" through the trunk. He was with the City of Miami police. The name embroidered in white on the black bar above his right chest pocket was T. Cruz.

"You were filming in Little Havana with UnMundo today. Am I correct?" he asked.

My lawyer in-laws, Drew and Sally, were in my head telling me not to say anything without legal representation. *Does a detective count?* Over the officer's shoulder, I saw Detective Pullman's black SUV coming up the street.

"Yes, that's right." I cocked my head and lifted one side of my mouth. *Certainly, the network pulled the proper permissions.*

"Did you witness an altercation between a Delvis Ferrer and a Cynthia Jordan?" Officer Cruz asked.

"Who?"

"Delvis Ferrer and Cynthia Jordan," he repeated.

I was stalling for time. I knew Delvis, of course, and I guessed the Cynthia person was the tour guide.

Detective Frank Pullman approached wearing his usual suit and tie. He was a dead ringer for Humphrey Bogart. If Bogart had been Black.

"Afternoon, Ms. Quiñones. Officer," Pullman said. He nodded his head like he was tipping a hat. "Detective Pullman, Coral Shores Police Department." Frank extended his hand.

Officer Cruz introduced himself as Tomas Cruz of the Miami PD, South Station. I watched the law enforcement posturing with amusement. Pullman didn't like that an officer from an outside department was on his turf without notifying Coral Shores PD. Cruz, young and cocky, wasn't going to admit his faux pas. The air was electric with tension. It felt like a human-made storm was on the horizon. The atmosphere shifted when Gordon arrived. Two Coral Shore PD against one MPD wobbled the scales. Thankfully, Gordon wasn't wearing his bike uniform. Spandex shorts didn't carry the same authority as the full pants and button-down shirt uniform. He'd recently been promoted to sergeant. I noticed Cruz clock the stripes on his sleeve.

"Cousin, everything okay here," Gordon said, giving me a kiss on the cheek.

"I think so," I said, returning his familial gesture.

"Let's get out of the weather. I think I smell coffee," Pullman said.

His nose wasn't that good. But he'd probably guessed correctly. I bet Mami was making café. I led the way and reminded them to wipe their feet on the welcome mat with the rainbow-colored bienvenidos. Manny, dry and changed, tackled Gordon in a running hug. My son adored his father's cousin. So much so that he'd dressed as a police officer for a couple of Halloweens.

Mami was, in fact, making coffee. When she saw me enter with three *guests,* she put out more demitasse cups. "Frank." She smiled and came around the counter that separated the kitchen from the dining room area. "¿Cómo está Claudia?"

Pullam answered that his wife was doing well and that they should have them over for dinner soon. Frank and Claudia were closer in age to my parents than to Robert and me.

The Miami police officer was off his game. He clearly hadn't anticipated the guards that flanked me as we settled into our seats at the dining room table. Pullman and Gordon had left him no choice but to sit on the bench side of the family table with Sirena's pink and lavender mermaid placemat and Manny's laminated map of the Caribbean with illustrations of pirate ships and sea creatures.

My mother served us café and placed a plate of Maria cookies on the table. She gave Manny a mug of warm milk with a few drops of espresso in it. She ushered him toward his room, promising him a story about her first attempt at arroz con leche. "Ni los cerdos querían comérselo. And you know pigs will eat almost anything."

Officer Cruz drank his espresso in two sips and then cleared his throat. "Ms. Quiñones." Pullman and Gordon looked at him. He straightened his back and continued. "Ms. Quiñones, can you please tell me about the altercation you witnessed between a Delvis Ferrer and a Cynthia Jordan?"

"Who is Cynthia Jordan?" I asked.

"She is a tour guide for Hop-in Red Bus," Officer Cruz said.

"There was no altercation. Some tourists ignored the signs and walked through our crew area. Delvis told them to leave," I said.

"What time was that?" he asked. I told him. "Did you see any other confrontations between the two?"

"No. I mean, the tour wanted to get into the restaurant where we were filming, but the manager had the door locked." I got kneed on my thighs from both sides. *What are you trying to tell me? Stop talking?* I got two more jabs. *Okay, I get it.*

There was a long silence.

Officer Cruz lost. He asked his question again.

I shook my head no and asked, "Why?"

Cruz's eyes went from Pullman to Gordon before deciding what to say. "Someone reported seeing Delvis Ferrer follow Cynthia Jordan into The Deco Theater."

"So?" I shrugged.

"Cynthia Jordan is dead," Cruz said with a flat affect.

Chapter Five

Officer Cruz left his business card, instructing me to call him if I *remembered* anything. *There is nothing to remember. Delvis told the woman to get out. I'm sorry the tour guide died, but my director had nothing to do with her demise. End of story.*

Gordon walked the MPD officer to the door. Their body language was chummy, but it was that put-on friendliness that wasn't real. When Gordon returned to the table, he had a little more information for us. Cynthia Jordan had had her head bashed in by a film canister. *Ow!* Her body was found by the police when they went to answer the theater's silent alarm.

"So, what does that have to do with Delvis? Or me?" I asked.

"It seems your director was yelling *angrily* at the woman shortly before." Gordon put air quotes around the adjective.

"Shortly before? What does that mean?" I asked.

"Velma," Detective Pullman said. "Don't even think about it."

"Don't call me Velma," I said.

"Fine, Veronica. Just stay out of it," he said.

Pullman had given me the nickname Veronica during the first investigation I'd stumbled into. It was a reference to Veronica Mars, a TV show I'd never watched. *When a woman dies next to you at a luncheon, and your BFF is accused of the murder, you have to clear your bestie's name.* The moniker stuck when, a few months later, another body came to my doorstep. *Okay, not exactly on my welcome mat, but my front yard. Actually, it was by a Halloween tombstone.* But ever since Puerto Rico, he'd begun calling me Velma. I knew the reference was from Scooby-Doo. Jorge had used it first. But it had been FBI informant Welmo who'd embraced it and shared it with Pullman. The two had been in communication because of my possible stalker but had stayed in touch due to the money laundering case I'd been a bystander to.

"I will stay out of it because there is nothing to get into. Delvis did not hurt that woman. Y pa' que tú lo sepas, I am more Jessica than Veronica or Velma. Bodies just show up in my vicinity. I don't go *looking for them*," I said in my defense. Mentioning Jessica Fletcher made me think that Mami and I could use a *Murder, She Wrote* evening like when I was a kid. *That would be fun. Popcorn drizzled with dulce de leche. Chifles. Merenguitos. Jupiña to wash it down. Yum.*

My snack food daydream was cut short by excitement from Tom. Robert had his key in the door. Even though Tom was not a full-time fur member of our house, he'd stayed with us enough times for him to consider us as an extension of his pack.

"Oh, good, just the man I wanted to see," Pullman said.

I gave him a raised eyebrow. "Oh, so that's why you were on my street."

Pullman stood to shake my husband's hand. It came with an upper arm pat-squeeze.

"Wait. What detective-y business do you have with Robert?" I asked.

Robert hugged his cousin and then stepped into the kitchen. I noticed that my husband's shoulders drooped. *Something has him worried.*

"Gentleman, care to join me?" he asked, showing them the pink, aqua, and yellow can he'd pulled from the fridge. "I have a guava ale, a dragon fruit IPA, and a pink grapefruit wheat." My husband was a recent convert to Miami's craft brewery scene. Our recycling bin had never been so colorful.

"Maybe later," Pullman replied.

Gordon passed, too. He was still on duty for another hour.

"Wow, what a day." Robert leaned against the counter and pulled the tab on his beer. The release of CO_2 was like a sigh. "Never could I have ever—"

Pullman let him have his dramatic moment. He waited for him to enjoy the first sip.

"Well, I have good news and bad news about the bones," Pullman said.

Robert pulled a stool from under the counter, propped his butt on it, and crossed his ankles. My husband looked dashingly handsome despite his rain wrinkled shirt and messy hair. It was normally GQ cover perfect. He'd obviously been running his hand through it all day. It was something he did when he was really worried. Bones at a construction site were undoubtedly worrisome.

"Let me have it," Robert said.

"The forensic team found a pottery shard. So, that supports the assumption that the bones are ancient." Pullman said.

"Can't we take Dr. Bell's word for it?" Robert asked.

"I'm afraid not." Pullman tilted his head and shook it slowly.

"So, that's the bad news, right?" Robert took another draw from his beer.

"No, that's the good news. The bad news is the county's forensic archaeologist is on vacation and out of cell range. She's on a mountaintop in Peru. It might be a few days before we can get her back to Miami." Frank drummed his fingers on the edge of the table as he leaned back in his chair.

"I knew as soon as I saw the bones that we'd have to shut down, so what's a few more days. I thought you were going to tell me they'd found more—like a whole graveyard or a structure." Robert ran his fingers through his hair. "One skeleton is a few weeks or a month max. But structures take months and years."

"The Miccosukee tribe has been notified." Pullman continued.

"They'll have a representative here in the morning," Gordon said. "Until we're given the clear to move the bones, I've got an officer guarding the site."

"You mean the mud pit," Robert chuckled. "That was why I couldn't get back to the game, babe. I had to put one of the country club's event tents over the site. It was a comedy. These guys can pick up a porcelain teacup with their claw bucket and set it on a table without a chip, but give them a few poles and a tarp and—" He exhaled.

"Poles at a golf course, *me-tal poles*, in a storm!" My hands thrashed through the air.

Robert put his beer down and came over to soothe me. "We got it up before any lighting."

A clap of thunder rattled the panes of glass in the French doors.

"I think that's my cue to leave," Pullman said.

"You're welcome to stay," I said.

"Yes, stay. Abuela always makes enough to feed a lacrosse team," Robert said.

"No, I need to get, but thank you for the invitation," Pullman said, pushing his chair in.

"Can I stay?" Gordon whispered in my direction.

I laughed. "Of course."

I watched Pullman's taillights disappear down the block, and then I closed the blinds. It was like night outside. I checked the time. It was a few minutes past five. Robert and his cousin were deep in conversation about a movie they both wanted to see. So, I stepped into my study to have a moment to myself. The room held most of my research books. It also had a small desk where my laptop lived. I sank into my reading chair and texted Delvis.

Are you ok? The police came by my house.

Delvis usually answered her text messages instantly, but there was no reply. Nor was there a someone-is-typing bubble. I gave it a minute. I tried reading the opening essay of Melissa Thompson's *Motherland* but couldn't focus on the meaning of the words. So, I flipped through the beautiful photographs in the Jamaican cookbook. The peanut and sweet potato stew looked delicious. There was a paragraph about its origins. Scanning it, I saw the author mentioned West Africa, the Spanish, and the "so-called" New World. I took an index card from one of the stacks I had strategically placed around the study and marked the page for a later read.

I checked my phone. No message. Delvis, who was younger than me by six or more years, was in the never-call-when-a-text-will-do camp. I texted her an emoji, an up pointer finger, and waited.

Uno, dos, tres, cuatro . . .

When I got to ten, I gave up and called.

Ring. Ring. Ring.

Pick up. Pick up. Pick up.

No answer.

Chapter Six

The next morning was not a sleep-in Sunday. Tom wanted to walk, and he told me with a cold nose to my cheek. I pulled on a pair of sweatpants and threw on an UnMundo T-shirt.

"Come on, boy," I said.

"Where are we going?" Robert yawned.

"Not you, mi amor," I laughed. "The dog. I'll be back in time for coffee."

Tom's tail swished across the floor like a windshield wiper as he waited for me to lace my sneakers.

"Babe, would you mind going to the site with me to meet the tribal rep? You're better at these culturally sensitive things than me." Robert rolled onto his side and reached his hand out to squeeze mine.

"I'm not sure what help I'll be, but sure, I can go with you as long as I'm free by noon. I have lunch with the squad."

"I'll have you back with plenty of time. Thanks, Babe." Robert tugged at me to meet his kiss.

We kissed and then kissed a little heavier. I pushed up on my elbow and away from the heat.

"You are so bad."

"That wasn't bad, that was *good.*"

"Stop. I have to walk the dog." I stood up. "Save it for later," I winked.

"I've got a golf cart with privacy shades." Robert made a Zoolander Blue Steel look.

Tom barked, something Vizslas don't do in excess. He really wanted me to hurry.

"Save it for later, handsome." I blew him a kiss.

Tom and I took our usual route through the neighborhood—Manatee to Seahorse, down to Hammerhead, then up on Queen Angel, careful to avoid my MIL's house a block over on Dolphin and Parrotfish. The storm had broken some branches. There were puddles everywhere that would evaporate by midday. As we walked over a purple carpet of fallen jacaranda flowers, concern for Delvis entered my mind. *Why hadn't she replied yet?* I texted Jorge. Even if he'd been out late in Wynwood or South Beach, I knew he'd be up to get ready for his Sunday brunch gig. My text was delivered but not read. *Be patient, Miriam. Jorge will reply soon.*

While Tom sniffed around an oak tree, I checked the *Miami Herald* for an article about the woman's death. The headline was "Death at The Deco." It sounded like the title of a mystery novel. I read the short write-up.

Saturday afternoon, a woman's dead body was found in the lobby of the historic Deco cinema. The details of the suspicious death have not been made public, but the Miami Police Department has identified a person of interest.

"Do they mean Delvis?" I said.

Tom gave me a quizzical look and rubbed his body against my leg.

"Don't mind me, Tom. I talk to myself all the time. And sometimes I forget to keep my mouth closed." I petted his copper head.

When we got back home, the house was vibrating with energy. The kids were up. Manny was helping Sirena build a tower, which

Camo was determined to knock down. I think that was the game, actually. My dad was in the backyard picking up storm debris. Mami was in the kitchen, and Robert was setting the table. I smelled Cuban bread toasting and eggs frying. Breakfast was loud but without spills or lizards. *Gracias a La Caridad.*

My phone sounded as I was getting into the passenger seat of Robert's car. It was a video call from Jorge or, rather, Cha-cha Minnelli.

"Hola, bella," I said to him.

"Ay, chica, I overslept," he said as he painted thick wings onto his eyelids. "Anyway, can you believe this thing con Delvis?"

"Did you talk to her?"

"No. Did you?" Jorge used the screen like a mirror and applied red lip liner to exaggerate his lips.

"No, and she hasn't answered my texts."

"That's no good."

"Estoy de acuerdo." I bit part of my lower lip and exhaled out the other side. "Did you talk to the police?"

He nodded as he brushed his lipstick on.

"What did you say?"

"Ay, chica. Officer Cruz was *so boring*. I couldn't even get him to crack a smile. Pa' nada.'"

"What did he ask you?" I tried to keep my annoyance in check. Jorge loved attention. And he loved to flirt. Having met Officer Cruz, I sensed Jorge's playful flirting would have made him uneasy. Most confident straight men read the room and indulged Jorge in his harmless fun.

"You know. Did I see Delvis fighting? Did Delvis say anything about the New York woman?"

"New York woman? *You mean* the tour guide."

"Sí, esa misma." Jorge pointed the tip of his blush brush at me.

We'd arrived at the country club before I could probe Jorge's memory for more.

35

"Babe, we need to get in there," Robert said.

"Is Roberto with you?" Jorge asked.

I turned the phone to my husband.

"Hi, Jorge," Robert said.

"Hola, guapo," Jorge said.

Robert blew my friend a kiss.

When I looked at the screen, Jorge was campily fanning himself.

"Have a good show. Please text me if you hear from Delvis," I said.

"Sí, sí." Cha-cha Minnelli ended the video.

Robert took my hand and led me through the golf course's maintenance buildings, where he got the keys to a golf cart from a peg board. As we zipped along the narrow road, I didn't see a lot of damage from yesterday's bad weather. But I did see the landscape crew feeding branches into a woodchipper. A large white tent was ahead of us just beyond a small mound with two sand traps. Robert took the cart off the path, and our speed slowed to a crawl. The ground was like a saturated sponge.

"We better get out. We'll have to walk the rest of the way," he said, returning us to the pavement.

The sides of the tent covering the pit were lashed closed, and a Coral Shores police officer was on duty, just as Gordon had said.

"Good morning," Robert said. "Is anyone in there?"

"No sir," the young officer replied. "The tribal rep should be here soon. Sergeant Smith is waiting to escort them."

"Can we wait inside?" Robert asked.

"I'm sorry, sir, no. You are only allowed in with a law enforcement escort. It's authorized personnel only." The twenty-something officer hooked his thumbs into his pant pockets. There was gray sandy soil dried on the sides of the officer's black patent leather shoes. *Uncomfortable. Has he been standing here all night?*

36

"I understand. It doesn't look like we'll have to wait long." Robert pointed to an overloaded golf cart making its way up the narrow asphalt road.

Gordon was at the wheel, and a woman in a striped shirt was beside him. Two others were behind them, shoulder to shoulder, on the small bench. As they drew closer, I could see the woman's shirt was embellished and not a printed pattern. The loose-fitting cotton shirt's collar had rickrack and ribbon that matched the white, black, red, and yellow band across the chest. The patchwork stripes ended in a row of footed Vs that looked like empty vases. *Or birds flying.* Gordon parked the cart on the path, and the foursome got out. One of the men wore a zippered camo jacket with white, black, and beige appliqued lines. The third tribal representative had grey hair and wore glasses.

"Robert, Miriam, this is Dr. Alice Cypress from the Preservation Office," Gordon said as he approached.

After Robert had introduced himself as the environmental engineer overseeing the construction, I extended my hand and introduced myself as Dr. Miriam Quinones.

"Are you the same Quiñones that wrote a piece about conchs for the AAA?" Alice Cypress asked.

"You read that?" I realized my raised eyebrows gave away my less-than-twenty-five- people-have-read-it emotions. I'd written the paper "Queen Conch and its Cultural and Culinary Importance in the Caribbean" as part of my dissertation. I'd been thrilled when the American Anthropological Association had published it. "Yes, that's my work."

"You cited one of my papers on the Calusa."

"*Yes!* It's an honor to meet you, Dr. Cypress."

"Likewise, Dr. Quiñones. Is there a particular reason they called you to this site? Have they found cookery?"

"I don't know. My husband asked me to come," I pointed to Robert.

Dr. Alice Cypress scrutinized Robert for a moment, making a decision about him that she didn't vocalize. But whatever she'd decided about him, her collegial manner toward me didn't change. She introduced her associates by name. The elder of the two had Osceola as a surname. And the younger man's last name was Billie. Even I knew that both family names carried a long history of tribal leadership. It was clear that this group of representatives were heavy hitters.

"Mr. Smith, please tell me about the discovery of the remains," Alice Cypress said. "Hadn't this land been surveyed previously? 1995, I believe. Which led to an excavation. Am I right?"

"Yes, 1995. The golf course went from a nine to an eighteen. We weren't required to do another assessment because it had previously been developed and surveyed. We weren't expecting to find anything but backfill and beer cans."

I gave Robert a stop talking about garbage look. This was a grave site. He needed to show some reverence. He got the message but didn't get the chance to correct his faux pas. Gordon stepped forward and instructed the officer guarding the tent to open it. The tribal representatives smudged the opening and sang as they followed Gordon into the tented area. Robert and I took up the tail end.

It was dim inside. Dankness, the precursor of mildew and mold, permeated the still air. My nose began to run, and I stifled a sneeze. *South Florida, nature's petri dish.* Gordon connected a plug to an extension cord wrapped into the tent's armature to keep it off the ground and dry. The work lamp drove the shadowy gray away.

Gordon inspected the bones. "Where's the piece of pottery?"

Chapter Seven

A murmur ran through the tent like a barefoot child chasing a bubble. I did not know where the pottery shard had been found, so I didn't know where to look. The crater-like indentation in the sandy soil was scattered with bones and bone fragments. I saw a few phalanges and part of a mandible. *Is that a patella?* It was hard to tell what part of the body the bones had belonged to as they were scattered and broken.

"There was a piece of pottery here yesterday. I saw it." Gordon glared at the young officer, who immediately went on the defensive and swore no one had been in or out of the tent. Gordon and the officer had a private conversation that caused the young man's brow to flop sweat.

"*Hello,*" a voice outside the tent called. A man with a balding crown and a scraggly ponytail stood in the triangular opening. "May I come in?"

I was no longer faithful to Catholicism, but I instinctually made the sign of the cross. Maybe it was because we were standing beside a grave. Or maybe because that man had spooked us all with his sudden appearance. *Como un vampiro, turning from a bat to a person in a puff of smoke.* I swallowed a giggle. My brain had gone from vampire to The Count. Sirena had been watching *Sesame Street* that morning as Robert and I had left the house. And the man asking for permission to enter—*like a vampire*—was not unlike the Muppet character. His head was round. He had pointy arched eyebrows and a goatee like the lavender puppet. But his vibe was that of an absent-minded professor, from his rat tail hair to his unclipped toenails to his cargo pants with bulging pockets.

"I'd like to observe if I may." The man stepped into the tent with his sandaled feet. "Dr. Gregory Vander Bell, Archaeology chair, Grove College."

"Dr. Bell," Gordon said with an air of relief. "You are welcome to observe, but we will not be moving the remains just yet. Do you know Dr. Cypress from the Tribal Historical Preservation Office?" Gordon motioned to the only other woman in the tent. Alice's face stayed expressionless, but a chill had certainly blown in.

Gordon introduced her entourage and then turned to Robert and me. "You remember Robert, right?"

"Bobby! I haven't seen you since you went off to college. I had drinks with your parents just last weekend at the department soiree. So glad you've come back to Coral Shores for good." Dr. Bell seized Robert's hand like it was the golden idol from *Indiana Jones*. I'd watched the original for the first time a few weeks back at Robert's insistence. *Is a giant stone ball going to chase us?* "And this must be your lovely wife, the ethnographer, Marjory has told me so much about."

I doubted Marjory had said anything nice about me or my profession, but I smiled, nonetheless. He'd stressed the *ethno* part, and it had felt a little like a microaggression, but I swept it off as an idiosyncratic flourish by a Muppet.

"Can we focus on why we're here?" Alice Cypress asked in a chiding tone.

"Of course, of course, of course," Bell replied stepping backward with each word until his heels touched the tent's wall. He clasped his hands, sloped his shoulders, and lowered his head. The spot he'd backed into was a place where rain had previously puddled. Dr. Bell began to sink. *Suck. Splat. Glop.* He lifted his silt-caked sandals and moved three feet to the left. "Sorry."

Looks were exchanged between the three Miccosukee members.

Ay, mi madre, they do not like him. I wonder why exactly. I mean, other than that he barged in here. And he probably wants to dig up whatever artifacts and remains are here and put them in his museum, which is not a popular thing with Indigenous folks in the Americas. Hello, 1990 Native American Graves Protection and Repatriation Act.

A gentle elbow from my husband and smoke from the purification smudge tickling my nose brought me out of my deep thoughts. The elder of the trio was reciting words that I assumed were a prayer. The language was not one I could identify by name, but its rhythm and cadence were soothing. The ceremony took only a few minutes.

After a moment of reverent silence, Dr. Alice Cypress asked Gordon and Robert some questions. I saw her point to Dr. Bell, which pushed Gordon into action like a domino kicking off a Rube Goldberg machine. Gregory Vander Bell did not want to leave and didn't make it easy. He danced around Gordon, insisting he could add valuable expertise. He tried to manipulate Robert with family ties. Twice, he exited the tent only to come back in to offer assistance with identifying the remains. Gordon had to eventually escort the professor off the premises.

I gave my respects to Alice and the other tribal members before the young officer drove them back to their car. Robert, as the only other authorized person to be at the site, was left to guard the grave until Gordon returned. I stood by the opening and said my own prayer for whoever was buried there. Tía Elba had been teaching me more and more about La Regla de Ocha. I knew from her that the orisha of graveyards was Oyá. I wished I knew the right words, the Yoruba words. But like the prayer the elder had said, in a language I didn't understand, feelings and intentions were a universal language. *May this person's spirit be free, and their earthly vessel rest in peace.*

"What are you doing?" I asked when I opened my eyes again.

"Documenting," Robert replied.

"It seems rude to be taking pictures after what we just witnessed. It's a sacred space."

"People take pictures of cathedrals." Robert continued to snap pictures with his phone.

"True, but this is like an open grave."

"What about saint's relics?" Robert raised an eyebrow.

I exhaled in exacerbation. "You must respect the culture of the deceased. And in this case, that means do not disturb."

"We don't know for sure if these bones are Tequesta. They could be modern. They could belong to a hobo that fell asleep in a sand trap forty years ago."

"A hobo? What century are you in, Roberto?"

"Babe, it's not far-fetched. The train tracks run along the property line of the club. In the nineties, the club had a problem with vagrants. Come on, I need a win. This project has had so many delays. It's hemorrhaging. Don't smash my hopes."

I rolled my eyes. His founding family 'Old Florida' roots were showing. "Didn't Gordon say the forensic team had found a pottery shard?"

"That's what he said, but I didn't see it."

"See what?" Gordon asked, looking over my shoulder.

"The piece of pottery," I replied.

Gordon grumbled. "The kid," he motioned to the officer dismounting from the golf cart. "Swears no one has been in the tent. I'm hoping the forensic team bagged it. It was right there by that big bone."

I looked at where he was pointing. Upper-level human anatomy hadn't been a requirement for my degree, but if my memory served me well, the partially exposed bone appeared to be part of the pelvis.

"Here, I have a picture." Gordon took out his phone and swiped to the picture. He enlarged it. A trapezoid-shaped terracotta chip with a crisscross pattern filled the screen.

"That certainly looks ancient," I said, giving Robert a stern glare.

"When did you say the county's forensic archaeologist was getting back?" Robert asked his cousin.

"She's on her way to Quito to catch a flight. It will be at least two days," Gordon replied.

He and Robert sighed.

"Come on, let's go home," Robert said. "No one is getting any answers from this grave today. Dead men don't talk."

They don't talk in words, but they do speak.

Chapter Eight

I wasn't pleased with my husband. *Humanity over profit.* But I also recognized that he wanted to be out from under the country club's hotel project. His dream of greening the club and golf course had turned into a nightmare. On the ride home, we talked. He thanked me for coming with him. Robert admitted he was super stressed about it all. He'd let his ego get the better of him to make insensitive comments about the remains.

"I thought my biggest problem was going to be trapping and relocating Bernice. I never would have predicted finding human bones. I did the soil survey and the land report. Any pre-Columbian—"

I interrupted him. "Pre-contact."

"Any pre-contact artifacts should have been discovered during the 1995 course expansion. That body should not be there. And I don't think it's Indian."

"Native American."

"*Native American.* Thank you." Robert gave my thigh a loving squeeze. "That is exactly why I asked for your help. I don't want to hurt anyone."

"I know where your heart is. Even though your nerves want to short circuit it," I said.

Robert put the car in park and leaned over to kiss me. "I love you, Miriam Quiñones. You're my pacemaker."

Groan.

"Ouch," Robert said.

I took his head in my hands and planted a big, messy kiss on his lips. "I love you despite your terrible dad jokes."

"Manny likes my jokes." Robert clicked the remote lock on his key fob.

"I laugh at my dad's jokes, too. That doesn't mean they're good."

"Oooo, I'm going to tell him," Robert said as we entered the house. "*Abuelooo—*"

"Don't you dare." I threatened him.

He winked. "I would never." He pulled me into a hug.

Manny and Sirena, hearing us home, ran into the living room and joined the embrace.

"¿Listos para ir?" I asked them. They replied like hungry pollitos chirping sí, sí. "We'll be back in a few hours. Relax. Watch a Marvel movie. You can't do anything to speed up the process."

"You're right. I think your parents want to borrow the car to go down to Krome Avenue to get some plants."

"You are a good son-in-law." I pecked him on the check.

"Well, they cook, clean, maintain the landscaping, and help with the kids. Lending them the car is the least I can do."

"I'll take your car. So they can take the SUV. It's better for hauling stuff. I bet they'll come home with enough plants to start their own nursery." *That's not a bad idea.* Mami *y* Papi had green thumbs. They could make anything grow. *Maybe not a nursery, that's a lot of work, but a plant-sitting business.* I filed away the idea to bring it up to them later. They were too young to be fully retired, and they'd appreciate a little income stream.

Robert moved Sirena's car seat into the back seat of his car, and we were on our way to Pepper's in a matter of minutes. I crossed the boulevard that separated the nice homes from the *very nice* homes. Ahead, framed by trees like a vintage postcard, was Biscayne Bay, with the sun shining on the blue-green water. A gust of wind ripped a palm frond off its trunk and sent it sailing onto the road. I slammed on my brakes.

"¡Mami!" Manny reacted to the hard stop. Sirena did the opposite. She broke out in laughter.

Oyá, is that you? The orisha of graveyards also wielded the wind. I wasn't one for superstitions and omens. Pero, I'd ignored a warning from the ancestors once before and it had almost cost me and baby Sirena our lives. *Oyá, if you are trying to tell me something. I need you to be a little clearer.*

I proceeded down the block, watching the sky for projectiles. Thankfully, it seemed to have been an anomaly. The weather was mild, with only a gentle breeze when we got out of the car.

"Mama-tee!" Sirena squealed.

Manny and I searched the water to see if it was true. My little mermaid had indeed spotted a manatee. I lowered her to the sidewalk, and we approached the railing for a better look. About ten feet from the seawall, there was not one but three sea cows. We watched the gentle, slow-moving herbivores swim by, then crossed the street to Pepper's house.

It didn't matter how often I'd been to her house, I was always in awe. Growing up in working-class Hialeah, my friends did not live in homes designed by world-renowned architects. Pepper Halstead's house looked like a modern art museum. It had two two-story rectangles with a glass bridge between them. A rooftop pool cascaded from the right-hand tower down the side into the lush garden between the structures. I thought her house looked like an H for Halstead.

The front gate was unlocked, so we let ourselves in. Gabriela, Pepper's ex-nanny, had graduated to full-time teaching at the Montessori school the kids attended, but she still lived with the Halsteads and helped out with childcare occasionally. Manny hugged Gabriela before joining his bestie, Sophia, who was building a Minecraft Lego set. Sirena wiggled her hand free from mine and ran over to Elliot, neck-deep in pink and lilac balls. I gave Sirena a hand getting into the ball pit. The girls began throwing the balls out and giggling.

"No te preocupes," Gabriela said in her Peruvian accent. "I'm watching them. Everyone is on the roof. Go and join them."

"Gracias," I said. The glass bridge was always a little scary to me. And it gave me a touch of vertigo, so I used the spiral stairs to get to the pool deck. It was too cool for swimming, but it was perfect weather to be outside—sunny with an occasional cool breeze.

"Por fin llegaste," Alma shouted exuberantly, causing her pashmina to slip off. It seemed she was right—I was the last to arrive. My BFF and I kissed each other on the cheek per Cuban good manners. Alma was dressed in a coral-colored flowy romper with strappy gold high heels. Fashion people called the style resort wear. In Miami, we called it everyday wear. Well, everyday for Alma. She had incredible style. Me, not so much. Gracias a La Caridad, Marie was dressed low-key like me in relaxed-fit pants, flats, and a long-sleeve blouse from Target.

"Hi, Marie. How is *Fritay All Day* doing with your new hires?" I asked about her Haitian restaurant on wheels. She and her husband Jamal had been running the food truck by themselves until recently.

"I think this new woman is going to work out. She's Haitian, so she's a natural with the spices," Maria answered.

"I'm so glad you're finally getting a moment to rest and relax."

Marie laughed. "Only for a few hours. We just signed a lease on a place. Small, but small is safe."

"Chica, that is super! I'm so happy for you. Let me know when you're ready, and we will do an *Abuela Approved* episode with you. Have you told everyone?" Alma and I had been friends with Marie since high school. She was one of the few Haitian kids in our predominantly Cuban school. She'd gotten to know Sally, Pepper, and Ana when we'd done a women's club gala pre-pandemic. *Never again!*

"Are you talking about the new place?" Sally, my SIL, was lounging with a Mimosa in her hand. *Or is that Pepper's infamous Saint Tropez sangria?* "I looked over the lease for her. It's a good deal."

"Thanks to you. You should really let me pay you for the consult. You saved us from that 'acts of God' clause," Marie said.

"Yeah, a leaking roof is the owner's responsibility, not the tenant's. I'll take my fee in akra fries," Sally said.

"Since when have you liked malanga?" I asked my very American-in-taste SIL. Malanga/Yautía, a root vegetable called akra in Haiti, was a Caribbean starch that made a delicious, slightly nutty fry with a dry, fluffy center, especially when cut into thick sticks. But the Haitian version puréed the malanga with epis (a wet blend of herbs and veggies) and peppers. The spicy batter is then molded into shape and cooked in hot oil.

"Ever since Marie's truck has been coming to Vana's softball games. That little kick of heat is so good. I'm addicted to them." Sally emptied her flute, refilled it from the pitcher on the rolling cart, and poured me one.

I took a taste. *Bellini, not Mimosa. Peachy good.* Our host, Pepper, gave each of us a martini glass of charcuterie. It was a new trend that I wasn't opposed to. It made it easy to snack while socializing. "I love this," I said to Pepper. "I'm going to suggest it to Yoli. But maybe instead of salami, gouda, and nuts, Manchego croquetas, jamón serrano, and olives."

"That sounds delicious," Pepper said. "Has your cousin found a place to hold her anniversary party?"

Everyone stopped munching and looked at me. They all knew about Yoli's bad luck.

"No. Another place pulled out on them. Pobrecitos. Yoli and Bette didn't get a party for their wedding because of COVID, and now it's looking like their anniversary party is going to have to be postponed, too."

"We can't let that happen, mi'ja. I have a listing that is standing empty. The owner just rented it out for a commercial. I bet they'd rent it to me for a party. Let me talk to them," Alma said.

Pepper joined me by the wall as I stood with my back to the bay, my martini of meat resting on the wide ledge at about elbow height. "Nonsense. She can have it here. How many people are on the guest list?" Pepper asked.

"I don't know, mostly family. Ours and Bette's. And some friends, maybe seventy-five people, a hundred at most." I shrugged my shoulders.

"We've had three hundred here. Tell her the problem is solved. Mi casa es su casa." Pepper's Oklahoma accented Spanish hurt my ears, but I loved her for trying and for her generosity. She was a true friend. "What's that in the bay?"

"We saw manatees when we got here. Are they back?

"Manatees aren't white." She pointed. "Is that a skeleton?"

I turned to look.

"¿Que, qué?" Alma shrieked.

The squad moved in unison like a choreographed dance troop to join us at the wall.

"It could be a plastic bag caught on a piece of wood," Marie said.

A mini yacht went full throttle as it passed the no-wake zone, causing a ripple of waves. The floating white thing disappeared and then bobbed up several times, making it hard to identify what exactly we were seeing. Finally, the wash pushed the thing closer to the seawall.

"That certainly looks like a skeleton," Sally said.

"Is it on a pool float?" Ana asked.

Okay, Oyá, I get you are trying to tell me something. Pero, coño, *enough with the bones.*

Chapter Nine

"Someone, *just not me*, should call the police," I said. *Ay, ay, ay. Frank is going to give me such mierda. Maybe I could just hide inside until it's over. But he knows our cars. There is no hiding— Miriam, you have to face the music.*

"On it," Pepper said. She had her phone to her ear. "An officer is on the way."

The six of us corkscrewed down the staircase. I whispered to Gabriela to keep the kids in the yard. The high hedge would block their view, but if Manny heard sirens or Gordon's voice, he'd be curious to see what was happening. Not knowing if there was any body remaining on the bones (*Eww!*), I wanted to spare the kids that trauma if I could.

Picture six slightly tipsy women—four dressed like celebrities and two like their underpaid assistants—walking across a street, a la Beatles album cover. That was us. If anyone had seen us, they'd have known *something* was up. Oddly, no one was on the promenade. And if anyone was on a balcony, they weren't paying attention. It was a gorgeous 75-degree day. Most of the boat docks were sans boats. Everyone was on the water, including, apparently, skeletons.

As we approached the railing, I could see that the bones were bones—well, a skeleton wearing board shorts.

"There's no skin or tissue on it," I said. *Gracias a La Caridad.*

"Have they been picked clean by birds and fish?" Ana asked.

"Or sharks," Pepper said with a little wobble in her voice.

"Pepper, look at the foam float. There aren't any teeth marks," Sally, always a voice of logic and reason, said. "Do you think the shark ate then placed the bones perfectly on the float?"

"Ay, mi madre, what if it's a balsero?" Alma asked. Despite immigration bans, people still risked their lives crossing the treacherous Florida straits to get to freedom and a better life. Homemade rafts and Frankenstein-ed boats washed up on our beaches daily or were intercepted by the Coast Guard. Not everyone survived the journey.

"How many Bellinis did you have before I got here, chica?" I said to my BFF. "Come on. Mira. Look. Clearly, that's a Halloween decoration."

The squad leaned over the rail to get a better look.

"Yeah, you're right," Alma said.

The others also agreed. The mood went from excited concern to what-is-going-on curiosity.

"But it's February," Pepper said.

"So?" Alma asked.

"So, where did it come from? No one has Halloween decorations up," Pepper added.

"Someone is playing a prank," Marie said.

"Probably. But that's a weird prank, right," I said.

A police car turned onto the street. The officer who got out was my cousin-in-law, Gordon. "Mrs. Halstead, you called in that there was a body in the bay."

"Not a body. A skeleton. We thought it was real, but now that we've gotten closer to it, we think it's a Halloween decoration," Pepper said apologetically.

Gordon looked at it for a long moment. The wave action jostled it, giving it life like it was dancing The Worm but, on its back, instead of its stomach. "I don't think that's a decoration. It doesn't look like plastic. Do you have a fruit picker or a long pole with a hook?"

"Will a pool skimmer work?" Pepper asked.

Gordon nodded. In the time it took her to get the skimmer, a bicycle cop had joined us. The village of Coral Shores had high property taxes and, therefore, a large law enforcement budget. The police were never more than a block away. Gordon directed the officer in shorts to jump down onto the rocks that lined the sea-wall. He then handled him the pole. The rocks had slick spots of algae, and the man nearly fell into the bay, but he was eventually able to coax the float close enough to grab it.

"What do we have here, Velma?" Detective Pullman asked, causing me to jump out of my skin. We'd all been so focused on the water rescue that none of us had noticed Frank's arrival.

Gordon, on his belly to help lift the skeleton onto the sidewalk, made an unhappy grumble.

"What is it?" Pullman asked him.

"This isn't a Costco special," he replied.

"Come again."

"The ladies thought it was a plastic decoration. But these bones feel real." Gordon rolled over and got up.

The skeleton was dripping salt water onto the concrete, making a halo not unlike a chalk body outline. I was reminded of the human bones Gordon and I had seen earlier in the day. But those were broken and shattered. These were articulated, connected at the joints by wires and screws. I'd seen similar ones mothballed at universities. It *could be* real human bones.

"Are those letters?" Pullman crouched to a squat. Using his pen, he flicked a piece of seaweed away. "S. M. I. T. H. Smith."

There were gasps followed by all eyes turning toward me.

"I think I have something else," the officer on the rocks said. In the pool skimmer's blue mesh was a bottle of Corona beer. Inside the bottle, there was a piece of paper.

Pullman took a pair of nitrile gloves from the inside pocket of his suit jacket. He popped the metal cap from the bottle and slid the paper out. Using his pinkies, he held diagonal corners down. On white velum, in red letters, was one sentence.

You're next, Smithie.

Pullman sighed. "Gordon, cordon off the area. We need to get forensics here."

By the time there was a yellow tape perimeter, there was also a crowd of onlookers. Most were innocent folks out for a stroll by the bay. But one man with a standard poodle was livestreaming or filming the scene. *Great! That will be viral news on the Around Town App.*

"Can we leave?" I asked Pullman. I didn't want to be filmed near a crime scene. *Is this a crime?* The thought that the person the bones belonged to had been murdered hadn't crossed my mind. *Wow, that would be some next-level creepy. Killing, then, eww, wiring the skeleton back together.*

"Yes, can we go back to my house? I have something in the oven." Pepper added.

Before nodding yes, Pullman eyed each of us like he was etching our likeness into his memory. We left the scene as a police van parked and blocked any future traffic.

Gabriela and the kids were in the kitchen eating lunch. Manny and Sophia asked if they could watch a movie after they finished. Pepper and I agreed it was a good idea to keep them inside until the activity beyond the hedge died down.

The squad followed Pepper to the teak table in the garden, each of us carrying some part of the meal.

"Well, that was not on my brunch bingo card," Sally said, breaking the silence that had fallen upon us.

"Drag queens, yes. Mimosas, yes. Quiche, yes." Marie motioned to the warm quiche Pepper had just set on the table. "But a castaway, nope."

"Where's Wilson?" Sally asked with a chuckle. The two shared a thanks-for-playing acknowledgment.

Ana expressed her confusion. *I'm a little confused, too.*

"The movie with Tom Hank." Sally's prompt hadn't helped me or Ana.

"Oh, the one where he is stranded on an island and his only friend is a volleyball," Alma said. "We watched it at Tatiana's house when she had that big sleepover senior year. Remember?"

"If you say so," I said. "All jokes aside, any ideas about who, what, or why?"

"Freaky, but it has to be a prank," Marie reiterated.

"And the Smith part?" Ana asked, looking from me to Sally. We were both married to Smith men.

"Smith is a very common name," Sally said. "It's probably the name of the manufacturer. It looked like one of those anatomically correct skeletons from a med school. I think your friend, Detective Pullman, is making a big deal out of nothing. I'm with Marie. Some teen found it in his grandparents' garage and thought it would be funny to put it on a float in the bay. One time, some kids put a piano on the sandbar."

"Oh my God, I remember that," Alma said. "It was the year I started my business in Coral Shores."

"Miriam, you're very quiet," Pepper said.

"I hope it's a prank. But Gordon was right. The bones looked real," I said.

"Duh. Of course, they *looked* real. They're made to be realistic. No seas boba. They don't make those things out of like dead people's bones," Alma said.

"Except—" I raised my eyebrows.

"Espérate." Alma put her fork down and leaned in. "Are you telling me they make them out of people bones?"

"They used to. The forensic anthropology department had a real one. It was from the 1920s," I said.

"Gross," Ana said before draining her glass of wine.

"Well, that puts a different spin on things," Sally said.

"Change of topic. Does anyone have a good book to recommend?" Pepper asked.

While Alma told everyone about a spicy romance novel she'd just finished, Sally whispered to me. "You know, Senior sometimes gets death threats. Do you think that was meant for him? I mean, the note could be read as a threat."

Our father-in-law, William R. Smith, Sr., was a prominent judge.

"Maybe," I whispered back. "Do you know if anyone he put away has gotten out recently?"

"I'll ask around."

A horrible thought crept into my mind.

What if the Smith isn't my father-in-law, but his son, my husband? The man who just unearthed a skeleton at the golf course. What if it's a message to Robert?

Chapter Ten

M onday morning, we ate breakfast inside because the patio was a maze of potted trees and plants.

"¿Abuela, cuales son esas?" Manny asked. He was at the French doors with Tom and Camo. They were all enjoying the new scenery. The cat was staring at a lizard. The dog's eyes were trained on a bird that was zooming in and out of the branches of an orange tree. *I think that's orange.*

"Compramos guayaba, limón, cachucha para frijoles negros, plátanos, banana, recao, cilantro, y varias otras yerbas," Abuela replied. I'd guessed the tree was citrus, just the wrong variety. It was a lime. In a few months, we wouldn't need to go to the grocery store for food.

"¿Qué es cachucha? I understood frijoles negros. I love them," Robert asked.

"It is the pepper you put in the black beans," she answered.

"Don't worry, Papi, it isn't a hot pepper," Manny said.

"Very good Manuelito, you recordaste." My mother beamed adoration on her nieto.

"Papi, recao is culanto which is *not*," Manny wagged his finger side to side. "the same thing as cilantro. I'm going to be a chef, so

I have to know these things." He climbed onto the bench and sat beside his Abuelo, who was dunking tostada into his café con leche.

I was doing the same thing with mine. Mami had sliced the Cuban bread into long biscotti-sized pieces so they'd fit into the coffee mug. All of us, minus Sirena and Robert, were dipping the buttered toast into our warm, sweet morning drink. We were as content as a dog with a bone. *Bones. Really, Miriam, you had to think of bones? I've got bones on the brain. The Smith carved into the bay skeleton—that has to be a company name or something. Right? That's not a message to Robert, right. Right?!*

"Are you going to the site today?" I asked my husband. Gordon wouldn't let anything happen to his cousin. *What do you think is going to happen, Miriam? The undead of Coral Shores rising from their graves like a horror film.* I shook off my creepy thought. Scary movies scared me.

"No. It's a complete stop work shutdown. There's no point. But I got an email over the weekend that might be a new client. They seem very eager. They want me to get started ASAP. They volunteered to wire a deposit to jump to the head of the line. There is no line, but they don't need to know that." Robert chuckled. "I'm meeting them at ten."

"I'm glad you have a new prospect on the horizon." Even though Robert's work had slowed, I wasn't worried about income. It was Robert's morale that had me concerned. The golf course hotel had been nothing but a series of headaches, and it was taking its toll. His forehead had faint creases where there were none before, and his easy smiles were now not as quick.

Abuelo took Manny to school so he could swing by the car wash and vacuum my car. Robert left for his office. It was nice to see a pep in his step. *I hope this new job is a smooth and easy one with no delays.* After I washed up the breakfast plates, Sirena, Tom, and

I went for a walk to give my mom a moment to herself before I left for the studio.

Thankfully, Sirena contentedly babbled to herself and didn't try to escape the jogger stroller, her trick de jour of late. I used the time to go over the day's recipe—croquetas. I always liked to give the viewers a little history and culture about the week's dish. We filmed the cooking part for the morning show, *La Tacita*, on Mondays. Then, on Wednesdays with Delvis, I'd record any voiceovers or added narration that was needed for the expanded Spanglish version that was *Abuela Approved*.

Delvis, you never texted me back! Everything better be okay. I guess I'll find out when I get to the studio.

I'd been deep in my head, letting the dog lead the way. When Tom stopped to take care of business, I realized we were on Marjory's street. Actually, we were in front of her house.

Am I imagining things, or did I see the curtains move?

"Hurry up and finish, Tom."

As I struggled to get the poop bag to open, I heard Marjory call my name. "Miriam."

Don't say a word to me, Marjory. You can see I'm picking it up.

"Miriam," she called again.

I showed her the knotted bag and pushed the stroller to leave.

"Miriam! Come here." Her curled finger beckoned me like Hansel and Gretel's would-be murderer, but she didn't step out of the house. "I need your help."

What game is she playing?

Against my better judgment, I pushed the stroller up the walkway to find out what she wanted. Robert and I had agreed that Marjory was on limited and supervised visits. Family gatherings were okay. It wasn't like we were going to keep her from seeing her grandchildren. But other Smiths needed to be there to keep her on her best behavior. When it was just me, she let the microaggressions fly like cannon fire. If it wasn't about speaking Spanish and my Cuban heritage, then it was about my *lowly* job as a "cook." She took every opportunity to remind me that The Smiths founded Coral Shores. They were elite and belonged. My parents and I were working class and didn't belong. I was taking a risk indulging the woman.

I locked the stroller's wheels, tied Tom's leash to the handle, and told him to stay. The dog looked at me with his golden eyes as if to say, "Curiosity killed the cat. Be careful."

"Thanks for the reminder," I whispered. I dropped the baggie on the step as I approached the door. "Good morning, Marjory. What is it you need?"

She poked her ash blonde head out and looked right and left. "I need you to do me a favor."

I could tell by how she closed her eyes that it pained her to say the words. She always looked everyone square in the eye like a ruler dispensing edicts.

"*Excuse me.*"

She huffed. "I need you to do me a favor. I need you to figure something out. You know, like you do."

I stared at her, blank-faced. *What is she talking about?* A beat went by.

"Please." Her tone was suspect, and her voice low.

I appreciated the please even if it wasn't entirely earnest, but my silence and befuddlement had been about the task.

"*Like I do.* What do you mean? You need me to decipher a recipe for you? You need me to interpret its cultural context?"

Marjory grumbled in exacerbation. "I need you to sleuth. You seem to be good at it. You figure things out before the police do."

The skill that I was most reluctant to use was the thing that now gave me value in her mind. I was stupefied. *What is happening here?*

"Will you help me or not?" A glimpse of the old Marjory shone in her tone. She wanted—no, needed me to do something that no one else could do for her.

The wind blew through the trees, and Tom whined. *Oyá, is that you with another confusing message?*

"Marjory, I need to get home. I have to be at the studio soon," I said.

"Come by this afternoon. I'll be expecting you." Marjory receded further into the shadows of the foyer and then shut the door.

"Qué carajo was that?" I said to myself as I toed the stroller brake. "Like, really, what was that about? I need to call Sally. That was just too bizarre. Is she losing her mind? Is she going senile? She was acting a little paranoid, *right.*"

"Mama," Sirena cried.

I snapped back to parent mode. "¿Què mi sirenita?" She'd dropped *or had thrown* her sippy cup. Since she was laughing, I hazarded a guess it was thrown. I picked it up from the sidewalk and placed it in the handle's cup holder. Tom sniffed and then licked the liquid that had spilled.

Coño. I'd forgotten to pick up the poo bag on Marjory's front steps as I'd left. She'd have a fit.

I followed Sirena's example and laughed.

"Oh, well. Too late to go back now."

Chapter Eleven

I watched the final minutes of the morning show's live broadcast from the makeup chair. Viviana applied more mascara to my eyelashes. I tried to flutter them dry, but it felt like I was lifting weights with my eyelids. She was good but not as good as Jorge, a thought I kept to myself.

"Bella," Viviana proclaimed.

"Gracias, tú eres una artista de alta calidad." I complimented her artistry. It didn't hurt to keep on her good side. It was better to hear chisme from her than be chisme she gossiped to others about. She'd powdered and zhuzhed every Latin American star that had been on UnMundo's *La Tacita* show for the past fifteen years. She'd seen and heard a lot of cellphone conversations. Today's celebrity was Jenna Ortega. I'd read the subtitles off the monitors above the mirrors and was impressed that she'd learned the cello for her latest role, a series about Wednesday from the Addams Family. Viviana couldn't stop talking about how nice the young star had been. I was glad that Hollywood had cast a Latina in the lead. It wasn't something I saw a lot of growing up, and I hoped that it would be different for Sirena.

Viviana nudged me to vacate the chair and move to the couch. *La Tacita* was over, and Ileana, the host, would need it shortly. She and her sidekicks were doing their goofy dance to the outro music, but on mute, it looked like a bloopers reel. They would be coming in soon to remove their makeup. The set lipstick was too bright, and the blush too severe for daylight. Usually, Delvis came to get me before the host made her way to Viviana's room. But that didn't happen today.

After a brief interaction with Ileana, which involved sharing a video of Sirena and a few photos of Manny, I went looking for Delvis. I found her leaning, back toward me, against the counter of the *Cocina Caribeña* kitchen. Her head was down, looking at something. When she moved to put it away, I saw that it was her phone.

"Jefa, everything okay?" I asked. She didn't react. "Delvis, everything okay? Are you ready for me?"

"Yeah, give me a second." She walked behind the citrus-colored wall. After a few minutes, she came back around. Her worry lines were deeper.

"What's going on? You didn't return my texts after the Little Havana shoot. The police came to see me about the tour guide. What exactly happened?"

"I'll tell you later." Delvis turned toward her crew and clapped. "Vamos gente. Let's get rolling."

Her camera and sound crew increased their speed by a fraction. Everyone's vibe was low energy and distracted. When the lights went from half to full, the pace picked up a bit. Cecilia helped me arrange the ingredients, measuring utensils, and serving plate. When we'd had to film in my backyard, she and my mom had often chatted about the Dominican Republic. My parents had lived in Punta Cana for a few years, near where Cecilia had grown up.

"Psst. Do you know anything about what happened in Little Havana after the shoot on Saturday?" I asked Cecilia.

"No tengo los detalles but I know it has Delvis in a bad mood. Ask Alex. He might know something," Cecilia advised. She freed a lock of my hair from under the apron strap. "You are making a lot of croquetas, no."

"Why, are you hungry?" I turned the heat on for the oil.

"Starving. Y también, they are my favorite."

"I got you covered. The first one has your name on it," I said.

Cecilia went to her position by the prompter. From her laptop, she played a song. Salsa always settled my nerves and helped me get into the cooking and talking flow. I froze when we had to film live. That was the reason we taped my parts for *La Tacita*. When we were on location or on my patio, it was different. I was much more comfortable. It felt almost normal, like being in front of a room of students. During my graduate studies, I'd taught several 101 classes as a TA—teacher's assistant. But being in the studio with the blinding lights, obstacle course of cords, and the camera's lens that stared at you like a cyclops' eye required extra help. Mary Poppins said a spoonful of sugar helped the medicine go down, and I agreed. After a few of Celia Cruz's shouts of ¡Azúcar!, my anxiety was gone, and I was ready to cook.

The time between 'Action' and 'Cut' flew by. While mixing the ham into the flour and egg batter, I'd given a little history on our culture's love of jamón, pork, and all meats porcine. The Spanish ships had brought pigs to the Caribbean. The animals did well, maybe too well. They adapted to island life and multiplied. They became a cheap source of protein.

Alex rolled the camera in for a few close-ups of the finished and plated croquetas. I'd arranged them with a few sprigs of parsley and wedges of lime. "Ya. Ese es el último shot," he said, reaching for one of the hot golden fingers.

I swatted his hand away. "I promised Cecilia the first one."

"Je, je." She stuck out her tongue and then took her time selecting one just to make him ache. It was all in good humor.

I passed the plate around to the other techs, making sure everyone got one. Our director was nowhere to be found. "Delvis, venga. Coge una." I called for her to come and get one.

"Where did she go?" I asked Alex.

"I don't know, but I'll take hers," he said.

I pulled the plate out of his grasp. He made pleading eyes and gave my cooking compliments. I sighed and gave in. "Fine. Here have Delvis', but you have to tell me what happened after I left on Saturday."

Alex chomped into the crispy brown exterior. The crunch was audible, as was his *mmm* when he tasted the creamy and savory inside. He dusted the crumbs from his lips. "Deliciosa."

"Thank you. Now tell me what I missed," I said.

"I don't know what happened, exactly. It was raining, remember. We were running like locos to keep everything dry. Some of the equipment was in the vans, y some under the tents. Pero the rain was so heavy que el techo de one of the tents split open." Alex mimed a deluge of water falling on his head. "It was crazy. We were all just trying to find shelter from the rain—las touristas, los homeless, los viejtios del parque. I remember seeing Delvis by the door to the theater. She was yelling at that tour guide lady, the obnoxious one that wanted to get into the restaurant. Remember?"

"Yeah. La misma that marched through our crew area blind to the tape and signs and UnMundo logos everywhere." I sighed. "So, then, what happened? Did Delvis y la mujer get into a fight?" I asked.

"No. Delvis said something. Then the lady said something back. Then Delvis went—" Alex recreated Delvis' movement—hands sweeping the air to say I'm done. "Then like five minutes later la policía llego."

"Pero wait, what happened in those five minutes?"

"¿Qué se yo?" Alex shrugged.

"So, you didn't see anything else after Delvis got fed up with the lady?"

"I don't think so." He thought for a second. "Honesto, I don't remember. I was worried about the cameras and the rain. Sorry."

"Nothing to be sorry about. Who was with you? Do you think they saw anything?"

"Maybe. I don't know. It was very chaotic. Just ask Delvis."

"I would pero she's disappeared."

"I just saw her walking to makeup," Cecilia said from the darkness. The set lights were still on full, which left the tech area in inky shadows.

I thrusted the empty croquetas plate at Alex and hurried, careful not to trip on the cables that were like jungle vines and the random set decorations that lurked like beasts out for blood, to Viviana's dominion. When I got there, Delvis was nowhere in sight.

"¿Delvis estuvo por aquí?" I asked.

Viviana was resting on the sofa like it was a chaise lounge. Her high-heeled feet were up, and her arm was draped on the spine of the retired, velvet set piece. All she needed was a scantily dressed Adonis with a feather fan. It was all very boudoir.

"Acaba de salir," Viviana answered that I'd just missed her.

I was about to turn and go hunt for her when Viviana asked what I'd made on the show. I was still in my apron. *Miriam, you are so rude. You didn't save any croquetas for Vivi.*

"Croquetas, déjame retrirve te unos antes de que el crew se las coman todas," I said. Vivi didn't need to know I was lying. The crew had already eaten all of them. But if I hurried and got back to the set before the cleanup was complete, I could fry up a few more. I hadn't used all of the mixture, and the oil was probably still warm. Viviana didn't hate me, but I wasn't one of her favorites, *especially after bringing Jorge on board*. Her favorite was the network's late-night comedian that I, well, all of us, thought she had a crush on despite the thirty-plus-year age gap.

Viviana heard all the gossip, if not direct from the source, then from the grapevine. It felt like Delvis was avoiding me. So, I needed to go about this in a different way. I needed intel, and I bet Viviana had some. I caught Cecelia in the nick of time. Literally, she had the bowl over the garbage and was about to scrap it with a spatula. I turned the oil to high, and by the time it bubbled with fizz, I had three little logs ready to fry. I placed the glistening croquetas on a folded paper towel to soak up the excess oil, thanked Cecelia for her patience, and zoomed off with my bribe—*I mean peace offering*.

Viviana was still on the sofa and alone. I presented the culinary treat to her. She inhaled them, excusing her ravenous eating as a skipped breakfast. *Sure.* I smiled. No one in Miami could resist a hot-from-the-fryer croqueta.

"Vivi, I'm worried about Delvis. She seems preocupada sobre algo. Do you know what is bothering her?"

The head of the makeup department swung her legs off the couch and patted the cushion for me to join her.

"She is in trouble. Pero I don't know que tipo de problema. Me preguntó por el número de mi primo, el abogado," Viviana said.

"*Your cousin is a lawyer.* What kind of law?"

She gave me a quizzical look.

"Real Estate? Bancarrota?" I listed a few other types of law practices. When I got to criminal her left eyebrow arched, and I knew I'd hit the answer.

Why does Delvis need the name of a criminal defense lawyer?

Chapter Twelve

After learning Viviana's chisme, I searched for Delvis one more time before leaving the studio. *Things must be serious if she's asking for lawyers. Delvis, I wish you would talk to me. My BIL is a fantastic lawyer. Coño, mujer. What is going on?*

My stomach growled on cue as I passed *Tres Sillas*. Yoli's café was officially called *Tres Palmas*. But Yoli and I had called it *Tres Sillas* all our lives because it had started out as a three-stool counter. That had been when Tía Elba y Tío Jose ran it. Yoli had taken it over five or so years ago and expanded it. Tia Elba, her mom, my mom's SIL, still came in daily to help in the kitchen.

There were no spaces by the restaurant, so I parked at the end of the little strip mall. As I passed the botánica, I left some coins at the feet of the Saint Lazarus statue. Six-foot-tall realistic figurines at businesses and homes were not uncommon in Miami-Dade's Cuban strongholds like Hialeah and Westchester. The saint synchronized to the orisha of sickness and health, Babalú-Áye, was always represented as an emaciated elderly beggar on crutches with dogs licking the sores on his legs. When Manny was younger, he'd ask to pet the old man's dogs. He was unbothered by their gaunt guardian. *Ay, mi príncipe, so sweet and good-hearted.* San Lazaro's story had something to do with a rich man who got his comeuppance in the afterlife while the beggar was rewarded with good health. *Or something like that.*

The metal bell tinkled as I pushed the glass door of the restaurant open. Bette was behind the counter, staffing the espresso machine and the ventanita, the walk-up window. She greeted me without missing a move in her coffee ballet—pack the grounds, slide the excess off, twist the filter on the machine, spoon the sugar, steam the milk, stir the café, pour, serve, repeat.

I sat at the counter on the stool closest to the kitchen. My cousin and tía wouldn't mind if I walked right in, but I didn't want to break their flow and cause something to burn. Soon enough, Tía came out. She held a plate with churrasco/grilled skirt steak accompanied by boiled yucca. Her eyes lit up when she saw me.

"¿Qué tal, mi'ja?"

I accepted her drive-by hello kiss. Once she'd delivered the steak to the waitress attending to the booths and tables, she came to get my order. I went with the daily special, fricase de pollo, even though the garlicky aromas of the steak had been tempting. Tía Elba made a delicious, rich, and tender chicken fricassee. She was back from the kitchen with my lunch in mere moments. That's the great thing about ordering the special: it is made and ready to serve.

"Tía," I whispered. "Have they found a place to hold the party?"

"Come. Eat, and then after, I will tell you." Tía patted my forearm like I was a little kid.

Bette got a moment of respite from window service and joined me for a chat. I didn't want to upset her by asking about the party planning, so instead, I asked about her sister, Omarosa.

"Are they still thinking destination wedding?" I asked.

"Ay, sí. My sister is crazy. She needs to give up that dream. No hay dinero pa esa bobería. Scotland! Imagine mi papá in a kilt." Bette laughed.

"Scotland? I thought it was going to be in Santo Domingo." I speared a piece of potato and ran it through the golden sauce.

"Ay, nena. She has been watching *Outlander*. Do you know that show?" She tucked a coily strand of black hair back into place under her headwrap.

"It's a romance with like time travel in it or algo." I wasn't confident.

"I don't know, pero she started watching it during the pandemic, and now that is all she talks about. She's read all the books, too. And then they did uno de eso DNA things because they want to have kids soon, and she was all worried about no se qué pero anyway. Gordon's came back con como 18% Scottish, and now every other word out of her mouth is Scotland this y Scotland that. Nena, do they even let brown people rent castles?"

I laughed. "Of course they do," I explained that Scotland was part of the United Kingdom of Great Britain, and that there were Caribbean diaspora from places like Jamaica, Dominica, Grenada, Trinidad and Tobago, as well as other places that had felt the impact of the British Empire like in Africa and India. "They could honeymoon in a castle. But a destination wedding is asking a lot."

"That's what Gordon says, too. I like him. Él es mi pana." Bette used the Dominican slang for buddy. "Y Mami loves him, también. She is teaching him to dance merengue."

My heart swelled. I'd kind of gotten the pair together. I began to think of castle-like places in Miami where they could have the wedding. There was Coral Castle, 1,110 tons of oolite limestone carved for a lost sweetheart. *Miriam, that's more like a rock garden than a castle.* There was Vizcaya, a favorite spot for quince photographs. It was a late Gilded age Mediterranean Revival estate built by the Deerings on Biscayne Bay. Gorgeous, but it had an Italian feeling to it. Then there was the Spanish monastery. *Not Scottish, but legit old.* The cloisters and chapel dated back some eight hundred years. William Randolph Hearst had shipped it to New York stone by stone. *Rich people and their expensive whimsies.* I'd forgotten how it had eventually ended up in North Miami, but it was a tourist attraction during the week and a church on Sundays. *That's a perfect place. I'm going to mention it to Omarosa.*

"Joven." A viejo at the window called to get Bette's attention. She left me to make him a colada, a large serving of espresso to share.

"¿Quieres un café?" she asked me.

"Un chin," I replied that I'd take a smidge.

Tía came out of the kitchen without her apron. "Acompáñame," she said.

I didn't know where she wanted me to go with her, but I understood it was a directive, not a query. I threw back my shot of Cuban coffee as I exited. We didn't go far. *Ay, Tía, I hope this isn't another surprise visit to the babalawo.* I skirted around Saint Lazarus and followed my aunt into the botánica. The last time she'd taken me there, it had been for a reading (like Tarot but with cowrie shells) by the babalawo. The honorific was a Yoruba word that meant 'father of secrets.'

"I need to buy a despojo for Yoli y Bette," Tía said. "This is too much mala suerte." Tía Elba believed in the power of despojo baths to defunk whatever bad funk had stuck to a person.

"They *have had* bad luck finding a banquet hall."

"Más que bad. Lo robaron el dinero." Tía studied the list of available fresh herbs written on the chalkboard above the counter.

"Wow, I can't believe they stole their deposit."

Tía exchanged a friendly greeting with the man dressed in white. Around his wrist and neck, he wore several beaded strands called elekes. *I think that and the white clothes means he is an initi-ate, a santero in training.* The man wrote down Tía's order and disappeared into a back room. While she waited at the counter, I perused the aisles. There were statues, urns, candles, bells, metal, fans, shells, and seed pods. The inventory was organized by orisha. There was a whole section of red. That was Chango's color. The blue was Yemaya. Purple was San Lazaro/Babalú-Áye. Yellow was Oshun/La Caridad de Cobre. I moved from one monochrome dis-play to the next until I stood in front of one that was rainbow. It had a lit candle, a bowl of black-eyed peas, and nine stalks of fresh gladiolas.

"¿Cuál es ésta? Is this Oyá?" I asked Tía.

Tía, the man in white, and the babalawo I'd met on a previous trip joined me in front of the multicolored display.

"Yesterday was her celebration day," the babalawo said in a thick Cuban accent.

"*Interesante.*" I thought I'd keep those words in my head, but obviously, I hadn't because I was getting looks from Tía, the initi-ate, and the babalawo. After an awkward silence on my part and hard, inquisitive stares from them, I gave in. "I think she has been trying to tell me something." I explained that I'd never thought much about the saint or her counterpart but that recently, I'd vis-ited a gravesite, and since then, it had been more bones and a lot of wind.

The babalawo said something in the Yoruba language that the initiate and Tía understood.

"Es tiempo para una consulta," Tía said.

Not again! The last time the ancestors gave me a warning, I hadn't taken it seriously enough. If I got another warning, I'd promised I'd take notes and follow their directions. *Lo juro.*

I sat on the floor opposite the babalawo with a straw mat between us. In Spanish, he asked me to explain what I'd felt and where I'd been when I'd thought about Oyá. When I told him I'd felt moved to say a prayer to Oyá during Alice Cypress's ceremony, he asked me a few questions about the bones and gravesite. He threw the cowrie shells and studied their positions.

"Son indios, pero no son viejos," he said.

The bones are 'Indian' but they're not old. I think I'll wait for a forensic confirmation on that one.

His next question to the ancestors was about the skeleton in the bay. The answer from the shells was confusing. He threw the shells again and got the same mixed answer. It was a maybe. Maybe the skeleton was related to the golf course gravesite, but maybe not.

"Pero sí son de la familia de tu pareja," he said.

His words gave me a chill. I hadn't told him about the Smith name etched into the femur. *Okay, okay. You've got my full attention now, Oyá.*

His last question was a request for advice. What should I do?

"Tienes que traer justicia y buscar la culpable."

Excuse me? I have to find the guilty and bring about justice.

Chapter Thirteen

"What's all that?" Robert asked about the bags in the back of my car.

"You don't really want to know," I replied, giving him a kiss. "I'll just say it's a Tía Elba thing."

"Well, let me at least help you with them."

I handed him the bags that contained groceries. Tía and the babalawo had instructed me that I needed to make an ebo/offering to Oyá. Ebos sometimes involved food but always involved work—a giving of one's labor. Since I work with food as a career, the babalawo said I should cook a food offering for Oyá. The orisha liked sweets like chocolate as well as spicy foods. I decided I'd make her a spicy black-eyed pea soup with sweet potato and coconut milk.

"How did your meeting go?" I asked.

"It was quick *and a little strange*." Robert unlocked the door.

"Strange how?" I inquired, as I made my way to the dining room table to set my bags down. Camo nearly tripped me, head-butting my ankles as I walked.

"*Well,* the developer came with his lawyer, which isn't unusual, but they insisted on paying me in full. Normally, it's half now and half when I submit my report. And then they wanted photos of us shaking hands and handing over the check. I guess it's for their website. I don't know. It was just a little much. *Is that a machete?*" Robert pointed to the wooden handle that had slipped from one of my botanica bags.

"Yes." I put it back in the bag. "It's a Tía Elba thing."

"Your phone is ringing." Robert motioned to my purse.

"Can you check who it is?" I had gladiolas in my arms that needed water and a vase.

"It's my mother." Robert looked at the screen like his eyes deceived him.

"Coño. She wanted me to drop by her house this afternoon. I completely forgot. Oh, well." I shrugged. "Don't answer it." I continued my search for a big enough vessel. "Camo, no." I scolded, noticing she was laser-focused on the gladiola tips hanging over the counter. "Those are not cat toys." I found the heavy glass vase and put the tall, tusk-like flower in it with some cool water.

Out of the kitchen window, I could see my parents playing tea party with Sirena. Papi had upcycled Manny's play cottage into a beach shack, complete with a sand pit yard and a surfboard painted on the side. When I'd left that morning, it had been devoid of foliage, but now it had banana and plantain trees around it. Tom, wearing a bucket hat, was asleep at my dad's feet. I grabbed my phone from Robert, opened the French doors, and went outside to capture the scene.

"Babe, is my mom—" Robert huffed the unsaid. "Do I need to have *another* talk with her?"

Sirena, seeing her dad, sprinted as fast as her little legs could manage toward him. Robert lifted her into an airplane zoomie and then hugged our giggly girl.

"I don't know what she wants this time, but it feels different. So, let me handle it for now." I snapped a photo of Robert and Sirena.

"I've got your back if you need me to intercede."

"I know, mi amor." I stroked his bicep.

"Niña, do you want me to pick up Manny?" Papi asked, tapping the watch on his wrist.

"No, yo pue—" My phone buzzed again. It was Marjory. *Miriam, the longer you avoid her, the louder she's going to get.* I changed my mind and gave him my car to go get Manny from his afterschool enrichment class. I texted my mother-in-law that I'd walk over to her house in thirty minutes. She replied, *GOOD.*

Mami helped me move the things for Oyá's altar into my bedroom and away from my curious mermaid. Mami warned me that a bedroom wasn't a good place for that particular orisha. "You do not want pelaya en tu cama." It took me a moment to make the connection. *Oyá is a warrior that can bring an angry storm. Yep, I don't want fighting in our bed.* "No te preocupes, your father and I will make a place outside for the saint. Me alegra que estes regresando a la fe."

I didn't burst Mami's happiness by telling her I wasn't one hundred percent a believer. My rational side told me that the supernatural was a flight of imagination, while my emotional side entertained the hope that something or someone had a road map.

Mami mused about the best location for the saint house. She decided to consult with Tía Elba about what direction it should face. As long as it wasn't in our front yard, I was fine with it. The neighbors, well, not Nelson, already gave me and my parents curious looks. The kind of looks that expressed they were putting up with our ethnic eccentricity, so we should not push it. One time, the *Abuela Approved* salsa theme blared from my backyard at eight AM, and from then on, we were labeled the loud neighbors. What would they think about a saint house with food, flowers, and candles in the front yard? *Miriam, is that so different from burying a*

St. Joseph statue in the yard to help sell a house? Alba says half her Coral Shores clients do it.

Papi tooted the horn as he passed me. I could hear Willy Chirno singing through the closed window. It was one of Papi's favorite songs. *We are the loud Cubans. Je-je.*

Marjory was waiting for me. I caught a glimpse of her in the window. It was creepy. She looked like a motionless guard, a stone sentinel. Before I could reach for the knob, the door opened.

"Did anyone see you? Were you followed?" Marjory turned the deadlock and activated the security alarm. She gave the sidewalk a quick survey before overlapping the heavy drapes in the front window.

"*Ummm. No. I don't think so.* Marjory, what is going on?" I followed her to the back of the house. All the lights were off there, too. The horizontal wooden blinds in the sitting room were shut. Only thin lines of sunlight pierced through the edges.

"Someone is trying to kill us."

Her exaggerated intonation, coupled with her flounce into a chair, made her statement almost comical. But it was evident from the altered state of the house that she believed it. *Is she being paranoid? Did someone give her some sleep gummies? Cannabis is legal in Miami-Dade, and THC causes paranoia in some people.*

"Well, Miriam, don't you have anything to say?" Marjory crossed her arms.

"Umm." *Don't you dare ask her if she's eaten gummies.* "Umm."

"Has the cat got your tongue? Say something, woman."

Deep breath. Do not react to her insulting tone.

"That *is* worrisome. Have you told the police?" I tried for a sympathetic pitch.

"Of course the police know! But that know-nothing detective couldn't find a snake if it bit him on the nose." The foot of her crossed leg waggled with so much energy that it looked like her shoe was about to fly off. "I gave him the notes, and he's done nothing about them. Nothing!"

"Detective Pullman is very good at his job. You can rely on him to be thorough." I knew that some of Marjory's heightened emotion was due to the fact that she resented having to trust a Black man. The woman needed to confront her bigotry. But there was also real fear.

Something Sally had said came to mind. Senior occasionally got death threats. Marjory's worry made sense if the notes were threats.

"Can I see the notes?" I asked.

"The police have the first ones, but I got another one this morning." She went into the kitchen. The refrigerator opened and closed. She returned holding a gallon-sized ziplock bag. In it, there was a deli bag of roast beef with a paper note. "This was in our grocery delivery."

I took the bag from her.

"Don't open it!"

"Don't worry, I won't. It was smart of you to preserve the fingerprints for the police."

"No. It's the meat. It's probably laced with poison."

Not impossible, but not likely either. I read what I could of the note. The receipt paper on which the message was scrawled was wet with pink roast beef juice. The message was only two words.

You're dead.

Chapter Fourteen

On the walk home, I mulled over what Marjory had told me about the four notes. The first threat had come to Senior's office at the circuit court via the interdepartmental mail system. It had been in a sealed, unstamped envelope. That letter had told him to retire *or else*. The second note had been left under the wiper of Senior's car while parked in the secure courthouse garage. The third note had been placed inside Marjory's car while it was in their driveway. The author was getting closer each time.

None of the notes mentioned why Senior needed to retire. *But, duh, it has to be about one of his court cases.*

"But is it an old case or a new case?" I began talking out loud. "It has to be a new one. The evidence has to be so overwhelming that they know the jury will give a guilty verdict. So, why not buy a juror or two? Que estúpida soy. It's about *what* evidence will be permitted. This is a case that hasn't gone to trial yet."

"Tall girl," a voice called.

I recognized the Jamaican accent before I saw the person. There was only one person who called me that and it was Patricia Campbell. She was strolling along with Gillian Brown.

"Welcome back, I haven't seen you two since—" I began.

"I know. I know. Thank goodness for the vaccine," Gillian interjected. I was surprised she didn't say anything about the National Health Service. Despite living in Coral Shores for over thirty years (She'd been Robert's high school librarian.), she was still very British. She took every opportunity to laud England as better at most things, especially its healthcare system.

"How is your family?" I asked Patricia. Her son and grandson lived in Miami. She visited him often, always staying with Gillian. They'd been friends for decades.

"Every'ting good. Gillian tell me you have a baby girl."

"The little mermaid," Gillian said.

I smiled. "Yes, her name is Sirena. You must come and meet her. And my parents!"

Patricia and Gillian walked the final block home with me. Manny remembered Patricia. He gave her a big hug and offered his assistance as a sous chef if she needed help cooking.

"I'm very good at chopping vegetables," Manny said. "Much better than when you showed us how to make ackee."

"Is that so?" She grinned delighted.

I introduced her to my parents and Sirena.

"Is Robert home?" Gillian asked. "I want to ask him if he's read the latest Ann Cleeves." Gillian and Robert shared a love of thrillers. She'd introduced him to the genre.

"I don't know where he has gone," I replied. "*Mami?*"

She answered me in Spanish, which she normally didn't do when English-only speakers were around. Robert had received a phone call and had gone to the site. *The state archaeologist must be back from Peru.*

"Well, maybe I'll see him at the exhibit opening," Gillian said.

"Huh?"

"Sorry, I assumed you and Robert would be in attendance since your family name is on the building."

"The archaeology department at Grove College has a new exhibit opening?" I made the leap.

"Yes, *Dr. Bell* is giving a lecture." Gillian's voice had a flutter.

I noticed Patricia rolling her eyes. I guessed Dr. Bell was Gillian's latest unrequited love.

"I'll ask Robert. He must have misplaced the invitation," I said. *I doubt we got one. I am not the socialite my mother-in-law wanted.*

"Manny, what is this I see? You making stew or akkra?" Patricia asked, referring to the bag of peas in the bowl I had set out on the counter as a reminder to soak them overnight.

"Mami's friend Marie makes akra," Manny said.

"Mi amorcito, Marie makes the Haitian kind with malanga. I think Ms. Patricia is talking about the Jamaican kind that is made with black-eyed peas."

"Yes, the fritter." Patricia nodded.

"The names are similar because they come from the West African word, a Yoruba word—àkàrà. In Brazil, you know they speak—" I started.

"Portuguese. I know. My friend João is from there," Manny said. *You've been mentioning this new kid a lot. Maybe I should meet his mom and invite them over.*

"Well, in Brazil, it is called acarjé," I said.

"Listen to you go, Doctor Tall Girl," Patricia said with joy.

"I want to try them all," Manny declared. "Can we make them tomorrow? Ms. Patricia, will you show me how?"

My mother, who'd been listening to my etymology lesson, came into the kitchen to rinse Sirena's sippy cup. She whispered to me that Oyá was called Yansá in Brazil. "Maybe she is very hungry. Mejor que tu prepares todas las variaciones." Mami closed the tap.

"Do you have palm oil?" Patricia asked. "They are better when you fry them in red palm oil."

I looked in the cupboard. I thought I had a bottle, but it appeared I'd used it and hadn't restocked. "No. But I have plenty of peppers." I showed her the wrapped tray of Scotch bonnets.

"Don't worry. Be happy. I'll bring oil tomorrow." Patricia was done with the discussion and the visit. She told Gillian, who'd been talking with my father about her skunk vine and air potato problem, that they needed to finish their exercise. "I will see you tomorrow, young man," she said to Manny from the walkway.

All the talk about fried food had me thinking we should have a fresh and light salad for dinner—watercress, avocado, tomato, and onion. Nelson's avocado tree had had an abundant year. Every few days, we'd find one or two of the green, football-shaped fruits in a bag hung on the side gate. Or sometimes Nelson would pass them to us over our shared fence. I looked out the kitchen window and noticed one high up in the tree that needed to be plucked before it fell and cracked like Humpty Dumpty.

Nelson is due back anytime now. I can put Tom in his backyard and grab the avocado. Nelson won't mind.

I leashed Tom and let my parents know I was going on an avocado harvesting mission. The dog strained the lead as soon as we stepped outside. His person was back. Tim Nelson was lifting his suitcase from the car idling in the street.

"Perfect timing. Come to papa, baby." Tim squatted and let the dog lick his face.

"How was your trip? Where did you go?"

"New York." He shut the trunk.

"Fun. Did you get to see any shows?" I asked.

"Not this time. I was too tired of sitting all day to sit another three hours for a Broadway show."

"*Huh.* What were you doing?"

"I told you." Nelson looked at me, then got embarrassed. "*I didn't tell you?* OMG, I'm sorry, I thought you knew. I've got a new job, executive director of the South Florida LGBTQ Chamber of Commerce. And my first project is to make our film festival more diverse. Historically, it's been very white gay-male centric."

"That is so cool! Congratulations!"

"So, I went to learn from the organization that does the New York one. Can you believe I was in New York City for five days and didn't see a single museum or even shop." Nelson dropped his bag inside. "But I did see some amazing films that I can't wait to bring to Miami." He reached to take Tom's leash from me. "Thanks for taking care of my boy, Tom of Finland."

"Anytime. You know my kids *and Camo* adore him." I smiled. "I saw a ripe avocado in your tree. Can I get it for dinner?"

"Oh, of course, you don't even have to ask. The picker is by the fence. Just secure the gate on your way out."

The muscles in my back and arms were trembling, but I succeeded in picking the avocado. Controlling an eight-foot-long PVC pole, hooking the stem with the bent coat hanger, and getting the fruit into the sleeve (a two-liter soda bottle) was not an easy task. I cradled the waxy green thing like it was a newborn baby. And with my free hand, I pinched and massaged my strained neck.

"You okay, babe?" Robert asked. He'd arrived home while I was in Nelson's backyard.

"Just a little sore," I replied.

"Here, let me." He put his warm hands on my skin and rubbed my trapezius.

I moaned. It felt so nice. I enjoyed the kindness and let him do his thing. He kissed the back of my head when he was done. "That was amazing. Gracias, mi amor." I turned and kissed him on the lips. "You look tired. What happened at the site?"

"One question has been answered. But a whole bunch of new ones are being asked." He exhaled. "The bones aren't ancient."

"That's good, right? That means you can continue with the build."

"Yeah, that's what I thought. But when they moved the remains, they found more bones. Those are *definitely ancient*."

"Are they human?"

Chapter Fifteen

The following morning, I asked Roberto if I could go to the golf course with him. He got excited and started talking about wedges and putters and handicaps.

"Mi amor, not to golf." I cupped his face in my hands. "I want to visit the site again. I'm sorry. *But I promise,* te prometo, that one day I'll let you take me, and we can hit tiny balls into sand traps. And I won't complain about the heat or anything." I kissed him, and he laughed.

"Babe, I knew it was too good to be true. I was pulling your leg."

I put my hands on my hips and dropped my jaw.

"Miriam Quiñones will walk hours, in the rain, to get to a remote village to interview someone about a recipe. But she has no interest in The Sport of Kings, the Marvel universe, or *Star Wars.* And I'm one hundred percent okay as long as she likes me." Robert slipped his arms through mine and pulled me close.

"I love you," I said.

"I love you, too."

"Me. Me. Me. Me." Sirena bounced, asking to be picked up.

"I love you, too, little fish!" Robert swooped her onto his hip.

"No fish. *Mermad*," Sirena said.

"Ay, que hermosa." I put my hand over my chest. The toddler cuteness wouldn't last much longer, and I needed to treasure it. In six months, she'd be starting pre-school. Mermad would quickly become mermaid, maybe even Ariel.

Robert and I dropped Manny at Agape Montessori, then grabbed a cappuccino at J's Java, the coffee shop that had just opened on Coral Shores' main drag. While we were waiting for our oversized—it was practically a soup bowl—cup of frothy good-ness, Sally came in with her girls. They'd gotten a late start and were grabbing a sweet breakfast on the way to school.

"Hi, family," Sally waved. She gave Vana some money to han-dle the purchase and came to our table. "FYI—I haven't' forgotten about what we talked about. I just haven't had time, but it's on my agenda for today. I'll call or text if I find out anything."

"Mom, Rae wants two cronuts. Tell her that is too much," Vana called.

"It's fine. Let her get whatever she wants." Sally rolled her eyes discreetly so her girls couldn't see. "Got to run. The principal has threatened to put me on crossing guard duty if they're late one more time."

"What was Sally talking about?" Robert asked. He had a bit of a foam mustache that made him look devilishly charming.

"Senior. I asked her to check if your father was on the bench for something big. Or if maybe someone he'd sentenced had gotten out recently."

"Any particular reason?"

I didn't want to worry him, but at the same time I didn't want to keep it from him—especially after seeing the situation firsthand. Marjory was truly afraid. "Senior has been getting ominous threats." Robert opened his mouth to speak, but I continued. "More than usual." He nodded that he understood. "That's why your mother was desperate to see me yesterday. She wants my help finding out who is sending them." His lips parted again. *Porbrecito looks like a fish.* "I know! I told her the police are good at their job. I'm not getting involved."

"If you'll let me speak," He cleared his throat. "There is a team at the courthouse whose sole purpose is to follow up on this stuff and keep the judges safe. Senior has had to use them plenty of times before. Ninety-nine percent of the time, they're paper tigers. I'll talk to my mom. She needs to let the professionals handle it."

Paper tigers. Eeny, meeny, miney, moe. Catch a tiger by the toe. Robert's word choice had sent me to the racist sorting song, which, of course, reminded me of Marjory's bigotry toward Frank. Thinking about Detective Pullman made me think about bones.

"Babe, what is going on in that magnificent brain of yours?" Robert asked. "I can practically see one thought kicking into the next one like a domino race."

"Funny you should say that. Did you know that dominoes were once made out of animal bones? Hurry up and finish your coffee. I want to get to the site."

I was curious. I wanted to see the food evidence they'd found. The forensic archaeologists had excavated a layer or two below the original bones to be thorough. And they'd found animal bones—deer, manatee, porpoise, and seal. Meaning that, in all likelihood, the area had probably been occupied by the Tequesta tribe. There hasn't been a deer or seal in Coral Shores in probably ninety or more years. *I wonder if it's an Everglades-sized deer or a Key Deer-sized one.*

We arrived to a beehive of activity. Workers were coming in and out of the tent carrying boxes sealed with evidence tape. Robert was granted permission to observe, but I was not. I ended up sitting in a golf cart with Dr. Bell, who had volunteered his expertise but had also been denied access. He was emphatic that he'd be called into service at any moment.

"The Caribbean monk seal went extinct sometime in the 1950s. The last recorded sea-wolf—that's what Columbus called it—was sighted in the wild in 1952 halfway between Jamaica and Nicaragua," Dr. Bell said. "We know from Fontaneda that the *sea-wolf* was a delicacy reserved for the elite."

"Fontaneda?" I asked, having tuned out his nonstop chatter. The name was obviously Spanish. The way the professor had said it, as if it was a well-known resource, made me nervous that I was losing my knowledge. *Not good, Miriam. Are you really ready to go back into teaching?*

"Hernando de Escalante Fontaneda. Do you know his story? Oh, so interesting." Dr. Bell refreshed my memory. Fontaneda was a thirteen-year-old shipwreck survivor, the son of a Spanish official, who lived with the Indigenous people of Florida for seventeen years.

"Oh, of course, I've read an excerpt or two," I said.

"I've seen the 1575 original! *Memorias de las cosas y costa de los indios de la florida.* I made the trip to the archives in Seville. I held the original writings. It was electrifying."

"What a privilege that must have been. Are you fluent in Spanish?" His accent when saying the memoir's title had been decent.

"Oh, no, not fluent, but I get by. My French is much better," Dr Bell said.

A woman with an air of authority came out of the white tent. She stretched her arms skyward, rotated her torso, and took several deep breaths of the cool morning air. Then she looked our way and marched up the slight incline to the golf cart path.

"Ah, see, here comes Victoria to get me. Her expertise is Incan trepanation." Dr. Bell checked to see if I knew what he meant. I did, but before I could get the words cranial surgery out, he was talking again. *He really likes the sound of his own voice.* "Brutal practice, drilling a hole in someone's skull with no anesthesia. I'll take my peaceful Tequestas over her bloodthirsty Incans any day."

"Dr. Quiñones? I'm Dr. Victoria Bustinza, but my friends call me Wayra." The petite woman extended her hand. "I understand that your anthropological specialty is food."

I smiled affirmingly as I shook her hand. She looked like she would fit in perfectly with the Indigenous people in the Andes, which made me wonder if Wayra was a Quechua name.

"I have something that you might enjoy seeing. Come with me," she said.

"Wayra, what about me?" Dr. Bell asked.

"Dr. Bustinza," she corrected him. "No, we don't need your help. You should probably get back to Grove. I'm sure the college needs you." After we were out of earshot, she said, "That man is so full of himself."

"So, you've met him before?" I asked.

"More times than I care to." She sighed. "Here, put these on." She gave me a paper jumpsuit, hair net, and shoe covers.

Once I was zipped up and ready, she escorted me into the tent. I saw that the indentation was slightly deeper now. The human remains were gone, and a mosaic of animal bones was in its place. I was looking at a rubbish pile. Five hundred years ago, the original inhabitants of this land had had a feast and thrown the bones into the garbage.

"May I take a picture?" I asked.

"Take as many as you like," she told me.

"Did you find anything else? Plant materials? Cutting implements?" I zoomed in with my phone's lens and saw striations on a bone where a human had cut the meat away.

"No, nothing yet."

"I'd be interested in seeing them if they do."

"I'll see what I can do for you." She left to assist a tech.

Det. Pullman and Robert entered from the opposite side of the tent. They were both wearing jumpsuits like mine. Robert's worry lines were back. Whatever Frank was telling my husband wasn't good news. Frank acknowledged my presence with a chin jut as they parted ways.

"Are you finished?" Robert asked.

"I think so. Dr. Bustinza was very kind to let me take pictures," I said.

"Wayra. Yes, she's nice. She told me her name means wind in *Che-something*."

"Quechua?"

"That's it."

Wind. Coincidence? Or Oyá?

Chapter Sixteen

"It looked like Pullman was giving you some news," I said as we sat down for lunch at the country club. The club was not my happy place. The first time I'd been there, a woman had collapsed into her chicken salad and died shortly after. My next experience with the Coral Shores Country Club wasn't any better. I'd been strong-armed into organizing the menu for Marjory's annual women's club gala, and it had nearly killed me. A love-sick killer locked me in a freezer after I had witnessed her poisoning the chef.

"Yeah, I don't know what to make of it." Robert replied.

The waiter came and took our order. I chose the Hawaiian Chicken. It was described as having a sweet glaze which sounded similar to the guava barbeque sauce used on pinchos in Puerto Rico. Robert ordered a bacon and blue cheese burger.

"Sometime soon, we should go to the fritas place in Little Havana. The one I did a *La Tacita* spotlight of. I think you'll like their burgers. That might be a fun outing for Mami y Papi, too. Papi could play dominos in the park," I said.

"Let's do it this weekend."

"Cool." Our table, by the floor-to-ceiling window, looked onto the greens. The boutique hotel's building site was out of view, hidden behind a few bunkers to the right of us. It was weird to be in such luxurious comfort after having just been in a forensic clean suit. *Actually, why were we in overalls in the first place? Victoria— sorry I'm not calling you Wayra until we really are friends—said the bones were Glades era, so like five hundred-plus years old.* "Mi amor, what has Pullman said about the human bones?"

"That's what we were discussing when you saw us. I don't know what to make of it. The bones aren't ancient. They found part of the jaw. One of the teeth has a metal amalgam filling," Robert said.

"That's good. It should help with identifying the poor soul. Do they have any idea who it is?"

"No. Frank said they'll review missing persons reports from the last forty years. But they don't have a lot to go on. The death could be accidental or suspicious. I got the feeling he was leaning toward suspicious."

"What gives you that feeling?"

"He asked me a lot of questions about the 1995 expansion— when the club went from nine to eighteen holes. I told him what I'd read in the records. He sure hmm-ed a whole lot."

Our lunch arrived. My plate had a grilled pineapple slice on it. Robert's burger was on a brioche bun and came with truffle fries. I stole one with the most parmesan on it. Delicious.

"Speaking of Frank. I think that's him driving down the path." I pointed to the golf cart going at top speed.

"Who's that with him?"

"Maybe Dr. Bell." I squinted my eyes to get a better focus. "Yeah, I think that's him." The golf cart stopped suddenly. "Oh wow." I pointed to the traffic obstruction.

"Bernice! Where have you been hiding?" Robert shook his head.

The reptile ambled across the path toward a large central pond with an aerator. All action had paused. All eyes were on Bernice. She was a living dinosaur. The scutes on her back reflected the sun like patent leather. Her underside was a creamy yellow, and her chunky tail had gray patterned bands.

"I wish the trapper was here. Damn. She's avoided all his bait traps," Robert said.

"I think that's because she prefers live prey," I said, covering my eyes as the creature slipped into the water to head toward a clueless Muscovy duck.

Pullman's golfcart resumed its travel. He parked it next to ours, and the two men got out. As I cut the juicy grilled pineapple into bitesize pieces, I watched them enter the restaurant via the glass side door. Dr. Bell and Pullman parted ways as soon as they entered. Gregory Vander Bell strolled to the bar and made some animated small talk with the bartender that was meant to be overheard. "I'm getting too old to dig in the dirt." He pushed his glasses up the bridge of his nose, flicked his rat-tail braid away from his neck, and sat on the far side of the oval bar.

"May I intrude?" Detective Frank Pullman asked.

"Pull up a chair," Robert said. "Join us. Let me get you a menu."

"No need for that. I'll only stay a moment. I have an update on the skeleton we pulled from the bay." He looked at me.

I balled the napkin in my lap anxiously. The babalawo had said the bay bones were related to my husband's family. I hoped they weren't an actual relative.

"They're real. Aren't they?" I asked.

"Yes," Pullman said.

Robert set down his beer glass. "You're saying the skeleton Miriam and her friends found in the bay is like a medical skeleton, not a Halloween decoration."

"Yes, and the bones are real, not plaster or plastic, real human bones." Pullman sat back and drummed his fingers on the armrest.

"So, where did it come from?" I asked. "Was the message in the bottle for Senior? *Or Robert?*"

"*Babe,* what are you talking about?" Robert gave me a puzzled look.

"I told you that 'Smith' was etched into the bones and that there was an ominous note attached," I clarified.

"*Um, no,* you didn't." My husband interrupted. "If you *had,* I would have told you that my great great-uncle Bartholomew Smith had a medical supply company in the early 1900s. So, the skeleton might be one of his. I think the family donated a few of them to the college fifty or sixty years ago."

"Yes, that's what we've determined. Gordon spoke to his father and solved that part of the mystery pretty quickly," Pullman chimed in.

"But what about the note? *You're next, Smithie.*" I asked.

"We found the author, a Grove student. Seems like it is a game between two fraternities. Each one tries to one-up the other with a prank. The swimming trunks belonged to the Sigma Tua president."

"Well, that's a relief," I said. "Is it okay to spread the news to the rest of the group?"

"You have my permission," Pullman smirked. "See how easy that was, Velma. You didn't poke your nose into it, and the police got answers and resolved the issue quickly."

"You don't have to worry about me. I do not want to get anywhere near a criminal investigation. Puerto Rico with the FBI was enough for a lifetime." I popped a piece of chicken into my mouth on an upside-down fork.

"I agree with Detective Pullman. Please let law enforcement handle it," Robert said.

"On that note, *Frank*—" He gave me an oh-no look. "Have you spoken to my mother-in-law recently?"

"Yes, and Senior. Why?" Frank leaned over the table.

"So, she told you about the last threat, right, the one in the deli meat?" I gave him a grim grin.

Both men looked at me with concern.

"I'll go over there now. Gordon has extra patrols monitoring the house. And the Feds are aware of the situation. People who try to intimidate judges are going to mess around and find out that the Feds don't play," Pullman said, pushing his chair back to standup. "Don't go poking around, Velma. Leave your mother-in-law to me."

"Gladly. And for the record, that is exactly what I told her. She needs to let you do your job because you are very good at it."

"You heard her," Pullman said to Robert.

"I'll testify to it under oath," Robert said.

They fist-bumped.

"Okay, that's enough, you two."

We all had a good-hearted laugh as Pullman took his leave.

"You didn't share the finer details about your visit with my mother," Robert said.

"I know, but in my defense, a lot has happened this week, and it's only Tuesday." I made the one sign with my pointer finger. "Saturday, someone died in The Deco theater near where we had been filming, and the police questioned all of us." I held up another finger. "You found bones. Three, Pepper found a skeleton in the bay. That was on Sunday. Then Monday, number four, your mother. Mi amor, that's a lot of weirdness for three days."

"Just promise me your *Murder, She Wrote* binge-watch with your mother is the closest you get to sleuthing."

"Lo prometo."

Robert informed the waiter he wanted to charge our lunch to his club account. I still wasn't used to the easy relationship Robert and his family had with money. At my core, I was working-class—a child of immigrants. I kept a mental tally and budget, especially at the grocery store. I had memories from my elementary school years of Mami at the checkout, having to take food off the bill because she'd gone over budget. It hadn't happened as much as I got older, when my parents had better job security and resources. But that instability had stuck with me. Robert was born with a silver spoon. He'd never known the fear of insufficient funds. Gracias a La Caridad that Manny and Sirena weren't growing up worried about having food on the table. Pero a la misma vez, I hoped they wouldn't take their privileged circumstances for granted.

Miriam, no te preocupes tanto. Your kids are going to be fine. Status isn't going to be what drives them.

"Babe, you have the faraway look."

"I was just thinking about Manny and Sirena. I hope they grow up to be kind human beings," I said.

"They will. They have you and the abuelos," Robert said.

"*And* you! You're a pretty good one. Actually, how did you and your siblings avoid turning out like your mom?"

"Teachers and coaches. Honestly, thank God for sports and the library. They saved me and Drew."

"What about Bill? He seems a lot like your dad."

Our waiter, busy with another table, hadn't returned with the slip that needed to be signed. So, Robert and I went to the bar to ask the bartender for the bill.

"Yes, he had more of Senior's time than me and Drew. But he has a lot of Marjory in him, too. He cares about heritage and legacy and all that *family name bs.* He's thinking of running for mayor." Robert signed the slip and handed the leather folder to the bartender. "Thanks, man."

"Bobby," Dr. Bell called from the other side of the bar. "I hope you and your lovely wife will be attending the museum's twenty-fifth anniversary celebration. Your mother has gone all out. Coral Shores society will be talking about it for years to come."

"I'm afraid we haven't been invited, at least that I'm aware of," Robert said, looking at me to back him up.

Don't drag me into this, mi amor.

"Pish-posh. Of course, *all* The Smiths are invited. Grove College wouldn't be where it is today without the Smithies." Dr. Bells slurred.

"We'll see if we can make it." Robert nodded politely.

"Another gin and tonic, sir," the bartender asked. "Are you ready to order some lunch?"

"Yes, yes." Dr. Bell took the menu and tapped it on the oak bar top absently.

We were a few steps from the door when Dr. Bell called us back into conversation. "Bobby, I'm at your disposal. I have a team of students. We could start excavating tomorrow. I imagine you want to get on with the build. We'd be fast."

"That's a generous offer. I'm not the one making the decisions at the moment, but I'll pass it along to Dr. Bustinza," Robert said.

Gregory Vander Bell smiled, but I could tell that was not the response he'd wanted.

Chapter Seventeen

"Mi'ja, come. Let me show you what I made," Papi said the moment my feet hit the pavers. He stood by the garage door waving to me to join him.

"Voy, Papi." I threw Roberto a kiss and pushed the car door closed. "¿Qué bolá, Papi?"

Stepping into the garage, I saw the project that had him so excited. The fresh white paint was drying with the help of a portable fan. He had repurposed a wooden wine crate I'd picked up at a yard sale to make the saint house. He'd unscrewed the box's hinged lid and cut a rectangle into it. *Papi is so crafty.* He'd then used the scrap wood to make a triangular pediment for the top of the box.

"Voy a poner este pedazo de acrílico en la puerta." My dad beamed with pride at his ingenuity.

The acrylic door would keep the statue and food offerings safe from wildlife. *The animal kind and the Sirena kind.* "Bella. Gracias, Papi." I gave him a kiss and a hug.

Mami entered the garage from the kitchen. "Sirena está durmiendo," she informed us. "¿Está seca?" She touched the paint to test it. "Perfecto. Hagamos esto antes de que la niña despierte."

"Dale," I said, agreeing we should get it set up before Sirena woke.

Papi took the box to the opposite side of the house, where he'd placed an ornamental concrete pedestal. I'd never seen it, but Mami told me they'd purchased it with the plants over the weekend. He used a strong adhesive to secure the box to the pedestal. Then, he attached the box to the exterior wall with a small L bracket.

Mami got the sixteen-inch Virgen de la Candelaria statue from my bedroom and instructed me to wash it with the bottle of fragrant water I'd brought at the botanica.

"¿Sabes que ella es la patrona de las Canarias?" Mami asked if I knew that the saint was the patron of the Canary Islands. No, I hadn't. But I was aware that a large percentage of the Spanish sailors that stayed in Cuba during and after colonization were from that region of Spain. And that there had been waves of immigration between Cuba and The Canary Islands ever since. Some were forced, like in the Blood Tribute era of 1678–1764. Spain sent subsistence farming families from the Canaries, known as Isleños, to their colonies in the Americas to keep up with the demand for sugar, tobacco, and rum in Europe. The Spanish needed cheap human labor in the "New World." The population of the Canary Islands fit the bill since they weren't considered *true* Spaniards. Fifty Isleño families were relocated to the Americas for every one thousand tons of cargo shipped out of the Americas. *Why are humans so awful to each other in the name of profit?*

"Sécala, bien," Mami scolded.

I went over every nook and cranny again to make sure everything was dry. Then, we placed a maroon mat on the floor of the little house and set the saint on it. I'd chosen that particular statue because I thought the painter had done a wonderful job. Not only was the dress beautiful, but the Madonna and child were painted in a warm, deep brown. Some referred to her as La Morenita or The Black Madonna.

A gentle breeze swept down the side yard. *Is that you, Oyá? Miriam, what has gotten into you? You are talking to spirits.* Returning from the kitchen carrying the vase of multicolored gladiolas, a stronger breeze hit my back like hands pushing me.

Miriam, let go of your critical mind and be open to the possibilities. I admitted to myself that the events of the last few days had been odd. Bones and death and more bones. Having a little guidance from the ancestors couldn't hurt. Placing the flowers beside the little house, I knelt down and arranged the rest of the ornaments. I put the machete and horsehair whisk behind the statue, along with nine pennies around the base. I closed my eyes, and when I opened them, my daughter was beside me.

"Mami. Mami."

"Sirena, ven pa'ca." My mother was by the play cottage with her hand on her hip. Sirena had slipped away from her.

"Mami. Ray-bow for pretty mami," Sirena said. She gave me one of the pieces from her garden-themed puzzle.

"Gracias, mi tesoro," I thanked her.

"No, mami no tuyo. Pa' ella." Sirena took the piece from me and placed it at the statue's feet. Like she'd said, it was a rainbow for the pretty mother.

Okay. Okay. I'm paying attention.

"Lo siento, mi'ja," Mami said, coming to retrieve Sirena.

"No te preocupes. I need to go get Manny anyway. ¿Quieres ir conmigo, Sirena?" I asked if she wanted to go along for the ride. My mother informed me that my father was already on his way to get Manny. "¿Qué hora es?" I looked at my phone for the time and was shocked. I'd lost track of time. *Did I go into a trance? Freaky.*

While Mami and Sirena played in the backyard, I pulled together the ingredients for the afternoon cooking session. Manny got home from school and came bounding into the kitchen. A moment later, the doorbell rang. It was Patricia Campbell, with her contribution of red palm oil.

"Hello, young man. Are you ready to cook with me?" Patricia asked.

"Yes! I've already washed my hands, but I need to get my apron," Manny said. He loved his personalized *Cocina Caribeña* apron. Delvis had had them made when shooting in the patio kitchen looked like it was going to be a forever thing. She'd even had one made for my mother, too. It had "La Abuela" embroidered in orange across the top of the lime green apron.

Patricia and I discussed a plan and decided that she and Manny would make the fritters while I prepared the stew. After draining the black-eyed peas that had soaked overnight, I gave her half.

"Start the oil so it will be good and hot," Patricia ordered, and I obliged. I admired the oil's vibrant color as I poured it into the pan. The deep tangerine tone of the oil comes from the beta carotenes in the palm nut.

At the breakfast counter, Manny and Patricia had their heads down on task. With Manny on his step stool, they were almost the same height. I clicked a photo of the pair from behind. *¡Ay, qué cute! I can see him using it in a cookbook someday.*

"Good job skinning the peas. Can you cut this onion?" Patricia asked.

"Sliced, diced, or chopped?" Manny asked.

"Diced, please, little chef. I'll cut the pepper."

Once everything was chopped, Patricia put the black-eyed peas, onion, green pepper, and Scotch bonnet into the blender. "Now, watch me closely. I only put a little water to start because you can always add water—"

"But you can't remove it," Manny finished.

Patricia let out a belly laugh. "What you don't know?"

To the mixture, they added salt and seasoning. After a quick blitz to incorporate everything, Patricia poured the slurry into a bowl and added the portion of onion and pepper she'd set aside.

"Do you know how to whisk?" She laughed at Manny's incredulous expression. "Of course you do. Alright, I'm watching. Make sure 'em nice and airy."

Manny whisked the batter like he was Jacque Pépin preparing an omelet. I took a few more pictures. The pair moved their station to the stove. I was still peeling sweet potatoes for my stew. Patricia spooned the batter into the oil, and Manny flipped the dough balls with a long-handled slotted spoon. In just a few minutes, they had a pile of caramel-colored fritters. We each ate one.

"Delicious," I said.

"So, fluffy," Manny said.

I set aside three for Oyá and told Manny to take the rest out to his abuelos and sister.

"What you need?" Patricia asked, seeing I hadn't made much progress. I gave her the calabaza pumpkin to cube.

I put the lid on the frying pot and left it to cool on the back burner. On the front burner, I sauteed onions, garlic, and ginger. Once the onions were soft, I added the pumpkin, sweet potato, and carrots along with vegetable stock. While that simmered, Patricia and I sat at the counter to enjoy a cup of coffee.

"I'm worried about Gillian," Patricia said.

"Is she sick?"

"Sick in the head." Patricia sucked air through her teeth. "She's in love with that long hair, Gloria Vanderbilt professor man."

It took a second. *She means Gregory Vander Bell.* "Are they dating?"

There was another toothy air suck.

"You don't approve."

Patricia tutted again and added a cut-eye, which was Jamaican for ¿Qué tú crees?—What do you think?

"The pandemic must have been very lonely for her," I said. "It's good that she's getting out of the house. Come on. What is it you don't like about him?"

I wasn't going to apply to be the captain of the Dr. Bell fan club. He was annoyingly full of himself. But I imagined that a librarian and an archeology professor might have a lot to talk about. They were close to the same age. And after Gillian had pined over a married man she could never have, at least her latest crush was single. *He is single. Isn't he?*

"He needs to cut that ugly lizard tail."

I laughed. "I agree. The ponytail is not doing him any favors."

"And he smells," Patricia said curtly.

I'd sat next to him in the golf cart most of the morning and hadn't noticed that he smelled terrible. It felt like Patricia might be jealous or sore that Gillian had less time for her now that Bell was in the picture.

"Both those things are changeable." I did a one-arm shrug.

It had been about fifteen minutes, so I checked the tenderness of the vegetables. The soup was ready for the next step. I added the peas, two cups of stock, and a can of coconut milk. The recipe called for turmeric, thyme, and allspice. Because Oyá liked spicy flavors, I went heavy on the Scotch Bonnet peppers. The kitchen filled with a delectable aroma that was both warming and sweet.

"Tall girl, I'll be on my way. I need to sit with my grandbaby," Patricia said.

I tapped on the kitchen window to get Manny's attention. He came in and gave Mrs. Patricia a hug.

"I hope you and Manny can cook together again before you go back home to Jamaica," I said.

"Yes, please," Manny said.

"Little man is going to be a big chef. Next time, I'll show you how to make bun. Yeah?"

Manny looked at me to fill in his knowledge gap. "It's a brown bread made with molasses and raisins. You eat it with cheese." He smiled and gave a thumbs-up.

Patricia hooked her purse on her arm and moved toward the door. Before she exited, she hissed. "Tall girl, keep eyes on our lizard-tail man."

Chapter Eighteen

Papi told me he'd affixed the door to Oya's house. So, I took a moment to deliver the ebo to her while Sirena played with her father and Manny helped Abuela make tostones. The frying oil from the akara was still good, and Mami liked to conserve resources. I took a small bowl of the stew plus the fritters to La Morenita/Oyá and set them on the maroon mat. The little house was crowded. I closed the plexiglass door and latched it.

"What am I supposed to say?" I asked myself.

I don't know, but say something before she brings a storm.

"Oyá, por favor, acepta esta comida en gratitud por tu guía y tu protección."

I held my breath, expecting a gust of wind. When it didn't come, I guessed that my simple prayer had been enough. Please accept this offering of food in gratitude for your guidance and protection. As I thought about my words, I noticed that the still-hot stew was causing the plexiglass to fog with condensation.

Is this a message? Am I supposed to interrupt the shape? Ay, ay, ay, Miriam, porfa. Orishas don't communicate via amoeba-shaped blobs on windows.

I laughed at myself and cracked the door open to let out the steam. I'd have to remember to close it later. I heard Robert setting the table for dinner. It was a cool evening, but the spicy stew would keep us warm.

"Ah, there you are," Robert said. "Would you like a glass of wine with dinner? I'm having a beer—maybe two or three. Wait until I tell you what happened at the site."

"Bad news, huh? Sure, I'll have a glass of wine. I think there's a bottle of Sauvignon Blanc in the fridge. It will go well with the stew."

"And the fish. Abuela made some *filetes mariposa*. Did I say that right, butterfly fillets?"

I kissed him. "Perfectly."

Manny, with Camo close at his heels, came outside carrying the tostones. "I made mojo de ajo to dip them in," he said.

In a few minutes, we were all gathered and eating. Sirena, my seafood lover, was devouring the fried yellowtail snapper quicker than Abuela could debone them. Camo was beneath her booster seat, patiently waiting for the inevitable crumbs.

"¿Quién quiere natilla?" Abuela asked.

Everyone, including myself, raised their hands. I loved my mother's vanilla cinnamon pudding. Actually, natilla was closer to a custard since it was made with egg yolks. After everyone had licked their desert bowls clean, the dominoes came out. We played the Cuban game, which used a double nine set. We all helped turn the fichas face down.

"Manny, dale agua," Abuelo said. It was the Cuban way of saying mix the tiles. Abuelo was training Manny to be his partner for Yoli y Bette's anniversary party domino tournament. He was teaching him strategy and slang. Each number had a nickname. One was *Lunar de Lola* because the single dot looked like a beauty mark. Four was *El Cuarto de Tula*, a song the Buena Vista Social Club made world famous. Cuatro/four sounded similar to cuarto, room.

Five was *Monja* because that's what it was in *La Charada*, a dream interpretation booklet that Cubans used to pick lottery numbers. If you dreamed of a nun, then put your money on number five.

"Me pegué," Manny said triumphantly as he laid his last tile on the table.

"Is that your last tile?" I asked. I was proud and a little sore. Team Manny y Abuelo had thrown some great tranques/blocks. "Count your points." Robert and I gave him our unplayed tiles. I liked that dominoes was not only a great family bonding time but also provided math practice.

"Ninety-five, one hundred and two, plus eight, that's one hundred and ten!" Manny smacked the tile onto the table.

Abuelo clapped. "Así va." He patted his nieto on the back. "Así va. Sí, señor. We are going to be champions." My dad was brimming over with pride.

"That's game. Okay, bath time, then bed," I said.

"But I want to read my book," Manny protested.

"You can read in bed *after* your bath," Robert said.

"Can I read a book to Sirena?" Manny asked.

How did I get such a sweet angel? "Claro, que sí, mi príncipe. But only one," I said.

"*Two?*"

Robert and I laughed. "Okay, two, but then bedtime."

My parents went inside to keep an eye on the kids. Robert refilled my wine glass and got himself another beer. I shoved my cold toes under his leg and wrapped the throw he'd brought me around my torso. The evening sky was dark blue and clear. Stars were beginning to show. It was a beautiful evening in Miami. Robert rubbed his hand up and down my shin.

"So, what happened today?" I asked.

"Babe, it was crazy." He shook his head. "So, after I left you at the house, I went to the office to get the golf course expansion papers, right, just to triple-check that I hadn't missed something in them about artifacts. *There was nothing to miss because there was nothing found.* But anyway, I'm two minutes from the club, and I get a call from Gordon. Dr. Bell is drunk and making a scene."

"No, me digas." My mouth was agape.

"Yes. And so that Gordon doesn't have to arrest him—you know he's one of mother's friends—Gordon wants me to come get him and take him home."

"Did you?"

Robert took a glug of his beer. "I did, but first, I had to calm him down. *And* smooth some feathers with Wayra and Dr. Cypress."

"*Dr. Cypress.* She wasn't there when we were there."

"I think she arrived while we were having lunch." Robert stretched his arms wide. His chest made a crackle-pop as he released the stress from the day.

"What did Bell say that got them upset?"

"You'll have to get the details from Gordon, but from what I gathered, *Dr. Gregory Vander Bell—*"

In my head, I heard Patricia's voice saying *Gloria Vanderbilt.*

"—insinuated that Wayra was a sicko who liked to drill holes in skulls." Robert wrinkled his nose.

"*Trepanation.* It's her specialty, apparently, *but she doesn't practice it.*" I chuckled.

"*And* he insulted Dr. Cypress. He said she was a frigid as an iguana in a cold snap."

My jaw dropped lower. "No, he didn't!" Iguanas enter a dormant "frozen" state when the temperature gets below forty-five and fall from trees. It is a surreal South Florida occurrence.

"Yes, he did! It seems like they have a history."

"Wow, I should have stuck around for the telenovela. That sounds bananas."

"Babe, the man would not stop talking. He just kept blathering about how he had better credentials than them. He has a museum. He should be running the dig. That anything found belongs to him—his museum. Blah-blah-blah."

His museum. Coño, mediocre white men claiming ownership of all the things yet again.

"How did you get him to leave?"

"I told him I'd see what I could do to get him access to the site. It's a lie that will probably bite me in the culo."

"I love it when you talk Spanglish." I made a *rawr* cat growl.

Robert danced his eyebrows up and down. We rearranged our positions so we could be closer. Our intimacy stopped mid-kiss.

Clink. Crash.

"Coño, I forgot to close the door." I jumped up and ran to the side of the house. "Please, please, please, don't be the statue." I prepared myself for a confrontation with a raccoon or a possum.

"What is it?" Robert had followed me.

"Camo! What are you doing?" The calico fluff ball was perched on the saint house like a gigantic gargoyle. "Why aren't you inside with your person?" I scooped her into my arms.

"That's cute. Your dad made a dollhouse for Sirena, huh."

I looked at my husband with pity. Pobrecito. All our years together and he was still clueless. "No, mi amor, it's a Tía Elba thing."

"Ooooh. So, better I don't ask. Umm, but what's that dripping?" He pointed to the corner of the box.

I handed him Camo and went in for a closer look. The bowl of stew was leaking but upright. *Que raro.* A piece of the bowl was missing. *How did you crack?* I searched the grass below and found a squarish chip of pottery.

"Another *cat*astrophe. Camo, you are a troublemaker." Robert mushed the cat, loving on her.

No, no, no. This isn't a meow kind of accident. This is an orisha kind.

Chapter Nineteen

My sleep had been, *appropriately*, stormy. I'd tossed and turned and had strange dreams. I was still mulling them over as I drove to work the next morning. One of them had been stressful but funny. I was chasing an iguana through a China shop, trying to save priceless crockery before it hit the ground. Patricia was in that dream shouting, *Tall Girl, git him.*

There was another dream, but it was much darker. I was having a hard time recollecting the images. They were just out of reach, kind of like when a word is on the tip of your tongue. But the mood of it had stuck with me. I'd roomed with a woman from Georgia for half a semester in college. She'd used an expression that described exactly how I felt upon waking from the macabre dream. *'Someone is walking over your grave.'*

"Deja de pensar. It will come to you," I said to myself.

"¿Qué Mami?" Sirena asked from the backseat.

"Nada, mi tiburón." My little mermaid was wearing a knitted shark fin beanie, gracias a Titi Alba. My best friend was madrina to my kids, and she loved being the fun aunt.

I turned on the radio. A Celia Cruz song was playing. It was the perfect thing to sweep away the gloomy dream dust that was dimming my light. Sirena and I sang along. Well, she mostly sang one word, tumbao, whenever it came around.

Traffic from Coral Shores to Hialeah was light, and we arrived at the UnMundo studios with time to spare. Wednesdays were voiceover days. I'd record the English/Spanglish that would replace the Spanish we'd recorded on Monday. *Cocina Caribeña* was a straightforward cooking segment for the *La Tacita* morning show. *Abuela Approved* used the same footage, but it got supersized with additional cultural and culinary factoids and some fun animation like a big head tiny body version of me and smiley-faced avocados and fruits. It was aimed at twenty-something Latinx or what some call the 'no sabo' generation. I didn't really like that term. It felt mean.

I signed in at the front desk. Folks had been asking when I was going to bring Sirena to work. Today seemed like the right day, and it gave my parents a break. UnMundo had an onsite nursery and playroom. I wished more companies provided childcare. It made showing up for work so much less stressful. As we walked through the halls, everyone we passed stopped to meet Sirena. Her outfit caused a few befuddled looks. Things were changing, but for the most part, Latinidad expected boys to be in sportsball blue and girls to be in princess pink. Sirena was definitely a princess, just not a pink one. She'd accessorized her outfit with the shark fin hat, a tutu, a mermaid cat mini backpack (stuffed with sea-themed squishies), and bright orange crab slippers. Like I'd said, childless Titi Alba was indulgent. Rosario, the head abuelita at the nursery, was overjoyed to see Sirena. My darling merchild didn't look back. She dove right into playing with the other toddlers.

I took the elevator to the recording room. Cecilia and a sound engineer were in the control room.

"¿Dónde está Delvis?" I asked.

"Ella tiene algo hoy," Cecilia replied nonchalantly.

What does Delvis 'have' today? And why didn't she tell me? It was highly unusual for Delvis not to be there. *Abuela Approved* was her baby. She liked to be in on all aspects of its production. The one time she'd had a doctor's appointment that couldn't be rescheduled, she'd pushed the time back for recording so that she could be present.

I entered the booth, put on the headphones, and looked at the script. It had notes and directions in Delvis' handwriting. *Adlib here. Laugh for the animation. Say Croqueta like ¡Azúcar!* She'd prepared everything as per usual. Was this the way it was going to be now? Maybe Delvis was letting go of the reins a little, making space for Cecilia to move up to assistant director. *No. Something is going on.*

"¿Lista?" Cecilia asked via the intercom.

I gave a thumbs up. We did a practice read, and then we recorded. My performance wasn't going to win an Emmy, but my adlib about béchamel was high energy. Cecilia didn't request any do-overs. *Delvis would have made me say that one line five different ways.*

When I left the booth, I went downstairs to makeup. Viviana always had the chisme. If anyone had the intel on the reason for Delvis' absence, it would be Viviana. I marched into the makeup room and was surprised to see Jorge there.

"Chica, what are you doing here?" he asked.

"Better question. What are you doing here?" I sat beside him on the velvet couch.

"Viviana has something today. So, she asked me to take her place." Jorge spun his phone on the cushion. The rainbow pattern on the case formed the words Gay AF when spinning.

"Hmm."

"¿Hmm, qué?"

"Did she say what she had?"

"No. And I didn't ask because you know how she is. I just got off her mierda list. No quiero regresar a la."

"I hear you. Have you heard anything more about Little Havana?"

"No. Is it rescheduled?" Jorge asked.

We looked at each other, confused.

"I'm talking about the police and the dead tour guide."

"Ooooh." His mouth formed an O. "I guess no news is good news, no."

"No se. Delvis has been acting weird. I think she's worried. She was asking about lawyers."

Jorge grimaced.

"I know," I said. We hugged, and I left him.

In the hallway, on the way to get Sirena, I bumped into Ileana, *La Tacita*'s host. She asked about my family, and I mentioned my youngest was with me.

"¿En el daycare? Quiero verla," Ileana said.

She walked with me to the nursery. *Miriam, if you act like you know more than you do you might find out a few things.*

"Pobrecita. I hope Delvis's situation isn't causing problems for the network," I said.

"No te preocupes. Viviana esta con ella ahora misma consiguiendo un abogado. The police are harassing her because they have no suspects." Ileana fanned the air like a fly was annoying her.

You guessed right. Viviana is with Delvis, introducing her to her lawyer cousin.

"Ay, qué chula," Ileana said upon seeing Sirena. "Me encantan esos cachetes." She made pinching movements with her hands. Sirena's cheeks were the cutest.

While Ileana fawned over my daughter, I helped Rosario make café. UnMundo was a Latin American company, so almost every department had a little espresso machine.

"Rosario, tengo que darle algo importante a Delvis, pero perdí el nombre del primo de Viviana, el abogado," I said.

I was fishing for the lawyer's name. Thankfully, she took my bait. His name was Ronaldo Lombardi. I looked him up quickly. His office was in the Brickell area. *Carajo. That's too far to drive and conveniently bump into them.* If I couldn't find out what was going on from Delvis, I'd have to try another route. *I'll ask Frank.* He had been ticked enough at the young officer who'd come on his turf unannounced, that maybe he'd followed up on the situation.

I texted Pullman an invitation to lunch. *Oxtail is the daily special. RU free?*

Frank texted back. *Your cousin's? CU in 30.*

Bette and Tía were ecstatic when Sirena and I came into the diner. Tía told her she was going to make something special for her. I knew that probably meant croquetas preparadas and a papaya milkshake. I left my daughter in their care and found a booth. Detective Pullman walked into *Tres Sillas* right on time.

"You know I'm not going to tell you anything about those bones, Velma," he said.

"Can't a friend ask a friend out to lunch?" I acted like my feelings were hurt.

"Do you think I was born yesterday?" He laughed. "And I can't make them release the site any quicker."

"Sit. I'm not going to ask you about the golf course skeleton. I'm sure Dr. Bustinza is working as fast as she can."

The waitress set down a basket of Cuban bread and two glasses of water. We thanked her in Spanish.

"So, this is just a friendly lunch," Pullman said.

"Yes." I smiled. "*Aaaand—*"

Pullman chuckled. "Out with it."

"Have you heard anything from the MPD officer that came to my house?"

Our lunch came. Rabo encendido had been the Wednesday special at *Tres Sillas* for as long as the restaurant had been operating. Even though Yoli had taken over the restaurant, her mom still made the daily specials. Tía made her oxtail stew in a pressure cooker, which infused the beef with complex flavors and the meat tender enough to fall off the bone. It isn't a stew served in a bowl. It is served over rice. The dark, velvety sauce should glisten like gold. And the carrots and potatoes should be as creamy as butter. Frank had a few bites before he answered my question.

"No. I haven't heard from Officer Cruz," Pullman said. He sopped up the sauce with a piece of bread. "Mm-mm-mm. This is good." He smacked his lip.

I gave him a look.

"Don't you think it's good?"

"Come on, Frank."

"Oh, what you meant to ask was do I have any information about the incident that I can share with you?" He took a sip of his Materva.

I tilted my head and glared at him. "Yes."

"Velma, last I checked, you haven't applied for a PI license."

I exhaled. *Miriam, que boba eres. In what world is Detective Frank Pullman a talker?* I decided to take a different approach, a more honest one.

"I'm worried about my boss. She's getting a lawyer," I said.

"That's smart on her part."

"What do you mean?"

"When law enforcement is formally questioning you, there are only two smart moves. Have your lawyer present. Or keep your mouth shut."

"But she didn't do it," I tapped the end of my utensil on the table.

"How well do you know her?"

"It's not in her nature." I signaled to Bette that we were ready for coffee.

"You said that she followed the tour guide into the theater. Unless you were there, you don't know what exactly happened. The death could be manslaughter. Example: The pair get into a fight—

"An argument. A verbal, words-only altercation," I interrupted him.

"Fine. They get into a verbal altercation. Your boss pushes the tour guide, who hits her head on the corner of the terrazzo stairs."

"*Is that how the woman died?* I thought it was a film canister."

Frank ignored me and continued with his hypothesis. "Then, because your boss is angry, she lets the woman bleed a little. She waits to call the police. Once she calms down, she regrets waiting, but still, it is her actions that caused the death." Pullman shrugs.

"No." I shook my head. "Not Delvis. That doesn't sound like her."

Our coffee arrived. Bette or Tía had added a palmier/orejas cookie to the saucer. Some people said the cookie looked like an elephant's ear. To me, they'd always looked like fat hearts. The ingredients were simple—puffed pastry and sugar. They weren't normally on the *Tres Sillas* menu. I touched the flaky wafer. It was fresh-from-the-oven warm. I looked over at the counter and saw my daughter with a cookie bigger than her head. It was shaped like an octopus. *Ay, Tía que cómica.*

I broke off a piece of my cookie and dipped it into my espresso. Frank sipped, then bit, then sipped. But it had the same effect. The cookie was a perfect accompaniment to the bold and bitter Cuban coffee.

"Can you at least tell me the cause of death?" I asked.

Frank brushed a crumb from his tie. "A blunt impact injury to the head."

"From the stairs or the canister?"

"*Velma.*"

"Just hear me out. Officer Cruz said that the woman had been hit by a canister, the metal box that a film reel is stored in. And you just said her head hit the marble stairs. What if there was someone else in the cinema?"

"I'm sure the MPD looked into it."

"Are you sure *sure*?" I asked.

"*Velma.*"

"What if someone was inside the cinema?"

"The closed. Shuttered. Not-open-for-business cinema?"

"Yes! Like in the attic or in one of the projector rooms."

Pullman cocked his head. "Who do you think was in the theater? Quasimodo?"

"*Frank.*"

"I know." He mocked. "The Phantom of the Opera." He acted like he had a radio on his shoulder and spoke into it. "We need an A.P.B. on a suspect. Six foot. White. Male. Last seen wearing a tuxedo. He may be wearing a mask."

Chapter Twenty

I stopped at Alma's real estate office on the way home from lunch. Partly for distraction—I couldn't stop thinking about Delvis. *She's not a murderer, accidental or otherwise.* But also to show Alma how much Sirena loved the hat.

"Hola. Are you super busy?" I asked as I entered.

Alma stopped whatever she was doing on the computer and rushed to Sirena. She made a please-don't-eat-me joke that had my daughter giggling. Then she took her to the supply room. When they emerged several minutes later, Sirena was hugging a dolphin plushie bigger than she was, and Alma had a brown box in her arms.

"Amiga, her birthday is still a month away," I said, noticing the Disney font on the return label.

"Shh! Soy un hada madrina," Alma said. She sat Sirena in the middle of the large table in the signing room, a glass-walled room where buyers signed contracts. "*Bibbidi-Bobbidi-Boo.*" Alma waved an imaginary wand in the air before opening the box. She threw packing material hither and dither, causing Sirena to laugh. When she finally got out the box's contents, I gasped. It was a set of twelve dolls—all the princesses.

Sirena grew silent. Her eyes were wide. You could tell she was amazed. She pointed to Tiana. "That's Titi."

I looked at the princess in green. It did bear a resemblance to her godmother, Alma.

She poked the plastic above Jasmine and said, "Mami." Marie was Moana. Pepper was the pink one. Sally was the blue one.

"And which one am I?" Ana asked. She'd been on a call and had just joined us.

Sirena pointed to the doll in the purple dress.

"Which one is that one?" Ana looked at the back of the box and answered her own question. "Rapunzel. I do like her shoes."

Alma got a pair of scissors and began freeing the dolls. Sirena hugged each one as it was handed to her. I took dozens of photos. Ana joined in the fun, too. She gave each doll a different voice and had them talking to each other about their castles.

While Walt Disney World was coming alive, I got comfortable and put my feet up. I flipped through the brochures that had been moved off the table and onto the dramatic vine plants and fifty-dollar-candle shelf. Alma specialized in multi-million-dollar single-family homes in Coral Shores. Ana, because of her Russian heritage, focused on million-dollar condos in Aventura and Sunny Isle. Some glossy promotional materials were booklets. Others were heavy card stock postcards. All of them were preconstruction—pay now, wait two years to move-in. One, a building going up in downtown Miami, offered 750 square foot, one bedrooms starting at six hundred thousand. An 'affordable' complex in Guyo Gables advertised leasing would begin by the end of the year.

"Where is Guyo Gables?" I asked.

"That's what they are trying to rebrand Little Havana as," Ana said. She was restyling Rapunzel's hair.

"No jodas," I said, half-joking, half-serious. "*Guyo like gallo. Rooster Gables.*" I looked at the address. It wasn't far from The Deco

Cinema. "No entiendo. It is clearly in Little Havana. Like people aren't going to be fooled when they literally have to cross Calle Ocho to get to the place."

"The developer wants people to think Coral Gables, the City Beautiful," Ana replied. "Mediterranean Revival, arched doorways, coral rock, landscaped lawns, you know."

I laughed. "What's next, Little Brickell? West Biltmore?"

"Probably," Alma chimed into the conversation.

"What's the lease on an affordable Guyo Gables apartment?" I asked.

"Three thousand," Ana said.

"¿Que qué? How can someone making minimum wage afford that kind of rent?" I shook my head.

"They can't, but digital nomads can," Alma said. She had Mulan doing a pirouette.

I'd only recently heard the term digital nomad. They were people who could work from any location with high-speed internet access.

"And New Yorkers," Ana said. "They are getting more space, and they love the weather."

"The weather is *great* in tourist season, but their opinion will change when summer comes," I said. Just thinking about the humidity and heat made me hot. I fanned myself with the flyer. "New Yorkers don't own cars. Most of them don't even have a driver's license. They are going to have a rude awakening when they get here. You can't get around Miami without a car." The county had buses, but most of the stops had no shelter. You'd either die of heat stroke or get soaked by rain waiting for a bus.

"They Uber," Ana said.

"I guess." I shrugged. I looked at the digital rendering on the advertisement. The modest apartment buildings had barrel tile roofs, arched entryways, and colorful planters. People with athletic physiques were pictured running and bicycling on the sidewalks. A compact car with a SUP on the roof was parked at a charging station on the side of the complex. The complex looked clean and sparkly, nothing like the real Little Havana that had a gritty vibrance. "They could have at least put a rooster in the ad," I said, flicking the postcard onto the pile.

"I know," Ana said. "The people are going to demand their money back when the cocks start their singing battles."

Alma and I threw our heads back and crowed *ki-ki-ri-ki*. My giggly girl joined in, too. *Ki-ki-ri-ki*. When we had read her the Cuban folktale *The Bossy Gallito/El Gallo de Bodas,* she had demanded we do the rooster crow every time he was on the page. *I know what bedtime story you're going to want tonight.*

I thanked Alma and Ana for taking a break to play with Sirena. We left them to their work and went to pick up Manny from Pepper's house. He went home with his bestie Sophia on Wednesdays. I parked and texted Pepper that we were outside. While we waited, I took in the bay. A motorboat was anchored at one of the little islands in the middle. I could see the sandy beach and little dock. It looked like someone had set up a hammock. A wobble of kayaks was paddling between the islands.

"Mam-a-tee," Sirena said, bucking in her car seat.

"No, mi ángel, quédate en tu sillón. No hay manatee ahora," I replied.

There are no manatees and hopefully no skeletons, either.

"Hey there, lady, how'd recording go today?" Pepper asked. She had Elliot on her hip.

Manny and Sophia were at the seawall railing. Something on the rocks had caught their interest. Sophia squatted and then got on her belly. She reached down to the rocks. I expected her to bring up a hermit crab, but instead, she had a glass bottle.

"Look, Mom! We found a message in a bottle," Sophia said. She rolled onto her back, bent her knees, and popped up to a standing position. Children are nimble creatures.

I got out of the car with my keys in my hand. Sirena protested that she wanted out. Instead, Pepper put Elliot in the backseat with her. Pepper and I exchanged concerned looks. "Part of the prank war?" I whispered to my friend. Her reply was a noncommittal grumble.

Sophia was trying to shake the message out of the bottle. Manny found a stick and gave it to his bestie. The twig snapped. There was an audible ahh of disappointment.

"Here, let me try," Pepper offered. Using her hairclip, a sleek barrette that looked like an ibis's bill, and with the bottle turned upside down so that the paper was in the neck, she clipped the paper, twisted it to make the coil tighter, and slid it out. The paper unfurled. A stiff wind almost carried it back to out to sea, but Pepper blocked the breeze and saved the page from tearing and flying away.

"What does it say?" Sophia asked.

"Is it a pirate map?" Manny asked.

Is it another anonymous threat?

We followed Pepper to the protection of the car. She plastered the page onto the passenger side window. Her hands formed a frame.

In unison, we read the message out loud. "Smithie, end it before I end you."

Chapter
Twenty-One

Pepper held onto the bottle and the note since it had been found by her kid basically in her front yard. I took a snapshot of it and called Gordon for her. Sirena was grumpy, and Manny wanted to chill with Camo, so the Quiñones-Smiths left before the police arrived.

We came home to an empty house. I guessed my parents had either gone for a walk or Robert had taken them to run an errand. *Ay, ay, ay. I hope he didn't take them to the garden center. Coño Miriam, you forgot to tell Alma about your plant sitter/stager idea.* I put a reminder in my phone to tell Alma and Mami about my inspired business collab idea for them.

"Mami, can I look at your cookbooks?" Manny asked.

"Claro que sí, mi príncipe," I replied.

Manny, with Camo in his arms, went into my study. I made Sirena some warm milk and put her in her play tent for some quiet time. When I checked on her a few minutes later, she'd fallen asleep on the mound of stuffed animals in the tent. I poked my head in on Manny. He was sitting crisscross applesauce on the floor with four cookbooks open in front of him. Camo was draped over his legs, staring up at him with adoration. I took a photo without disturbing the tranquility.

I went into the kitchen with all intention to plan our evening meal, but Delvis texted.

I heard recording went ☺

Before she ghosted me again, I called her. *Come on, come on, answer the phone.*

"Hi."

"Hi."

There was a long pause.

"Are you going to tell me what's going on? Maybe I can help," I said.

Delvis sighed but didn't say anything.

"Jefa, I have experience with this kind of thing—you know, the police and dead bodies. Let me at least tell you what not to do." I waited for my boss to reply.

"I've got a lawyer. It's going to be fine," Delvis said. She was unconvinced and putting on a brave face.

I tried a different tactic. "Good. Hiring a lawyer is smart. What does your lawyer think about the evidence?"

"There is no evidence. The police are grasping at straws." Delvis's voice grew stronger. "They have nothing, and that's what's so frustrating. No video. No prints. Nada. Because I didn't do it! That lady was alive when I yelled—" She took a breath and rephrased. "Cynthia Jordan was alive when I told her not to go into the theater."

I sensed that the lawyer had already coached Delvis on how to say certain things.

"So, what happened after I left? Cynthia Jordan, that's the tour guide's name, no." Delvis made a noise of affirmation. I continued. "What did she want? Why did she go into The Deco?"

"It was raining, and I *think* she wanted to take her tour into the theater because, you know, the walking part of the tour was rained out. I told her the place was closed. She kept pulling on the door and knocking on the glass. I told her to leave. The Deco was private property, and she was also in our crew-only area, so I told her to move along. I turned my back on her and went to help the crew strike. The next time I looked in that direction, I noticed The Deco's door was open. Between you and me, de verdad, I was pissed. The lady had been so pushy and demanding all fricking day that I was going to give her a piece of my mind *and* call the cops on her. I literally had just pressed call on 911 when I saw her bleeding on the lobby floor," Delvis said.

"How did she get in?" I asked. "It was locked, *right*."

"I assume it was. Maybe she jimmied it loose."

"Did she break the glass? Did the lock look like she'd messed with it?" I asked. *How did she get in?*

"I don't remember, to be honest. I didn't think to look. I just went inside to tell her I was calling the cops on her for breaking and entering. But I guess the place had a silent alarm because the police were already on their way before I called. The dispatch heard me scream when I saw the blood."

"That's good. That proves you didn't do it."

"You'd think that, but no. They say there are seven minutes between the alarm and my call—enough time to have killed her." Delvis sighed.

"How exactly did she die?"

"I don't know what she did. Maybe she tripped, you know the lights were off and with the rain, there wasn't a lot of sunlight from the doors. I stumbled over something myself. It took a second for my eyes to adjust to the darkness."

"So, she tripped and fell."

"Yeah, I guess. She tripped and *fuácata*." Delvis used the Cuban onomatopoeia equivalent of whack.

"What did you see? Describe the scene to me."

"Her head was on the first step of the stairs. You've been there, no. The lobby has those terrazzo stairs that take you to the balcony seats."

"Was she on her back or chest?"

"Her back."

"*So, she tripped backward.*"

"I guess so."

"Did you see a film reel container?" I asked.

"Yeah. There was one on the floor near her head. It was open."

"Do you remember hearing anything? A noise? A door? Footsteps?"

"Just my heart. It was beating out of my chest. The dispatch was telling me to stay calm that help was on the way. Next thing I remember the police are entering the lobby."

"You didn't sense that someone else was in the building?"

"*You mean the killer.* Great, now I'm not going to get any sleep. The killer probably saw me. They know my face. Great."

I had not meant to scare Delvis, but the only plausible explanation was that someone else had been in The Deco. If the police weren't looking for the killer, then I guessed I'd have to. *I'm not letting Delvis get blamed for this.*

Delvis and I talked for a little while longer. I asked her to take me through her movements one more time. Nothing much changed. We ended the call on a work note.

"Don't forget about *Ria's Rotis*," I said. I wanted her to schedule a spotlight at a Trinidadian place I'd found. "I'll see you Saturday for the shoot."

"If they haven't arrested me by then," Delvis said.

"Cállate. You are *not* going to be arrested. I'll see you the day after tomorrow." I ended the call and looked at the time. *Oops. I better think of something easy for dinner.*

I opened the fridge to check if my mother had already prepared something for dinner. "Delvis is not going to get arrested." I moved the milk carton. "I'm not going to let that happen." I pulled the meat drawer open and lifted a tray of pork chops to see the use-by-date. "She did not kill that lady." I mumbled.

I put the chops down and moved them onto the vegetable drawer. Nothing was inspiring me. "Someone had to have seen something. Delvis is not a mur—" I shut the fridge door and found four sets of eyes waiting for me to stop talking to myself.

"Delvis is not a what, Mami?" Manny asked.

"Delvis is not a mur—, a mermaid," I said. *Quick thinking, Miriam. I'm sure Manny bought it. Roberto, not so much.* My husband's face told me he saw right through me. I needed to change the subject. "Familia, pónganse los zapatos vamos a comer afuera. ¿Quién quiere fritas para la cena?"

Manny clapped. My parents nodded amicably. Robert raised his eyebrow.

"Mi amor, hamburgers. *Yum!* You love a good hamburger." I hooked arms with him and escorted him out of the kitchen.

"Babe, what's going on with Delvis?" Robert asked.

I bent and looked inside Sirena's play tent. She fluttered her eyes open and yawned. "Venga mi sirenita vamos a pasear." I waved for her to come out so we could go on our outing.

"*Babe.*"

"*Mi amor.*" I kept my back to him.

"*Babe.*" He spun me around. "Delvis is not a *mermaid.*"

"Me, *mermad,*" Sirena said proudly, pointing at her chest.

"Yes, you are, my darling," Robert said. "Go to Abuela so she can help you get ready to leave." Our daughter toddled away. "Miriam, I know what you were about to say."

"Mud-duh. I was going to say 'mother' in a funny way." I grinned.

"You were about to say," Robert lowered his voice, "*murderer.*"

"*No.*" I wagged my head. "But I'll tell you what I am going to murder —a hamburger."

Chapter
Twenty-Two

Three generations fit comfortably into the Pacifica, reminding me of the how and why I had become a mini-van mama. I drove, and despite a little bit of workday rush hour traffic, we got to Little Havana in half an hour. Papi helped distract us from frustration when, at one point, we were at a standstill on the highway. He sang the Cuban folksong *Guantanamera,* and the rest of us sang the chorus. Even Sirena joined in on the 'guajira' part.

I dropped my family off at the restaurant and told them to get us a table while I parked. It was a ploy on my part. I was still thinking about Delvis and The Deco. *Who opened the door? Was it the tour guide? Or was someone inside?* I wanted to see what the lock looked like. Was it easy to break in? Luckily, I snagged a space near the theatre. There was a band setting up in the open area by the domino park, where our UnMundo crew had been on Saturday. I walked by the cinema and stopped to look in through the glass doors. The lobby was dark, and there was a chain and padlock that hadn't been there before. The short, heavy chain was looped through the double doors' handles. I tugged the handle even though I could see the lock's tongue spanning the gap between the doors. Air was flowing from it. I put my ear to the crack and listened. *Miriam, por favor, no seas estúpida. If someone is in there, they aren't making a racket. They'd be as quiet as a mouse. They'd be hiding.*

Mi familia were at a round table reading their menus when I entered the restaurant. After we'd ordered, I told my parents that there was going to be live music by the domino park.

"Qué divertido," Mami said, looking forward to the fun. "Luis and I met at a dance." She told Robert the story of their meeting. They were in a quinceañera court. Mami was friends with the girl turning fifteen and Papi was friends with her date. The court met for weeks in advance to learn the classical dances and the choreography for the more contemporary disco tunes. They were paired together because of their height but didn't like each other initially. "He had two left feet."

"Two years later, we met again at another quince. Pero by then, I was a *very* good dancer," Papi said.

My mother laughed and agreed. "*Very* good."

I'd heard the story before. They'd danced to the same song, the classic danzón "El Bombín de Barreto," two years prior, which had left my mother's toes sore. My father had been so embarrassed by his dancing that, in the interim, he'd been practicing. He'd taken an afterschool job cleaning a dance studio so he could learn and practice.

Our fritas were delivered to the table. Everyone dug in, and all conversation stopped. Robert cut Manny's burger in half and then cut that half into bite-size pieces for Sirena.

"This is delicious," Robert said once he tasted his frita.

I was passing him a napkin from the stack of extras the waiter had left us—fritas were juicy and messy—when the chef came to our table. I introduced Yuvisleidys to my family as one of the queens of Las Reinas. Mami complimented her on the restaurant's Cuban nostalgia décor.

"Sería perfecto para la aniversario de Yoli y Bette," Mami said to me in an offhanded way.

The chef asked who Yoli and Bette were. I relayed the troubles that my cousin and her wife had been having finding a place to rent for their anniversary party. I also mentioned Yoli had a small restaurant in Hialeah. Before I knew what was happening, Mami had Yuvisleidys and Yoli talking on the phone. It was settled. The party would be at *Las Reinas*.

Robert paid our bill, and I led the way to the domino park. A bandstand had been erected, and the musicians were tuning up. The Deco's neon was on. *It wasn't lit an hour ago. Is it on a timer?*

"Mi amor, keep an eye on both the kids. I'm going to get the umbrella from the car just in case," I said.

Robert looked at the sky. "I think we'll be fine."

"Better safe than sorry." I tapped my father on the shoulder. "Papi, pregunta si tú y Manny pueden jugar." I pointed to a domino table that had only two players, a pair of older women. The one facing us had a red polka dot scarf over her curler-ed hair.

"Vamos compay," Papi said to his domino buddy, Manny.

I watched my family enter the fenced playing area. *Remember to get the umbrella, Miriam.* I went to the car and got an umbrella to maintain my subterfuge. The real reason I wanted some time away from my family was to snoop. *Someone had to have seen something. Maybe there is a custodian. Maybe that's how the neon got turned on.*

I walked slowly from the residential street where I'd parked. There were plenty of places for an assailant to hide. The Deco had an alley with a small dumpster. The killer could have run out the back door and jumped into the trash. Or they could've escaped into a neighboring business. *Ooo! What if the killer is a business owner? Maybe someone annoyed with the tour guide's obnoxious megaphone.* I beat the purse-sized umbrella against my thigh. *Or maybe a homeowner tired of having a noisy bus in front of their house every day.* I looked at the modest houses that abutted the commercial area. A row of shade trees separated the alley from the sidewalk. The public space between The Deco and the domino park was pedestrian-only. So, it essentially made the residential street a dead end.

I moved into the shadow of the trees and leaned against a trunk. The bandleader announced that the program would start in a few minutes. I studied the back of the cinema and the other businesses. There were three places between the cinema and *Las Reinas.* Next door to The Deco was a guayabera store that sold fine linen shirts to the locals and less expensive poly-blend versions to the tourists. Then, there was a rum tasting room. I saw an employee carry a box of empty bottles outside. The last store had peeling paint beneath a leaky window unit AC.

A gallo crowed. I followed the direction of the call. *Ki-ki-ri-ki.* It was in the tree beside the one I was leaning against. It crowed a third time. A rooster from a street over replied. "Por fin tu socio respondió," I said looking at the proud bird preening its feathers.

"Ese se llama Naco," a weathered voice said.

I pretended that I hadn't been surprised by the speaker. The voice belonged to a woman leaning over her fence. She was throwing corn onto the sidewalk for Naco and his flock of chickens to come to dinner. Naco flew down from his roost once the hens and chicks came out from the bushes. While they pecked at the corn, he kept an eye out for danger. Occasionally, he puffed out his chest and fanned his wings to intimidate all creatures big and small.

I struck up a conversation with her. She'd lived in the house since 1992. First with her husband and now with her sister. I asked her if the area had changed much.

"Sí y no," she replied. In Spanish, she told me, "The neighborhood was like the ocean, always the same water, but the fish changed with the tides—sometimes the tides brought in sharks."

Her analogy was poetic and a little peculiar. I thought about the advertisement for *Guyo Gables* that I'd seen in Alma's office. The address was nearby. *What is her opinion about it?* My time was running short. I needed to get back to my family. I had to stay on task. *Ask her about The Deco.* I used a que lastima the neighborhood is changing angle to ask her about the cinema. Why had it closed? Had she heard if it was going to reopen? Was someone taking care of it?

The woman was chismosa. I learned that the back door to The Deco was sometimes left unlocked. Once, a local character named El Marinero, because he wore a sailor's hat, had taken a box of candies from there to sell on the street. Officials from the city went in and out of the place. A few students from the college had keys to the place. Even though The Deco was closed for business, it was still being used by the college.

A trill of horns and drums swelled. The band set was starting.

"Buenas noches. Me llamo Miriam. Gracias a por conversar conmigo" I said to the woman.

"Un placer. Mi nombre es Gloria. ¿Puedes darme una foto?" she asked for a photo.

Qué boba eres Miriam. She watches UnMundo.

I took a selfie with her and watched as she posted it to her Instagram account. I got a notification on my phone that my *Cocina Caribeña* account had been tagged. I quickly looked at her feed. It was all Naco. Gloria's account was a Naco fan account. I smiled inwardly. I clicked on an image that was an edited video of the gallo 'dancing' to salsa. *The video shows part of The Deco's backdoor.*

"¿Gloria, de donde sacaste esta video?" I asked her how she'd taken the video.

She showed me a wildlife camera attached to the fence. It was below the top cross rail, slightly camouflaged by the ixora foliage. I asked her if the police had questioned her about an incident last Saturday. They hadn't. She'd heard the activity—the police cars, the fire rescue. But because of the heavy rain, she's mainly stayed inside watching her telenovelas. She'd spied me early that Saturday before the rain.

"¿Ese sábado tú viste algo del guía turístico?" I asked her if she'd seen the guide that day.

She gave me an earful about the disrespectful tour guide. Gloria's feathers were ruffled more than Naco's. She tick-tocked her head right and left with her hands on her hips, complaining about the tourists. They littered. They came into her yard and picked fruit from her trees. The music drifting from the park's band was the perfect soundtrack for Gloria's angry dance. She looked a little like Naco.

Ay, ay, ay. Ella está bien encojonada. Is she mad enough to be the killer?

Chapter
Twenty-Three

My phone kept vibrating. *Robert! I'm on my way. I promise.* I said goodbye to Gloria and Naco. I finally looked at the messages. They were photos of Papi y Manny playing dominoes. I ran over to the park and got to see our son put down the winning tile. The crowd that they'd drawn burst into applause.

"Manny, wow, impresionante." I patted his back. It was an impressive win.

"El es un bárbaro," Papi said. The Cuban expression was a compliment, kind of like the fire emoji. It meant they were reaching great heights and were unstoppable.

The senior citizens who made up the domino club joked that they were going to bend the membership rules for Manny. There was a group photo and some more good-hearted teasing. It was hard to see my father's eyes; his smile was so big. He was so proud of his nieto.

Mami handed Sirena off to me. The band was excellent, and she wanted to get in a dance before we called it a night. She whispered something into my dad's ear. He said something in Spanish to his new friends that got a laugh.

"Viejo," Mami called out to Papi. "Voy a buscarme un nuevo compañero de baile."

Papi hammed it up and rushed over to her "before she found a new partner." The band was playing classic Cuban dance tunes. A flutist played a short intro, but as soon as the violins took over, I knew it was a danzón.

"You are in for a treat," I said to Roberto. "My parents are amazing together. Danzón is casi como el tango. It's romantic. There's fancy footwork and turns."

"But it's slow," Robert said.

"It builds." I swayed along to the tune, cocking my hips with each beat of the timpani drum.

Sirena, standing in front of her brother, was mesmerized by the live music. Her head swiveled from the bass to the coronet to the guiro. She got so into it that she played an imaginary clarinet.

The floor cleared as the song intensified, and as my parents' prowess became evident. Everyone wanted to watch them. They were incredible—beauty in motion. The next tune was a cha-cha-cha, which made sense since it evolved from the danzón. The dance floor filled again. My parents kept dancing.

"We should get back," Robert said. He gestured toward Manny, who was yawning.

"I know." I kissed my husband's cheek. "Just a few songs more. *They're having such a good time.*"

No longer having a clear view of the orchestra, Sirena ran into the dance area to get to the stage. I followed her into the churning sea of bodies. I had to sidestep and spin to miss elbows and avoid my toes getting broken. She had a knee on the stage steps when a police officer got her attention.

"She's mine. Sorry," I said, reaching out to grab Sirena by the waist. When the officer stood from his crouched position, I saw his face. It was familiar. *Great.* The face belonged to Officer T. Cruz from the MPD. *Wait! That is great. I can tell him about the video.*

"She's yours?" Officer Cruz said.

We were behind the wall of sound, but it was still hard to hear him. I jerked my head to signal we should move away from the band.

"Yes. This is my daughter, Sirena," I said.

He studied my face for a second. *He doesn't remember me.*

"I'm Miriam Quiñones. You came by my house the other day." I swung Sirena to my other hip. *Niña, you are getting too big to carry.*

"Yes. I remember." *He looked up at The Deco in neon.* "What are you doing here?"

Don't you mean at the scene of the crime? "Family night out. My parents are dancing."

He watched them dance for a moment. Even though there were other dancers, they were the stars.

"Hmm. Well, keep the little one close to you. Please." His tone was as friendly as a scorpion.

Sirena kicked and squirmed like she wanted down. She reached her arms over my shoulder. I looked and saw that Robert was walking toward us with Manny. I let my little mermaid down and watched her clumsily run to her father. We communicated in parent sign language that we were switching kids. Manny came over to me and the officer. Having a family member, Gordon, in the service had made Manny interested in all police. I think he liked the uniform and the fresh-from-the-barber hairstyles. *Miriam, suggest a father-son trip to the barber.*

"Officer Cruz, this is my son, Manny," I said.

"Mucho gusto," Officer Cruz said, extending his hand. Iceberg Cruz was melting. His tone was kind and sincere.

Manny shook his hand and replied in Spanish that we had a cousin who was a sergeant. Whatever melting of the iciness had begun reversed itself. I slid in with some rambling about Manny loving the police and having dressed up as one for several Halloweens.

"What were you this Halloween?" Officer Cruz asked.

"José Andrés," Manny said.

"Who's that? Does he play fútbol?" Cruz asked.

Manny and I both said, "World Central Kitchen." When that didn't turn on the light bulb, we added in unison. "The Bazaar on South Beach."

"Oh, *the tapas guy*—that Spanish chef who's always on the news."

Manny and I did slow nods. *Mi príncipe, don't you dare roll your eyes.* I pulled Manny into a side hug to hide his facial expression from Officer Cruz.

"Um. Were you able to find the perpetrator?" I pointed to the cinema with my lips.

"The MPD does not discuss open cases."

"There are so many cameras and phones and tourists around here. I'm sure you're still reviewing videos and interviewing people." Officer Cruz's annoyance was palpable, but I kept on. "Oh my goodness, you must have to watch so many hours of TikTok and Instagram and Facebook." I chuckled and hoped it sounded natural and not forced. "Like Naco, the salsa dancing gallo. He's a Calle Ocho celebrity. I think he lives around here. Maybe in that house on the corner." I pointed to Gloria's place.

Officer Cruz squinted like he was in one of those Western movies that Papi liked. I even thought I heard whistling. *Miriam, porfa, that's a flute.*

"¿Mami, cuando nos vamos a ir?" Manny asked. He sounded tired. It was a lot of activity for a school night. "Camo, necesita su treat."

"Pronto mi amor. When this song finishes," I replied. *My son and his cat. Camo will survive a night without her evening treat.*

The tune crescendoed and then ended abruptly. A man in a sailor's hat had gotten on stage. *El Marinero.* He took the mic and began to sing. *He doesn't have a bad voice.* The band recognized the song and jumped in. It was the salsa song from the 80s, "Juanito Alimaña", about a robber that people in the neighborhood knew about but were too afraid to report. *What are you trying to tell us, Marinero?*

"Come on, Manny. Let's get your abuelos," I said.

"Y Papi y Sirena también. No los podemos dejar." Manny said.

I smiled. "Don't worry, mi amor. We aren't going to leave them."

"Goodbye, Officer Cruz." Manny shouted above the song, but Cruz hadn't heard him.

When the song ended, I corralled my family. The crowd clapped for an encore. As we exited the scene, there was a commotion. The band began playing that iconic chase tune. Looking back at the dance area, I saw Officer Cruz had jumped onto the stage. He was pointing and barking at El Marinero, who was bobbing up and then down in the sea of people like a whack-a-mole.

Ay, Miriam. No blunt objects to the head analogies.

Chapter
Twenty-Four

The morning after our Calle Ocho outing, my parents were cooing like flirty love birds. I decided they might enjoy having the house to themselves for a few hours. I retrieved our hurricane radio from the supply box and dialed it to the Latin oldies station. The first song was a romantic ballad. They hummed along, occasionally locking eyes to sing to each other. When Mami fluttered her eyelashes, Papi stood a little taller. *Ay, que cute. Okay, I need to get us out of here.*

Robert and Manny had left, so I packed a few playthings in a satchel, put shoes on my mermaid, and buckled her into her car seat.

"¿Pa' donde quieres ir?" I asked Sirena. I had no good plans for the day. If I had thought to put on workout clothing, I could've dropped her at the Rec Center's childcare room and gotten in a little exercise. The park was an option.

"El-li-ot. El-li-ot," Sirena said.

"¿Quieres ver a tu amiga Elliot?"

"¡Si!" Sirena clapped.

I shot off a text to Pepper asking if we could pop by for a coffee. She replied instantly with a line of hearts and coffee mugs. I backed out of the driveway and drove to the bay. Our short journey was, thankfully, omen-free. There were no flying tree branches or hurricane gales. *Coño, I forgot to check on Oyá this morning. Please, don't send me any more dispatches from the other side.*

Pepper must have been watching for us because the gate opened before I could ring the buzzer. She was happy to have the companionship. Elliot was cutting her last molar. Needless to say, the child was dissatisfied with life. We put the kids in the sand pit and sat outside with our coffee. Pepper had some freshly baked *pink* minimuffins and offered me one.

"Mmm," I said after I'd tasted one. "Strawberry? And rosewater?"

"Yes! Is it too much? A little rose goes a long way. I don't want them to taste like soap," Pepper said.

"They *do not* taste like soap." I smiled. "When did you become such an adventurous baker?"

I washed down the last crumb with a sip of coffee.

"I've been watching *The Great British Bakeoff*." My friend grinned.

Elliot wailed and got red-faced, which caused Sirena to shake with laughter like a voice-activated toy. Little Elliot threw what was in her hand, a plastic shovel, at her. It landed in Sirena's lap and did the trick. She stopped laughing. My almost three-year-old looked from her grumpy playmate to the adults with a plea for help.

"Is there any old Cuban folk medicine for tooth pain?" Pepper asked.

"You could rub rum on her gum like my abuela supposedly did with me, but I don't suggest it."

"Yeah, probably not a good idea. I think I have a box of popsicles. Is it okay if I give one to Sirena? You know they always want what the other has."

I nodded that it was fine. She returned with a blue freezer pop that she'd cut in half. The ice seemed to alleviate the ache, and soon, the girls were back to playing.

Pepper peeled the pink metallic paper from a muffin and bit into it.

"So, have you heard anything from Pullman about the message in the bottle?" I asked.

She nodded, holding up a one-second finger while she chewed. "The first one or the second one?"

"The one Sophia found."

"She found another one this morning."

I went slack-jawed.

"I haven't called the police about it yet. Between dropping off Sophia and *Molar Molly* over there, it slipped my mind." Pepper sighed.

"What does it say?" I scooted to the edge of my seat.

"I don't know. I threw it to the floorboard. We were late."

"*Pepper*, if you ever need a morning ride for Sophia, you know you can call me." I patted her on the knee.

"*I know.* The keys are on the hook in the kitchen if you want to get the bottle from the car."

I stood up so quickly the momentum caused me to misstep and make an ungraceful spin to catch myself. Pepper chortled.

"Easy there, Velma," she said.

I gave her an I-don't-like-teasing look and went to retrieve the bottle. The key fob was where she said it would be. I went out the back of the house to their car pad. The bottle had rolled under the seat and lodged itself between the metal frame and something soft. I contorted so I could get a better grip. I pinched the soft thing and tugged. *Ewww, yuck. It's cold. And fuzzy.* I held my breath, hoping it wasn't a once-upon-a-time-alive critter. I sighed in relief when I saw it was a purple unicorn squishy toy. Manny had a few of them. His were food themed and had cutesy faces. I placed it in the cupholder and stuck my arm back under the seat. I twisted the bottle, scrapping the glass against the metal bolt until I'd dislodged it. It was the same brand of beer. *Did this guy drink a whole six-pack?*

Unlike last time, the message slipped out as soon as I broke the wax and tipped it upside down. *Frank is going to burst a blood vessel.* I untied the string that held the rolled note. I slipped it back into the bottle. *Miriam, saving the string will not save you from reprimand.* Unfurling the note, I read the one-sentence message.

Don't be a fool, Smithie.

The message was not as threatening as the previous two. I held it up to the sun, flipped it, and looked at it every which way. There was no signature or other words. Was it a silly fraternity prank, or was it something more sinister? Was it a message to Senior? *Miriam, you are sounding paranoid like Marjory.*

"Did you find it?" Pepper asked, hearing me approach.

"Yep. And a purple unicorn," I said.

"That's been lost for months!"

I put the bottle and paper on the stone table between our chairs. "We—I mean, you. *You* should report the find to the police."

"*Really?* I was going to chuck it. We know it's a part of that frat game. What does this one say?"

I repeated the sentence from memory.

"I wonder how many messages in bottles he threw into the bay. Not the most foolproof joke. What if it got taken out with the tide and floated to Nassau or Cuba—or Greenland?"

She was right. The bottle wasn't guaranteed to make it to its intended recipient.

"What did Detective Pullman say when you gave him the second bottle?" I asked.

"You know he isn't much of a talker." *Chuckle.* "He put the bottle in a bag and thanked me."

"Did he tell you the name of the student?"

"Nick Forte or Fortis *or Forton.* I don't know—For-something." Pepper jumped up. "Elliot, do not bite her! That is not how we treat our friends."

In typical Sirena fashion, my daughter did not take it seriously. "Maybe it's time for the pod swing," I suggested.

We helped the girls into the hanging chair that was low to the ground for safety's sake. It was made of blue tent material with yellow trim around the opening. It had a cushioned seat and a pillow. The pod hung on a chain that allowed it to spin. Pepper gave it a gentle push. In quick time, Elliot settled down and dozed off.

"Pobrecita, she tired herself out crying," I said.

"I know. The first tooth and the last tooth are the worst. She fussed all through the night. Even Sophia was cranky this morning because of her caterwauling."

The swing's sway slowed, and Sirena waved that she wanted out. I held the pod still so she could crawl out, then set it to rocking again for the napping Elliot.

"We're going to go. Thanks for the coffee," I said, hugging my friend goodbye.

"Thank you for the distraction." Pepper bent to speak to Sirena. "Elliot will feel better soon. Sorry she wasn't nice to you today."

"Eat." Sirena pointed to the muffins.

I laughed. "Don't feel bad," I said to Pepper. "See, she's already moved on." I peeled a muffin and gave it to her.

We showed ourselves out. "Now, where do we go, chiquita?" I said, getting behind the steering wheel. "¿A casa? ¿Al parque?"

"*'Scuela,*" Sirena said. She meant her brother's school/escuela.

"No, mi amor es muy temprano para recoger a Manny." I told her it was too early. *But we could go to another school.*

Chapter
Twenty-Five

As I drove to Grove College, I lambasted myself. It was a fool's errand. What was I going to do if I actually found Nick For-something? And why did I care? It was like Grove College had popped into my head, and I couldn't get it out until I went there. The person in the guardhouse directed me to the main visitor parking. The lot was full, so I circumnavigated the campus for a visitor's spot. The unplanned sightseeing took me past Greek Row. *Which frat house is Nick's?* I saw the Fine Arts building, the Student Union, and the library. They were all painted cream and had decorative friezes in muted shades. Before it was a college, Grove had been a pineapple and fruit tree grove. There were fruit sculptures dotted around the grounds to commemorate that history. Finding them would be a fun way to pass some time and a way to teach Sirena the names of the fruits.

"Gracias a La Caridad," I said, seeing a car leaving a spot. I zipped in after it and parked. I took out Sirena's umbrella stroller from the trunk, belted her into it, and gave her a few toys and a baggie of O's. As I clicked the lock button on the fob, a gust of wind rattled the brown metal sign in front of us. The words Museum Parking Only were in white reflective paint. The gale was so strong that the pole and sign looked and sounded like a rattle-drum. "Okay, Oyá, I hear you. You want me to go to the museum." As soon as the words were out of my mouth, the wind ceased.

I pushed the stroller along the walkway, following the signs to the Sciences building. Along the way, we passed a giant pineapple sculpture done in a cubist style and a kinetic mobile of oranges. According to the sandwich board sign outside the three sets of doors, the Grove Museum of Florida History was on the fourth floor. Students had sticker-tagged the sign along the edges. The hodge-podge of pop culture characters and band logos gave the impression of tattooed arms sticking out of a muscle tee.

I asked a student where the elevator was. The presence of a mom and a toddler seemed to confuse them, but eventually, they mumbled 'down that way.' The elevator stopped on the second floor, and several students got on. They disembarked on the third floor, where a non-student person got in.

"Can I help you find someone?" they asked, pressing the four button.

"No. We're just going to the museum," I replied.

They kept glancing at me as they held the elevator door for us to exit.

"The museum is right there." They pointed to the right. "Um, pardon me, but do you have a YouTube channel?"

Okay, so the looks were about that, not a mom and stroller on a college campus.

"Yes. It's called *Abuela Approved.* Do you watch?" I asked. My show appealed mainly to Latinx Gen Z and millennials on the cusp. They didn't look like any of those things, but looks don't always tell the whole complex truth.

"I'm not a subscriber, but *yes,* I have watched it. A student showed it to me." They chuckled. "She wants us to offer more *relevant* anthropology courses."

"I didn't know Grove offered an anthropology degree," I said.

"We don't. Our focus is archeology, but we have a few two-hundred-level classes." They looked in the direction of the museum. There was a faint sigh. "Let me introduce myself. I'm Lyle Murphy, Dean of Arts and Science."

"It's a pleasure to meet you. I'm Dr. Miriam Quiñones—" While I hesitated on whether to add the Smith part of my name, the dean jumped in.

"Yes, I know. I looked you up after I saw the show. Your specialty is the Caribbean. We have a growing number of students from the Caribbean. Do you think you might be interested in giving a guest lecture?"

"Hmm. I'd have to give it some thought."

"Please do. Here's my card." He handed me a business card with an embossed pineapple on the back. "Email me, please. I'd really like to discuss this further," he said, motioning me down the hall to the museum entrance. He held the door for me to get the stroller through.

I assured him I'd be in contact and tucked the card into my bag. *That's an idea. Maybe I'll guest lecture. It's less time-consuming than adjunct. Hmm.*

"Lady. Ma'am."

I blinked out of my daydreaming. A student with two messy ponytails and puffy headphones around her neck was behind the reception desk. She was trying to give me a sheet of beige paper.

"Ma'am. Here."

I took the page. It was actually two sheets stapled together.

"There are two exhibit halls. Early Florida is through there, and Settled Florida is this way. You can go forward in history or backward. The exhibits connect in the middle." The young woman disappeared below the chest-high counter.

Deciding to go to the Settled Florida hall first, I stepped from the linoleum into a carpeted corridor.

"Gran-gran," Sirena said. "Grandy"

I told her she was right. The people in the portrait were her grandparents. Inscribed above the ornate golden frame, in decorative cursive, were their names—The Honorable William R. Smith, Sr. and Mrs. Marjory Edith Smith. A PBS voice read the names in my head. *This program was made possible by the generous donations of . . .*

I skipped the modest exhibit about the founding families of Coral Shores. I'd learned more than I'd ever wanted to about the Smiths, Pimpkins, and Weathermans when I'd first moved to town. One of the Pimpkins had tried to frame my BFF, Alma, for the murder of a Weatherman. It was a memory I wish I could forget.

The next display focused on the fruit groves and tomato planters. There were produce crates, porcelain plates with grapefruit blossoms painted in the center, and newspapers of the time.

"Casa. Jugar. Jugar con casa," Sirena pleaded.

"No, mi amor. Eso no es para niños." I explained that the dollhouse-sized model of a 1907 general store was not for playing. I read the description beside it. The one-room structure had been built on stilts to keep it from flooding. Coral Shores, called Seal Shore Town until 1896, had been swamp. The Smith Brothers General Store had stood on what was now called Reef Drive. "The structure was destroyed by the 1926 hurricane that devastated the young city of Miami."

"Coco-dee-yo." Sirena pointed to the five-inch alligator in the resin water below the store.

"Cocodrilo." I gently corrected her.

Bernice's great great-auntie, probably. I'd made myself laugh, but then my thoughts went to a darker place—the remains at the golf course. Had they been identified yet? Was there a name?

We turned a corner and continued our time travel. There was a single placard for the 1700s recounting the land swap of *La Florida* by the Spanish to the British in exchange for Havana. The 1500s had more space devoted to it. There was a free-standing glass case with a featureless muslin mannequin in armor and weapons. A conquistador's helmet was on a pedestal beside it. A screen played a short video about Juan Ponce de León. An early map of Florida and the Caribbean had been animated with ships and fantastical sea creatures. It transitioned into the fabled quest for the Fountain of Youth.

Miriam, cálmate. Chill. You do not need to give your preschooler a lesson on Ponce de Leon's brutality to the indigenous people. Slaughter and slavery aren't age-appropriate for someone making two-word sentences.

I forced myself to take a deep breath and hold it to the count of ten. The Settled Florida hall's muted lighting and carpeted floor ended in a square-shaped room. Directly ahead was the entrance to the other half of the museum. To our right, there was a gray drinking fountain between two doors. The door marked *Ladies* had a silhouette of a woman in a bonnet and regency-like dress. The one marked *Gentlemen* had a man in a waistcoat holding a riding crop. To our left, there was a door with a lock. Above it was written *Special Collections*.

Sirena threw her toy out of the stroller with a giggle. *Oh, no, little one. We are not going to play this game.* I set the wheel brake and went to retrieve the dollar store mermaid doll that had skidded across the linoleum tiles into a corner. The hollow blue tail was made of molded plastic. It hinged at the waist where the human part began. The maid had dark brown skin and wavy black hair. Her painted shell bra was white with ridges of glitter glue. Abuela had bought it for her on one of their excursions. Sirena loved it. The doll I had in my hand was number three. The first one had gotten lost at the park. The second one had had its tail chewed by Tom. It wasn't the dog's fault. Sirena had shoved it in his mouth. I didn't want to search all the dollar stores in Miami-Dade County for a replacement number four. I stuck the blue fish-woman into the stroller's mesh pocket.

As I toggled the brake free, the door to the Special Collection opened. Inside, it looked like a library. Some shelves held books, and others archival boxes, the kind with handles and a place for a label. There was a worktable with an open box on it.

"Mrs. Smith, what a delight to find you here," said Dr. Gregory Vander Bell. He shut the door swiftly, causing a whoosh of air.

Achoo.

"Bless you," he said. "Or, as your people say, salud."

I ignored the uncomfortable benediction and thanked him.

Sniff. Sniff. Sniffle.

"I'd love to give you a personal tour, but I'm afraid I'm in the middle of something important." Dr. Bell gestured over his shoulder. "It's rather exciting. I'm going to unveil it at the celebration this weekend. You and Bobby will be in attendance, correct."

Achoo.

Dr. Bell padded the pockets of his cargos. "Oh dear, I don't have a handkerchief."

"Don't bother. I'll get a tissue from the bathroom." I pushed the stroller over to the ladies' room.

"I hope it's not a cold. You won't want to miss the museum's silver celebration." His voice ascended like the Sesame Street Muppet he resembled. There was a gleam in his eyes. Again, I sniffled.

"Okay," I said as the bathroom door swung behind me. I dashed into a stall and grabbed an arm's length of tissue paper. I blew my nose and sneezed once more. Sirena found my noises hilarious. *I hope it's allergies and not a cold.* My sniffling waned. We were halfway out the door when Sirena said she had to go. She was still accident-prone. So I was glad she wanted to go in the right place at the right time. We washed our hands and were ready for the next part of the museum. Opening the door, I stopped. Dr. Bell was re-entering the Special Collections room. I didn't want him to stop us again. Sirena was being pretty patient *and quiet* for a toddler, and fate shouldn't be tempted.

All I saw was his stringy braid swish across his back as the collection's door shut. Another whoosh of air blew into the alcove. *Sniff. Sniff.* I pinched my nostrils with the rough tissue paper and stopped the oncoming sneeze.

What is in that room? Moldy plants and mummy dust?

Images of Dr. Bell being chased by an Egyptian mummy zipped through my mind. Of course, there wasn't a mummy—Egyptian, Chilean, Aztec, animal, or bog, for that matter in the Grove Special Collection. *Or is there?* The college literally had skeletons in their closets. That's how one had ended up in the bay. Maybe someone donated great-grandmother's souvenir from her honeymoon on the Nile. *That's a disturbing thought.*

I was so caught up in my ponderings that I wasn't taking in the part of the museum that should've been more interesting to me, the pre-European contact part. 1492 was a date seared into my brain. It was a pivotal point in the history of the Caribbean. But the people native to Florida and the Caribbean were less familiar to me. I'd referenced the Calusa tribe in my paper about conchs, but they were a southwest Florida tribe. The Tequesta tribe, according to the foam-core poster I was reading, were localized to the Miami area and were more peaceful than the Calusa.

I stopped in front of a long, low, coffin-like display case displaying several vertebrae and partial ribs of a whale. Sirena pressed the button that was at her eye level. A theatrical recording played. It described a ritual whale hunt that was part of a chief's funeral rites.

"*Wh-ell.*" Sirena looked at me with curiosity.

"Whale. Ballena." I translated the new word into Spanish. Being a mermaid, she had an Animales de los Océanos picture book that Manny often read to her.

I maneuvered the stroller around the skeleton and over to a mural depicting a circular village on the shores of Biscayne Bay. The homes in the painting were round with conical straw roofs. In the foreground, beside a long dug-out canoe, a bare-chested man held colorful parrot fish on a plant-material cord. The shelf in front of the drawing had shells, fish vertebrates, wooden mallets, and other artifacts 'Found while digging the Coral Shores canal.'

I pushed Sirena around the corner into the last and final room. A multi-shelved case held dozens of pieces of pottery. It looked like a gigantic curio cabinet with varying heights and box-like sections to accommodate the different-sized objects. I marveled at a shallow bowl that was like a plate. The description informed me that only five pieces were authentic. The rest were recreations. In the center of the case was a bulbous pot. It was complete except for one missing shard. All of its pieces were authentic.

A clap of thunder broke the reverent silence. And then the lights flickered. We were plunged into darkness.

Chapter
Twenty-Six

The emergency exit lights were the only thing that had power. They cast creepy red pools of light. In a matter of seconds, there was a powering-up wind and then a pop. All the lights came back on except for the spotlights in the case. Then, a signal lamp, the one above the pot, flickered to life. *That's weird. Did the power outage fry the others?*

The student with headphones called from the front entrance. "You're still here." Her tone was flat, like she was perturbed. "You will need to exit the museum."

"Sure, okay. Is there any particular reason?" I asked.

"We are running on generators. All museum patrons must evacuate to the lower lobby until full power is restored. Those are the rules," she said.

I pushed the stroller to the elevator before it dawned on me that it would be out of service. We went back to the museum desk.

"Excuse me, where are the stairs?" I asked.

The young woman came out of the reception area, closed the wide glass door that had been propped open, and locked it at its base. She tucked the key into the ID holder on her lanyard. The name on her Grove ID card was Ilmi. She began walking without any indication to follow her. When she stopped halfway down the corridor and looked at me, I scooted into motion. We turned a corner, and there was a set of wide stairs.

It took me a second to decide how I was going to get down three flights of stairs with a toddler and a stroller. Ilmi studied me as I undid Sirena and folded the stroller. With the 'lightweight and convenient' stroller awkwardly under my arm, I took my daughter's hand and began taking the steps sideways with her in front of me. We rested after making it down the first flight without tripping. I adjusted the stroller to better grip it, but I felt it slip from my arm. Ilmi was suddenly beside us. She took it and continued the rest of the way with us.

The second floor seemed to be classrooms. A river of students began to stream down the stairs. I stepped aside to wait for the flow to subside. Ilmi stood with us in silence. When there was only a trickle of people, we continued our descent. On the ground floor, Ilmi opened the stroller for me. Her ID holder spun, and I saw the sticker on the back of it. It read Neuro-Spicy. *I think that means Neurodiverse.* Knowing that bit of information, I corrected my earlier quick judgment that she was an indifferent college student giving *an old* an attitude.

"I think we'll go ahead and go. There's no sense waiting for the power to come back on," I said. "Where's the main door? I'm a little turned around."

Ilmi started walking away again without warning. This time, I followed instantly. She took me to a door I recognized.

"Thank you," I said.

Ilmi nodded her head and shrugged slightly.

"My name is Miriam Quiñones, and this is Sirena." Sirena waved and smiled at the mention of her name.

"I'm Ilmi. Okay, bye."

"Ilmi. That's a lovely name." I wanted to ask her about the department while I had her on the chance that I did get the opportunity to give a guest lecture. "I've never met anyone with that name."

"It's Finnish," Ilmi said. "My grandmother is from Finland."

"Cool. How many years have you been a student at Grove?"

"This is my last year." She removed a sensory toy from her hoodie's pouch.

"Is archeology your major? Is that why you're working at the museum desk?"

She nodded.

"Is Dr. Bell a good professor?"

"No."

Her bluntness was jarring but refreshing. And I *had* asked.

"What is it you don't like about his classes?" I asked.

"Him and his toenails."

"Oh." I didn't have a comeback because I kind of agreed with her. I didn't really like the man either. *Wait, where is he? Shouldn't he be in the lobby, too?* "Speaking of Dr. Bell. I saw him go into the Special Collections room. Will he be able to get out? You locked the museum door."

"He has keys to everything," Ilmi said. Then, without any prompting, she told me he had been spending a lot of time in the Special Collections, and he'd suspended all access to it.

"Is it a research library? Could I use it if I went through the proper channels?"

"Perhaps. You'd have to ask the dean."

I just might do that.

"I have to leave now," Ilmi said. She strode away.

"Thank you for your help," I called after her.

Sirena and I took the accessibility ramp. Outside, there was no evidence of a storm. The sky was clear. I touched the grass, and it was dry. Perhaps the sound I'd heard had been a transformer blowing, not a thunderclap.

"Leche," Sirena said.

I checked the time. "¿Tienes hambre?" When she was hungry, she asked for milk even though she hadn't had a bottle in months. *Mami better not be sneaking her a bottle.* My stomach growled with the thought of lunch.

I decided to try the Dominican bakery that had opened near the Caribbean supermarket. It was a mile or so from the college. I took a number and let Sirena enjoy the sugary sights in the case. A slice of bizcocho de piña had my daughter mesmerized. The cake was a rich yellow with a layer of pineapple marmalade between the two layers and frosted with meringue.

"Ciento veintitrés," said the woman behind the counter.

"Un jugo de naranja, dos quipes y una empanada de pollo," I ordered.

Sirena splatted her little hand on the glass. My parents had lived in the Dominican Republic. They might enjoy an authentic bizcocho. I told the woman I'd take a small pineapple cake to go.

"¿Qué quieres escrito?" she asked.

I was flummoxed.

"¿Hembra or varón?" She grinned. Her brown face glowed with warmth.

She wanted to know what color frosting, pink or blue, to write the message in. It felt like the woman really enjoyed cake artistry. I hated to tell her that the cake wasn't for a birthday. It might break the woman's heart. *Heart! I'll ask for a heart. Love is always something to celebrate.*

"Un corazón simple. En rojo o morado," I told her.

The woman's eyes twinkled. She quickly boxed our lunch and flicked the switch on the juicer. In Miami, fresh orange juice was a thing. I put Sirena on my hip so she could watch the oranges roll down the chute, get sliced by gravity, and juiced by the wheel.

After I'd paid, Sirena and I moved to the eating counter to enjoy our lunch. I tore the crunchy exterior to make it easier for little teeth before giving Sirena her quipe.

"Cro-queta," Sirena said. She took a bite and made a this-doesn't-taste-like-what-I-thought face.

"Luce como una croqueta pero se llama quipe y tiene carne," I informed her.

She took another bite but was unconvinced. I halved the chicken empanada and switched with her. I liked quipes. The fried snack was made of bulgar wheat and ground beef, similar to a Lebanese kibbeh but with different seasoning. Between the 1880s and the 1930s, a steady wave of Syrians, Palestinians, and Lebanese migrated to the Dominican Republic. Naturally, their foodways created new dishes in their adopted home.

Sirena ate most of her lunch, leaving only a wedge of crust. We shared the jugo. I dusted the crumbs from us and the counter, then went to collect the cake. It was in a white box with the lid open. The woman proudly showed me her work. It was a heart of purple and red rosettes. It was beautiful and made me wish there was an occasion to celebrate.

Chapter
Twenty-Seven

"What time is Gordie getting here?" Robert asked.

"It should be soon," I replied. We were outside. There was a chill in the air, but it wasn't cold. I had on a cotton shawl I'd bought in Cartagena de Indias.

The Colombian city on the Caribbean coast had been an important port to the Spanish. The same model of conquer and enslave had been imposed upon the fishing village of indigenous peoples as in every land that Spanish boots had touched in those centuries. Captured Africans were trafficked and sold in the walled city's plaza. Their faces were visible to this day in their descendants. About a quarter of the country's current population identified as Afro-Colombian.

Thinking of the Caribbean's Indigenous and the Africans displaced to the Americas by Europeans, my mind drifted to casta paintings from the late 1700s. They were made in the Americas, mostly Mexico/New Spain and sent overseas to quiet the anxieties of Spaniards. I'd studied them because of their food iconography. The illustrations depicted a caste system. There were sixteen categories—sixteen tableaus showing couples and their offspring. The prodigies were defined with words like mulatto (African and

European), mestizo (Indigenous and European), pardo (Ibo-European, Indigenous, and African), zambo (Indigenous and African), and other such terms that were used to place people in a hierarchy with white Europeans at the top.

Snap.

Snap.

Jiggle.

"Babe, what planet are you on? Tatooine?" Robert asked. "I asked about your day, but you were zoned out."

"Yeah, I was thinking that if it were 1773, I'd be labeled a prada," I replied.

"Italian."

"What? No, not the fashion brand. There's this painting. It was like a catalog of commodities the Viceroy of New Spain sent home to the King." *Commodities. Ownership. Take. Take. Take.*

"Babe," Robert jiggled my leg again. "I love your big brain, but I need you to be here, in our backyard in Coral Shores, in the twenty-first century. An animal is getting into your saint box, and I don't want to disturb whatever voodoo thing you've got going over there."

"It's not Vodou," I replied. *But it's not not Vodou.* I stood and went around the side of the house to see what he was hearing. If there had been an animal, reptilian or mammalian, it had scurried away. The saint house's door was rocking.

"Fur or scales?" Robert asked, holding a broom.

"Neither. I don't think it was an animal," I said.

"Then what was it?"

"Probably the wind." *Or Oyá telling me her bowl is empty.* I kissed him and shooed him off to put Mami's broom back where he'd found it before she got mad at him. I took the bowl to the kitchen to clean and refill it.

A pot of frijoles negros was simmering on the stove. Oyá liked dark-colored things, so I ladled in some of the seasoned black beans. The garlic, cumin, oregano, and culantro smelled delectable. On the counter in a gallon-sized freezer bag, pork chops were marinating in mojo for Papi to grill once Gordon and Omarosa arrived.

I placed the fresh ebo in front of the saint statue. "I promise to save a slice of bizcocho for you," I said, remembering Oyá preferred sweets. I knelt and tried to think of something else to say. I wished I had a song or the appropriate Yoruba prayer, but my mind was blank. I held the space for a few more moments, then latched the little door.

"Primo," I heard Manny yell.

"Primo," Gordon replied.

I waved to Omarosa and Gordon to come into the backyard. They detoured to the kitchen to give saludos to my parents. Gordon had brought a mixed-six of craft beers. In Spanish, he offered one to my father. His conversational Spanish was improving. Omarosa had gifts for each of the kids.

"You know that's not necessary," I told her.

"I know, pero I was at Books & Books today and couldn't resist." She gave each of them a book wrapped in playful paper.

Manny helped his sister, who was trying to rip into her gift. He carefully lifted the sticker that taped the paper together. Sirena then wrecked his fastidiousness by clawing the paper off the book.

"Pato," Sirena said, showing me the book.

"Eso es una gansa," I told her the bird on the cover was a goose, not a duck. The gift was a collection of bilingual nursery rhymes called *Mamá Goose*. "Dale gracias a Titi," I told her to thank Omarosa, and she did. Sirena gave me the book, and I flipped to the index chanting *Tin Marín de Do Pingüe*. The counting song wasn't listed in the book.

Omarosa picked up the chant and sang the next line with me. *Cúcara mácara titere fue.* But we each sang different lines after that.

The Dominican and Cuban versions of the rhyme were not the same. I recalled the video that Jorge had sent me with a Venezuelan guy's theory that the rhyme was actually about a murder. I masked my discomfort about it and laughed with Omarosa about our word salad.

"Mira, Mami," Manny said. He'd finally unwrapped his book and folded the paper. *Mi hijo es único.* He was one of a kind. What kid took such care with wrapping paper? "Gracias, Titi. Is this about baking?" he asked, examining the cover that had a girl holding a spatula with winged pig cookies flying around her.

Omarosa's toothy grin shone against her dark red lips and brown cheeks. "Yes. It's about a Mexican family in Texas with a magical bakery. It's a girl character, but I know how much you like cooking," she said.

"I don't care that it's a girl. I love it." Manny hugged her. "*Love, Sugar, Magic: A Dash of Trouble,*" he read the title aloud. "I'm going to start reading it right now. Do I have time before dinner?"

"Abuelo hasn't started the grilling yet, so you have about fifteen minutes, antes de que tiengas que venir a la mesa," I said.

Manny ran to his room to read.

"Li-bo," Sirena said.

"I think she wants you to read to her," I told Omarosa.

"Okay. It will be good practice," she said.

"What? You aren't." My mouth hung open.

"Nooo. Not yet. Pero pronto después de la boda."

"Oh, that reminds me. Bette said you want a *castle theme*. Have you looked at the monastery on West Dixie by Greynolds Park? It might be the perfect place for the wedding," I said.

"Ooooh, that's a good idea." She gave me a thumbs up as she followed Sirena to the living room couch to read to her.

I heard the rice cooker ping that it was done. Mami told my father it was time to start the chuletas/pork chops. I offered to help slice tomatoes or avocado for the salad, but Mami waved her knife for me to vamoose. Gordon and Robert were in the yard chatting. They had beers in their hands. I poured myself a glass of albariño and joined them.

"Bustinza says she'll have her report finished by tomorrow," Gordon said.

"But that doesn't mean we can start back up. The archaeologists are still digging," Robert said.

"Have they found anything more?" I asked. "Since the food waste."

"I don't think so. But boy, are they looking," Robert said.

"Bell really wants to get in on the dig. He has your mother," Gordon raised an eyebrow at Robert, "and the mayor putting pressure on us. But it's out of my control. Once the state and the Tribal Preservation Office are involved—" He blew a puff of air out the side of his mouth. "I mean, maybe if we'd called him first, he'd have some leverage, but . . ."

"I ran into Dr. Bell today," I said. "Sirena and I went to the museum. There's a *big* oil painting of your parents. I feel like you could have mentioned that your parents donated a *wing* to a museum." I took a sip of my wine.

"Babe, it's not a wing. It's a hallway. Honestly, I'd forgotten about it. It happened like twenty years ago. It's not like it's called The Smith Museum. She just donated a little money for paint and carpet." Robert shrugged off the donation like it was the same thing as buying a box of chocolate bars from a St. Brigid's student. His relationship with money was as a deep and full well. Mine was walking a mile to fill your bucket and hoping you didn't spill any on the walk home.

"Speaking of Smith donations," I said to Gordon. "What's the story with the bay skeleton?"

"Just a frat boy having a laugh," he replied.

"Did you interrogate him?" I asked.

"Slow down, Rizzoli," Gordon laughed.

"Who's Rizzoli?" I whispered to my husband. He replied that she was an intense police detective from a show called *Rizzoli and Isles*. I sighed. *I'm cursed.* Pullman had started the nickname thing, and it had become a curse.

"The guy was just pranking a rival fraternity. No harm done, thankfully. Imagine if a propeller had run over it. There would've been bones on the shore and washing up on people's docks. It would have been hundreds of phone calls." Gordon rattled his empty can of brew. "I mean, I know he gave you and your friends a scare. I can get him to apologize to you all personally."

I thought about it. I wanted to ask Gordon about the messages in the bottles. But the plural part might get Pepper in trouble, and I didn't want that. Something about the easy explanation of a frat prank did not sit well with me. It was the notes. They seemed to be about something. *Smithie.* I was about to ask Gordon who Smithie was, but Papi had put the meat on the grill. The sizzle and the caramelized goodness hit the men in their stomachs. Robert and his cousin licked their lips. Their attention was drawn to the grill like paper clips to a magnet.

"I'll ask Pepper and the rest of the squad. What's the kid's name?" I asked.

"Nicholas Forte. He's a Theta Mu," Gordon replied. "You want another one?" He rattled the can at Robert.

"Sure." Robert gave his cousin the can. "Forte. That's the business name of my new client."

Dinner under the stars was wonderful. Manny regaled the table about the first chapter of the book. "Mami, there were a few words I didn't know how to say," Manny confessed. "I know what they mean, just not how they sound."

"That's okay. Sometimes, I come across words I don't know how to pronounce. If you write them down, we can look them up together," I said.

"I think I still have my old Webster. Well, it's at Mother's," Robert said.

"What's a Webster?" Manny asked.

"It's how old people looked up the definition of words before the internet," Gordon said. He was a few years younger than Robert, and he never let him forget it.

Robert mimed an uppercut. Gordon threw his head back like it had landed. They both laughed. And whenever there was laughter it got Sirena's giggles going.

"Time for cake," I said.

"¿Quién quiere café?" my mom asked.

I told her to sit and relax. My coffee was just as good as hers. Papi made a face. He liked his drinks sweet, and I made my café with one spoonful less than hers. He swore it was two spoonfuls less.

As I waited for the cafetera's water to boil, I took eight dessert plates from the cupboard. I glanced out at the table and saw Robert removing the dirty dishes. Gordon had his arm around Omarosa, and she was leaning against him. Mami y Papi were telling them the story of their wedding. Manny and Sirena were listening, too. I loved the family scene.

"Babe, the coffee is spitting," Robert said, coming into the kitchen with a stack of plates.

"Coño," I cussed. I flicked the cafetera's lid closed and poured a few drops into the sugar. I combined the two ingredients into a paste with a spoon. The sound of the sugar crystals against the little metal pitcher was musical, like the sultry scrap of a güiro.

Robert loaded the dishwasher as I finished portioning out the espresso. He carried the tray of demitasse and dessert plates. I brought the cake.

"¡Bizcocho!" Omarosa said. "Dame un pedazo grande por favor."

"Con gusto," I said. I made the first cut and then looked at her for approval before I made the next cut. She pinched the air, signaling I could go a little bigger. I sliced the rest and served it. Before I gave Sirena hers, I cut it in half and put part onto a saucer for Oyá.

"This frosting is just like your mom's," Gordon commented to Omarosa.

"It's called suspiro," she said. Using her finger, she stole some of the frosting from his piece and ate it. She made a dramatic, eyes-shut intake of air. "Because it tastes so good it steals your breath."

Mami y Papi's shoulders shook with je-je-jes.

"Más dulce," Sirena said, having finished her piece. Her little hand was doing the gimme-gimme at the half piece I'd set aside.

"Voy a compartir contigo," I told her. I used the side of my fork to carve a chunk from my slice for her. The sponge cake was rich yet airy. I'd seen it made and knew it took two sticks of butter and half a dozen eggs. I licked the crumbs from my fork and tasted a hint of orange zest.

Amongst six adults, two kids, and an orisha, nothing was left but the silver cardboard cake disc. I excused myself and snuck around the side of the house with Oyá's piece before someone tried to eat it. The latch gave me problems, but I eventually got it open. As I moved the bowl of beans to make space for the cake, a chicken bone rolled to the edge of the box. I put my hand out to catch it as it fell.

Where did this come from?

Chapter
Twenty-Eight

Friday morning, after everyone had left, my phone alerted me to a text message.

Can I come over for coffee?

I replied that he could. Thirty seconds later, the doorbell camera let me know Pullman was walking up the front path. I opened the door and greeted him. "Were you staking out my house, waiting for everyone to be gone?"

"That is a possibility. Is the coffee ready?" Pullman smiled sin vergüenza.

I rolled my eyes at him and waved him inside. He sat at the counter and kept quiet as I packed the grounds into the cafetera. "Have you had breakfast?" I asked.

"I could eat," he replied.

I cracked an egg into a frying pan, microwaved some of last night's rice, and heated up a two-inch strip of grilled pork. "Desayuno a caballo." I placed the plate in front of him. We each took our plates (mine was just a buttery tostada) to the dining room table. "So, to what do I owe the honor?"

"I need to talk to you about your mother-in-law," Pullman said as he pierced the adobo-seasoned egg, letting the yolk run into the rice. "Her fears are not unwarranted."

My heart sank to my gut. Marjory might be infuriating, stubborn, bigoted, elitist, and wishing for the Reagan years, but she was Robert's mother. And if her fears were valid, that meant Senior was in danger.

"Someone is legitimately threatening Senior and Marjory? Why? And what are you doing about it?"

"The Feds have it under control. They know who it is. But—"

I waited for him to say more, but he took a bite. I fluttered my hand, telling him to hurry up.

"But, in the meantime, I need Mrs. Smith to stay put."

"What do you mean stay put? I don't think she's left the house. *Has she?*"

"No, she hasn't left the house. But she plans to tomorrow for some museum party. And," He did it again. I drummed my fingers while he chewed. "And she plans to take a gun with her as protection. We can't have that. We do not need a firearm situation. She is a menace to herself and to others." Pullman wiped his mouth and pushed his plate away.

I stared at him, dazed. He was absolutely right. Marjory Edith Smith should not be armed. "What do you think I can do about it?"

"I want you to go over there with me. Tell her you will go to the museum thing in her place. It is critical that she and the judge stay in their home until given the all-clear," Pullman said.

"And what makes you think she'll listen to me?"

"You have a way about you. People trust you. They confide in you. She asked for your help. I believe that you can convince her this is you helping her."

Camo jumped into Pullman's lap. She purred and butted her head against his abdomen. I took a moment to process what he'd said. *He has a point. She asked for my help.*

"Okay, I'll do it."

"Good. Now, on to the other reason for my visit."

I wrinkled my forehead. "*Other.*"

"*Yes, Velma.* Other. It seems that Officer Cruz and the Miami Police Department have made an arrest in The Deco murder." He scratched the cat's head.

My heart shot up from my gut and back to my chest, where it began to beat hard and fast.

"And it appears you had something to do with it."

Camo jumped down and went to the French doors. She pawed at the glass, asking to be let out. I cracked the door wide enough for her to slip out and go lizard hunting. The sky was overcast, but it didn't look like rain. The sun would burn off the haze in another hour. I left the door open to let in the sixty-five-degree air.

"*I* had something to do with it," I said, returning to my seat.

"It appears Officer Cruz took your advice. He spoke to the neighbors that share the alley. Two of them had cameras." Frank scratched under his jaw with three fingers.

"*Really.* So, did they get the guy?" *I hope it isn't El Marinero.* I had no idea who the murderer was, but I knew it wasn't Delvis. If she had wanted to hurt someone, she'd film an expose or documentary about them. She wouldn't be physically violent. She'd slay, but in the artistic way.

"I don't have the details. It's not my jurisdiction, but it is my understanding that someone from the City of Miami planning department is in custody."

"A city employee. *Wow.* I did not see that coming." I took our cups and plates to the sink. "*Any idea why?*"

"No, and it's none of my business. We'll read about it in the news. Won't we? Velma." Frank gave me a stern look.

Camo came back inside with something in her mouth. *I hope it's a dead lizard and not a half-alive one. I hate seeing the poor things suffer.* She leaped up on the counter. "No," I yelled, waving a dish towel in the air. "You are not allowed up here." The cat dropped what was in her mouth and jumped off. I braced myself for a man-gled anole. It wasn't a miniature dinosaur. It was a three-inch bone bleached white from exposure. *Is there a dead raccoon in my yard?* The French door slammed shut. *Oyá?* I remembered what the Babalawo had said 'Son indios, pero no son viejos.' The orisha kept bringing me back to the bones at the golf course.

Frank was going to give me yet another face, but if I didn't ask, who knew what the next message from Oya would be.

"Frank, any updates from forensics? Do they have a name?" I asked. I whisked Camo's gift into the trash, locked the back door, and acted like I was getting ready to go. If I was helping him with Marjory, he could help me in return. "Gordon was over here last night for dinner. He said that Dr. Bustinza would be filing her report today." My intention was to sound nonchalant.

"No ID, but we have a year range. The team is cross-referencing the age with missing persons from that time. We should have a name soon."

"Oh, good. What year?" I hooked my purse onto my arm.

Frank grumbled. "*Velma.*"

"I'm simply curious because it's Robert's project. Ese hotel ha sido un dolor de culo." I used Spanish to show how frustrated I—we were with the project's delays. I hoped it would garner some sympathy from him.

He held the front door for me. As I locked it, he looked at something on his phone. "The report says the remains are male, twenty to twenty-five years of age. They estimate the body was placed in the ground no earlier than 1990 and no later than 2000 due to trace chemicals that match an industrial fertilizer popular during that decade."

"Interesting." I took the few steps down onto the walkway. "Should we go in your car?"

"Yes, unless you'd like to take *The Mystery Machine*, Velma."

Chapter
Twenty-Nine

I wanted a snappy comeback to Pullman's Scooby Doo barb, but I couldn't even remember all the names of the characters. There was Shaggy, the pretty girl, and the jock. *I wish I'd watched more cartoons. That's the first time I've ever thought that.* I chuckled to myself.

Frank took a roundabout way to my in-laws' house. He drove three blocks north, then turned back around and drove past her house three blocks south. Along the way I noticed more traffic than usual for our quiet residential streets. We passed the same shark-skin gray Maserati twice. And the black SUV in the driveway cattycorner to Marjory's house had its windows tinted so dark that they'd get stopped by a state trooper for a violation. *Feds!*

"Are they being watched?" I asked. I'd chosen the wrong term, but Pullman understood my question. He gave a micro-nod that I'd come to know meant that I was right, but he couldn't officially confirm anything.

"Your father-in-law is a *federal* judge," he said, cutting his eyes my way.

"If they're under protection—surveillance—guard, *whatever it's called,* then why can't they go to the museum thing?"

Frank shifted the car into park and left the motor on idle. He turned to me and spoke in a low tone that screamed 'I don't like repeating myself.' "She has a gun. She plans to take it with her. That is within her rights. She passed the background check, and she has a permit. We cannot legally take the gun away from her. *You've met her.* She's a ticking bomb of misplaced righteous indignation on a good day. One wrong move, and she'll wave that pistol around like she's *Tony Montana*." He cut the engine. "Just follow my lead. Convince her that it isn't safe for her to go out tomorrow night and that you should go in her place."

"If it's not safe for her, is it safe for me?" I asked.

"*Velma*, would I put you in harm's way?" Frank asked, sounding hurt.

I felt like I'd disappointed my father. Of course, Frank would never put me in jeopardy. I was usually the one putting myself in danger and getting reprimanded by him for it. But it gave me an idea for how to pitch the notion to Marjory.

Without knocking, Frank and I were let into the house by a man in a dark suit. His cologne was eau de I can snap your neck. *Ay, ay, ay. I bet she's treating him like he's her butler. Pobrecito.*

"Who's there?" Marjory called from the TV room off the main hall. It was the room that the grandkids played in when there was a family gathering.

"Just me," I said, entering the room.

Marjory was seated in one of the leather wingback chairs.

"Do I have you to blame for all this?" Marjory waved her finger like she was casting a spell.

She shut the James Patterson book she'd been reading and placed it on the candlestick side table. To do so, she had to move the gun that was resting there. It was a ludicrously huge semi-automatic that looked like it weighed as much as a bowling ball.

She put the gun on top of the book, with the muzzle pointing toward where I was sitting on the couch. The back of my neck grew damp with perspiration, and my armpits were like toaster ovens. *Deep breath, Miriam. This is precisely why Frank asked you to help him. She is loca, loca, loca.*

I didn't take her bait about the 'all this.' Instead, I took charge of the narrative. I was sorry that I was going to have to throw Frank under the bus, but it was the only option.

"Marjory, you were right. The Coral Shores Police Department was not taking the situation seriously." I glanced at Frank. "Thank goodness the FBI are. How are you and Senior holding up?" I leaned in with my hands clasped in my lap.

My mother-in-law shifted uncomfortably, unsure of how to answer. Our relationship was usually her attacking and me setting a boundary. My leading with kindness and sympathy put us in new territory.

A different man in a suit came into the room. He was holding a drink in front of him like it was an unpredictable wild animal that might bite him. "Your Arnold Palmer, Mrs. Smith. Exactly half lemonade and half tea."

I know that voice. Welmo! It had been two years since I'd seen him. What was he doing in Miami? Last time we'd spoken was during the money laundering trial of Alma's boyfriend. The one who had targeted her with plans to use her real estate company in his cryptocurrency washing machine. Welmo was Delvis's cousin from Puerto Rico. Was she aware that he was in town? *Miriam, focus! You can find out about Welmo later. You have Marjory dangling. Reel her in.*

We acted like we didn't know each other. But I caught his wink. He deftly turned the gun's muzzle toward the wall as he stepped away from her royal highness. *Gracias.*

Marjory took a sip of the drink. Since she didn't complain about it, I guessed he'd gotten the ratio right. I swooped in and rode the moment of pleased-ness.

"How are you and Senior handling the stress? I know it must be difficult having the FBI in your house. But thank goodness they're here to catch the criminal that's threatening your life. You're the matriarch of the family. You hold this family together."

Miriam, que comemierda eres. I was laying it on thick, but it was getting the desired results. My mother-in-law's ramrod affect softened. She relaxed into the chair.

"It's been awful. Before my men arrived, it all fell to me to keep the house and Senior safe. *That man* has the self-preservation of a tadpole. Can you believe he's been to the courthouse every day this week? He's in court as we speak. They say he's being guarded by undercover officers. But that is nonsense. William Robert Smith, Sr., is in line to be on the Supreme Court. His life is being threatened. He should have had a secret service agent assigned to him for protection since the get-go."

There was a lot to unpack. *My men.* Humans aren't property. *The Supreme Court.* Was that true? Was Senior going to be appointed to the Supreme Court? Maybe of Florida, but not the United States of America. *No puede ser. Ask Robert about it later. Stay focused.*

"You are absolutely right. He *and you* are too important to lose. They need to keep you safe for the future of the country." *Ay, Miriam, por favor, that's going too far.*

Marjory was smiling and nodding. She was eating it up. I had her in the palm of my hand.

"It's too risky for you to leave the house until this lunatic is caught. Let me help you. I know you have some social events. Let me go in your place. *Let me be the target.* You're too important to the family."

It felt like Frank, Welmo, and the front door suit all had their eyes fixed on me. The room was quiet. Marjory swirled her drink. The ice cubes sounded like gongs.

"That's not a bad idea," she said.

I gripped the sofa, not wanting to give away my satisfaction and win.

"*But*— I should really be there. You don't understand what's at stake. Bell needs to be taken down a notch. He's forgotten who butters his bread." She drained her glass and shook it at Welmo for him to take the empty glass back to the kitchen.

Take Bell down a notch. What does that mean?

"Is it something Robert could do?" I asked.

Marjory blustered. "My Bobby. No. Bill could. It's a shame he's out of town. He'd be perfect. He understands leverage and politics."

Qué carajo is she talking about?

"*Grove College politics.* I had a lovely conversation with the dean yesterday," I said.

"Lyle? You know Lyle?"

I didn't know know him, but I was going to bluff. Marjory was intrigued. I had her back on the line. "Remember, Rob—" I hated calling my husband Bobby. He didn't like his nickname much either, but whatever it took. "*Bobby* and I were academics before we moved back to Miami. Academia is very political. Tell me what you need me to do."

Marjory tilted her head and thought about it. "Hmm. I've been after Bobby to take more of a role in the family's legacy. And you—" She gave me a look like I was wearing a bikini in a snowstorm. "You're an archaeologist, so you speak their language."

Anthropologist, not Archeologist, but I'm going to let it slide.

"What do you need *us* to do?"

For the next thirty minutes, I got a lecture about Dr. Bell getting 'too big for his britches.' The more Marjory talked, the looser she got. The museum that she (and Senior) had 'paid for' was supposed to be more about 'our history' and less about 'Indians.' I balled my hand into a fist and stuffed it behind a pleated velvet pillow. I alternated between secretively flipping her off and clawing the fabric of the fancy throw pillow. *Miriam, you are doing this for Frank. And for Robert. And for the kids. You can't change Marjory. Only Marjory can change Marjory. And she can't change if she's dead. And we don't want her to accidentally kill someone, either.*

Once she was satisfied that I understood her game plan—withhold any future monetary donations to the college until the Settled Florida part of the museum was doubled—I was dismissed. The suit in the hallway was about to open the door for us when Marjory called. "Buy a new dress. There's nothing in your closet that is appropriate. You're representing The Smiths. Dress like it."

"What, like the band?" Frank chuckled under his breath as we stepped out of the house.

I gave him a puzzled look.

"The Smiths. The English band from the eighties. Never mind." He unlocked the car for us. "You did good."

"You're not mad at me? I kind of threw you under the bus," I said, clicking my seatbelt together.

"*Miss Marjory,*" Frank used an exaggerated Southern accent, "is never going to like 'the help.' My feelings aren't hurt. You used psychology. You played to her ego. You were very crafty." He accelerated into the lane. "I might have to change your name to *Martha Stewart.*"

"Don't you dare!"

Chapter Thirty

When I got back to my house, I texted Alma that I needed help picking an outfit. She replied with a GIF of a little Latina girl in a vest squealing, 'I'm so excited.' She enjoyed fashion and was always happy for me to be her dress-up doll.

My parents weren't back from their errands yet. They tried to stay out most of the morning on Fridays so I could test the following week's recipe without Sirena begging for my full attention. But since we had a guest chef for next week's segment and we were filming another Little Havana spotlight tomorrow, I had a rest day.

I went into my study and opened my laptop. If I was going to play chess at the museum celebration, I needed to do my research.

Meow. Camo stretched and pawed my thigh.

"Jump up, girl."

Camo bounded into my lap, made herself comfortable, and shut her eyes.

"Where to start—hmmm"

Meow. Camo chirped like she was annoyed that I'd spoken.

"Okay. Okay. I'll be quiet."

I read Lyle Murphy's bio on the Grove College website. But I had to go to a higher ed news site to get actual information. He'd been hired away from a prestigious college in the northwest two years ago to improve Grove's image and recruitment. *Changing it from what to what?* I did a quick search for the answer—from a small college for rich kids with a low bar entrance standard to an economically and culturally diverse student body. That's what he'd meant by a growing number of Caribbean students. *Hmm. Pienso que me va a caer bien este tipo. He gets it.*

Next, I did a deep dive into Dr. Gregory Vander Bell. He was born in Ohio, attended the University of Colorado for undergrad, and done his graduate work at Indiana University. He'd taught at 'Ole Miss' for a year. *That's not very long. Did he not like it? Or did they not like him?* Then, he was hired by Grove for the 92/93 academic year.

The internet was around in the early 1990s, but it was a far cry from its current manifestation. 'Rate My Professor' certainly wasn't a thing, nor Reddit. If I wanted the dirt on Bell's early career, I needed to search the school newspaper. *Hold on, Miriam. Before you do that, see if you know anyone in the department.* The University of Mississippi was a football school, but it had a good sociology and anthropology department. When I'd been looking for a job before Robert and I decided to move back to Miami, I'd applied for an associate professor opening but hadn't gotten an interview.

I looked at the department's faculty page. One of my cohorts' faces stared back at me. *¡Qué suerte!* "I guess Wyn got it. Good for her!"

Meow. The cat protested. She twisted and reknotted herself.

"Sorry, Camo. I didn't mean to disrupt your nona. Qué vida you have."

I shot an email to Bronwyn Green and returned to my internet search. Coral Shores had a weekly newspaper called the *Shores Sentinel.* They'd recently digitized their archives thanks to funding from the Women's Club. I knew this because Marjory had bragged about it. My mother-in-law was a past president and active member of the organization. I entered Bell's full name into the search bar and got fifty-plus hits. *Wow. Slow news days.* The results were in chronological order, starting with the most recent. The first write-up was merely a listing for a library talk. It looked like he gave one yearly. I found an article about a trip to England. He was leading a study abroad semester during which the undergrads got to assist in excavating a Roman site. I skipped forward, technically backward, to 2005.

Bing.

Wyn had replied to my email. She confirmed that she still had the same phone number and would be happy to help if she could.

I looked in my contacts under W, B, and G but couldn't find her name. I typed in her number, and her name came up as *Folk Medicine Chica*. I laughed and remembered that because of her area of interest, folk medicine, she could be slightly annoying. If you had a cut or a headache or stubbed a toe, Wyn was ready with a root that would cure it. With a name like Bronwyn, one might expect a white woman with Welsh or wannabe-Welsh heritage, but no. She was a Black woman from the Blue Ridge Mountains. I texted her *Hola*. She texted back, and the generic initial in a circle updated to her current avatar—a photo of her in a straw hat with a sunflower on the brim. After we'd caught up on each other's lives. I asked if she could ask around about a former professor. She replied that she'd ask the department administrator, who'd been there for eons. I thanked her, put down my phone, and returned to reading the *Shores Sentinel*.

The 2005 news pieces were much of the same—talks and trips. I went back further to 1998. Bingo. The grand opening of the museum was the front-page story. There were several photographs. I zoomed in on the grainy black and white scan. Marjory and Senior, along with the heads of the other founding families, were behind a wide ribbon. The then-president had an oversized pair of scissors about to cut the ribbon. Even though the image was captured twenty-five years ago, Marjory looked the same. She had the same bob and an almost identical style—a sweater set worn with trim trousers and flats.

The headline read "Grove College Digs History." I skimmed through the article. The original collection was an assembly of hodge-podge items from the founding families' personal belongings, such as planters' diaries, the sales ledger from a general store, memorabilia from Florida's East Coast Railway (Henry Flagler's train), and a signed Ernest Hemingway novel. The last paragraph mentioned that Dr. Bell had acquired some 'Indian artifacts' (shells, turtle carapaces, and animal teeth) for an upcoming exhibit. There was an image of him. He was younger, fitter, and had a lion's mane of hair. But like Marjory, his fashion sense was the same. He was in cargo pants and sandals.

My phone notified me that someone was walking up the front path. I looked at the video and saw no head, only a bouquet of flowers. *It's not our anniversary.* I went to the door to accept the delivery.

"These are for you, mi salvadora!" Delvis thrust the enormous pom-pom of hydrangeas, roses, and orchids at me. The flowers were in every shade of purple. "You saved me."

"Thank you. They're gorgeous. Umm, but I don't know what you mean," I said.

She followed me to the dining room table, where I set the vase and flowers down.

"My lawyer called to tell me I am no longer a suspect. No orange jumpsuit for me." Delvis was giddy. "You did this. You!" She pointed and did a little dance. "How'd you find a video of the killer escaping when the police couldn't?"

"Have they caught him?" I thought back to my conversation with Frank. Turning the handles on the double doors, I moved us outside. I opened the beverage cooler and offered Delvis a soda. She took a Materva, and I chose a Jupiña.

"I don't know. I don't care. I'm just happy to be free. So, how did you find the camera?"

I told her about Gloria and Naco. She made me promise to introduce her to Gloria tomorrow after the shoot. Delvis wanted to thank her.

"I am so relieved. Mujer, when I tell you, mi'ja, I was having nightmares. Like, for real nightmares that I was going to end up in a documentary about wrongful convictions. Like, can you imagine I finally get a film award, and it's not for a film I directed but for one I'm the star of because I've been rotting away in jail for something I didn't do, and then, like, one of my film students, like, makes a documentary about me. No-no-no-no-no. Te lo juro, I was losing my sh—" Delvis stopped to breathe.

I was glad to see Delvis back to her old self. "You don't think it was El Marinero?" I blurted out. *I hope he isn't the killer. I kind of liked him.*

"How do you know El Marinero?"

I told her about his performance the other night. "He has a good voice."

Delvis laughed. "He's a character! I have like thirty seconds of him cantando in my Calle Ocho film. So sad that the film festival is postponed."

"Oh no, I'm sorry. Can't the organizers find another venue? Like what about the Olympia theatre downtown." The 1926 Mediterranean revival theatre was on the National Registry of Historic Places. It was kind of a miracle that the gorgeous old building hadn't been redeveloped into condos. Miami was not good about preserving its history. *Miriam, you sound like Marjory.*

Nelson let Tom out to the backyard to play catch. We heard him saying, "Get it! Good boy!"

Dominoes, Danzón, and Death

"That's it!" I yelled. "You need to talk to my neighbor. He's part of the LGBTQ film festival. He'll know of a place. Nelson. Nelson. Can I come over? I want to introduce you to someone."

Nelson went to the place in the fence line where we could see each other's faces. "Come on over," he said.

Delvis and I went out my side gate and into my neighbor's yard. I made introductions and explained the situation. The two began talking about juries, distributors, and other things that had nothing to do with my sphere of reference. So, I left them to their chatting and commiserating. I closed the latch on Nelson's gate and went back to my house.

Entering, I saw Camo eyeing the satin bow around the cylindrical vase. "Oh, no, you don't missy-poo." I took the flowers into my study.

My laptop had gone to sleep. Entering my password, the *Shores Sentinel* website came back into view. I clicked the arrow to go to the next page of search results. "Nada interesante." I clicked to the last page. "¿Qué es esto?" The headline read, "Grove's Dr. Bell Excavates Golf Course." I tapped the hyperlink, and another front page spread with grainy photos came up.

Trill. Trill. The door cam alerted, but I didn't look.

Ring. Ring. The doorbell rang. "Delvis, why didn't you just come through the back?" I said as I zoomed in on the black and white photo on my screen. My butt was out of my chair, but my fingers were still on the touchpad. "Voy."

Tap. Tap. "¡Coño!" I startled at the noise. I looked out the window, expecting to see a tree branch or a bird. "Alma!"

My BFF bent over in a maniacal laugh.

I gave her a you-are-twisted look and went to let her in. "Chica, you scared the caca out of me," I said, swatting her on the upper arm. "What do you have in those bags?"

"Duh, your outfit for the thing tomorrow." Alma dropped the bags onto the blue sofa.

"How?" I was astonished.

"I called in an emergency to my personal shopper." Alma plopped onto the long ottoman and crossed her ankles.

"Since when do you have a personal shopper?" I put my hands on my hips.

"I sold a house to Tamara Casini—"

"Never mind, I don't need the details." *All her stories start the same way.* I laughed.

Crash. A noise came from the study.

"Camo!"

Chapter
Thirty-One

I ran into the study. Camo, the flowers, and the vase were on the floor. The cat was bunny-kicking the bow with her hind legs. I sighed. Then I realized my laptop was askew. The flowers must have hit it on the way down.

"Please, no water," I said as I lifted it. A droplet of water formed at the corner as I tilted it.

Alma picked up the flowers. "I'll get a towel."

I showed her the real problem: my damp laptop. *Pitiful whine.*

"¡Arroz! Hurry, take it to the kitchen." Alma pushed me out of the room.

Having loosened the bow and ribbon, Camo bounded off with it in her mouth like she'd nabbed a snake.

I turned the laptop off, dried it the best I could, and then put it in a plastic container with a whole bag of rice.

"Ay, ay, ay. I have everything backed up, but still," I sighed and slumped onto the kitchen counter.

"I know what will cheer you up." Alma pulled me from my moping and into the living room. "I think the black dress is going to look amazing on you." She grabbed the bags and used her chin to point me to the bedroom.

As I kicked off my shoes, I got a text from Delvis. She was still talking to Nelson. There were emojis and exclamation points, so I knew things were going well. *See you tomorrow at seven.* I replied with a thumbs up.

"¿Todo bien?" Alma asked.

"Si, algo sobre el trabajo," I replied, setting my phone on the nightstand. The small altar on a shelf by my bed needed dusting. The orisha, Yemaya, was the protector of children and mothers. While I was pregnant and during Sirena's first year, I had been very good about *feeding* the orisha. "Dame dos segundos." I said, holding up two fingers. I took the glass of water and the burnt-out candle from the altar. After rinsing the glass in the kitchen, I refilled it with fresh water. The blue votive had a layer of film, which I wiped off, and used a knife to dislodge the metal disc that had held the wick upright. In our hurricane stash, I found a fresh candle. Then I looked in the fridge for something Yemaya would like *to eat.* She liked watermelon. I didn't have melon of any kind, but I did have some dulce de fruta bomba/candied papaya.

I tucked a dust cloth under my arm and took the offerings to my room. Alma had busied herself laying out the dress on the bed. I cleaned the saint and the shelf, then put the fresh offerings on it. From the hiding place where I kept it, I took out the lighter and lit the candle. It flickered and shone through the wavy blue glass, giving it an ocean vibe. Yemaya was often pictured as a mermaid, that was why I also had shells on her altar.

"This should really be in Sirena's room," I said partly to myself. "Whenever she gets a room to herself."

"Chica, I told you I can find your parents an apartment. I saw a nice little condo in Normandy Isle come up for rent."

"We're going to build Mami y Papi an extension. Roberto's fighting with the village about the plans. But as soon as he gets the permit, we will start work. The village will let us build a room above the garage, but we'd like to build them a little efficiency in the backyard." I stripped down to my undies and chose a dress from the bed.

"Pfft. The village does not like *in-law quarters*. I had a buyer for a double lot ready to sign when the inspection came in. The owners had built a spa in the garage—*like a five-person in-ground hot tub*—without pulling a permit. The inspector told the village, and they ordered it to be backfilled and returned to its original garage state. The buyers rescinded their offer. They loved the hot tub. I found them a property in Morningside. You will not win that fight. If the village dice que no, it's no."

"I'm beginning to think you're right. I just hate the idea of them having to climb the stairs." I slipped a one-shouldered red dress over my head.

"You could give your parents this room and you take the new room," Alma said.

The dress slid down around me. It hugged my hips, and the length of it fell to the floor. It was very formal. "Esa no es mala idea. We were already thinking it would need an en suite." I went to the mirror. I did my best Jorge impersonation. "*She's giving prom.*"

My BFF cackled. "Yeah. Next." She pointed to the green dress.

The emerald dress was cocktail length, hitting at my knee. It had three-quarter sleeves with a wavy, rolled hem. The neckline was high with a shallow scoop. "I feel like this is too conservative. The neck is too high. ¿Entiendes?" I tried to pull it away from my throat. "I feel like I can't breathe."

"It's giving mother of the bride." Alma made duck lips and nodded.

"I like the belt, though."

"Not enough reason to love what you hate. Next!"

I tried to put on the next dress, a wildly patterned bodycon. I couldn't get both my arms into it. "This is way too tight. It can't be the right size. I think it's for you." I wrestled it off and threw it into Alma's lap. The pattern had chains and Italian baroque motifs. It was more her style than mine.

Alma looked at the tag. "You're right, it's my size. I'll try it on later." She smoothed it and put it aside. "Try this high-low."

I took the burgundy dress and stepped into it. Turning around, Alma zipped the back for me. It was a handsome dress with a subtle pattern and flutter sleeves. "Este no esta mal. I wish it was in a different color. This feels like a Christmas party dress. *Right.*"

"Agreed. Okay, I saved the best for last." Alma unwrapped the tissue from around a black dress. "It's a V-neck, which looks great on you. The back is open but not too sexy. It has ruching y, mira, it has a wrap belt like the green one."

Everything about the dress was right. I put it on, and it looked like it had been tailor-made for me. "I love it. Classic, elegant, con un poquito de sexy." I plumped my boobs, and we both giggled. "Y la más importante—I feel confident. Like I'm Miriam Quiñones de *Cocina Caribeña,* not Miriam Smith, Marjory Smith's daughter-in-law." I turned on my tiptoes to admire the way the dress fit my fundillo.

"Here." Alma gave me a pair of heels from the closet. She went to my modest jewelry box and selected a gold lariat necklace with diamonds at the ends. It was last year's anniversary gift from Robert that she'd helped him select. I wasn't supposed to know that, but BFFs don't keep secrets. She handed me a pair of small gold hoops and a pair of diamond studs.

I put one in each ear. "Which one works best?" I covered one side than the other.

"Diamantes." We said in unison.

The alert for the doorcam sounded, and we heard the front door open. My parents were back with Sirena. Alma poked her head out. "Put that on a hanger. I'll pack the rest in a second. Voy ayudar a tu mama con las compras." Alma unzipped me and then went to help.

A warm paw slapped my foot. "Camo, so that's where you went to hide. I do not appreciate what you did to my flowers *or my laptop*." I shimmied out of the black dress, hung it in the closet, and put my regular clothes back on. Kneeling beside the bed, I looked under it for the purple ribbon. It was all fun and games, having caught a 'snake.' But if she ate it, that could be dangerous. Stormy, the woman who had given Manny the kitten, had warned me about strings and things. "Undigestible and deadly," she'd said. "Let her eat a lizard tail but never a ribbon." I reached my arm under and felt around for the satin *snake*.

Camo thought I was playing with her. She batted my hand sans claws. "Gatita, this is not a game."

At last, I got a good grip and pulled the ribbon away from Camo. I stood, and the calico zoomed out from under the bed, chasing the tail. Mistakenly, I flicked it across the bed like I was casting a fishing rod. She jumped on the bed, her claws millimeters from snagging the emerald dress. *¡Ay, Caridad!* The cat launched off the bed, landing on the floor, ready to repeat the chase in the opposite direction. I hastily rolled the ribbon up, stuffed it in my pocket, and tried to shoo Camo out. She evaded me by running back under the bed. I wrapped the dresses in their tissue and put them in their bags to protect them from claws. To a cat, snakes came in all kinds of disguises, especially ribbons and belts.

Chapter Thirty-Two

Mami insisted that Alma stay for lunch. She'd bought three medianoche sandwiches at Sedano's, the Latin grocery store. She cut them in half and served them with Chifles chips. It was a simple yet satisfying meal. Sirena ate only the bread and pickle from her portion. Papi took the ham, roast pork, and Swiss cheese from her plate and stuffed it into his sandwich.

"'bue-wo," Sirena said. Her little face was written with aghastness.

I took the pickle from my sandwich and gave it to her as compensation.

"¿Mami, qué más hiciste?" I asked her where else they'd gone that morning.

"We went to El Home De-po pero no tenían el tamaño de maceta que queríamos," Mami replied.

My parents had all sizes of pots in the garage, so it made me wonder what size pot they'd been looking for. It dawned on me that as much as they loved living with us and helping with the kids, they probably missed the large property they'd maintained in their last job. My parents came from a long line of guajiros. Cultivating plants was in their DNA. *Miriam, now's your chance to tell Alma about your idea.* I pitched the plant stager business idea to my parents and Alma. Mami y Papi didn't quite understand why people would want to rent plants. I explained that it was like hiring a decorator for a wedding or a quince.

"Chica, that is brilliant!" Alma made a flourish with her hand. She was so jazzed by the idea that she wanted to take my parents to see one of her properties that needed sprucing up. "It's been on the market for two months without a nibble. The house has mega potential pero, ahora mismo sin muebles y luces, it looks boring and plain, you know. It needs to feel alive. The plants will do that. Such a good idea. I wish I'd thought of it earlier."

"*Excuse me,*" I jabbed.

"Estoy bromeando, chica." Alma laughed. "But seriously, franchise potential. We need to set your parents up with an LLC ASAP. After I show them the house, I'll take them to my office. They can use the courtyard to store their plant inventory, like a greenhouse or whatever. We are going to make it rain!" She mimed throwing dollar bills.

Alma put the dress bags into the trunk of her car. Which reminded me to throw away the ribbon in my pocket and check on my laptop. *Ay, ay, ay. Camo.* Sirena and I waved goodbye to her abuelos and madrina, and then I read to her from the book Omarosa had given her. Continuing with our tradition of 'Mami communicates in Spanish and Papi in English,' like we'd done with Manny as he was learning language, I read her the Spanish version of the rhymes. Pretty soon, my little mermaid drifted off to sleep. I moved the ottoman closer and made a pillow barrier to protect her from rolling off the couch in her sleep.

Now, what was I doing before today's dose of beautiful chaos?

I used my phone to search for how long the rice trick took. I huffed an exaggerated sob. My laptop was out of service for at least twenty-four hours. The thought of joining Sirena in nap time crossed my mind, but then I got a text from Welmo.

Can I come over?

Yes. 🐸 is sleeping, so don't knock or ring.

A few minutes later, Welmo was at my door. I let him in and gave him a hug.

"Have you had lunch?" I asked in a low voice.

He shook his head no.

So that we could chat at a normal level, I turned the living room TV to a relaxation video called *Sonidos de El Yunque*. A chorus of coquis sang, interspersed with rain and the occasional bird call. Welmo's face lit up at hearing the sounds of his homeland. Puerto Ricans adored their unique little frog that sang co-kee. We moved to the kitchen, where I warmed up the remaining half of the medianoche sandwich.

"Primero, how long have you been in Miami? Segundo, does Delvis know? Because I saw her today and she didn't say anything. Also, did you know about her little problem? It's solved now, pero you could have helped her más fácil que yo. Third, estás viviendo aquí? Are your wife and kids here?" I rattled out my questions rapid fire.

Welmo held up a finger. "Only a week. I just got the permanent assignment to the Miami field office. It was between Miami and Tampa."

"They wouldn't let you go back to PR, huh," I said as he munched on a plantain chip.

"No, not with as many *ex*-police officers there that know my face." He raised his eyebrows. He'd help bust open a police corruption investigation in his old precinct. He held up two fingers. "No, my prima doesn't know—*yet*. This thing with your suegros got hot very quick. I haven't had time to look for an apartment for Ive y los niños."

"Alma can help Ive with finding an apartment." Alma had had to testify in the money laundering case, too. I was confident she'd want to help the guy that helped save our lives. *Well, him and a whole SWAT team.*

"¿De verdad? *Alma can help me?* Porque I have no free time to go see places y todo eso."

"I can text her now si quieres," I said.

"No, I'll call her later. She doesn't need to know I'm working on your suegros' case." Welmo wiped his mouth with a paper napkin.

"Speaking of my in-laws. I'm sorry Marjory is treating you like a servant." I started a pot of drip coffee for us. I'd bought a bag of Yaucono brand not too long ago. It was the only Puerto Rican brand available in Miami. Welmo's visit was the perfect time to use it.

"She is, cómo se dice, amargá,"

"Disagreeable. Bitter."

"But I also understand that she is scared. She should be. The threat against Judge Smith is real."

"If the threat is against Senior, then why have all those agents watching Marjory?" I poured the coffee into mugs. The sugar shaker was already out. I got the milk carton from the fridge.

Welmo stirred two spoonfuls of sugar and a big glug of milk into his coffee. "Judge Smith follows instructions, ella no."

I had to laugh. *Marjory, you are the problem. Always!* "I can see that. So, do you know who's making the threats?"

"Sí."

"Can you tell me who it is?"

Welmo gave me a look like I was Juan Bobo. *Of course, he can't tell me.*

"Pero, what I can say is that we are close. He is becoming impatient y errático. He will show himself soon. So, for that reason, I will be attending the museum evento with you." Welmo sipped his café cautiously as steam curled from the mug.

"What do you mean? As my date? Everyone in Coral Shores knows Robert, that will not work. *Oh,* you mean como escondido. You'll be there, but I won't see that you are there."

"No, I mean I will be with you and your husband. I will be your visiting brother." Welmo grinned.

"Yo no tengo hermanos."

"We know, but the culprit doesn't."

"*We.* The FBI or you and Pullman?"

"Detective Frank is a very good man. He likes you very, very much."

That was a non-answer answer. I got the feeling Frank had coordinated my extra security. To be honest, I didn't mind. I wondered if Frank had mentioned the messages in the bottles to him. *Say something!*

"¿Pullman te ha dicho algo del mensaje en una botella?" I showed him a picture of the first message in a bottle. "They said that a college student did it as a joke. Pero then—" I swiped to the other message. The one that Pepper had in her car.

"No, I have not seen this." He took my phone and enlarged the picture. "Mándamelo." He handed it back to me, and I sent him the photo. "Now, tell me what is my prima's problem."

I recapped Delvis' troubles and emphasized that she had been cleared.

"Why did she not call me?" Welmo looked like his feelings were hurt. "I will ask Frank for the details."

"Pero, por favor, do not put my name in it, please. Y, don't tell him you got that photo from me."

Welmo gave me a quizzical look. "*¿Por qué?*"

"Porque, I am not getting involved in the investigation. I am not a Velma. Ni una Veronica. Ni una Jessica. Soy Miriam, minding my own business."

"Okay. I will not use your name. What time will you leave for the museum tomorrow?"

I shrugged. "Six-thirty. I think it starts at seven."

"I'll be here at six. We will ride together."

I gave him a thumbs up and saw him to the door. We hugged goodbye.

"Thank you for the lunch, Velma." Welmo winked.

Chapter
Thirty-Three

Early Saturday morning, I got a text from Delvis asking if I could bring Manny to the shoot with me. He was still asleep but due to wake up at any moment. Even though I was cien por ciento sure he'd say yes, I went to his bed and asked him.

"Mi príncipe," I said, giving him a gentle shake. "Do you want donuts and ice cream for breakfast?"

Manny's eyes popped open, and he stared at me as if he wasn't sure if I was real or a dream.

"Do you want to go to work with me today? I am visiting a donut shop, and Delvis wants you to try the sweets on camera." I stood from my stooped position, putting a fist on my hip and cuffing my other hand around the wrist.

Manny threw off his Pusheen bedsheets. They were a gift from "Tía" Alma *because cat and food.* The print of the bed set was the chubby kawaii cat as various breakfast foods. My son sleepwalked to the bathroom without a word. On his return, his hair was brushed and shiny with gel, a little too much gel. He traded his PJs for blue pants, a cream-colored polo shirt, and his little chef jacket.

"Listo," he said.

That was the only word he said. He marched into the living room and stood by the door, holding my bag and keys. I giggled and snapped a photo that I sent to Delvis.

"Mi amor, I'm still in my bata." I touched the lapels of my robe. "And I haven't had my café."

"Mami, we can get coffee on the way." He put my purse on the ottoman and pushed me towards my room to change. "Apúrate. It's not nice to keep your director waiting."

Este niño. Ay mi madre.

My mother felt pity for me and made me a to-go tumbler of café con leche. She made one for Manny, too. His was mostly milk with just a drop of espresso. "Gracias, Abuela," Manny said as we got in the car with our tumblers and a piece of pan de maíz each. The sweet cornbread was wrapped in a paper towel.

That day's location was several blocks south of The Deco. As I drove past it, I gave gratitude that Delvis was out of that sticky situation. Of course, she didn't kill the tour guide on purpose or by accident, but their verbal brawl had been intense. *I'm sorry the woman is dead. What was her name? Cynthia something. Cynthia Jordan. I hope justice is served, Cynthia.* Thinking about justice took my brain to court, and that took me to judges, and that made me worry about Senior.

"Welmo and The Feds will keep him safe," I said to reassure myself.

"What Mami?"

"Nothing, mi príncipe." I smiled at him. "Mira, we are here."

One of the crew had been posted on the sidewalk to watch for us. He motioned for me to roll the window down, and I did. He explained how to get to the UnMundo tent. I followed his directions and went around the block where the alley had been cordoned off for our staging area. Someone in an UnMundo crew shirt lifted the barricade and showed me where to park.

Manny and I went directly to the makeup tent.

"Hello, Jorge," Manny said.

Jorge had one eye done and the other almost complete. He'd drawn a high eyebrow and used purple glittery eyeshadow. "*Manuel.*" Jorge looked at me, puzzled.

"Delvis requested that he be in the shoot," I explained. Manny climbed into the canvas chair Jorge had vacated.

"Not me. Manny, I think you are great, ya tú sabes, pero it was Ileana, la jefa, who asked if you could be the taster today," Delvis said, coming into the tent. She looked tired, but her body and voice were hyper. The iced coffee in her hand looked like a *Miami Especial*—a whole colada mixed with sweetened condensed milk. There was enough caffeine and sugar in the drink to party for days.

"*La jefa de La Tacita.*" Manny's cheeks glowed with pride. He sang *La Tacita's* opening jiggle.

"You better be paying this young Latin King," Jorge said.

Delvis and I nodded not to worry. We'd made sure Manny and his abuela got paid for their guest appearances on *Abuela Approved.* Delvis had pushed for it. Manny's paycheck went directly into an IRA account that Robert's oldest brother, the financier, had helped us set up. His uncle had harrumphed when I'd demanded that the investment fund avoid buying shares in weapons and firearms companies, but he found one that we all agreed upon.

"¿Qué le pusiste en el cabello?" Jorge asked me in an accusatory tone. I slyly moved my pointer finger like an inchworm at the culprit. Jorge understood and changed tone. "Manny, your hair looks increíble, pero I think we can make it look espectacular." Jorge began spraying my son's hair with water to loosen the glue-like gel.

"Miriam, ven conmigo," Delvis said.

I told Manny to stay with his *Tío* Jorge while I talked to the director. I went with Delvis to the OB (Outside Broadcast) van.

"Thank you for introducing me to *Timbo-land*," Delvis said with extra flavor.

"*Nelson?*" Wow, they must have bonded over tequila shots to be special nickname friends already.

"He is dank." Delvis sat on the stool bolted to the floorboard and spun on rotation.

Delvis was a couple of years younger than me, and I was a soccer mom, but I'd never heard dank used any other way than moldy-wet-stinky. *Don't ask. Look it up later.* "Yeah, he's a great guy. So, was he able to help you with the film fest?"

"Yeah. He's talking to them about maybe, like combining the festivals. You know power in numbers. Marginalized voices uniting." Delvis pressed some keys on the keyboard and clicked a file name on the screen. "Timbo is a film nerd. We talked for hours, and I left so inspired that I went back into my footage to find the stuff I shot of El Marinero. Did you know he's gay? He was a Marielito."

I didn't, nor could I have learned that personal history in my short interaction with him. But I did know that Fidel had vilified homosexuality. He made 'sanitariums' (quarantine camps) for HIV+ folk. Many gay men were 'allowed' to leave Cuba during the 1980 Mariel boatlifts. Fidel Castro eventually apologized for his treatment of LGBTQs, but not until 2010.

"Timbo nagged me to make a short for his festival. So, I went looking for the footage—cause I knew I had more of him singing—and mira la que me encontré." Delvis hit the play button. El Marinero was on the screen. The sound muted, but I could tell he was belting out a ballad. Delvis tapped at two figures in the background.

"Who are they?" I leaned in for a closer look. It looked like the couple were arguing. One of them had a brown bag. *A lunch sandwich?* The other one was crisscrossing their hands in a gesture of refusal. Then the one with the bag threw it at the guy, and money flew out.

Delvis stopped the tape and zoomed in on the couple.

"That's the tour guide!" I blurted out. The image wasn't sharp enough to see her face, but the mini-amplifier was easy to identify. "Who's she with?"

"I don't know. He's in the shadow of the building, and we were using a shallow depth of field to focus on El Marinero. You can't see any of his features, but I think he's looking at us. Like he realized he was being filmed."

"Who is us?"

"Me and Fi." Delvis noticed I hadn't heard the name before. "Fi is my cinematographer. Ella esta brutal."

Fi might be awesome, but she wasn't UnMundo crew that I knew of. "If this guy—" I pointed to the blurring oval on the scene. "—was looking at you guys, could he recognize either of you?"

"Fi had a Sony PXW covering her face. I had the mic, so I was in front and close to El Marinero. Do you think I should show it to the cops?" Delvis asked. She was nervy-turvy, bouncing her leg up and down.

"Yes," I affirmed in a very maternal, do-right tone. "That could be the killer." *I also think you should tell your cousin, a full-fledged FBI agent. But since you don't even know he's in Miami, then I'll tell him!* "Do you need Officer Cruz's number? He's the Calle Ocho cop that questioned me and Jorge. I have his card in my purse."

"Oh, I know Cruz. I went to school with his sister." Delvis snorted. "Bro loves a badge. He was our school's hall monitor. Dude would march you to the principal's office for not having a hall pass."

Chapter Thirty-Four

Jorge used his talents to contour my face so I looked like myself on screen instead of a pufferfish. I was completely okay with my weight. I loved the body that had grown two kids. I loved my full lips and hips. But the expression 'the camera adds ten pounds' was accurate, and for me, it was all in my face. The first few times I was on *La Tacita,* I'd barely recognized myself when I'd seen myself on screen. Viviana had done my make-up with minimal contour. She'd improved at making me look like me, but Jorge did it effortlessly.

"Bella," Jorge said, removing the protective tissue from around my collar. "That lipstick should last through all the eating, pero if you need a touch-up, aquí estoy."

I gave my friend air kisses.

"You know I'm only staying so I can get a donut. La fila for Dulce's siempre es around the block. And you know how I hate to wait in line. Tell the owner they need a VIP line for fabulous people like me—" Jorge made a pose. "—y mi amiguito Manuel." He and Manny high-fived with flair.

Jorge went back to his own makeup as Manny and I left the tent. It had been a little jarring having a half-Jorge, half-Cruella

Deville styling my hair. I'd have to check Jorge's Instagram to see the final masterpiece. He'd be clean-faced by the time Manny and I returned to the tent.

It was the first time Manny had shot on location. He was used to our outdoor kitchen, where the camera was stationary. It took a few takes to get the opening shots of us walking into the donut shop. The front of *Dulce's Donas* was a mural, a street scene of humorous characters with speech bubbles. The one above two women with their foreheads touching said, 'tengo chisme.' There was a man in a sailor's hat singing. El Marinero. His bubble had *Dulce's Donas son dulce* on a music staff with notes flying into the sky. The clouds in the sky were donuts with icing that dripped into raindrops. A cat was on a table with its mouth open and tongue out to catch the sweet rain. The man with an umbrella sitting at the table had a thought bubble that read 'guayaba y queso' with question marks. In the foreground, there was a mother with two squabbling kids. Between them a donut was falling to the ground. At the corner of the building, under the window, a spotted dog was peeing. Manny giggled when he saw that part of the mural.

We took some B-roll shots by the gallo sculpture on the side-walk in front of the treat shop. The giant rooster wore an apron with the donut shop's name on it. The sculpture was painted in high-gloss pastels. Delvis took a few snaps with her phone to post on *Abuela Approved* socials.

Inside, we were greeted by Dulce, a forty-something Cuban woman, and her twenty-something daughter, Jasline. Over the counter, I asked the mother-daughter team what had inspired them to go into the donut business. Dulce had made custom cakes out of her home kitchen as a side hustle. "So, she had the skills," Jasline said. "Mi mama es muy talentosa."

I love that she is speaking in Spanglish!

Dominoes, Danzón, and Death

Dulce interrupted and continued the story. While they were in Orlando for a trip to the parks, they made a visit to *Voodoo Dough-nuts*. Then they went back the next day and the next. "Los sabores eran un poquito raros pero deliciosos." The non-traditional flavors were intriguing, which gave her the idea to experiment with Caribbean flavors. Soon, the orders for donuts outpaced those for cakes. She needed a bigger space, one with industrial fryers.

The pandemic hit about six months after they'd opened for business. Jasline took to social media to promote her mom's place. She made process videos of how the donuts were decorated. She and her mom did all the dance challenges. Within a few weeks, they had a steady line of delivery scooters at the curb.

Each week, they had a special flavor. Sometimes, they were holiday-inspired. With Valentine's a week away, they had heart-shaped donuts filled with a sabayon passionfruit cream. For Navidad, they'd had coquito and crema de vie donuts. It was Jasline's idea to keep a score board as to which flavor sold more. And she had a poll on their website where people could vote on which flavor they liked better. Crema de vie was the Cuban answer to Puerto Rico's coquito. It was heavier and more like eggnog.

"¿Cuál ganó?" I asked.

"El coquito," Jasline said. "Because it had a lot of rum in it. We carded people. You had to be 21 to buy it."

Her mother told her to stop joking. It was only extract.

Manny asked what the flavors of the donuts in the display case were. Jasline pointed to each one as she listed their everyday flavors: Guayaba Glaze, Maria Cookie Crunch (drizzled with condensed milk), Dulce de Leche, Flan-retto (flan and amaretto-flavoring), Coconut-Tamarind, Marmelada con Natilla (Orange marmalade and pudding), and Mango with Candied Lime Rinds.

"Yo quiero probar una," Manny said on cue.

Dulce told him that if he helped her finish the last batch of donuts, he could take a dozen home. We took a short break to let the crew set up in the kitchen. Looking out the store's window, I saw that a line of patrons had formed. An UnMundo PA was outside, explaining that Dulce's Donas would be opening an hour later than usual. All of the patrons stayed. I walked out and thanked them for their patience. One woman asked if someone famous was inside. I told her I was the host of a show filming a spotlight about the place. She craned to see if a 'real celebrity' was in the shop.

I smiled graciously and again thanked them for their patience. *Gracias a La Caridad, I have thick skin.* I chuckled as I opened the shop door.

The donuts we'd be helping make for the camera were their gluten-free variety. Dulce had made the dough from a blend of chickpea/garbanzo and cassava/yuca flour. It had to rise, be cut, then be left to rise a second time. Dulce took a rack of ready ones, put the entire rack into a flat cage, and then into hot oil. She turned them halfway through. The hot donuts were then left to cool.

Manny and I put on food safety gloves for the finishing steps— glaze and topping. Dulce gave Manny (who was on a step stool) a spouted bowl of espresso glaze. She told him to pour the glaze over the donuts. He hesitated, afraid it would make too much of a mess. "No te preocupes," she said with a wide grin. The pan beneath the rack would collect the drips. Manny did an excellent job after his worry had been soothed away.

I took a spoon and dipped it into the unused glaze. "Sabe igual que una taza de café." It tasted just like a shot of Cuban coffee. Next, he sprinkled panela/brown sugar on top. The sprinkles weren't cylindrical like the ice cream kind. They were more like crumbs. I asked Dulce about them. She showed us how she made them by grating a cone of brown cane sugar.

We took the tray of finished gluten-free donuts to the display case. The final shot of the day was Manny and I eating our donuts. I ate a coffee one, and he had the Maria Cookie Crunch. Jasline packaged a sampler box especially for Manny to take home, letting him choose the flavors he wanted. The owners had several boxes ready to go for the crew. When we exited, they turned the sign from closed to open. The line that had doubled clapped with appreciation.

"Mami, I didn't know which flavor Abuelo would like best, so I got him the same as Papi," Manny said.

"Which flavor is that?"

"Flan."

"I think you made the right choice. Your father and grandfather love flan." I tried to muss his hair. It looked soft and product-free, except it wasn't. *How does Jorge do it? He's a wizard.*

"¿Donde están mis donas?" Jorge asked. He was applying serum to his face in little dots. The glitter-glam look was gone.

"Delvis has some boxes for the crew," I said.

"I have one for you, Tío Jorge," Manny said. "Here." He carefully took the donut from the box. It had a yellow glaze and rainbow glitter. "Do you like it?"

"*Like? Love!*" Jorge exclaimed. "¿Cuál es el sabor?"

"Banana. The glitter doesn't have a flavor, but it is *eat-able*."

"It is very me." Jorge took a chomp of the donut. "*Mmmmmm.*" He stomped his feet.

After we'd cleaned our faces and Jorge had brushed the product from Manny's hair, we said goodbye. On the way to our car, we passed the OB van. Delvis and Officer Cruz were inside, viewing the footage. Manny caught a glimpse of the screen.

"That's the singer from the domino dance," Manny said.

"Sí, mi amor." I clicked the car fob, and the alarm beeped off.

"He was singing about a robber." Manny climbed into the back seat.

"You have a good memory. It's a famous salsa song called 'Juanito Alimaña'," I said, looking out for pedestrians in the make-shift parking lot.

"Is that why the police officer is there? Is he going to arrest Juanito?"

Yes, if Juanito is the one who killed the tour guide.

Chapter Thirty-Five

Manny and I arrived home to find Abuelo grilling chorizo for lunch. Robert was seated by the play cottage. He held a trapeador (a Cuban "T" shaped mop) in his hand. Sirena wore a T-shirt dress with a mermaid body painted on it. A pearl choker was sewn around the collar, and the shell bikini top had iridescent sequins. It had been a gift from Alma and was a little too large. Roberto or Abuela had tied a knot so she wouldn't trip herself.

"Who are you supposed to be?" I asked my husband.

He leaned the mop toward me and deepened his voice. *"Don't you recognize my triton?* I'm Neptune, God of the Seas."

"Is Jason Momoa here, too?" I winked at him.

"Different character universes. I'm Roman. Aquaman is from Atlantis, a Greek myth." Sirena gave him a starfish sand mold. He put it on his chest. "Do you know Neptune is not only the god of the ocean but also of *the wind and storms?*" He used a dramatic baritone.

A gust blew through the yard.

Oyá, he didn't mean anything by that.

"See my power." Robert smirked in a charming, rogue way.

"I'll take your word for it. Greek and Roman mythology weren't my thing as a kid," I said. Growing up, we had our own gods and goddesses, the orishas. I hadn't paid too much attention to them other than the occasional story/pataki that Tía Elba would tell me, but now I was all ears. "I need to check on something." I pivoted on one foot to get to the side of the house. "Where's Mami?"

"She's doing something with Alma," Robert replied in his Neptune voice. Another gust of wind kicked up, and he waved his trident like he was commanding it. Sirena laughed and squealed, "'g-in."

No, no, no. Let's not do it again. I rushed over to the saint house. This time the door was shut, but in the bowl, instead of frijoles negros there were bones—chicken and *pork*. "Is that from the chuletas we had Thursday night? Mami, are you doing this? It can't be Sirena. Her little arms can't reach that far in. *Right.* Right." I scratched my head. *Miriam, you are making up stories in your head. Woo-woo stories, chica.* I tried to unlatch the door to remove the bowl, but my fingers felt a small suitcase lock. "Okay, that has to be from Mami or Papi," I said, relieved there was an explanation to the bowl of bones. "Oyá, as soon as I find the key, I'll get you some fresh food." *Miriam, you are going loquita. You are talking to a statue.* As I turned to go, I laughed, "As long as the statue doesn't start talking back."

Clink.

Tink.

Thud.

Sounds had come from the saint house—the *locked* saint house. I knelt on the ground to be at eye level. A bone had hit the plexiglass and chipped the bowl in the process. *Impossible.* There had to be a mouse or a frog or some critter in there. It had probably hid as I approached. *Or maybe there's a hole in the bottom that it crawls in and out of.* As I tilted my head to look for a hole, my phone vibrated in my pocket.

I glanced at it quickly and stood. It was a text from Wyn. *Call me.* Anything to distract me from the bone mystery was welcomed. Dialing as I walked into the house, I went to my study and shut the door.

"That was quick," Wyn said.

"Is this not a good time?" I asked.

"No, you're good." Her cadence, with its molasses pauses and undulating pitch, had changed somewhat from the high and bright mountain accent I recalled. The University of Mississippi was near Oxford, William Faulkner country. The area had a dramatic literary history that seemed to have seeped into Wyn. "I was just about to sit down to lunch—ham, red-eye gravy, biscuits, and potlikker greens. Wish you were here to share a meal with me."

"Mmm. It sounds delicious." I responded, not lying. I'd read about, but never tasted, the coffee-based gravy. "I can call you back later."

"Naw. It's piping hot. It will keep a second. And what I've got to tell you is a juicy nugget."

I raised the volume and put my phone on speaker. I wanted my hands free to take notes. Picking an index card from a stack, I clicked a ballpoint pen and was ready to write.

"Your professor left on *suspicious* terms. There were allegations of impropriety." Wyn paused before continuing in a hushed tone. "Some Chickasaw artifacts went missing. Nothing was ever proven. But, *girl*, you know where there's smoke, there's fire."

It took me a beat to digest what she'd told me. Dr. Bell had stolen Native American artifacts from the university. Could that be true? I needed details.

"Um. Huh. Do—" I started and stopped, sputtering with befuddlement. If what she was telling me was true, that cast a shadow over his current role as the director of the Grove Museum.

Miriam, get your thoughts in order. Wyn's lunch is getting cold. "Do you know what he *allegedly* took?"

"Well, the story goes that, and this is why they couldn't prove anything for certain, but the school was helping with an excavation of some mounds over in Starkville. And they'd found some metal pieces that had probably belonged to the Spanish, because there was a battle that happened around those parts. The Chickasaw ran them off, but anyhow—the Native folk took the horseshoes and ax heads and whatnot and turned them into other things, as one does, right. Well, like I was saying, one day, they had a dozen doodads in the pit, and the next morning, there were only ten. That happened a couple of times, and each time, your professor was the common denominator."

"This is giving me A. Head. Ache." I rubbed my forehead.

"Mix yourself up a little corn meal and salt into a dough and put that on your forehead for a spell. Ma Jaspers taught me that. I don't know if it's the ingredients or the weight of it that's doing the fixin', but it does work. And it's better for you than a Tylenol." Wyn's chuckle was lyrical, like a chorus from a hymn. "I've got to get going. Listen, don't be a stranger. Let's catch up soon, alright."

"Yes, definitely. Thank you for the information." I ended the call and blew out a huff of air. My bottom lip vibrated with the force. I stared at the doodles and scribbled words I'd made on the index card: Cornmeal and salt?! Root witch. (With a hat and star drawn beside the words.) Chickasaw. Stolen?! (I'd doodled a horseshoe.) Bell. Theft. (I'd circled the two words in a tornado.)

I hummed as I pondered my next step. *Does that mean Dr. Gregory Vander Bell is a thief? Is that why he's so interested in the golf course find? Is he trying to steal something from it? Or maybe he already did? Miriam, the missing pot shard!* He'd been there the day Dr. Cypress performed the smudging ceremony. He'd appeared out of nowhere and hadn't been invited to attend either. Had he stolen the shard that very morning?

I closed my eyes and tried to replay the scene in my head. Robert and I had gone through the lawn and maintenance area. We had taken a golf cart to the site. There was a guard outside the tent. The Tribal Preservation Office representatives got there. Gordon let us in the tent. He plugged in a cord for the lights and noticed the piece of pottery was gone. Then Dr. Bell appeared. *I remember getting the feeling that Alice Cypress didn't care for Bell. What does she know? Does she know something but can't prove it?*

I heard the doorknob turn.

"Mami, almuerzo is ready. Abuelo told me to get you," Manny said.

"Voy," I replied.

Manny, with Camo at his heels, went to the patio. I followed, though at a slower pace. The memory film in my head urged me to see something that I was missing. It glitched between two images—the bottom of Bell's cargo pants and his sandaled feet—*Gross. Get a pedicure, sir.* —and finger bones. *Bones. Bones. Bones. They won't leave me alone.*

Outside, I sat at my usual spot. Abuelo and Manny served a build-your-own type of lunch. Robert cut up a sausage for Sirena while I made a sandwich for him. Abuelo had already sliced the Cuban bread into three-inch buns. I stabbed a steamy chorizo with my fork, butterflied it, and put it on the open bread. I spooned on the green chimichurri sauce and closed the sandwich. I repeated the process for mine. Manny had his own way. He preferred slicing the pork sausage into rounds to dip them into the sauce, then using a piece of bread to sop up the drippings.

I bit. I chewed. I mmmed. The fatty ground pork was flavored with cilantro, cumin, and garlic. The casing had a nice tooth to it.

My father was a grill master. "Delicioso," I said. "¿Dónde compraste el chimichurri?"

"I made it," Manny said proudly. "Abuelo me enseño."

Abuelo nodded in acknowledgement, indicating that he had indeed taught his grandson how to make the famous Uruguayan condiment.

"What's in it?" Robert asked.

"It has parsley, garlic, oregano, red vinegar, salt, olive oil, red pepper flakes, and some diced onion. I made it with the chopper. Don't worry, Papi, I didn't use the big knife," Manny assured his father. The chopper was a pint-sized food processor, literally two cups, I'd bought just for him.

"*Luis,*" Mami called from the side of the house. "Abre el portón, por favor." Papi got up from the table and went to open the gate. In a few seconds, Mami, Papi, and Alma paraded into the backyard carrying half-dead potted plants. "Estas matas son casi huesos, pero yo voy a revivirlas," Mami said, determined to save them.

Basta con los huesos. I don't need more bones. Not even plant ones.

Chapter
Thirty-Six

"Babe, should I put this container in the fridge?" Robert asked, as he loaded the dishwasher with our dirty plates that had sat on the counter for a few hours. Alma had stayed for lunch. She already had my mom plant staging. They swapped several dry and brown plants for vibrant and healthy ones for one of her listings—a townhouse that needed a little TLC.

I replied from the living room, where I was keeping an eye on Sirena. She'd gotten up from a short nap and was playing with her Little People figurines. "What's in it?"

"I don't know. It's kinda heavy. *Rice.*" He shook it. *"Dry Rice."*

"Oh, no, don't put it in the fridge. That's my laptop. I almost forgot about it." I retrieved it from the counter and opened it on the dining room table.

"Did you spill coffee on it?" Robert's tone was jokey.

"Not this time. This was all Camo. She toppled a vase of flowers, and water splashed on the keys. Not a lot, but better safe than sorry." I cleaned the dust from it and pushed the open rice bin away. *Please turn on.* I lifted the screen and pressed the power button. *Come on, work-work-work.* The welcome and log-in page appeared, allowing me to breathe a sigh of relief.

"Mami, 'rriba," Sirena said. She held a toy in each hand, keeping her from using her hands to climb onto the bench. I helped her up. She put her toys into the rice and began playing like it was a sandbox.

After I'd logged in, a window popped up asking if I wanted to resume my previous session. I clicked yes. In an instant, the *Shores Sentinel* headline 'Grove's Dr. Bell Excavates Golf Course after Survey Finds Whale Bones' filled the screen. I read the puff piece that speculated about dinosaur bones. The blockbuster Jurassic Park had come out in 1993, so dino mania was still a thing in 1995.

The newspaper's reporter made it seem like Dr. Gregory Vander Bell was world-renowned, describing him as a preeminent expert on 'Indian Tribes of the Southern United States.' The article was written a few days after three whale vertebrae had been found. There was a plea for community volunteers to help support the student archaeologist with a meal train of refreshments and meals. I scrolled to the image under the headline. Dr. Bell was in the foreground. His hair was fuller, but he wore the same style of glasses. The photography credit was given to G. Brown. *It couldn't be.*

"Mi amor, what did Gillian do before she became your school's librarian?" I asked.

Robert closed the washer and pressed the on button. "I don't know. I can't say it's ever come up in conversation. Why?" He came to stand behind me and look at the screen. I pointed to the name that I had enlarged. "Could be. Ask her tonight. I'm sure she'll be there." He kissed the top of my head and squeezed my shoulder. "Is that from the 1995 dig?"

I uh-huhed and reduced the page back to normal size.

"Oh, look, there's Stormy." He pointed to a willowy figure behind Bell. "I'll have to ask her about the '95 dig."

Me, too. As a member of one of Coral Shores' founding families, Stormy Weatherman had a lot of insider gossip. And as a person that had come to reject that elitism, she wouldn't mind spilling it to me.

Robert had given me a quizzical eye when I'd told him we were attending the Grove Museum silver celebration. "Won't my mother be there?" he'd asked with concern. I'd explained that she and Senior were laying low by order of the Feds. He accepted that without pressing for details, and I hadn't wanted to explain why we were bringing FBI security with us. Because telling people I had a long-lost brother felt wrong, I'd informed Alma and Welmo that they were each other's date to the event.

"I'm jumping in the shower," Robert said. He put his lips to my ear and whispered, "Do you want to join me?"

A shivery thrill tickled my neck, and I closed the computer. "That is an excellent idea." I let the abuelos know they were on kid duty while Robert and I got ready. We took a long, very relaxing shower.

"Mr. Environment, weren't you worried about our excess water usage?" I winked at him.

"One point two five GPM, water saver. You thought my five-hundred-dollar shower head was extravagant—Wait, what was it you called me? A gastador. Let me know if you've changed your mind." Robert gave me a devilish expression.

"I have definitivamente changed my mind," I said. I slipped my hand under his towel to squeeze a butt cheek.

"Are you asking for round two, Mrs. Quiñones-Smith?"

I kissed him. "As much as I'd love it, no. We're going to be late if we don't stop messing around."

Robert pouted. I pulled the towel from his waist and swatted his derriere with it. We fell onto the bed in an embrace. "I love you, Miriam Quiñones."

"Y yo te amo, *Roberto Esmith*." I purred in my most campy, exaggerated accent. *E-Smith. Smith-E. I wonder if Welmo has looked into the messages in the bottles.*

Robert and I got dressed. He helped me with my necklace and I with his collar. Welmo and Alma arrived on time—a real feat for my BFF. She was always on time for business appointments but ran on *Latin Time* for social events, which meant anywhere from thirty minutes to two hours late.

After kisses to the kids and gratitude to the abuelos, we left the house. Alma rode in our car, and Welmo followed behind us in his big black SUV. He'd said it was for precaution. In case he got called away. I got the feeling that that was a half-truth.

The Grove College parking lot had a line of cars. Students in fluorescent vests were trying to direct people to self-park, but it seemed everyone wanted to use the valet service.

"Are you ladies okay to walk a few extra steps?" Robert asked.

"As long as it's not rainy, I'm fine," Alma said. "I can even run in stilettos if I need to. *Verdad*." She tapped my shoulder.

"She can run and jump hurdles in those things, especially if her purse spills and her lipstick is rolling away." I laughed, remembering a night on South Beach when we were twenty one.

"Mujer, that lipstick cost me half a paycheck. *Sixty dollars.* The case was sold separately. Cle de Peau number three-ten. That red looked amazing on me. *Right*."

"Okay, if you say so." I shrugged.

"Oh no, you didn't." Alma reached to the front seat, acting like she was going to pinch my arm. I undid my seatbelt and moved out of the way.

"*Children*," Robert jokingly warned. "This is a high society event. I expect you to behave yourselves."

Alma and I froze and stared.

"Oh my God, I sounded like my mother," he said.

Alma cackled. I fanned my face to stop the tears of laughter from ruining my eyeliner. We'd calmed down when a knock on the glass startled us. It was Welmo. He'd parked a space over from us. He opened the door for Alma and held out his hand as she got down from the car. The four of us walked from the back of the parking lot toward the lights and activity.

"Miriam, por favor," Welmo said, motioning that he wanted a quick word.

In Spanish, he told me to stay with Robert. I was not to leave him alone. If I needed the restroom, I should go with Alma, and he'd stay with my husband.

"Me tienes preocupada," I said. "Is there something you aren't telling me?"

"Nothing to worry about pero that note you showed me. Well—" Welmo tik-tocked his head and pursed his lips.

"¿Qué? Tell me." I whisper-shouted.

"The man threatening your suegro has a son that attends *this* college."

So, it wasn't just a fraternity prank after all. Ay, ay, ay.

Chapter
Thirty-Seven

Welmo and Alma walked behind us. I could hear them chatting in Spanish. Alma was asking what kind of home he wanted for his family. Welmo said his wife, Ive, would be missing her large family. So, if there was an area that was family-oriented with schools and parks, it might help Ive make friends. "Y cerca de la playa. Our kids love to build castles and dig in the sand." Alma told him she had a condo on Key Biscayne to show him. Very family-friendly, it was the perfect place.

I hope tonight is uneventful. Mr. message-in-a-bottle, Nick Fa-Fa, or was it Fo, whatever his last name is, I hope he doesn't show up with a pirate sword.

"Babe, are you okay? You tensed up," Robert said. He stroked my hand to loosen the viselike grip I had on this arm.

"Sorry." I let go. "I'm just stressed about having to represent your mother at this thing. I am no Marjory."

"Thank heavens." His tone was light-hearted. "Babe, you have a TV show that goes into millions of homes—"

"Nine point three million," I said.

"Nine point three million homes, you've got this. And I've got you." He put on an aristocratic affect. "*I'm to the manor born. I've*

216

been trained to hobnob and eat canapes since I was in diapers." Robert kissed my temple. "Have I told you how stunning you look in that dress?"

"Yes, but I don't mind hearing it again." I smiled coquettishly.

"Mrs. Quiñones-Smith, you are stunning. I am a very lucky man."

I hope we're all lucky tonight.

Our foursome moved from the asphalt to the sidewalk and joined the stream of guests strolling into the building. We had the elevator car to ourselves.

"Remember to stay in the museum. No moonlight walks. No going down dark hallways," Welmo said.

Robert furrowed his brow. It was like it had finally dawned on him that we had an FBI escort, which was a serious thing. He was about to say something when the elevator doors opened.

A jazz quartet was playing outside the museum lobby. A curtain had been erected to hide the hallway behind the band. The reception desk had been made into a wine bar. Young people, likely students, in Grove College polos and black pants passed by us with trays of appetizers disappearing into the Settled Florida exhibit side. A photo-op station with a 'Grove Museum Celebrates Twenty-Five Years' backdrop took up one side of the lobby.

"Oh, fun, a step and repeat!" Alma said.

"A what?" I asked.

She pulled me into the photo line. Welmo shook his head no. Robert, Alma, and I stepped into position. The photographer snapped three shots and pointed to a guy with a clipboard.

"Hello, Ilmi. Nice to see you again," I said. The photographer was the student with the Finnish name I'd met the day Sirena and I had visited.

"Hello," Ilmi said. She looked at the viewscreen of the fancy camera and told the clipboard guy what photo numbers we were. "51, 52, 53."

"Your names, please," the guy said.

"Alma Díaz, Miriam Quiñones—" Alma said.

"Can you spell that?" he asked.

Alma took the clipboard from him and wrote our names on the photo list.

As we moved to the wine bar, I thought I heard the guy say Robert's name under his breath. *Miriam, you are being paranoid.*

The bartender looked discombobulated by the simple order. *Probably faculty or staff.* Robert handed us our drinks: white for Alma and me and sparkling water for Welmo. He put a twenty-dollar bill in the tip jar and took his glass of red wine.

The Early Florida Wing was closed, but the guests seemed content with the wine and self-serving history of the Settled Florida hall. The L-shaped exhibit space resembled a river with rocks. The Coral Shores society were the rocks, and the servers with trays of prosciutto melon balls, cheese on toothpicks, and brie puffs were the current flowing around the chatty groups.

"Let me take a picture of you and Robert in front of the portrait," Alma said.

I gave her a you-can't-be-serious look, which she ignored.

"Better to give Marjory proof before she asks for it. You look great, and you're doing your job representing the family," she said to me.

She goaded us to pose like Marjory and Senior. As we stood there mimicking the oil painting, I thought I saw Ilmi's assistant sneak a peek at us. *Is that guy looking at Robert?* Once Alma had had her fun and released me from the torture, I moved to confirm what I'd seen. Welmo stepped in front of me and gently turned me like a dance partner might.

"The party is this way. Let's stay together," Welmo said.

I flared my nostrils. "I think the guy at the photo station is watching Robert."

"No te preocupes de eso. That's my job, Velmita." Welmo's smile was all business. "Go mingle. I will be close by."

A man in a blue suit and red tie had Robert in an ear lock. I joined my husband and was introduced to the man—Mayor Titwell. His nose had the blood vessel blooms of a heavy drinker. After the appropriate niceties, Robert excused us from the conversation, claiming to have seen someone we needed to speak to.

"Thank you," I said.

"I played golf with him last month," Robert whispered. "You know, I'm trying to get our extension approved, so I let him win, and now he thinks he's ready for the Masters."

"That's the green jacket one, right," I said.

"You *do* listen." Robert winked.

"We better find someone to talk to." I searched the crowd. "I think I see Stormy over there."

I signaled with a chin jut to Alma and Welmo that we were moving farther into the party. Alma was in shmooze mode, which was how she'd won Realtor of the Year annually. She had two couples engaged in lively banter. Welmo left her and tailed us.

Stormy saw us and dispatched her date to find her a stuffed mushroom. "Two of my favorite people," she said with her arms stretched out in welcome.

"Good evening, Mrs. Weatherman," Robert said.

"Don't make me mad, Robert. How many times have I told you to call me Stormy," she said. Stormy's diamonds caught the light as she shook her finger at him. She was dressed in a cream and black pant suit that had probably been bought in Milan.

"Hello, Stormy," I said.

"Give us a hug, darling." As we embraced, she asked, "Is that awful woman here with you?"

I knew she meant Marjory. There was no love lost between them even though they acted with civility toward each other in public. "She will not be in attendance this evening," I replied.

"*Thank, Dagda.*" Stormy patted me on the forearm. "He's an old god." Her eyes twinkled. Since the passing of her daughter, Sunny, she'd plunged into Irish paganism.

"Miriam, weren't we going to ask Stormy about that newspaper article you found," Robert said.

Stormy put weight on her back leg and peered at me with anticipation.

I took a breath. "Well, where to begin—"

As I floundered for a starting point, Robert spoke up. "Miriam found a *Shores Sentinel* article about the 1995 dig. You were in the background of a photograph. Were you part of the dig?"

Stormy closed her eyes like she was remembering a jolly time. "I *was*. That's partly why I'm here tonight. Between you and me, I can't fake that I like any of these *friends* anymore."

"Can you tell us about the dig? Do you remember anything odd about it?" I asked.

"Odd? In what sense?" Stormy said.

At that point, our heads were close together like we were gossiping teens.

"Do you remember anything odd about Dr. Bell, in particular?" I asked.

A sardonic laugh bubbled from her. "Vander *is* odd on a good day." Stormy remarked, taking a sip of her wine. "You have to understand that the discovery was exciting. *Everyone* in Coral Shores was talking about it. Vander was Grove's Indiana Jones. He didn't have Harrison Ford's looks, but he was young, thirty or thirty-one, and the students looked up to him like he was a god. Do I think Vander had the experience to handle an excavation of that size?" She hummed and looked skyward. "Probably not. He and Alice were at each other's throats most of the time."

"Dr. Alice Cypress was part of the excavation team." If they had history, that explained the cold and angry stares I'd witnessed during the ceremony.

"No, not the team. She was his girlfriend. She was studying at Florida State. *I think.* Anyhow, she came to see the dig. You know, she's Seminole."

Miccosukee, actually. And oh my gawd, they dated!

Stormy kept talking. "At first, Alice tried to talk him into working with someone that had more knowledge. She told him that he needed to include the tribe. Uh, I remember there was this one screaming match that was vicious. I think that was the straw that broke the camel's back. They broke up a few days later. The next time we saw her, she was holding a NAM sign."

NAM? Native American Movement, perhaps. "What was the fight about?" I asked.

"Something about the Seminoles being latecomers to Florida. He said they have no claim to the Tequesta and the Calusa lands and lineage." Stormy rolled her eyes. "In my opinion, they have more *claim* than we, European settlers, do. But, to be honest, I don't know that I was enlightened enough at the time to have said as much. I was just happy to be furloughed from the PTA and digging in the dirt." Her male companion returned with an hors d'oeuvres-laden napkin. She took it from him and gave him her empty glass. "Do be a dear."

Robert looked at his near-empty glass and motioned he would join the gentleman in his libations quest. *Miriam, don't leave Robert's side.* I had so many questions for Stormy. Before I'd made up my mind whether to go with my husband, he'd left. I felt Welmo's eyes on me. I shrugged in my defense. Welmo looked from me to

Robert, gave me a don't-leave-that-spot warning look, and went after Robert.

"I wondered whatever happened to the new boyfriend. You know, I thought Alice was doing it just to get under Vander's skin. I should ask her when she gets here," Stormy said.

"Dr. Cypress is going to be here?"

Stormy chuckled like a devil had possessed her. "She didn't know about it. Maybe her invitation got lost in the mail, but I rectified it. I called Lyle and made sure she was on the guest list."

Calling Dean Lyle Murphy was a power move. *Stormy, you are a trickster. A little Coral Shores Loki. Oh, Robert would be so proud of my Marvel reference.*

"Oh!"

"Did you remember something?" I replied to her utterance.

"Yes. There was another big fight. It was about the time that Vander shut the dig down. It was between the love triangle—Alice, the new boyfriend, and Vander."

"Was it about their relationship?"

"No." She shook her head like the details were all coming back to her. "It was about a piece of pottery, or a bone, or an artifact, I don't quite recall, but something significant had gone missing."

Chapter
Thirty-Eight

I knew it! It appeared that Dr. Gregory Vander Bell had a pattern. He liked to take things that did not belong to him. Bell hadn't learned anything from his Ole Miss slap on the wrist, and there he was, in a similar situation a year or so later—artifacts there one day and gone the next. *But what if the argument was about the Mississippi cloud of doubt, not something that had happened at the golf course find in 1995? Miriam, check your facts. Don't accuse the man of grave robbing. Yet.*

Bell was pompous, jealous, a status-seeker, and in need of a pair of toenail clippers, but until it was proven, it would be unfair to call him a grave robber. The 1995 dig had followed state guidelines and standards. Right? *Right.* Robert had read the report. I needed to ask him what exactly they'd found. *Where is he? He should be back by now.*

My heartbeat revved from school zone to highway speed. I scanned the party guests. I saw Alma, Patricia, Gillian (*I need to speak to her*), and one of Marjory's Women's Club friends, but not my Roberto. *Welmo is with him. He's fine. He's protected.* The air in the room changed like a fierce wind had pushed open a door. Looking down the exhibit hall toward the lobby, I saw Robert's

'Square and Flair' brown hair bobbing above the cluster of people at the hall's entrance. *Gracias a La Caridad, he is tall.* The crowd parted, and I saw that Victoria Bustinza was with him. Welmo was two steps behind him.

"Babe, look who I found—Wayra," Robert said.

I smiled and greeted her with a Latin American kiss on the cheek. "¿Cómo estás, Victoria? It's lovely to see you again."

"And with no mud on our shoes," she said. She wore a burgundy satin shirt, flowing black pants, and patented leather stilettos. Her loose curls were pinned to one side with an ornate comb.

"Wayra just told me the good news," Robert said.

"We've identified the remains," she said. "His name will not be made public until authorities have contacted his relatives in Canada."

"*Canada.* Wow, he was a long way from home," I said.

"Yes, Quebec, so there might be some language hurdles. I don't know. The police have contacted someone from his band," she said.

"Band? He was a musician. How did you figure that out?" Robert asked.

"He was First Nations. In Canada, they use band, not tribe," Victoria clarified.

"*Son indios, pero no son viejos.*" The babalawo's words sounded in my head like a phantom tune.

"Ironic and sad that his remains were buried on that particular site," she said. Robert and I gave a curious look, prompting her to continue. "There is no doubt that the site is Tequesta."

Robert sighed. "The ninety-five survey said it was undeterminable. The animal bones that kicked off the dig in the first place were common to the area. No evidence of human habitation was found." Robert ran his hand through his hair. "They found the whale spine and bones of a few other species. Turtle. Manatee. Deer, maybe."

"I didn't start working for the State until 2010. I don't know who was in charge," she offered.

"Bell was," I said under my breath.

"Really?" Victoria looked at me.

I nodded.

Someone who knew Robert stopped to chat. With Robert out of the discussion momentarily, Victoria and I stepped back to continue talking.

"Bell handled the survey that became a dig," I said.

"The same exact area?"

"I believe so."

"He must not have done a very thorough job. They found animal bones then, and now we've dug a little deeper and found an activity area with food evidence. What year was that?"

"Nineteen ninety-five."

"Three years before the Miami Circle was uncovered. If Bell was green, maybe he didn't know what he had." She shrugged. "Was there peer oversight?"

"I don't know. Robert has read the report. I've only read an article about it in the local paper."

A long hmmm emitted from Victoria Bustinza. I joined her. Something was fishy, and it wasn't the bacon-wrapped scallops that we were being offered. I popped one in my mouth. The umami of the shellfish and the salt of the crisp bacon were delicious.

"Sorry about that," Robert said. "That was Henry, one of my brother's friends. So, what were we talking about?"

"The first dig," Victoria said. "Who was on the survey team?"

"No team. It was only Dr. Bell and his students," Robert replied.

"That seems unusual," she said.

Robert tilted his head to one side and raised his shoulders in a nah. "Coral Shores was *and really still is* a small town. The club is private. Everyone that was on Grove's Board of Trustees probably played golf there. I can completely see how things were encouraged to be quick and tidy without too many questions and outside interference. It was the nineties, after all."

Victoria and I expressed our disappointment in the lack of scholarly professionalism.

"Ladies, I'm not approving of it, but it *is* a possible explanation." Robert smiled smugly. "And now, because they cut corners then, the hotel is further delayed." He drained his wine glass. "Let's talk about something more pleasant. Wayra, tell us about Peru."

Victoria began telling us about her yearly trek to Peru. The number of people in the small hall had increased, as had the volume. I wondered when the speech and applause part of the evening would happen. As if my supplications had been heard, the clinking of wine glasses called for silence. From the end of the hall near the research library and bathrooms, Dr. Bell's voice asked us to follow him into the Early Florida exhibit.

Almost half of the attendees went to the bar, possibly anticipating a lengthy program. I expected that there would be at least two or three speeches. Donors had to be thanked. *¡Carajo! Was Marjory supposed to say something? ¡Coño! Am I supposed to say something? If I'm asked to say something, I'll just—* "throw Marjory under the bus."

"*Excuse* me," Patricia Campbell said. "You making devious plans to get rid of your mother-in-law, Mrs. Marjory." She laughed.

I covered my mouth and laughed, too. "No. But I don't want to give a speech for her." I'd fallen a little behind Robert and Wayra. Alma had her arm hooked into Welmo's. "It's nice to see you here," I told Patricia.

"T'is Gillian's doing," she replied.

"Where is she?"

Patricia rolled her eyes. "She's making a fool of herself." She pointed with her mouth toward a podium that had been placed by the whale box. Behind the wooden stand, a curtain had been hung to block one-third of the exhibit hall. *What's behind the wizard's curtain?* Dr. Bell was adjusting the goose neck microphone stand. Gillian, standing in the front row, held two wine glasses. She gazed at the man like he was a movie star. Once Bell had gotten the mic's height right, he took his drink from her without gratitude.

I asked Patricia, "Was Gillian ever a photographer?"

"You mean professionally? You'll have to ask her. I thought it was a hobby. She's got boxes of albums. Labeled by the year." Patricia's expression told me she thought it was a bit excessive. "I'd better join her before she throws her underpants at him." She sucked air through her teeth.

I watched her excuse and pardon her way to Gillian. I found my group along the wall close to the divider and joined them.

"We lost you for a second," Robert said with a wink. He pulled me to him and rested his hand on my hip. We heard the door that led to the lobby being tried, then a voice of authority instructed them to go around.

Qué carajo is Dr. Gregory Bell hiding behind the curtain?

Chapter
Thirty-Nine

D r. Bell tapped the mic, and the crowd fell silent.

"Good evening!" he bellowed, causing reverb.

Gillian dashed to the rescue. She lowered the volume on the speaker and motioned for Bell to push the microphone away from him a tad.

"Thank you, Gillian," he said.

I guess he has manners when people are watching.

"Let's try this again," he said. There was a titter of laughter from the crowd. "Good evening. It is wonderful to have you all here to celebrate Grove Museum's twenty-fifth anniversary."

There was a round of applause. He then went into a brief history of the museum. He acknowledged the generous donations of family items and heirlooms that had seeded the Settled Florida exhibit. *Gracias a La Caridad, it looks like I don't have to say or do anything!* Robert waved when the Smith family was mentioned. Bell thanked the board of trustees for their support. He acknowledged Dean Lyle Murphy but didn't invite him to the dais.

"In 1999, a year after we opened, Grove College asked me to grow the museum into something more. President Morris, God rest his soul. *He was a brilliant man.* President Morris asked me to build an enviable collection using my expertise. *Those were his words.* He put me at the helm, set my compass to the horizon, and instructed me to go forth and find treasures that would bring glory to Grove."

Alma put her head to mine and whispered, "Qué comemierda." I expressed that I agreed. With no one to contradict his side of the story, he was laying it on thick.

"I began the Early Florida collection," he swept his arm dramatically, "with the *Eubalaena glacialis* that I found here in Coral Shores." He pointed to the whale display. There was another round of applause. He glazed over the specifics of the survey turned excavation. He mentioned the hopes and disappointment he and his students had had for the site. He said he'd turned those dashed dreams into a burning passion to find and acquire native artifacts for the collection.

I tugged Robert's sleeve and spoke softly. "*They only found animal bones in 1995.*" He nodded. "*No human artifacts.*" He shook his head. I tuned back into Bell's pontificating.

"Over the years, I've acquired the largest collection of Tequesta pottery from private collections and brought it to public display," Bell said.

From private collections. That's an odd brag. What are the provenances? I tried to recall the information tags by the pieces of pottery. Had any of them read "donated by" or "from the collection of?" The only thing I remembered clearly was the power outage.

"And this evening," Bell's voice lifted. "I add a new acquisition to the collection. A one-of-its-kind specimen. Without further ado—"

I chuckled to myself. It had been so much *ado* already.

Bell snapped his fingers at Gillian. She shuddered from her starry-eyed brumation and pulled the cord on the curtain. A pedestal with a lit acrylic cube was revealed. The audience ahh-ed and shuffled to glimpse the small item on display.

"I present to you a Glades I era pipe. Look at the delicate visage," Bell said, encouraging patrons to move into the no longer partitioned area. "Imagine the hands that sculpted that beak in five hundred B.C.E. It's an incredible artifact. A few pipes have been found in the Belle Glades but none with avian motifs."

A murmur of "five hundred B.C.E" serpentined through the audience. I used my phone to find the date range of the Glades I period. It was 500 B.C.E to 750 C.E, a period of one thousand two hundred fifty years. Bell was using the oldest possible year for full effect.

"Is it a parrot?" the woman looking at the pipe asked.

"It's a seagull," her female companion said.

"I believe it to be the Tequesta *god of the graveyard*," Bell said.

"They worshiped *a bird*," the first lady said. "How fascinating."

"Where did you acquire such a sacred item?" a female voice asked from the back of the hall.

I craned my neck to see who had posed the question. The voice belonged to Dr. Alice Cypress. I quickly looked at Bell to see his reaction to the uninvited guest's appearance. Gregory Vander Bell was not happy. *Is that nervousness, or is he angry?*

Bell adjusted his reaction and cheerfully said, "That's a long, boring, academic story. I know everyone is tired of hearing me yammer on." He forced a laugh.

"That's the most accurate thing he's said all evening," Victoria Bustinza said.

"Sparkling wine is being served," Bell said into the microphone. "A toast to Grove Museum. Twenty-five years!"

"Cheers." Several peopled toasted.

Victoria stood on her tiptoes to beckon her colleague, Alice, to join our group. People parted for Dr. Cypress and avoided eye contact like she was the grim reaper or, perhaps more aptly, a goddess of the graveyard.

My skin became clammy thinking about the analogy. Oyá was also a cemetery deity. She was one of three orisha that held the keys to the graveyard. Alma, Welmo, and Robert got in position to see the clay pipe, leaving me with Victoria and Alice, three women with PhDs who all had experience with the dead. It felt like a supernatural concurrence. *Ay, ay, ay, Miriam, you are taking it too far. There is no woo-woo here.*

We made small talk until the curious had had their fill. Alice walked around the pedestal, looking at the pipe from every angle. She shifted onto her heels and stood stone still. The serious look on her face contrasted with the vibrant beaded barrettes in her hair.

"What is it?" Victoria asked Alice.

"I'm not sure," Alice replied.

The three of us stared at the two-inch terracotta item. I read the identification card, which didn't deviate from what Bell had told us. Clay. Bird. Glades I. Tequesta. The negative space of the elevated white card practically swallowed the sparse information. But there was some new information. The piece had been found in Arch Creek. *That's near here.* It was donated to the museum by Anon.

Good old anonymous. Private collection anonymous.

"Hmm," I said. "How often do collectors want to stay anonymous?"

"Not often, but often enough," Alice said.

"Some collectors donate for prestige and others for the tax break," Victoria said.

"But this piece," I gestured at the bird pipe. "This piece is unique. Wouldn't the donor want to brag to their peers? That's what these events are all about, no?"

Victoria chuckled.

"If the provenance is shady," Alice said flatly, "it might stir up unwanted questions."

Victoria and I looked at Alice.

"There's something you're not saying," I said.

"Spill it, Dr. Cypress," Victoria said.

"Not until I have all the facts. I need to check something in our archive," Alice said.

"Let me know if you need an assistant. I miss reading dusty old pages," I said. "I don't miss the sneezing and stuffy nose, but the work is always enlightening."

Alice drifted off and found Stormy. Victoria left to examine the whale bones. I stood by the pipe for a few seconds more. *Little bird, do you have a dubious provenance? No, that wasn't the word Alice used. Shady, that was the word.*

Robert and Welmo were with Alma. I caught Robert's eye and signaled I was ready to go by making my fingers walk. He replied with a thumbs up. As I weaved around folk, I checked the white cards for donor names. Five out of seven were anonymous.

"One more photo," Alma said. She pushed Robert and me to stand in front of the large pottery display. She left-righted us until she was pleased with our positioning. "That's good. Send Marjory the one you like best."

I looked at the photos she'd texted. "They all look the same to me. Pick one for me. Porfa." I made a pleading face at my BFF.

"Fine," Alma said, rolling her eyes.

"Babe, are we ready?" Robert asked, placing his hand on the small of my back.

"I am if you are."

Alma and Welmo fell into step, and we exited the exhibit hall.

"Miriam," a voice called to me in a British accent.

I turned to find Gillian chasing after me.

"I have a cookbook for you. Do you mind stopping by mine tomorrow to collect it?" Gillian asked.

I told her I would, and then we left. Others had the same idea. There was a wait for the elevator, so I led my group to the stairs. A few of the fitter or perhaps more impatient of the crowd followed us. I overheard chit-chat about the event—primarily complaints that the wine was of the 'Two-Buck Chuck' variety.

Ilmi's assistant nimbly weaseled through the stair congestion. At the bottom of the stairs, he looked over his shoulder at us. Or at least that was how it seemed to me. *Mi'ja, what has that kid done to you that you are so suspicious of him?* To be fair, he could have been looking at someone behind us on the stairs. He hurried out the door.

We were out of the building a few moments after him, but I couldn't spot him on the lit path or in the inky stretches of landscaping.

"Bobby," a man in a blue suit said.

Robert stopped to speak to the man.

The man spoke with a wheeze. "I expected your parents to be here. Are Marjory and Senior alright?"

We'd been prepared with an answer for such a question. "Nothing serious, just a mild cold, but Senior has a full docket, so caution's the better part of valor," Robert said. The part about Senior was adlib.

"Send them my regards," the man said, slapping Robert on the arm.

There was movement from the cocoplum hedge. *Probably an iguana.* I took the keys from Robert. He'd had more wine than me. Welmo, in turn, took them from me. I was about to protest that I'd barely had a glass when a figure darted from the hedge and tackled Robert.

"Ay mi madre," Alma yelled.

The attacker was on Robert's chest with a fist raised. Welmo bear-hugged the man to immobilize him. It was the photography assistant. Robert back crawled on his elbows and got out from under. Welmo threw the man on the ground and pinned his hands behind his back. The instincts of a former police officer. Campus security came running up soon after.

"What just happened?" Alma asked me. "Who is that guy?"

"My name is Nick Forte. You killed my father, prepare to die," the guy said, being lifted to a stand by campus security.

"He's quoting *Princess Bride*," Alma said.

I gave her a *qué carajo* look.

"The movie with the sword fights, Andre the Gaint, and the 'as you wish' prince."

I shook my head.

"Ay chica, it's a pop culture classic. Pero, never mind that. Why is this pendejo quoting Inigo Montoya at your husband?"

"I have no idea!"

Welmo had an inaudible conversation with the campus police. He then made a phone call. Robert dusted himself off and refused the offer of a first aid check.

"I'm fine," he said, walking stiffly toward us.

Welmo intercepted him to tell him something.

"Detective Pullman is on his way to escort you and Alma safely home," Welmo said, handing me my key fob. "I'll take Robert home after he has made his statement."

"Are you going to tell me what this was about?" I asked.

Welmo shook his head. Robert pursed his lips and shrugged his shoulders.

"Babe, it will be ok. I'm fine. Go home. Kiss the kids. This won't take long," Robert said.

Won't take long. Pfft. Famous last words.

Chapter Forty

As I suspected, Robert did not get home quickly. He had to give a statement to campus security, Coral Shores police, and then the FBI had questions. I was in bed when he finally rolled in at 1 AM.

"Mi amor, I made you something to eat," I said the next morning, closing our bedroom door with my foot to keep Camo out.

"What time is it?" Robert rubbed his eyes, sat up, and propped a pillow behind his back.

"Ten. Mami y Papi took the kids to Pepper's to play." I set the tray on the bed and handed him a mug of café con leche.

"Just what I needed," he said, savoring the sweet and milky coffee. *Crunch.* He bit into the toast with cream cheese and Mami's mermelada de toronja. I'd made my version of tortilla Española with the leftover maduro and jamón from the meal my parents had fed the kids last night. My husband took a forkful of the crustless egg pie. "You know this is one of my favorite things."

"I know." I smiled. "How's your chest? Are you sore? The guy looked like a windmill."

Robert rubbed his chest. I saw him flinch. He tried to hide it, but it was obviously tender.

"He landed a few good ones." He continued eating.

"You didn't tell me much last night," I said. *Miriam, let the man eat in peace.*

"I told you everything I know. The guy is the son of the man who's been threatening Senior. He has some crazy idea that Senior is out to get his father." Robert drank a sip of coffee.

"Isn't it the other way around?"

"I know, but you can't make crazy make sense." He took the last bite of tortilla. "Pullman said he'd come by today to update us. Unless something changed overnight, the Feds are still camped out at my parents' house. The kid wouldn't tell the police where his father was hiding, so my parents are still under protection." Robert put the tray on the floor so I could snuggle beside him.

"Pobrecito Welmo. Another day with Marjory," I said.

"Nah, my mother is treating him like a hero. I stopped by there last night. She kept *calling and calling.*" He gave me the you-know-how-she-is look. "I told her how Welmo pulled the guy off me and saved me from a black eye or worse. Her opinion of him changed immediately. She rushed to get him a lemonade and offered to make him a pimento cheese sandwich."

"Like I said, pobrecito Welmo."

We had a good chuckle.

We took advantage of the empty house and kept the bed warm. *Okay, hot.* Afterward, Robert took a long shower. I scrolled through Alma's text messages, looking at the photos she'd sent from the evening. She'd managed to take a few of the arrest, too.

"Everything, okay?" Robert asked, a towel around his waist. "You look very serious."

"Just going over last night's pictures," I said.

"That reminds me. I had this weird dream. You know, one of those where you're aware that your brain is telling you to remember something important when you wake up."

I nodded.

"We were at the museum." He explained as he ran his fingers through his damp hair. He looked upward, searching for the dream's details. "The exhibit hall was packed with people—like shoulder to shoulder, no room to move. Oh, yeah!" Robert pointed at me enthusiastically. "You, Wayra, and Dr. Cypress were holding hands and dancing around one of the displays, singing a nursery rhyme."

"Do you remember which one?" I asked.

"No, because it was in Spanish. Wait-wait-wait, what's that one Abuela is always saying about the penguin?"

"Close, but it's not a penguin. Tin Marin de dos pingüe," I said. I tried to rub away the goose bumps forming on my arms.

"That's the one. So, you three were singing and going round and round so fast that it created a whirlwind, knocking everyone down like bowling pins. That part was really weird because I remember feeling like I hit the ground, too."

"Mi amor, you did hit the ground *hard* when the guy ambushed you. Maybe that was your brain dealing with it in the dream."

Robert shrugged, suggesting it was plausible. "Then, after the people were on the floor. Were they dead? I don't know. They definitely weren't moving. Anyway, you three sang another verse of the rhyme, and Dr. Cypress pointed at something. Oh yeah, I remember, that was creepy."

"What?"

"Her finger bone grew kind of like Pinocchio's nose." He made a face. "Like the bone shot out of the flesh and went across the room to point at—" Robert made the gimme-gimme hand movement. "Let me see that one of us. The last one Alma took."

I handed him my phone. He enlarged whatever was on the screen.

"That piece, above our heads. I swear it looks like the piece we found at the golf course," Robert said, showing me a piece near the lip. "That's what Dr. Cypress was pointing at in the dream."

"Espérate. I don't think that piece was there the day Sirena and I went." I tried to remember what I'd seen the day the lights had gone out. We were in front of the multi-shelf display. *The bulbous pot had a piece missing. I remember there was a trapezoid shape missing from the lip.*

"Where's my phone?" Robert asked. He dug in his suit jacket and found it. "Gordon sent me a photo of it. There. See."

I studied the blurry image. It looked like the photographer's hand had moved when he'd shot it, or it was low light. But the crisscross hatching was clear enough. And it matched the design of the museum's pot.

"This is the missing piece of pottery that Gordon had words about with the night guard. Right?" I asked. "Who are you texting?"

"Gordie. When he didn't say anything else about it, I figured that forensics had bagged it and taken it away." He tossed his phone onto the bedspread and went to put on clothes. A few seconds later, Gordon replied with a simple "No."

"Gordon says Forensics doesn't have it," I said, filling in the gaps.

We held each other's gaze.

"But like, all old pottery looks alike, right," Robert said. "That dream was just my brain mixing up everything from the last week."

"Puede ser. Maybe." *Oyá, I get you messing with me, pero, por favor, don't send my husband any more dreams.* The saint house was literally on the other side of the headboard wall. *I'm paying attention. Lo prometo, I am trying to understand what you are telling me.*

"Bell is odd, but come on, he's not a—"

"*Thief.* You think he stole the shard from the site," I said.

"I'm not saying that."

"Um, you kind of are." I twisted my lips to the side and raised my brow.

"Bell's one of you guys. You know, an academic, a lover of knowledge, a preserver of history, you types are by the book." Robert pulled on a gray graphic T-shirt.

"Thank you for the halo, but not every professor is a saint." I stood and gave him a quick peck on the lips. "What's the place on the shirt?"

"*The Ox*. It's The Oxford Bar in Edinburgh. It's in the Inspector Rebus novels," Robert explained.

"Which reminds me, Gillian has a book for me. I think I'll go by before the kids get back." *Miriam don't forget to dig in her photo boxes for pictures of the dig.*

Chapter
Forty-One

B efore walking to Gillian's, I checked the saint box. There were
no new bones, flying China, or other metaphysical appari-
tions. I gave Oyá fresh food and asked her to keep her woo-woo
directed at me. *Se volvió loca, Miriamcita.* I strolled to Gillian's
humming "El Cuarto de Tula."

Patricia answered the door. "Tall girl. The spice bun aroma
bring ya." Her Jamaican accent was as jolly as her laugh.

I smelled the nutmeg, allspice, and cinnamon of the paschal
quick bread.

"Ah, Miriam," Gillian said, poking her head out the kitchen
passthrough. "Just in time for a cuppa."

I heard a teacup being placed onto a saucer. Gillian came out a
few moments later carrying a tray. She set it on top of a mound of
newspapers, magazines, and books that occupied the sitting room's
coffee table. The Union Jack tray was at risk of sliding down the
hill of reading materials. Gillian stabilized it with a Paddington
Bear decorative pillow on one side and a tartan print scarf wedged
under one corner.

"I believe you take your tea with lemon," Gillain said, pouring
the steaming liquid from a cat teapot. It reminded me of Vaquita

in Old San Juan, Doña's black and white street cat, patterned like a Holstein cow.

"Yes, please," I replied, taking the saucer with the wedge of lemon. I added two cubes of sugar, stirring them until dissolved. Patricia and Gillain both took their tea with milk. Patricia served the sliced brown loaf with a triangle of orange cheese. I was sure the processed cheese was a Jamaican brand named Tastee that came in a large can. Patricia had probably brought it with her, as I hadn't seen it in any of the Caribbean markets in Miami.

Taking a bite of the moist, dark brown bread, I tasted the unique flavor that the stout beer used in the bake added to the complexity. The mild cheddar cheese gave the perfect tooth to the bite. "Delicious," I complimented the baker.

"Oh, before it slips my mind." Gillian popped up from the sofa. She returned in a flash with a recycled Christmas gift bag. Poor Santa had a gash across his face that probably should be looked at by a doctor. "Here we go."

I pulled the cookbook out of the bag. It was a spiral-bound cookbook from Antigua and Barbuda from 1974. The yellowed pages had a few small tears and creature nibbles, but other than that, it was in fine shape. "Thank you. This is a needed addition to my collection." I flipped through the thin volume, saying the dish names. "Fungie. Pepperpot. Souse. Goat Water. Ducana. I can't wait to try these. Have you had Fungie? It's similar to polenta but made with okra water." I felt that the bag had something else in it. "Another cookbook? Nooo, it's a crime novel. Is this for Robert?"

Gillian tittered. "No, it's for you. He mentioned you were interested in the Rizzoli and Isles series. That's not the first, but I believe it is one of Tess Gerritsen's best."

I read the inside flap—a museum, archeology, a recently discovered mummy, cryptic messages. *Hmm. This sounds all too familiar.* "This looks interesting," I said. *This is your opening, Miriam. Ask her about the photographs!* "Wasn't the museum's celebration wonderful last night? The piece they unveiled! Amazing. Such a treasure." *Mujer, she has the hots for Bell. Get her talking about him.* "Such a kudo for Dr. Bell and Grove."

"It's a real feather in his cap," Gillian said.

I bristled at the expression but tried not to show it. The saying came from European colonists to the Americas who observed that some Native tribes' leaders and warriors were distinguished by the number of feathers in their headdresses.

The floodgates had opened. Gillian didn't need any prompting. She began to gush about *Vander.* "I'm so happy for him. He has worked tirelessly to bring Grove notoriety. He really thought the 1995 excavation was going to produce something more substantial. It's not that the whale bones weren't an impressive discovery but pottery—evidence of human habitation." She gasped dramatically. "Well, that would have put him in *National Geographic* and on the cover of *Time* magazine."

Patrcia and I gave each other sidelong looks. Gillian was delusional if she thought Gregory Vander Bell, PhD was man of the year material.

"He was devastated when he'd had to throw in the towel on the golf course dig," Gillian said.

That's the puerta, chica. Ask her why the dig was shut down.

She gestured with her tea hand, sloshing a few drops onto her skirt. "If he'd only been allowed to continue, he would have found those human bones."

She doesn't know the remains are not ancient.

"Why was the 1995 excavation terminated so quickly? Digs usually take months, if not years," I said.

"I think the protests had something to do with it," Gillain said, turning her nose up.

"There was a protest? Was it large?" I asked.

Gillian shook her head. "No. It was only a few radicals, but I'm sure the founding families put the squash on it. You know how it is. No one wants news vans. Coral Shores is very private."

"Do you remember anything about the individuals that were opposed to the dig?" I couldn't bring' myself to say 'radicals.' That sounded so 1960s.

"I'll do you one better." She set her cup down and wobbled up from the too-soft sofa. "I've got photographs."

"See. I told ya. She got boxes of 'em," Patricia said in a low voice. Her eyes glistened with amusement.

We heard cardboard sliding on the wood floor. Boxes were opened only to be followed by a maddened sigh.

"Found it!" Gillian huffed in, carrying a heavy storage box.

Patricia and I scrambled to clear a space before she dropped it on the tea set. Patricia took the tray to the kitchen, and I stacked the magazines and papers on the floor beneath the table.

Gillian lifted the lid off and tossed it aside. Her excitement was palpable. The air around her vibrated. "I was a stringer for the local papers. Not just *The Shores Sentinel* but *The Miami Herald* and *The Palm Beach Post*. Mostly for society events and the *lifestyle* section, but occasionally I'd cover a car accident."

"I had no idea you were a photojournalist," I said.

"Oh, don't be daft. I was a librarian with a Canon," Gillian said, self-effacing. "But it was fun!" She raised her shoulders to her ears and grinned. "I stopped when the editors demanded I switch to digital. Alright, here we go." She opened a folder filled with 8 x10 black-and-white photographs.

She laid the first two glossy papers to the side. They looked like what my computer folders looked like when view was on the medium icon selection. There were rows of small pictures framed by the distinct notched film borders, but it was hard to see what was in the photos. A few of the squares had been circled with red grease pencil.

"What are these?" I asked.

"Contact pages. They're made by placing the negative directly on the photographic paper. You sandwich them with a piece of glass on top, then expose them. That is what I would turn into the editor. The circles are the ones he selected for print." Gillian pointed to the red. "I don't think the choices were always the best, but c'est la vie, comme ci comme ça."

"Do you view them with a magnifier?" I asked.

Gillian plunged her hand into the box and began rooting around. Patricia cleared her throat and gave me a marble-handled magnifying glass.

"Here it is," Gillian said, holding a shot glass-like object to her eye.

Between Gillian's monocle and my inspector's glass, it felt like I was in an old-timey movie.

"Hold on," Gillian said. "This one will do you better." From behind a pillow, she retrieved a rectangular plastic magnifier that had an LED light.

I took it and began studying the images. There were two types: wide shots of the landscape and close-ups of dirt. I moved onto the second sheet. That one had people. The editor's choice was a humorous one. It was a golfer in the background giving a disapproving look at the person in the excavation crater. The next frame had the golfer *jokingly* swinging as if they were going to hit the field crew who was in the hole. *Pégale, pégale que ella fue.* The violent nursery rhyme sang in my head. 'Hit her, hit her. She did it.' Ice spiders crawled up my spine. *Was that how the person died? Were they hit in the head with a golf club? So brutal.* I tried to see the face of the crew member, but it was concealed by a hat and hair.

Gillian chuckled happily. "Here's one of Alice and Vander. I'd forgotten that they'd liked each other once upon a time. When he saw her last night at the party," she gasped for effect. "I thought he was going to blow a gasket."

The 8 × 10 image was crisp. The black was squid ink, and the white was polar ice. In between the two extremes were shades of silver. Alice Cypress was young. Her black hair was loose, with a few strands caught wisping in the breeze. Bell was not handsome, but even in the stasis time capsule moment, there was a magnetism about him in his youth. "Why don't they like each other?" I asked.

Gillian hmmed. "Don't quote me, but if my memory serves me correctly. She switched sides."

"*Sides*," I said.

Patricia made a tooth suck.

Gillian took another folder from the box and leafed through it. She withdrew a photograph of a picket line. "There. There's Alice, and that's the Mohawk." She tapped her lips with her finger, taking a second to think. "Oh, it's coming back to me. He spoke French. And he'd been part of something similar up there—a land dispute about a golf course. It had turned bloody. Perhaps that's why the dig was cut short, to avoid something similar."

I looked at the man in the picture. In it, he was alive and virile. How soon after it was taken had he been killed? And why? Who killed him? *Did Bell kill him?* My mind was filled with hunches, questions, and images—the clay pipe, the museum identification cards, the research library, Bell in the tent, Oyá's persistent messages. The dam had broken, and I was paddling to keep my head above water.

"Do you have the contact sheet for this one?" I asked. Gillian found it and gave it to me. I looked at them with the magnifier. "This one. Did you print this one full size?"

"What number is it?" Gillian asked.

"Twelve," I replied.

She turned the folder around to review the backs of the pages. Each photo had a date, letter, and number written in small, uniform handwriting on the back. I noticed that some pages had more information—names and locations, maybe.

"Roll C. Exposure twelve." Gillian held it at arm's length, giving it a critical eye. "The composition isn't bad, but the girl blinked."

I wasn't concerned with the student in the foreground. I was interested in the action behind her. Over her shoulder on the golf mound, almost out of frame, there were two men in an argument. Bell had hands on the man from Quebéc. It looked like he was giving him a shove.

"Can I borrow this?" I asked. "I want to show Roberto what the golf course looked like in 1995." My excuse helped ease her hesitation.

"Of course. Take the whole file. There are better ones than that one." She put several folders into a Publix grocery bag and tied the handles before adding it to the gift bag of books. I thanked her and Patricia for the tea and cake, then left.

As soon as I was on the sidewalk, I did a search for 'Quebec Golf Course Land Dispute 1990s.' The first result was a Wikipedia page titled *Oka Crisis*. I read as I walked and nearly tripped where a root had buckled the sidewalk. Catching myself before I fell face first, I stopped to finish reading the encyclopedia entry. A Kanien'kehà:ka (the preferred name of the Mohawk people of that area) community near Montreal had stopped the expansion of a golf course into their lands and burial grounds. It had taken seventy-eight days. The Royal Canadian Mounted Police had been called in, as well as the Army.

"Wow! Like super wow," I said aloud. A miniature schnauzer yapped. I looked up to realize I was blocking the way. "Sorry."

"It must be interesting," the dog's walker commented.

"Yes. Very. The Mohawks resisted. And they won!"

The woman gave me a wide berth and yanked her dog to leave *the crazy lady* alone.

I need to talk to Alice!

Chapter
Forty-Two

I got home, kissed the kids, then shut myself in my study. I put my *Do Not Disturb I'm in Reading* doorknob hanger, a hand-crafted Mother's Day gift from Manny, on the handle. It was bilingual and had "Estoy leyendo No molestar" on the reverse side.

Alice had not replied to the email I'd sent the moment I'd left Gillian's house.

Chica, it's Sunday she might not check her inbox on the weekend.

"I know. I know. I know. Chill out." I mumbled.

I cleared the floor and laid the 8 x10 black-and-whites on the rug in order. Essentially creating a supersized contact sheet. The first set was pretty boring—glamor shots of the dig pit, tools, and establishing shots of the golf course. I took the photo of the tools out for a closer look.

"Nice composition, Gillian." The closeup was of the brushes of varying sizes: a pointy bricklayer's trowel, a chisel, and a rock hammer set. "That looks deadly." The hammer had a thin pick on one end and a blunt cross-hatched head on the other. I'd seen a rock-hound use the tool to crack open a geode. It was easy to wield and effective. *Ay, gracias a La Caridad, I survived that date. Who thinks a five-mile trek to a cave is a good first date?*

Dominoes, Danzón, and Death

I put the tools picture aside and laid out the next set, the one with the golfer pictures. I looked at the series of four images. The field tech was unaware of the golfer swinging a club at his head. *Is interrupting a golf game a motive for murder?* "No. I don't think so." I moved on to the images of Alice with Bell. There were three total exposures 17, 18, and 19. The one Gillian had shown me, exposure 18, was the better one. I took all three and added them to my stack.

The second folder held the picket line images. There were six or seven protestors with signs. It was hard to read the slogans on them, but one was clear and facing the lens. GRAVE ROBBERS was written in all caps. I turned it over to read the details.

April 9th, 1995

Roll C

Exposure 2

Coral Shores Country Club

Florida-Native American Movement protesters

A quick search led me to a website for the group. The page hadn't been updated in several years, but there was a paragraph about the Coral Shores find in the history section. *In 1995, F-NAM defended the sacred land of our Tequesta ancestors. Sacrificial whale bones, cookware, and a pipe bowl were found during the expansion of the Coral Shores Country Club Golf Course. F-NAM was joined by First Nations faithkeeper Pierre Deer Maracle.*

"That has to be him." I snatched up the picture of "Alice Cypress with French Mohawk" from the floor. "Is your name Pierre? Are you Pierre Deer Maracle?"

A knock at the study door startled me.

"Babe, I know you're working, but Frank is on his way over," Robert said.

I cracked the door open a smidge. "Did he say why?"

"He has an update. I think they caught the guy." Robert looked behind me at the grid of photos. "Whatcha doing in there?"

"I'll show you later. How soon—" I didn't have to wait. Detective Frank Pullman rang the doorbell. I closed the study door and went to greet him. "Coffee?"

"You read my mind," Frank said.

I told my parents we were having an adult conversation in the dining room. Mami said she'd keep the kids in the yard until we were through. I closed the double doors. Pullman waited until the cafetera was on the stove to start talking.

"It took a while, but we got him," Pullman said.

"The man that's been threatening Senior," Robert said.

"Yes. The kid that attacked you didn't crack, but his mother was very helpful." Frank, seated at the counter next to Robert, crossed his arms over his chest. It was his way of letting us know that was all the info we were going to get until coffee was served.

I creamed the sugar into a paste, poured the black espresso into it to make the delicious foam, and then portioned out our shots. I rolled the air with my hand to get Frank to continue.

"The mother, divorced from the father, was very eager to help in exchange for leniency for her son," Pullman said. "They took the guy into custody this morning at 6 AM."

"Where was he hiding?" Robert asked.

"At the girlfriend's condo. A sugar baby arrangement." Frank shook his head, disapproving of the Miami phenomenon that took advantage of too many young women.

"Can you tell us the man's name?" Robert set his demitasse down.

"Teodoro Magnus Forte," Pullman said.

Robert's face went pallid.

"*Mi amor*," I said, putting my hand over his. He looked like he was unwell.

"Teo Forte is my new client," Robert said.

"Yes, about that," Pullman scratched his jaw. "Mr. Forte's plan was to blackmail your father into throwing the case."

"Senior? *Never.*" Robert declared.

"I'm confused," I said. "How?"

"He was going to implicate Robert," Pullman pointed his finger but didn't move his arm from its resting position. "In the defraud charges, thinking Senior would protect his son from a scandal."

"The stunt with the check," Robert grumbled.

"What exactly is Forte in court for? Senior doesn't discuss his cases," I said.

"He's in federal court on conspiracy to defraud charges. His development company *allegedly* stole millions in tax credits and grant monies that were incentives to build affordable housing for workforce residents. Basically, he inflated the costs of materials in the contracts. And then, when the apartments were put on the market," Pullman blew a puff of air. "The twenty percent of units that were supposed to be affordable were at the top end of the mandated range, making them out of reach for the intended occupants."

Like those three-thousand-dollar units at Guyo Gables. Cabrón.

* * *

"And now the Feds are also looking into his PPP loans," Frank added.

"If he had all that money, why didn't he leave the country? Why did he turn to violence?" I asked.

"I've met him. I didn't know who he was at the time." Robert looked at Pullman, emphasizing that point. "He definitely had a big ego—most developers do, to be honest. There is something about having your name on a building that makes you think you are a superhuman. He invited me to go out on his racing boat.

Those things are deadly. They're like F-1s but on the water. Anyone that drives them has to be a little crazy."

"You weren't planning on going, were you?" I asked.

"*Babe.* I've got two kids and a gorgeous wife. I like my life." He kissed my hand." I *love* my life. Now, if he'd asked me to play golf at Doral, I would have said yes."

"So, what happens now?" I asked. "Teo will get jail, hopefully. What about Nick, his kid? Did the dad tell him to attack Robert?"

"No. That was an impulsive act on Nick's part. He was expecting Senior to be there. He had a note in his pocket that he planned to give Senior. It was similar to the ones in the bottle. The skeleton in the bay was his idea, too. *Maybe a bid to get his father's approval.* Just speculation. The Forte family dynamics are movie-worthy. I got the feeling the kid hates the mom for the divorce, and the mother hates the father for the numerous affairs. The divorce has been contentious."

There was a shared moment of quiet to let the information settle in. I was glad Senior was out of danger but not so glad that Marjory was free to roam the streets of Coral Shores once again. It had been nice knowing Marjory was housebound and under guard. And I felt a little sadness for Nick Forte. *I hope he gets some help.*

"Thanks for the coffee," Pullman said, standing to leave.

Miriam, you should show him the photos.

"Umm. Do you have any updates about the man—the bones?" I asked.

"His family is being contacted," Pullman said.

"How did he end up buried in the golf course?" Robert asked.

Gracias, mi amor. That is a good question, and it's better coming from you than me.

"We don't have an answer to that. Yet." Pullman began walking to the front door.

"Is there a cause of death?" I ventured.

"Dr. Bustinza is examining the skull," he said.

"*You found the skull*! I thought only part of the jaw had been retrieved," I said.

"The skull *surfaced* this morning." Pullman had his hand on the handle.

I narrowed my eyes at him. "Where? Who found it?"

Pullman gave a wry laugh. "Bernice." He left without expounding on the news he'd dropped.

"*Bernice.*" Robert and I said in chorus.

Chapter
Forty-Three

B ernice's distant cousin, a brown anole, was sunning on the
patio bench. Camo sensed her archenemy's presence, woke
from her nap, and went into predator mode.

Robert had called Gordon to get the story about the skull's
discovery. I tried to listen in, but he was pacing as Sirena tugged at
his pant leg, asking to be airplaned. He finished with Gordon and
scooped Sirena up by the waist. She put her arms out and tensed
her body into a plank. Robert zoomed her around the backyard,
making plane sounds. When she 'landed' on the grass, she rolled
around giggling and demanding another flight.

"Sweetie, Papi's tired, maybe later. Go play with your brother,"
Robert said.

Sirena tootled over to Manny, who was on a blanket looking
up at the clouds. She collapsed onto it, still giddy from fun. He
pointed to the sky and began telling a story about the shapes. I
watched with pride at the tenderness he showed to his sister.

"So, you want to hear the story?" Robert asked as he sat next to
me. He'd gotten a seltzer from the patio fridge. He offered me the
first sip. I took the can and nodded. "A groundskeeper saw Bernice

with what he thought was a deflated soccer ball. She was taking it to her nest. I guess she was adding it to her golf ball collection."

"How did they get it away from her?" I asked. I'd seen her jaws. They meant business.

"They threw some golf balls into the pond to get her away from the nest, then they netted it with a pole net. That's how they do it. They clean her nest out every week."

"That sounds dangerous."

Robert shrugged.

"Remind me never to let you take the kids golfing." I chuckled.

"The groundskeepers know her. They weren't taking too big a risk. Actually, they were trying to keep her safe from indigestion. It was only when they got it out of the net that they saw what it was—the skull was tangled in pond grass. That's when they called the police."

"When did they find it?"

"Early this morning."

"Wow."

"Wow, is right." Robert sighed. "That hotel is never going to get built at this rate. Hey, did I see photos of the golf course on the floor of your office?"

I was about to answer him when my phone vibrated. It was Dr. Alice Cypress. "Hold that thought, mi amor. I need to answer this." I touched the green circle and put the phone to my ear. "Alice, thanks for calling. Will you be in Miami today?"

I retreated to my study.

"I'm actually on my way there now," Alice said. There was road rumble, like tires going from gravel to asphalt. "Why?"

"I have some photos from the 1995 dig I'd like to show you. There's one of you with a Pierre Deer Maracle." I sensed a change of energy at the other end. "Do you think he might be the body that was found at the golf course?"

"I've suspected it from the beginning. Text me your address. I'll be there in forty-five minutes."

While I waited for Dr. Cypress to arrive, I made a plate of bocadito sandwiches. Mami had made a bowl of the cream cheese, pimento, and sweet ham spread to prove to Yoli that they could have the anniversary party in the backyard with homemade party food, in a pinch. The pyramid of dinner roll sandwiches disappeared in minutes, as did my family. Mami y Papi were going to see a property Alma wanted them to stage. *Qué bueno que their plant business is happening.* Robert said he was taking the kids to see their cousins. He wanted to talk to his brother about 'stuff.' *He's worried about the Forte stuff. I hope he hasn't cashed that check. Yeah, good idea, mi amor. Talk to your abogado brother about the legal ramifications of it all.* Before I could get the dirty plate to the kitchen, my family had left me alone.

Meow.

"I see you, Camo. I know I'm not alone-alone." I scratched under her chin.

Howl.

A gust of wind blew through the patio.

"I hear you, Oyá. Sí, sí, you are here, too." I went to the side of the house to give the orisha the attention she was demanding. Inside the *locked* saint house, there was a bocadito. I shook my head, baffled by the magical meals. "Who is doing it? *Mami. Papi. Sirena.* Qué sé yo." Another gust of wind whipped through the yard. I went into the house feeling like it was pushing me inside.

Ding-Dong

"Alice. Thanks for coming," I said, answering the door.

"I was on my way to Coral Shores anyway." Dr. Alice Cypress stepped across the threshold.

"The skull?"

"The skull."

We both sighed.

"So, you have some photos of Dear Pierre?" she asked.

"Is that what you called him?"

Her reply was toned with warmth and remembrance. "That's how he first introduced himself to me. *Deer, Pierre. Pierre Deer.* When he vanished, I thought it was me. I thought I'd scared him away. We'd had a *passionate night.* I might have said the L word." Alice rolled her eyes.

I imagined a twenty-seven-years younger Alice, one who was in love with a handsome guy. The Alice from the black and white photograph. *Show it to her!*

"Have a seat." I motioned to the sofa in the living room. "Someone told me you were dating Bell around that time."

"That's what he told people. We'd gone out a few times. Once he called me his 'real-life Indian princess'," I started to doubt my judgment. I think he got off on telling people we were a couple. Like it somehow legitimized his credentials."

I got the stack of set-aside photos from the study and sat beside her. "Is this him?"

"*Yeees.* I've never seen this photo. Who took it?"

I told her about Gillian. She vaguely remembered the local paper being there.

"Why was he down here?" I asked, pointing to Pierre.

"F-NAM asked him to come."

"*Native American Movement.*"

"The Florida chapter." She nodded. "They thought we might be able to fight for the golf course like the Kanien'kehà:ka." She looked at me then continued. "Mohawk. Do you know what Mohawk means? Maneaters. Cannibals. Mohowawog in the original Narragansett. The Dutch mispronounced it as Mohawk. That was never the name they called themselves. Kanienkehà:ka means people of the flint. Bell called Pierre a *radical* Mohawk—that did not go over well."

I'd learned about the name's origin from my internet search about the Oka Crisis. I made a mental note to practice pronouncing and using the preferred name. "So, what happened? Did F-NAM protest the dig?"

"F-NAM didn't get the chance. The dig shut down almost overnight. I never found out if that was the college or the country club. The Florida chapter was small and loose. They didn't really have an elected leader. When Pierre left, whatever organization they had just fell apart. He was their rockstar. He'd been part of the original group that started the physical protest to stop the land development in Oka. They put a shack in the middle of a forest road and refused to leave. They demanded nation to nation talks with the Quebec government. It didn't go peacefully. The Canadian army marched on them. Pierre told me about it." Alice stroked the image of her once-upon-a-time boyfriend.

"Why *did* they stop the dig? They'd found enough to warrant further excavation, right."

"The animal bones should have been enough. Whales were not a common meal. Hunting a whale was a dangerous endeavor. An animal of that size was for a special occasion. There was a rumor that someone had found a piece of pottery. *I* never saw it. Bell took me off the excavation team. I was told it was an order from above—only Grove students and faculty were authorized. We had a fight about it. It was the last straw for me, and if I'm honest, it's probably what drove me into Pierre's arms."

"There are some pictures of the excavation site. Let me get them. You might see something I missed in them." I returned with the folders.

Alice studied the black and whites. "These bring back memories. I remember Pierre talked about sneaking onto the property late at night to see it for himself. He thought there was something to the rumor. What is this?" She set the folder beside her and held the photo in her hand close to her face, then at arm's length. She turned it upside down and then right side up. "Does that look like the tip of a pottery shard?"

I took the photo from her and mimicked her actions—looking at it from all angles. "I think you're right."

We then scrutinized every shot on Roll A and found a few more shapes that might be something. *Y también, they could be rocks, Miriam.* Roll B, the one with the golfer, didn't have any close-ups of the dirt. Alice was visibly repulsed by the one shot of her and Bell together that looked chummy. Her energy changed when we reviewed roll C.

"That's Mitchell from the Ft. Pierce rez." Alice tapped the image of a tall man with dark skin. He looked like a Gullah-Geechee man I'd once interviewed in South Carolina about rice and West African food traditions in the South. "That's Dot. She's bird clan like me. She's a teacher at Ahfachkee." Alice's cadence code switched from professional to less guarded. She named the others in the F-NAM protest shots. She lingered over the few that had Pierre in them—especially exposure 12, the one with Bell shoving Pierre. "I didn't know about this fight. Looks like Vander is pushing Pierre off the dig. Are you sure there aren't any more shots of them arguing?"

"I didn't see any on the contact sheet," I said, giving her the sheet with the rows of negatives. "Would you like some coffee or a glass of water?"

"I'd take some tea if you have any."

While the water heated, I prepared the mugs and honey. I'd decided to join her as a cup of tilo/liden tea might do me good. It was the Cuban remedy for anxiety and stress. Things were definitely getting more stressful. Gillian's photographs had raised a lot of questions. Was pottery discovered at the site? Did Pierre sneak onto the site at night? What were Bell and Pierre arguing about? Why did the dig end so abruptly?

As we sat at the dining room table, breathing in the delicate notes of the healing tea, Alice got a text message from Dr. Victoria Bustinza asking for a video chat.

"Hi. I'm with Miriam," Alice said.

Alice propped her phone against her mug horizontally to be hands-free. I scooted my chair closer to her and waved at Victoria, who was in a lab. Behind her, on a tray, was the skull. Victoria gave a thumbs up, letting us know it was okay for me to be in on what she was about to tell us.

"The partial mandible aligns perfectly." Victoria flipped the lens and gave us a close-up of the jagged fracture. "Now that we have a complete skeleton, I can confirm the cause of death." She moved the view to the back of the skull. "Sharp force trauma to the parietal. Possibly from a pickaxe or gardening tool."

"Wait a second," I said, jumping up to get Gillian's photograph of the tools. "Could this be the murder weapon?"

"Try to hold it still," Victoria said.

My hands were shaking from the adrenaline.

"It looks like a likely candidate. I'd have to test it for size," Victoria said. She turned the camera lens so we could see her face once again.

"What do you think happened? Did the jaw break before or after death?" Alice asked.

"The victim could have been fleeing or taken by surprise. The blow to the back of the head could have easily taken them down. The break was here." She pointed to the underside of her chin. "He might have landed on a protruding rock. After the tissue decomposed, the mandible could have been easily separated from the rest of the skull. Especially if there was predation."

"Do you think Bernice had it this whole time?" I asked.

"*Bernice.*" Alice wrinkled her forehead.

"Bernice, the alligator. The skull was found in her nest," I explained.

"No. The more likely scenario is that it was thrown in the pond recently, and the alligator dislodged it from the bottom," Victoria said.

"*Recently.* How long?" I asked.

"Not very long. A few days. *A week.* I didn't see any evidence of dissolution or degradation from being submerged for a long period." Victoria covered the remains with a white paper-like cloth. "I'd like to examine the tools in that picture."

"Do you think there might be trace DNA?" Alice asked.

Victoria shook her head. "But you never know. There would have been substantial hemorrhaging."

"Has Pierre's family been reached? I think he had a younger brother," Alice said.

A flash of shock passed over Victoria's face. "You knew him? I'm sorry for your loss. The Canadian authorities notified the brother this morning."

"Please give him my contact information. I'd like to help return Pierre to Kanesatake," Alice said.

The video call ended. I offered Alice another cup of tea, but she refused.

La pobre. She is grieving not knowing her boyfriend was here all this time and that he was murdered. Qué cosa tan horrible.

"Do you think it was Bell?" The words were out of my mouth before I could soften them.

"Yes. *But why?* Was it an accident or deliberate?" Alice straightened her back and lifted her chin.

"Do you think Pierre saw something that night? Pottery or some other artifact?" I collected our mugs and took them to the kitchen. *Miriam, didn't the F-NAM site say something about a bowl?*

"Maybe, but why hide the find? What was it? And where is it now?" Alice brushed a strand of her black and gray hair from her forehead. "A lot of our artifacts vanish into private collections. Maybe Bell had plans to sell whatever he'd found, and Pierre was going to expose him."

"You know, Bell left another college under a cloud of questions."

Alice's eyebrow shot up. "Go on."

"Ole Miss, his first teaching job, some Chickasaw artifacts went missing from a dig. A friend of mine works at the university. She wasn't there at the time, but she spoke to someone who was, and well, it seems everyone knew, but no one could prove it." I put my fist on my hip and leaned on the counter.

"I need to talk to Dot. Maybe she remembers something I've forgotten." Alice got up to find her bag. She rummaged for her car keys. "I'll let you know if I find out anything. Can you interview the photographer about that picture?"

"The tools?" I fanned the photo in my hand.

"Yes. We need to find that pickaxe," Alice said as she left.

I looked at the writing on the back for the first time.

April 6th, 1995

Roll A

Exposure 7

Coral Shores Country Club

G. Vander Bell's tools

It's been twenty-five years. Could he still have them? Where should we look for them?

Miriam, there is no we. Call Frank. Call Gordon. Tell Alice. Tell Victoria.

Chapter
Forty-Four

S oon after Alice left, the kids got home. Robert filled me in on his chat with Drew and Sally. Since he hadn't deposited the check, there wasn't much to worry about. *Gracias a La Caridad.* The rest of Sunday was family time. Papi grilled shrimp and mariscos for dinner. Sirena ate her weight in seafood. Camo tried to steal a fish filet from Abuelo's prep tray. At some point, I got a text from Delvis informing me filming was postponed a day. She didn't explain why.

If that wasn't weird enough (Delvis never took time off), I got a phone call from Lyle Murphy, Grove's Arts and Sciences Dean. He apologized for calling me on the weekend and confessed he'd gotten my number from my MIL. *I don't know if I can forgive him for that!* The purpose of his call was to ask if I could come by his office for a conversation. With my schedule suddenly cleared, I told him I'd be there at ten.

"So, chica, is this an interview?" Alma asked. She was my stylist, especially when I was nervous about how to present myself.

"Que sé yo. We are having a *conversation.* I don't know if he wants to offer me a guest lecture spot or if he wants my opinion on *diversifying their courses,*" I said.

"Mi'ja, no free labor. What is your consultation rate?"

"Huh?"

Alma flipped her hair off her shoulder. "Know your value and charge for it. You need to know the dollar amount before you go into that meeting. Don't give away your expertise for free. You worked your culo off to get those degrees. *Hello,* you still have student loans, no."

She wasn't wrong, but she wasn't exactly right. When Robert had gotten his trust money, he'd offered to pay off my loans. I'd agreed because my interest rates were higher than average. I had gotten scholarships and grants, but I'd gotten loans for the remainder. Having a Spanish last name and no generational wealth like homeownership, my options had been limited. I'd promised to put the same monthly payment amount into a college fund for the kids. In theory, I had three more years of *payments.*

"Gracias, amiga, you are always watching out for me. Now, *what* should I wear?" I opened the closet doors.

"Cual es el vibe that you want? Host of a television show with millions of fans, *or* serious professor who has their nose in a book."

"Something in between." I shrugged grandly and dropped onto the bed.

"Cálmate, a vision is forming in my head." Alma swirled her pinched fingers in front of her forehead like she was mixing a potion. "Wide-leg pants, a chain belt, a striped button-down, a sweater, and close-toed pumps."

"Do I have those things?" I laughed.

I watched as Alma mixed and matched things from the closet and dresser drawers into her vision. Once I was fully accessorized, it was perfection. The colors were rich and warm instead of my usual bright and tropical. The gold chain belt gave the right amount of TV personality bling. The shirt, a silk-blend suit shirt that was too small for Robert, gave the look the business edge it needed.

Instead of a sweater around the shoulders, Alma had found a large triangle scarf, a gift from Marjory that I'd left in the box. At the last moment, she swapped my thin gold necklace for a mid-length strand of pearls.

"Wow, this is incredible. Was this really from my closet?" I chuckled. "Oh, my goodness, I know who this reminds me of—" I turned to look at my friend dead in the eye. "Jessica Fletcher."

"¿Qué que? The old lady who solves mysteries. That outfit is not old lady," Alma said offended.

"Amiga, Jessica Fletcher always looked amazing. Very classy and sophisticated."

"Okay, fine. Classy, but Miami classy con style, *e-please.*" She buffed her manicured nails on her blouse then blew on them.

I looked at the time. "Coño, I have to hurry."

"Here, put this on." Alma gave me a lip stain. "The color is called rosewood. It will give you a little color without the lipstick shine because we are keeping it classy." She winked. Then she had me walk through a cloud of perfume.

"I've got to go." I dashed to the entry hall to get my purse and keys. I opened the door and closed it. "I forgot to say goodbye to Sirena." I kissed my daughter on the head, then went to leave again. "Oh, I'd better tell Mami when I'll be back." I did and got out the door. "Should I bring my CV?" I asked, poking my head back into the house.

"Chica, why are you stalling?" Alma cocked her hip.

"Am I? I am." I exhaled a huff of frustration at myself. "Would you come with me?"

"*To your interview.* Mi'ja, that's not how interviews work." She thought about it. "Okay, sí, I *was* at your UnMundo interview pero, that was different. That was me introducing one friend to another friend."

"*Y*—I really need my best friend right now."

265

"What are you nervous about?" Alma said, already collecting her things to go. "Are you having PTSD about Roberto's attack?"

I locked the door, and we got in the car. "That, and I don't want to run into Dr. Bell." The radio blasted when I started the engine. I lowered the volume and backed out of the driveway.

"¿Por qué? Because you are about to take his job. Aaah, so it is an interview."

"No." I swagged my head. "Listen, I know it sounds crazy, but I think he might have killed a man."

"Crusty-dusty dude with the gross toes that needs to stop wearing sandals in public? That Dr. Bell?" Alma crossed her arms over her chest. "I can see it." She nodded curtly.

I told my BFF about the skull and the pickaxe theory, as well as some of what Alice had said about Pierre and Bell.

"Chica, this better not turn into a SWAT team on the roof situation like last time," Alma said.

"Yeah, let's not do that ever again!" We were laughing about it now, but it hadn't been funny when it had happened. Guns were never funny, especially when the holder of the weapon, Alma's boy-friend, had it pointed at your BFF. Alma hadn't seen a guy for more than one or two dates since then.

I turned into the Grove parking lot.

"Okay, pero seriously, what do you want me to do if I see the guy?" Alma asked. "And what am I supposed to do while you are *conversing* with the dean? Because it's not an interview, right."

We made a plan as we walked into the building. She'd go to the museum while I talked to Dean Murphy, and I'd text her when I was finished. If she gave me the all-clear that Bell wasn't around, we'd meet at the elevators and leave together. But if Bell was roam-ing around, she'd distract him so I could make my escape.

The dean's office was in the corner of the building on the same floor as the museum. The hall seemed mostly administrative, with professors' nameplates and office hours posted on the doors. I looked for Bell's name but thankfully didn't see his office. *I bet his office is by the museum. Maybe it's in the research library.*

We were greeted by a receptionist. She informed me that the dean was expecting me but wasn't yet out of his morning meeting. She motioned to the closed door behind her. Alma quietly asked if I wanted her to wait with me. I told her I'd be fine. She took a fruit-flavored candy from the bowl on the coffee table and left. Panic struck me as soon as Alma stepped out of view. What if it was a staff meeting, and Bell was in there? *Cálmate. It's not like he knows you suspect him, Miriam.* The dean's door opened before I'd finished leafing through the alumni magazine on the coffee table. A middle-aged woman holding a stack of folders exited and went into the smaller office adjacent to the dean's.

Dean Lyle Murphy approached, and I stood to shake his hand. "Thank you for waiting. Come meet my assistant," he said, introducing me to the woman who'd just left his office. After pleasantries, she began clacking away at her keyboard, letting us know she had work to do. "She's not happy with me at the moment." He used a stage whisper. "We're adding ten new courses, and she has to find classrooms and space in the schedule." He led us to the sitting area in his office. "Which brings me to why I've asked you here. Would you be interested in teaching at Grove next semester?"

When I didn't reply instantly, he added that it would be a two-hundred-level anthropology course of my choosing. And if my *Abuela Approved* filming schedule allowed, there was a three-hundred-level course, too.

"Is this part of the new courses you mentioned? Or would I be replacing a current professor?" I asked.

The dean got up and shut his office door. "This is confidential and not ready for prime time." He leaned forward as he settled into the green leather chair. "There are some forthcoming changes that will take the department in new directions. A certain tenured professor will be asked to take early retirement."

He means Bell. He's sixty at best. Early retirement. Why?

"Grove has the potential to be more than it is right now." Dean Murphy tapped his fist on the arm of the chair. "We want to welcome Caribbean and Latin American scholars to use our research library. The current department head has refused to open it to visiting scholars. It is stunting our growth."

Qué raro. Is he keeping it all to himself? Bell's status hunger. So maybe he's found something in there that he wants to take full credit for. Or, Miriam, perhaps he's hiding something like stolen pottery or a murder weapon.

"What do you think?" He crossed his legs. "You don't have to decide right now. But I do hope you will consider it. Can I answer any questions for you?"

I asked him about the current courses and their popularity. I asked what the enrollment numbers and demographics were. *Miriam, now is your chance. Ask him to see the research library!* "I'd love to see the research library. Can that be arranged?"

"Of course, it would be my pleasure." Dean Murphy checked the time. "And now's the perfect time. Class has just started. We won't encounter any resistance." He got a key from a pineapple jar on his desk and twirled the ring on his finger. "Right this way."

I followed him through the halls, glancing at every open door. Dean Murphy had seemed to imply that Dr. Bell was teaching a class at the moment. In the museum's lobby, I saw Alma chatting with Ilmi. Alma lifted an eyebrow at me. I replied with wide eyes and a discreet hand movement that meant *I'll tell you later.*

"We are very thankful for Marjory and Senior's generosity," he said as we went by their portrait. "I hope that support will continue even with the program's new direction and planned changes to the museum. I'm sure having you on staff will help reassure Marjory that her family legacy is safe."

Don't be so sure.

"I was at the event on Saturday. I don't remember you mentioning anything about new plans," I said.

"No," he laughed nervously. "We didn't want to bite the hand that feeds. The founding families section of the museum is going to have a new home—probably in the alumni offices. Not everyone will be happy about the move."

"Ah," I said, knowing he almost certainly meant Marjory.

Chapter
Forty-Five

The dean fiddled with the sticky key until the lock finally turned. "There we go." He pushed the door open. A motion sensor turned on the overhead lights.

Achoo!

"Bless you," Dean Murphy said.

I sneezed again.

"Dusty books."

"Yes, I'm sure that's what it is," I said. There was a free-standing double-sided bookshelf filled with old books, many with flaking and disintegrating bindings. I pinched my nostrils and sniffled. "Who is the collection manager? Or do you have a catalog librarian?" A special collection, research library, or any similarly limited access part of a library usually had someone(s) who oversaw it and kept its inventory. I'd met some amazing special collections librarians who had been assets to my research. No way I would have found what I'd needed in the short time allocated at some of these collections without their insider knowledge. They knew where all the buried treasures were hidden, or rather shelved.

"The original collection." He pointed to the dusty old books. "When it was at the main library, had a dedicated librarian. But for some reason, perhaps budget cuts—I'm not sure, it was a decade before my time—when the collection moved to the museum, around '97-'98, it fell under the control of the department head cum museum director."

"Hmm, if you want to open it up to visiting scholars, it *really needs* a dedicated librarian," I said, looking behind the double-sided stacks and realizing there were more. There were five in total, each with a Y-shaped handle used to crank them forward or backward. The moveable system provided high density in a compact space. Only one row could be accessed at a time.

"I agree. Do you have someone to recommend?" Dean Murphy asked.

"I might." *Gillian would be ideal.* "She was at the event the other night. She's well-liked and connected in Coral Shores. She might be just the diplomat you need. Gillian Brown, do you know her?"

"I do, not well, but we've been introduced. I'm going to make myself a note. Thank you." He took out his phone and entered the note. "I've got a meeting in a few minutes; please stay as long as you like. I'll leave you the key. Drop it off to my assistant when you're done." Dean Murphy put the key on the worktable.

I thanked him and told him I'd get back to him about his offer within a week. As soon as the door clicked shut, adrenaline shot through me. *Find the pickaxe. Hurry before Bell gets out of class.*

"Ay, coño, Bell," I said to myself. I called Alma and explained the situation. "If you see him, text me, and then distract him so I can get out of here. I don't want him to know I've been in here. ¿Claro?"

"I got your back, Velma," Alma said.

"Para con eso," I said, mustering as much tolerance to the ribbing as possible.

"Does that make me Daphne or Shaggy?" My BFF snickered.

"Ay, ay, ay, ay, ay. I give up. Just stay in the lobby and keep watch. Gracias." I disconnected and slipped the phone into my pocket so I could feel it vibrate if she texted.

Alone in a room full of historical items, it felt like every book, box, and bone was whispering at me.

"Where do I start?" I whispered back.

The flat files seemed the logical place to start. The chest-high cabinets of gray metal took up the entire wall opposite the stacks. I put the strap of my purse over my head to wear it crossbody, then pushed it behind me. From a container on the worktable, I took a pair of cotton gloves and put them on.

The exterior label of the first drawer was coded. Not knowing the organizational system, "20:CS:BI:13:MS" gave me no clue about what was in the drawer. I pulled it open and found a silver spoon, an ivory baby rattle, and a smocked bonnet. *Este no es.* The next drawer had animal teeth, molars of a prehistoric horse, maybe a camel. *Closer.* I started opening the drawers two by two. Some had papers, others had items, but all were small. *Miriam, move on. These drawers are too little to hold it.* The cabinet was about twelve or fourteen inches deep. The pickaxe in Gillian's photograph probably had an eighteen-inch handle.

I shifted to the floor-to-ceiling wall of boxes. Again, the numbers and letters on the label were no help. The archival acid-free storage boxes were all different sizes. *Try that long, flat one!* I opened the lid of one that was the right size and found ribs nestled in tissue paper. This one had a handwritten tag in the box.

Found Seal Shore 1872, Caribbean Monk Seal. Donated by The Smith Family

Robert's ancestors? I tried to take a picture of the tag, but the glove was a hindrance. I removed the glove from my left hand and awkwardly took the photo. I peeked into all the boxes I could safely reach, leaving the shelf above my head alone. It was too risky, and I didn't want to drop anything. The contents of the boxes varied greatly, from a Seminole palmetto fibers doll to a gambeson, the padded jacket Spanish soldiers wore under their chainmail. With my gloveless hand, I snapped an image of the doll and tag to share with Dr. Cypress. The final box I looked in had a sea turtle shell.

Found Seal Shore 1872, Sea Turtle Carapace. Donated by The Smith Family

The shell was gorgeous, and I wondered why it wasn't on display.

"Where are you, Mr. Pickaxe?" I mumbled. *Try the stacks. Maybe he hid it in the stacks.* As a graduate student, I'd had an irrational fear of moveable bookshelves. What if I was too lost in a book to hear the mechanism begin to turn? I'd be squished between the bookshelves like peanut butter and jam between bread. *Shake it off, Miriam. You've faced real danger. Books are not dangerous.*

If Bell were going to hide a box in mobile shelves, he'd probably do it in the next to last. *Right?* I turned the Y-shaped steering wheel, and the second stack glided on the track. Once all four shelves were squeezed together, I slipped into the row between the fourth and fifth bookshelf.

Achoo!

I wiped my dripping nose with the cotton glove I'd removed earlier.

Jackpot! That's not acid-free and archival.

On the bottom shelf, there was a plastic tub with "ARCH 101 Demo Tools" written on it in Sharpie. *¡Fo! Has he been showing the murder weapon to his intro students for twenty-five— no twenty-seven years. Gross!* I removed the lid with my still-gloved right hand. Inside, there were various tools of the trade, including one, two, *three* pickaxes. *Victoria will have to test them all.* I took pictures of the box and a bird's eye view of the jumble of tools. Then,

I gingerly moved the tools and brushes to take a photo of each pickaxe.

A text message from Alma popped up on the screen. *He's here! I couldn't stop him! He's in the BR.*

"Carajo. Oyá, I could use un poquito de orisha intervention. Maybe not a power outage, pero algo. Ayúdame," I mumbled as I reached for the lid I'd placed atop the shelf above. In my frenzy to close the tub and get the cajaro out of there, I knocked a book onto the floor.

Achoo.

"¿Qué es eso?" *Miriam, shh!*

A modern-day spiral notebook was hidden in a hollowed-out, crusty old book. I held my sneeze as I retrieved it from the library floor. *You don't have time to investigate. Take it!* I didn't know if it was Oyá or Velma in my head, but it definitely wasn't Detective Frank Pullman. He would have told me to call him and not touch anything. I put the notebook into the book and stuffed it into my purse. I returned the mobile shelves to their original positions.

My hand was on the doorknob when I remembered Dean Murphy had left me the key. *I wish I could see if the coast was clear.* I cracked the door a few centimeters. *¡Alma! Gracias a la Caridad.* My BFF was in the hallway. She waved me to hurry. I tiptoe ran toward the settler wing, keeping my heels from tap-dance announcing my escape. As I turned the corner into safety, I sputtered to a stop. Ilmi was beside the conquistador mannequin with a finger over her mouth. We heard the bathroom door swing open and close.

"Mr. Bell, your speech the other night was educational. I have a question," Alma said at full Cuban volume.

"Doctor. It's Dr. Bell."

We didn't hang around to eavesdrop. Ilmi and I speed-walked out of the exhibit hall. At the lobby desk, I asked Ilmi for a favor.

"Please return this to Dean Murphy's office on your next break," I said, handing the key to her. "And don't let you-know-who see you."

Ilmi zipped the key into the doll-sized strawberry print backpack hooked to her belt loop.

"Yes," she said flatly. But I swore I noticed a slight smile.

Chapter Forty-Six

"Where are you?" I said as I typed the words into the text message.

Alma didn't reply.

I'd been in the car long enough for her to have made it out. While waiting, I sent the pickaxe images to Alice and Victoria. *Miriam, you should send them to Pullman. It's the right thing to do.* I crafted a no-soy-culpable "I didn't touch anything I just happened upon it" message to Frank and attached the images. *He's not going to believe you.* And I let Victoria know I'd informed the detective.

Tap. Tap. "Let me in," Alma said.

"Ay, mi madre. What took so long?" I asked.

"He wouldn't shut up. I asked one simple question y ese tipo went on and on and on."

"Thanks for saving me." I said, backing out of the parking space.

"Duh. I wasn't going to let you get caught, mujer." Alma combed her hair with her fingers. "Did you find something, Velma?"

276

I groaned. "*Je, je, je.* Basta con el Scooby Doo, porfa."

"You're no fun." Alma fake-pouted. "*Soooo.* Did you, or didn't you?"

"I did. I found—well, at least I hope I found—the murder weapon."

"Where is it?" Alma got my purse from the backseat. "Is it in here?"

"No, loca. I took pictures and sent them to forensics."

"So, what's this?" Alma pulled the cracked leather book from my bag.

My nose began to itch, and I pinched my nose to ward off a sneeze. "I don't know yet. But it is something. Open it."

"*Whaaaat?* Is it a secret journal? Is it in code? Que cool. You really are Velma."

"Amiga, cálmate. You are way too excited. I shouldn't have taken it because now I have to explain how I got it in the first place—if it turns out to be something and if not, then I have to sneak it back in there without him knowing, that is, if he doesn't figure out it's missing before I get the chance." I gulped for air.

"*Ummm.* You need to chill. And breathe. Come on, deep breath. Inhale. Hold it. Exhale slowly." Alma did it with me. I had to admit it helped. I was calmer by the time we got to my block. "Your in-laws are in here un montón de veces," she said, looking at the notebook pages.

My serenity flew out the window. "¿Que, qué?"

"Marjory Smith. Douglas T. Smith. William M. Smith. Smith, Smith, Smith. Oh wait, here's a Weatherman and a Pimpkin."

The car jerked us forward when I stomped on the brake. I turned off the engine and unbuckled my seatbelt to lean over the console to see into the notebook. "Let me see." She wasn't exaggerating. There was a list of Coral Shores founding families' names with dates and catalog letters like the one on the flat file drawers.

"What are all the letters for?" Alma asked.

"I don't understand the cataloging system yet. I have to figure it out."

"I think you mean *crack the code*." My best friend grinned.

"Be serious. Nothing about this is good. Something—" I waxed-on-waxed-off the air above the notebook. "—is fishy."

"*Jinkies.*"

I gave my BFF a puzzled stare, to which she laughed, handed me the book, and exited the car.

"I've got to show a house in fifteen minutes." Alma threw a kiss. "Good luck, *Velma.*"

I was too curious about the spiral notebook to be frustrated with my friend's jokes.

As I closed the secret compartment book, dust and debris floated up to irritate my nose. *You've been very sensitive to molds and pollens lately. No, not really. The other day, Mami shoved flowers into my face, and I didn't sneeze. I'm only getting stuffy-sneezing occasionally.*

"And it coincides with being around Gregory Vander Bell!" There was the first time I met him in the tent and then at the museum when he'd just come from the Special Collections room. "It's the book. He must have handled the book right before, and the dust particles stuck to his clothes." I sniffled and opened the glove compartment to get a mask from the leftover pandemic stockpile.

I walked into the house wearing the blue mask and holding the book away from my clothes. Sirena, who was chasing Camo in circles, stopped, bubbled up with giggles, and wilted onto the living room rug. Camo hopped on the ottoman to watch, curious and dubious of the young human.

Dominoes, Danzón, and Death

"Mami, doctora," Sirena said, kicking her little legs and rolling about.

"Sí, tu Mami es una doctora de antropología," Papi said from behind his *El Nuevo Herald* newspaper. Robert had gotten him a subscription for Christmas. "No te sientes bien." Papi remarked, noticing the blue mask.

"Es este libro. Muy polvoriento," I explained. "Voy a leerlo afuera en el patio."

I did just that and took the book outside to read it in the open air, passing by our dining room table covered in Party City bags to the open French doors.

"¿Qué son todos eso bolsos?" I asked my mother.

"Son para el party," Mami replied. She was getting a malta from the drinks fridge. "Elba is coming by later to make the table decorations. Son todos blanco y negro como los dominós."

Mami told me she'd made potaje de lentejas for lunch. I told her I'd get a bowl as soon as I'd finished studying this important book.

"¿Vas a regresar a la universidad?" She asked, bewildered.

"No," I laughed. *Pero, maybe yes, Miriam. Not like she thinks for another degree, but maybe to teach.*

Mami left me to my studies. I removed the notebook and put the book shell as far away from me on the table as I could. Taking off the mask, I breathed in the fresh and verdant South Florida air. "Okay, mysterious journal, what secrets do you hold?"

The cover and first page were blank. They gave no clue as to the ownership. *Come on, Miriam. It's safe to assume it belongs to Bell.* I turned to the second page and began reading the list. The hand-writing was neat and even, with each numerical entry following a discernible pattern. Number, Description, Origin, Year, Donor, Donation Date. As Alma had noted, the Smith name was prevalent on the list, but so were the names of the other founding families.

4. Fendograf fountain pen. Gold-fill. Art Deco motif. Owned by Joseph T. Pimpkin. Used to sign Coral Shores charter. (?) Approx. 1920
   • Donor: Marjory Edith Smith, February 1997
8. Pineapple crate. Weatherman Growers label. Approx. 1911
   • Donor: Cecil Donald Weatherman, March 1997
13. Key, brass, stamped with initials FECRY. Florida East Coast Railway. Approx. 1930
   • Donor: Marjory E. Smith, March 1997
22. Army uniform button. Miami Minutemen. 1898.
   • Donor: Samford Pimpkin, May 1997

The list continued for two dozen pages, with most of the items related to Coral Shores and Miami history from the late 1800s to the mid-century 1900s. The catalog kept the same information pattern, with the only variation being an occasional star in blue ballpoint ink. All other markings and information were in black ballpoint ink. The Smiths were responsible for seventy to eighty percent of the donations. It was no wonder that Marjory and Senior had their portrait hanging in the museum.

"Niña, tienes que comer," Mami said. She was at the patio doors with lunch.

I got up to get the plate from her. "Gracias, Mami. Huele delicioso." The brown lentil stew smelled smoky and rich. My mother made her version with chorizo, potatoes, carrots, calabaza, and ham. Tía Elba's recipe, the one served at Tres Sillas, didn't have chorizo or calabaza, but it did have tocino/fatback bacon. Gilda crackers were tucked around the bowl, and a spoon was in the stew.

"Come," Mami ordered me to eat. "I remember you always forgot to eat when you were *estudying* for a test."

"Mira, Mami. I'm eating." I dipped the scalloped edge hard cracker into the stew and took a bite. The bland crackers were slightly concave, making them great for holding the thick soup.

Mami nodded in satisfaction that I was consuming nourishment. She returned in a few seconds with a cup of soup. "Para la santa," Mami said.

"I'll do it," I said. I took the food offering and the tiny key from her. My mother had braided bread ties together to form a key ring of sorts. At Oyá's house, I set the cup down to undo the little lock. The box stank of old food. "Fo." I wafted the stink away. "Oyá, I think you need some fresh air. I invite you to have lunch with me." I carefully maneuvered the statue from its house and took it and the cup of lentils to the patio table.

"Buen provecho," I said, saluting the saint with the spoon.

A short burst of breeze blew over the table, ruffling the pages of the notebook I'd pushed out of the way of our meal.

"Is that you?" I looked at the saint. *Miriam, you keep talking to that statue like it's a person. Estas loca.*

A longer breeze blew. I got my phone from my purse and weighed the pages down, giving the saint an okay-that's-enough glare. As my hand released the phone, the screen lit up. "That's weird." Instead of the normal locked screen, there was the image of the flat file label. "That is definitivamente your doing." I gave Oyá a raised eyebrow.

"What are you telling me?" I ate a spoonful of stew.

"What am I supposed to see?" I tapped the spoon in the saint's face.

I stared at the letters and numbers, 20:CS:BI:13:MS, on the screen as I ate another spoonful. "What do you want me to see about the code?"

The phone sat horizontally on the notebook, underlining entry number twenty. "Okay, if the first number is the number. Then what does CS stand for? *Coral Shores.* Okay, let's go with that for now. So, what does BI mean?" I thought about the items in the drawer—a rattle and a bonnet. *Baby Items!* Comparing the image and the entry, the rest of the code came easily. 13 was the year the items originated, 1913. MS stood for Marjory Smith, the donor. But Coral Shores wasn't in the written entry, nor was CS. *Do I have that part wrong? It could mean something else.*

"I'll ask a librarian." I pushed the call icon on Gillian's contact page. After an exchange of pleasantries, I got to the point. "Gillian, do you have any experience working with special collections? Not just books and documents, *but historical items*."

"Oh, my giddy aunt. As it happens, I worked at Graceland for six months," Gillian replied.

"*Elvis Presley's home*," I said, unsure how I recalled that factoid about the rock-n-roll star.

"Oh my, it was a gas. The fan mail always made me blush." Gillian tittered.

I imagined a young Gillian reading some teenagers' spicy love letter to The King of rock-n-roll. "Perfect. I think you can help me. Is there a standard method in cataloging a collection?"

She thought a moment. "The order might vary, but usually, the item is given a number associated with a grouping or a collection of items that belong together because they are the same type of thing or were acquired or donated together. Then there might be a few simple descriptive words like, say, embroidered handkerchief or war medal."

"Could those be abbreviated?" I asked.

"On a tag, certainly. The master list will have a detailed description."

"Okay, so number, collection, description. What else?"

"The date of the item is included. It's important to know the age of a piece. And then the donor's name is included to keep the chain of provenance," Gillian said.

"Thank you. You have been very helpful. I promise to get your photographs back to you soon."

"No rush. They'll only go back into their box. Keep them as long as you need. Toot-a-loo." She ended our call.

I looked at the list again, drawing my finger across the writing as I read left to right. I could feel the indentions from the heavy hand that had written it.

"Catalog number. Item description. Date. Donor."

Why was there a handwritten list hidden in a hollowed-out book? A proper inventory would be printed from a database, *surely*.

I read and reread the entry for the baby items I'd seen in the flat file. It matched the photo except for the addition of the CS and the blue star. "What does the star connote?"

I leafed through the notebook, looking for an answer. In the latter pages of the notebook, the list was written in blue ink. "Do the blue stars correlate to the blue list?" Again, I ran my finger across the words, except this time, the ink color was blue.

20. Bowl (three pieces), Indian (Tequesta), From private family collection. Approx. 1913
    • Donor: Marjory E. Smith, May 1997

"Espérate. *The Smiths had Tequesta pottery*. Where did they get it?"

I quickly cross-checked the starred entries with the blue list. There were a lot of Tequesta artifacts with the Smith name attached to them. And I noticed that the black ink with blue star catalog codes were very similar to the blue ink catalog codes. It was like a ghost list.

Dread washed over me.

"I need to speak to my mother-in-law."

Chapter
Forty-Seven

"Well, it's about time."

There was no hello from Marjory, only a guilt trip that I hadn't called to check on her sooner. I held my tongue and apologized. She hadn't been the one that had been tackled. Robert had. She'd been sitting at home being waited on hand and foot. *Ay, el pobre Welmo.*

"So, what did Lyle want with you? Has he offered you a position? You need to stop chasing stardom and stop galivanting to foreign countries without your husband. Robert needs you. The children need you. It's time for you to be *respectfully* employed."

Miriam. Do. Not. Take. The. Bait. She is never going to forgive you for Sirena's birth in D.R. She is an unhappy person who wants to control what is not hers to control. I remembered the breathing exercise Alma had done with me. Inhale. Hold. Exhale. *Avoid. Deflect. Take back the narrative.*

"Thank you for giving Dean Murphy my phone number. We had a lovely conversation. But that's not why I called today," I said. *Did I hear a little gasp of dissatisfaction?* "The other evening, when Robert and I were representing *the family* at the event, I noticed

284

you had donated a multitude of pieces to the museum. I had no idea The Smiths had amassed such a large collection of Native American artifacts."

"*Amassed.* We didn't acquire them. Our family lived them. We built this town. Robert's forefathers took this land from swamp to city," Marjory said with her usual contempt.

Ay mi madre, this woman thinks The Smiths are the native Americans.

"I know. Robert is *very* proud of his heritage. He's told me so many stories about the founding of Coral Shores." I fibbed. Robert rarely mentioned he was from a founding family. I changed my approach. "Is that where The Smiths found the *Indian* pottery and artifacts? In the swamp."

"*Pottery.* I gave the museum a few pieces of English China I had in the cabinet. And an etched crystal coupe that had belonged to Charles and Marion Deering," she said. "The Smiths and my mother's family, The Pimpkins, were invited to the estate on many occasions." The Deering estate was a Gilded Age mansion on Cutler Bay in South Miami that was now a state park that hosted arts and culture programs.

Marjory still wasn't getting what I was saying.

"Did you donate three pieces of Tequesta pottery—" I checked the blue list. "A sea turtle shell, a pottery knob, a perforated shell ornament, a wooden pestle, a bone awl, a shell ladle—"

Marjory interrupted with sounds of dismay. "What utter incompetence! Bell is a fumbling idiot. I gave him important pieces of Coral Shores' history, and he's lost them. Goodbye. I need to have a word with Lyle and the board."

"Perhaps you should wait," I said.

"*Excuse me.*"

"What I meant to say is perhaps you should speak to Senior and Drew and probably Gordon before you call the college."

"Why on earth would I need to speak to Cousin Gordon first?" she asked.

"Well, you could talk to Detective Pullman if you'd rather." *Ay, Miriam, que mala eres. You didn't need to say that.*

Marjory grumbled. "I cannot abide that man."

"I know, but you might need his help with this. I think Dr. Bell is using your name to cover up his improprieties," I said.

"*I beg your pardon.*"

"I think he stole Tequesta artifacts from the 1995 excavation and has slowly been putting them on display at Grove, saying they were acquired from private collections."

"What does that have to do with me?" She huffed.

"Bell is forging the provenance of the pieces. He is using your name and the Plimpkins' and the Weathermans' to make a fake document trail for the items he stole. This is a legal matter. He is a thief."

Marjory was quiet.

"Please, do not call the dean until after you've spoken to Gordon."

"I'll think about it," she said, then hung up.

"Ay, ay, ay. That woman me saca las canas," I said.

"Don't let Marjory give you gray hair," Detective Pullman said.

I looked up. "How long have you been standing there?"

"Long enough. Were you going to take your own advice? When were you planning on calling me?" He pulled a chair out and sat.

My mother came outside and set demitasses of coffee in front of us.

"Gracias por el café, Carmen," he said.

"De nada. Would you like a little tortica to go with it? I just took them out of the oven," my mother said.

"¿Hiciste torticas de Morón?" I asked.

"Si, *eshape* like fichas for the party," she replied.

The Cuban shortbread cookies were good but not something my mother made regularly. And she was making them rectangular to look like dominoes instead of the standard circle cut. Mami y Tía Elba were really going all out for Yoli and Bette's party.

"Carmen, I would love to try a cookie," Frank said.

My mother hurried back with three cookies on a saucer.

"Gracias, Mami," I said.

"Thank you, Carmen," Frank said.

I reached to get a cookie. Frank pulled the plate out of my reach.

"So, when were you going to call me?" he asked, dunking a cookie into his espresso.

"You were next on my list. I had to confirm before I told you what I'd uncovered. *Don't give me that look.* I sent you the picture of the—" I lowered my voice. "—murder weapon."

"About that. We're working on a warrant. Are we going to find your fingerprints on it?"

"No," I answered, thankful for the archive gloves.

"What have I told you about breaking and entering, Veronica?"

"I was let in. Look at the security footage if you want. Dean Murphy let me in." I held my head high.

"And what about that old book." Frank pointed to the leather-bound book at the end of the table.

"I borrowed it from the library." *That's not a lie.* "And that's how I found this." I turned the notebook toward him. "I think Bell found a small Tequesta site on the golf course in 1995. And when Pierre—Alice and I have been talking—when Pierre confronted Bell about it, probably telling him the artifacts should go to the Miccosukee, they fought. Bell lost his temper or panicked or both and hit him on the head with the pickaxe. Then, to cover his tracks,

287

Bell closed down the dig, hid the artifacts for later, and buried the body with the animal bone."

Frank passed me the last cookie. "Alright, Velma, that's a pretty good deduction. Now explain the other part, what you were telling your mother-in-law." He motioned to the notebook but didn't touch it.

I explained my theory that the starred items had been reclassified as something else in the blue list. "But I'd need to go back to the museum to confirm it," I said.

"I don't think so," Frank said, shaking his head.

"Then let Alice check," I said. "At the event on Saturday, she mentioned she thought there was something shady going on with there being so many anonymous donations of Tequesta pieces."

Frank agreed that we should call Dr. Cypress. I put her on speaker and let her in on the notebook I'd uncovered.

"I spoke to Dot. She remembers Pierre saying he'd seen a bird pipe," Alice said. "And he said he'd return it to the tribe himself if Bell didn't do the right thing. I think Pierre said something to Bell that night he disappeared. I think he told him to give the pipe to us. And I think it got him killed."

"Do you mean the pipe unveiled at the silver celebration?" I asked.

Frank scratched the stubble on his chin. He was having thoughts that he wasn't going to share with Alice or me. But I guessed what he was thinking and vocalized it.

"Remember when you were doing the smoke ceremony?" I asked Alice. "Remember how Bell was there, uninvited? What if he was there already? Maybe he got there earlier to recover something. Gordon said there was a piece of pottery missing. And Robert thinks it is now on display in the museum."

"Hmm." Frank said. "Dr. Cypress, Dr. Quiñones, let's take this to the station so I can get your statements."

Chapter
Forty-Eight

"**B**abe," Robert whispered. "I need to check on something at the club."

I rubbed the sleep from my eyes and looked at the time. "Mi amor, it's 1:37 AM. Can't it wait?" I stretched then turned onto my side and curled into a ball, tucking the sheet under my chin.

"It will only take a few moments. If I don't go, I'll toss and turn until morning worrying about it." Robert tied the laces of his shoes and stood.

I flung off the sheet and made myself into an X as I yawned with my entire body. "Okay, then I'm going with you."

"*Babe.*" Robert gave me the *you are being ridiculous* look.

"*Babe.*" I mimicked him. "Like I can sleep now. I'll have a nightmare about you wrestling Bernice or something," I chuckled. "Give me two seconds to dress." I slipped on an UnMundo track suit, stuffed my bare feet into a pair of canvas slip-ons, and pulled my hair out of my face, securing it with a large claw clip at my crown. "Ready."

Robert kissed my cheek. "You are the hottest ride or die."

"I want to say the same about you, but I'm pretty sure that's throw-up on your shirt." I pointed at a discolored spot on his chest.

Robert pulled the T-shirt away from his skin.

"Sirena or Camo? Ewww, don't smell it!"

"Smells sweet. I think it's juice," Robert said. He took a hoodie from the closet and put it on. "Let's go."

The Coral Shores streets were quiet. The village looked like the cover of a magazine. Every house had a pristine lawn, a warmly lit front walkway, and palm trees wrapped in fairy lights. We were at the club within a few minutes.

"What exactly are we checking on?" I asked as we walked toward the maintenance building.

"One of the club's security guards texted me that he thought he saw someone lurking around the excavator." Robert took a key chain from the peg board and a flashlight from a nearby table.

"Why didn't they go check it out?" I got into the golf cart with Robert.

"Insurance reasons." He turned the key and the battery buzzed on. "I texted the night officer—"

"*The site is still under police guard,*" I said.

"Maybe not. He didn't reply to my message." Robert drove the cart onto the path.

The breeze was crisp as we zoomed along the asphalt lane. I zipped my jacket up, protecting my neck and chest from the cool air. Unlike the lawns in the neighborhood, the greens had no lighting. It was pitch black beyond the cart's head lamps, which weren't much stronger than candles. But the night sky twinkled with stars, making it feel a little romantic.

"Stay here, I'll be right back." Robert pressed the brake pedal to the floor, engaging the parking brake. We were on the top of a little hill past the excavation site. "Please, stay in the cart. I don't want you twisting an ankle. There's a sand trap and a small water hazard down there."

"*Me. Go out there. With the snakes and the things and the things.* No. I'm not leaving this seat." I laughed, scrunched into the seat, and put my feet on the metal dashboard. "*No te preocupes.* I'm very comfortable right here." I watched Robert until he became a bouncing ball of light in the distance. The sounds of frogs and crickets soon became overwhelming. I took out my phone and distracted myself from the eerie night sounds with Jorge's social media posts. He was putting on glittered eyelashes when I sensed something move in the tall grass to my left. *Bernice!* I paused Jorge's video and listened to the night.

Groan.

"Do alligators groan?" I whispered to myself.

The noise came again. I pointed my phone's light at the patch of tall grass. The reeds swayed. A hand shot out.

I gasped.

The hand fell to the ground. *Groan.* Another hand shot out. It grabbed the ground and pulled. A head emerged. It was the night officer.

I jumped out of the golf cart and ran toward the man. My shoe sank into the soft grass as soon as I stepped off the little road and I tumbled onto my knees. Florida humidity had made the gentle slope into a slip and slide. I dried my grass-stained palms on my jacket then carefully crawled forward.

"Are you okay?" I asked. "What happened?"

"Help me." The man's voice was weak.

"Are you stuck?" Memories of cartoon quicksand filled my head.

"Bleeding," he said.

I dug my heels into the tender earth, grabbed his arms, and pulled him out of the weeds and onto the road. The golfcart's headlights showed the damage I hadn't seen in the dark. The hair on the back of his head was matted and glistening. He'd been hit with something and, by the looks of the dark stain on his back, he'd bled a lot.

"You need to see a doctor. Let's get you to the hospital," I said. I called Robert's phone. A ringtone came from the cart. His phone was on the bench, pulsing with each ring. *Coño. It must have slipped out of his pocket. What am I going to do? I can't lift him by myself.* "Stay here. I'll be right back."

Groan.

Using my phone's light I went in the direction I'd seen Robert go. "Ro—" I stopped myself from shouting more. *No, seas boba, Miriam. Don't draw attention to yourself. Someone hit that man over the head and he's probably still out there.*

I carefully made my way to where the excavator was parked. If Robert was there, I couldn't see him. "Robert," I whispered as quietly as possible.

"Babe?"

"Shh." I felt my way around the machine to where Robert was. He was leaning against the excavator's metal tracks with one shoe off.

"I got a rock. What are you doing here? I told you to wa—"

I put my finger on his mouth. "Shh. Someone is out there." I made a whirling motion with my pointer finger. I cupped Robert's ear and whispered into it, explaining that I'd found his night officer.

Robert grabbed my hand and we dashed in the direction of the golf cart.

"Where's the cart?" I said looking up and down the path. "Don't tell me he drove off."

"There." Robert pointed to a pair of lights shining into a tree. Robert took off in the direction of the accident.

I was about to follow him when I saw a light. There was a bouncing dot of light playing at the base of the tent. *Who is in there? Coño. Grave Robbers.* Without thinking, I ran to the tent. I flattened myself on the ground and looked under the canvas wall. Dr. Gregory Vander Bell was on his knees in the crater, chipping at the earth with a small trowel. From his vest of many pockets, he removed a beaded barrette like the ones Alice liked to wear. I was about to press record on my phone when the screen lit up with Robert's face.

"Who's there?" Bell shouted.

I declined the call, stuffed the phone into my jacket, and got to my feet.

Bell lumbered out of the tent. His headlamp moved spastically from left to right searching the night. "Come out, come out, wherever you are."

His chanting voice gave me piel de gallina/goose bumps.

Bell slowed his head movement, keying in on one area. "I can hear you breathing."

I held my breath and stepped farther into the dark.

Bell moved two steps in my direction before turning and walking away from the tent.

¿Qué hago? What do I do? Before I talked myself out of it, I slipped into the tent. I needed to know what Bell had been up to. *Was he planting evidence? Does he know the police are about to arrest him?* I inched my way around the edge of the crater, listening for Bell's return. When I got to the far side, an arm went around my waist and a hand covered my mouth. I was about to kick my assailant's shin when a hot breath filled my ear.

"Babe. It's me. Shh," Robert whispered.

I stopped kicking, swiveled around, and hugged him. Robert motioned for me to come with him through the flap he'd come through.

"Not so fast," Bell said.

The hair on my neck prickled.

He flicked on his headlamp and blinded us frozen.

When my eyes adjusted, I saw that he was throwing a small camp shovel from hand to hand. There was a gooey sheen on it. The officer's blood most likely.

"Get back in there," Bell said.

Robert and I walked backward into the tent.

"Bobby, why did you have to marry *such a little troublemaker?*" Bell asked.

"Doctor—" Robert began to speak.

"Shut up! I have to think about what to do with you." Bell menaced with the shovel.

Robert stepped in front to shield me. "Doctor Bell, you've been such a good friend to the family. I'm sure we can come to an arrangement." Robert spoke quickly to get his offer out before Bell shouted again.

"Go on," Bell said.

Robert cleared his throat. "Let us leave and we were never here."

"Bobby, I trust you, but not *Doctora Quiñones.*" He strutted toward us brandishing the shovel. "I'm surrounded by know-it-all women."

Robert turned, trying to keep me behind him. But I stepped up beside him.

"Victoria! Alice! And you!" He jabbed the metal tool in my direction.

I tried not to flinch. "Is that Alice's barrette?" I motioned toward the black, red, and yellow hair clasp in the hole.

"A memento," he said. "From when she was my Indian Princess." He laughed. "Funny, it should be found at the murder site. Maybe she killed *Deer Pierre.*"

"You know that's not true," I said.

"A little forensic evidence," his headlamp beamed on the barrette, "is all I need to cast a sliver of doubt."

"What about the pickaxe I found?" I asked.

Robert gave me a stern side-glance.

"And the false donor records?" I asserted.

Robert continued to glare at me.

"The college won't want a scandal. I'm certain the board will want things kept quiet. There won't be any charges filed, much less a trial. *And the murder of a radical Indian by his radical Indian girl-friend.* Too bad, so sad." Bell chuckled.

"Hands in the air!" Seargent Gordon Smith yelled.

The tent was flooded with light from both sides as police officers entered.

"I called Gordie when you didn't answer," Robert said.

"Gracias a La Caridad." I kissed my husband. "Gordon, I owe you a flan," I said.

"What about me, Veronica?" Pullman walked into the tent holding an evidence bag in his gloved hands.

"You get one, too," I said.

"And me? I'm the one that called the police," Robert pouted. "And the ambulance. The guy needs a few stitches but he's going to survive."

"Everyone here, *that is not a murderer*, gets a flan!" I said.

Chapter
Forty-Nine

The rest of the week had been a blur between the party preparations that had taken over my house and the Grove Museum investigation that filled the headlines. Forensic evidence proved that the pickaxe in the special collection library was the murder weapon that killed Pierre Deer Maracle. Gordon found a shoe print in the video he and Robert took that matched the size and sole pattern of Dr. Bell's sandals. He was also able to identify the missing pottery shard to the one recently displayed at the museum. Alice accompanied Pierre's remains back to Canada on Thursday. While there, Pierre's brother gave her a letter he'd sent the day before his murder. In it, he'd draw a sketch of the bird pipe and outlined his plan to demand Dr. Bell return it to Native hands. Upon being confronted with the existence of the letter, Gregory Vander Bell confessed. He'd killed Pierre over the bird pipe that he thought was lost. Pierre had it in his pocket the whole time. It had been buried with the body for twenty-seven years. When Bell went to the new dig site to dispose of the evidence that could identify Pierre, he found the pipe and other pottery. Bell threw the skull into the pond.

Brrring.

Dominoes, Danzón, and Death

My phone rang. Omarosa took the tray of domino-shaped cookies from my arms so I could answer it. We were at *Las Reinas de Las Fritas* with minutes to decorate before the guests arrived.

Brrring.

"Hello, Dr. Quiñones. I'm sorry to bother you on the weekend," Dean Lyle Murphy said. *Umhum. You said the same thing last time. Maybe I should start looking at the caller ID.* "But I wanted you to hear it from me." *He doesn't know I know. Thank you, Frank, for identifying the source as a prominent female Ph.D. of which there were three—me, Victoria, and Alice.* "The professor we were offering early retirement to was Dr. Gregory Bell. We've suspected he'd been falsifying the provenances and the proveniences of some of the Early Florida acquisitions."

"How long had you suspected him?" I asked. Calle Ocho was noisy with tourists and traffic. I turned the volume up on my phone to hear better.

"We'd been watching him for a year. The anonymous donations of rare pieces had accelerated leading up to the museum's twenty-fifth," Murphy said. "I hope this will not impact your opinion of Grove College. We, I, really want you to join the faculty."

I'd been so busy that I'd forgotten I'd promised him an answer within the week. *Miriam, you are going to have to tell him you were the one who found the notebook. Yes, but not today.*

"Dean Murphy, I'm at my cousin's anniversary party. Can I stop by your office on Tuesday to discuss the offer?" *That will give me a chance to discuss it with Delvis, too. Can I teach and film the show? Can I make it work?*

"Of course. I'll see you on Tuesday. Enjoy the party. Congratulations to the happy couple," he said.

I slipped my phone into my pocket and went into the restaurant. Tía and Mami had been there for hours already. The tables were decorated in black and white. Four domino playing tables had

297

been brought in and placed at the front of the restaurant near the rolling window that would be kept down for the private party. Manny had been given the task of setting up the tables for play. He was turning over the tiles and singing along with the band that was warming up. Gordon and Sirena were also enjoying the musicians. Sirena, standing on Gordon's feet, danced in front of the stage. The smell of caramelized onions and hamburgers floated in the air. The party was ready for guests.

"¿Dónde estan Yoli y Bette?" I asked Tía Elba.

"Están en camino," she replied. "A, allí están." She gestured to the door.

"Primas," I yelled. "Felicidades." I gave them each a hug. Bette, dressed in a blue body contouring dress, looked fabulous with her coily hair bouncy and shiny. Yoli wore a white linen guayabera that had dominos embroidered on the pockets.

Yoli gave Manny a pat and asked him if he would be her domino partner.

"Sorry, Prima, but I'm Abuelo's partner," Manny replied.

Out of the corner of my eye, I saw my dad beam with pride.

Someone knocked on the glass wall.

"Guests are here!" I shouted.

"Let's get this party started," Yoli clapped.

I stationed myself at the door and welcomed people as they arrived. I recognized some folks like Bette and Omarosa's parents, but others were friends I was meeting for the first time. Everyone had a smile on their face and joy in their heart. Alma took over door duty when she arrived so I could get a drink from the bar.

Mami had sent Robert on a special mission. When I saw him come in through the back exit, I was surprised by who he had with him. It was El Marinero. Mami had told Yoli about him, and she'd invited him to sing at the party.

"I wasn't expecting to see him here," Delvis said from behind me.

I gave her a hug. "I feel like I haven't seen you in a month."

"I know. Sorry about canceling the shoot this week. I'm glad we had a few episodes banked so that we could cover." Delvis took a sugar-rimmed mojito from the bar.

I took one of the bocaditos Mami had made. A tray of fritas sliders was coming out of the kitchen. A friend of the couple was placing paper boats of mariquitas on each table.

"What a wild week," Delvis said.

"I had a wild week, too. But you go first," I said.

Delvis pushed her blue hair out of her eyes. "So, remember how your buddy Nelson encouraged me to submit a short film to the LGBTQ festival. Well, guess what I found in my outtakes? That lady, the tour guide who was killed, she was paying off a city official. Wait, you saw a little of it in the production van, right. Okay, so Fi and I went through all the film we'd shot. Turns out the city official was in a lot of it. Not just the sandwich bag bit that you saw. I showed what I had to the cops. They talked to El Marinero and finally believed what he'd been saying all along. The city official had been using The Deco as a drop site. People would leave him money in a certain film canister that was in The Deco's lobby. The same canister that he ended up hitting her over the head with because of the sandwich bag fiasco I'd mistakenly filmed."

"Oh, my goodness, was he coming for you next?" My jaw dropped.

"*Maybe*," Delvis said. "The cops asked me to lay low for a few days while they investigated it. They arrested him yesterday. So, what was wild about your week?"

"Oddly enough, it also involved an arrest," I said.

"Explain, please," Delvis said.

"Later, let's enjoy the party," I said as the band stuck up Celia Cruz' *La Vida es un Carnaval*. "Remind me to ask you about our production schedule for spring." I danced toward the domino tables to watch Papi and Manny play. "I might have an academic gig to work around."

THE END

Recetas / Recipes

Frita Cubana / Cuban Hamburger

A frita is much more than a variation on the hamburger. It is about the perfect combination of elements. There is a special sauce, a cracker-crust airy bun, and fried shoestring potatoes. The history of the Frita Cubana begins in Havana in the 1920s, arriving in Miami in the 1960's. Burger Beast has a history of this delicious street food and cultural icon. (https://burgerbeast.com/frita -cubana-recipe-history/) My version substitutes turkey for beef. Feel free to use beef if you prefer it, but pork is a must.

Servings: 8

Ingredients:

Cuban bread buns or bakery buns
1 potato or a can of shoestring potato sticks
Cheddar cheese
Meat patty/burger
Special sauce

Sauce:

1 cup ketchup
⅓ cup water
1½ teaspoons cumin

1½ teaspoons paprika (sweet or smoked)
¼ cup white vinegar
2½ teaspoons sugar
½ teaspoon each salt & pepper
1 tablespoon hot sauce (Tabasco, Frank's, Cholula original or
    similar)

Patty:

1 lb ground turkey
1 lb ground pork
1 teaspoon cumin
2 tablespoons garlic powder
1 tablespoon onion powder
¼—½ onion grated or finely chopped
2 tablespoons ketchup
3 shakes of hot sauce
salt & pepper to taste

Mix the sauce and set aside. Combine the patty mixture making sure the spices and different meats are well integrated. Divide into eight patties. Cook in a well-oiled pan at medium/ high or grill. Put a spoonful of sauce on top of the raw patty. Cook thoroughly flipping them once. Melt a slice of cheese on the burger at the end.

If you are making your own shoestring potatoes, fry them as you are cooking the meat and allow them to drain/dry.

Lightly toast the inside of the bun. Liberally spread the sauce on each side. Place patty on bun, pile high with fried shoestring potatoes, and drizzle a little sauce over them. This burger is meant to be messy. It is a many napkins meal! Enjoy!

Bocaditos

Growing up, bocaditos were a required finger food at all backyard parties, weddings, and quinces. The name translates to "little bites." On any given Saturday in Miami, there will be an order pickup line that goes out the door of the neighborhood Cuban bakery. The party food is packaged in cellophane-wrapped trays. A party of 25 gets one tray of assorted pastelitos and one tray of bocaditos. That's probably enough for a small office party. But if you have a backyard of hungry kids, you'll need several trays of these tasty sandwiches as most kids (and adults) grab one for each hand and come back for seconds. You may want to size this recipe up.

Servings: 12

Ingredients:

1 package (12 rolls) of King's Hawaiian Sweet Rolls
8 oz package of cream cheese
½ cup mayonnaise
2–8 oz packages of diced ham
1 jar of diced pimentos

Let the cream cheese come to room temperature. Drain the pimentos and reserve the liquid. Combine the cream cheese with the mayonnaise then add the pimentos and ham. Use an immersion blender, food processor, or simply a fork and knife to make sure the ham is minced. If your spread is too thick add a little of the pimento brine. Spread the paste onto the rolls.

Miriam's Tortilla Española

Tortilla Española is traditionally made with potatoes. It is delicious hot or cold. Many Latin American bakeries sell it in their cases. The crustless quiche is perfect for breakfast, lunch, or dinner. Several times in this series you've read a scene where Miriam whips one up quickly using leftovers. I and, in turn, Miriam substitute maduros/sweet plantains for the potatoes. If you can't find maduros in the frozen food aisle (and don't have fresh) then use leftover French fries, roasted potatoes, or hashbrowns. This dish is very forgiving once you find the correct cooking temperature and amount of oil to use.

Serving: 2

Ingredients:

3 eggs
5–6 maduros/sweet plantains
Diced or sliced ham (cooked bacon or prosciutto work well, too)
Oil (olive oil or vegetable oil)

Pour enough oil into your 8-inch skillet to coat the sides and have enough for frying. *This is the part you might not get right on the first cook. It takes a little more than you think.* When the oil is hot, fry your maduros until golden. Try to flatten them into the same thickness. I arrange them in a flower shape. Turn them and lower heat medium to low-medium. Place your ham between or around the maduros. Pour in your scrambled eggs. Do not stir. Once the liquid gets a few bubbles and the sides have begun to solidify put a lip (or plate) over the skillet. Lower the temperature and be patient. You can check on the progress but do not turn up the heat. Once the middle is cooked, remove from the stove, and use a knife to loosen the sides. Put a plate over the skillet and flip the tortilla onto it. If you've used enough oil, a beautiful fluffy omelet with a maduro "flower" will be on your plate. If you haven't been generous with the oil, then it might stick but it is still delicious!

Palmeras

Palmeras are sometimes called orejas as they look like elephant's or pig's ears, but the cookie is French in origin. In France, it is called a palmier because it resembles a palm frond. I've put a Cuban twist on this easy-to-make cookie by adding a guava glaze. The Puerto Rican version uses honey. Other variations use cinnamon, chocolate, or coconut flakes.

Servings: Approx. 12 cookies

Ingredients:

1 package of frozen puffed pastry (defrosted in refrigerator)
Granulated sugar
Guava paste

Preheat oven to 400 degrees. Sprinkle sugar onto your workstation. Use a rolling pin to stretch and flatten the sheet of pastry. Flip and repeat adding more sugar to work surface, if needed. Fold the pastry ends in 1/6th, and then fold them again meeting in the center of the sheet. Place in the fridge to chill for 10–15 minutes. Use a sharp knife to cut the folded roll into 12 even slices. Place the slices on a parchment-lined baking sheet. The slices should look like similar to a V. They will spread as they bake to look like a heart or ear. Bake for 10–12 minutes. Flip the cookies and bake an additional 4–6 minutes until sugar is golden and caramelized. While the pastry is in the oven, melt a one-inch cube of guava paste with a tablespoon of butter. Brush a thin layer of glaze onto the cookies and allow them to cool.

Cuban Natilla

Natilla is a thick, flavorful, and delicious custard. Legend has it that we have Spanish nuns to thank for this dessert. It came to Latin America with colonization and each country has their own variations. Some recipes call for coconut, honey, or raisins. Others use brown sugar in place of white sugar. This version is the Cuban Natilla that I grew up with. There are quicker versions which use condensed milk but I find those too sweet for my liking.

Servings: 4

Ingredients:

3 cups of whole milk
Rind of a lime
2–3 sticks of cinnamon
¼ cup cold water
4 tablespoons of corn starch
½ cup sugar
5 egg yolks
Optional: vanilla extract and cinnamon powder.

This recipe calls for a double boiler. I use a 2.5 quart oven-safe glass mixing bowl on a 5–6 quart pot. Start by heating the water. It needs to be boiling when it is time to use it.

Put the cinnamon sticks and the rind of ½ a lime into a small pot with 1 cup of milk. Bring to a boil then remove from heat. Let it steep for 10 minutes. Strain a set aside.

Dissolve the corn starch in the cold water and set aside.

Blend your egg yolks and sugar in your double boiler bowl. Add 2 cups of cold milk and the corn starch slurry. Stir. Place the bowl on boiling water. Slowly add the warm strained milk to the bowl. Stir often (constantly) for 45 minutes until it thickens. It feels like it is never going to happen so, don't lose faith. In the last ten minutes it comes together into a pudding consistency. Turn off heat. Optional: Stir in one cap of vanilla extract and cinnamon powder to your liking.

Portion the warm custard into serving bowls. (Hint: Those glass or ceramic yogurt jars work great.) Chill overnight.

Author Notes

Dominoes, Danzón, and Death has Miriam back home in the fictional village of Coral Shores in Miami on the banks of Biscayne Bay. As with the other books in the series, I combine historical facts and contemporary issues into my stories. Modern day Miami was built on Tequesta land. A quick internet search for "Miami Circle" and "Henry Flagler's Royal Palm Hotel" will be an eye-opening history lesson. I chose to highlight that part of Miami's history because it is too often hidden. Recently another large Tequesta settlement was found in downtown Miami next to the Miami River that opens into Biscayne Bay. The site was going to be developed into multi-million-dollar condos. To read more about the battle around the site's preservation search "Brickell Tequesta site."

My goal was to honor the ancient Tequesta whose lands I live on. I see the physical remnants of their civilization in my everyday outings. There are mounds and circles all along Biscayne Boulevard and on the shores of the bay. If you would like to do a deep dive, I suggest starting with HistoryMiami Museum and the University of Florida's digital archive.

Raquel V. Reyes

While the Tequesta tribe may be history, Indigenous peoples are not. The Miccosukee and Seminole tribes mentioned in this story are thriving cultures in Florida. Please make it a point to visit some of their cultural institutes like the Ah-Tah-Th-Ki museum.

The character Pierre Deer Maracle is not a real person but the Oka Crisis/ Kanien'kehà:ka Resistance is fact. If you'd like to know more, there are several good articles and essays about the tribe's successful resistance to land developers and the reclamation of their lands.

A special thanks to fellow mystery writer, D.M. Rowell, for her sensitivity read and insights. She is a Kiowa storyteller and author of the Mud Sawpole Mysteries.

310